Watermark

Watermark

by Jennifer Farquhar

Copyright © 2018 by Jennifer Farquhar

Publisher's note:
This book is a work of fiction. Names, characters, places and incidents are either the product of the author's imagination or are used fictitiously, and any resemblance to actual persons living or dead is entirely coincidental.

Library and Archives Canada Cataloguing in Publication

Farquhar, Jennifer, 1974-, author
Watermark / Jennifer Farquhar.

ISBN 978-0-9958235-7-0 (softcover)

I. Title.

PS8611.A765W38 2018   C813'.6   C2018-902063-6

Printed and bound in Canada on 100% recycled paper.

Book design: Maurissa Grano
Cover Design: Jennifer Farquhar and Maurissa Grano
Author photo: Erin Michalski

Published by:
Latitude 46 Publishing
info@latitude46publishing.com
Latitude46publishing.com

We acknowledge the support of the Canada Council for the Arts, which last year invested $153 million to bring the arts to Canadians throughout the country.
Nous remercions le Conseil des arts du Canada de son soutien. L'an dernier, le Conseil a investi 153 millions de dollars pour mettre de l'art dans la vie des Canadiennes et des Canadiens de tout le pays.

Canada Council   Conseil des arts
for the Arts   du Canada

MIX
Paper from
responsible sources
FSC
www.fsc.org   FSC® C004071

~To Thanos, Tessa, Zack, and Hannah~

Lament

A superstition exists among Mikinaak Islanders that after a child dies, his spirit will communicate with the family through dreams. At night, the spirit may request provisions for the journey to the afterlife—sweets, coins, perhaps a pocketknife. The mourners honour these dream requests.

But sometimes a complication arises: the young spirit is unable to reach its destination. Disoriented and forlorn, the spirit may plead with a living relative for companionship. The family has little choice but to deny the spirit its request.

PART ONE

CHAPTER 1

Leaving Toronto, 1994

We drive the seven hours to Mikinaak Island in near silence, watching the landscape stumble backwards in time. Walmarts make way for crippled A&Ps, grocery stores decamp and leave their general store cousins to man the roads, then general stores abandon the scene and all that is left is a boarded up gas station that hasn't whiffed a drop of fuel since Pierre Trudeau was Prime Minister. Paved roads wither into gravel nuisances that ping a hailstorm against the chassis of the car, and the Escort is now sullied by fine white dust. By the time I spot the swing bridge that links Mikinaak to the mainland, it seems conceivable that the five-dollar bill in my pocket could purchase a couple of steak dinners and malt shakes at the local diner. Not that I have an appetite.

The bridge, however, looks newer than I remembered it, more secure. Eighty meters of metal beams saluting the sky, reinforced steel girders signaling its capacity to bear great loads. Nine hundred tons of wasted reassurance for a limnophobic like me. I am grateful to be in the driver's seat, despite Zane's insistence that he can drive, *should* drive to practice for his road test. Because the task of focusing on the road in front of me is a much-needed distraction from the water.

When I learned I had inherited the island house from my mother, my first instinct was to burn it to the ground. I even went so far as to think up an accomplice. Surely that fish-mutilator Tubby McCallister had spawned a new generation of grubby little criminals by now. But in the end, I spent money I didn't have on a cleaning crew to look after the task of ridding the house of its memories, and the unfortunate life of a broken woman.

Then I contacted a realtor, and my family home has sat on the market ever since.

I brought up the topic of the house as Zane was tending to his chili pepper plants which I had failed to water the previous week while he was in the hospital.

"I have some bad news for you, Zane. We need to move again."

"Already saw the notice, Momsidius." Zane didn't look up from his plants.

Momsidius, Momosa, Mombabwe. I hadn't realized how much Zane's nicknames meant to me until recently, when they had begun to fade from his speech. Except Marines. That one I wasn't so keen on, which he knew.

"I'm so sorry this is happening again, Zaner."

Zane looked up, his earnest grey eyes locking on mine, and I glimpsed the sensitive little boy who scarcely showed himself anymore. My arms ached to reach out and take him in an embrace, to somehow grasp onto the sweet side of my son before it disappeared again behind his quiet, pensive exterior.

"Don't sweat it, Madre. Who knows, maybe Medica going under will turn out to be the best thing that could've happened to you. I bet you'll land a new editing gig any day now. Or maybe this is the push you need to bust out of the science copywriting ghetto.

You could try publishing those stories you're always working away on at night—the ones you never let me read?"

"My getting fiction published is about as likely as winning the Lotto 649, sweetie."

"Need me to go grab a newspaper and start looking for cheaper apartments? I hear the Jane and Finch neighbourhood is lovely this time of year—only fifteen homicides this month." A tiny grin crept across Zane's face.

Warmth filled my chest, and I knew, as paltry a crumb as it was, I would return to this rare Zane smile later to savour it.

"Actually, Zane, I know a place where we can stay rent-free."

He stopped spritzing his plants, and turned to face me, head cocked sideways.

I took a deep breath. "Zane, your grandmother died two years ago, and left her home on Mikinaak Island to me." I paused to let the information sink in. Which part would be the most shocking for Zane? The fact that he had a grandmother? A lineage? Or the fact that I owned a home when we had been trudging from one shoddy apartment to the next.

Zane examined his fingernails as though our family history was inscribed on them.

Here we go again.

"Family on Mikinaak Island." He let out a low whistle. "That's one fuck of a humdinger. You're a secretive dame, Marina McInnis."

"Zane, you know how I feel about swearing."

He gave a curt nod.

"We really don't have any other options, Zane. Plus—you'll have all the space you need to grow your own garden."

"Give it up, Marines." His voice took on a dejected tone that hurt even more than his anger. "Might as well ship me off to Siberia." He stormed off to his bedroom.

Of course I knew he'd be upset. Zane loved the city for what it did so well: provide infrastructure for the roamings of a brilliant, restless loner. He cherished the sprawling University of Toronto library where he spent his free time researching whatever captured his imagination on any particular week; enjoyed nothing better than his trips to specialty seed shops to comb through hand-wrapped packets of heirloom seeds for his container garden; prized the freedom of the subway system that I finally started to let him ride on his own two years ago. In a moment of weakness at his constant hounding when he was fourteen, I told him that he could ride the subway alone once he committed the entire subway map to memory. That same evening he sat me down, pulled four coloured pencils from his back pocket, and sketched the sixty-some stops on the four different train lines of the Toronto Subway map in fast strokes, only raising his head to smirk at me once he had completed a smartass perfect legend at the bottom of the map.

But at some point, Zane's explorations had crossed the line into risk-taking I could no longer handle.

Zane was the type of child who always had bruises and broken bones. Sounds terrible, but there it is. When he was a toddler, Zane was *a going concern* according to my well-meaning neighbours who could hear him leap from the dresser to his bed through the thin walls. When he was ten, they were calling him *hell on wheels,* just not to my face. The emergency room doctors at Toronto General had become familiar with Zane's file by then, their initial concern replaced by tired smiles as Zane recounted his wrestling move, or his performance crooning a Bryan Adams power ballad at the top of his lungs using his fork as a microphone. He had leapt from the kitchen table for a grand finale for that particular trip to the ER, his tongue taking on four equidistant piercings. "He's lucky he didn't lose an eye," the doctor had said to try to comfort me. Which did exactly the opposite. Knowing Zane, next time it *would* be an eye.

If Zane wasn't exploring the world, he was edgy and volatile, so I gave him as much freedom as my nerves would allow. Usually to my chagrin. Just last year he climbed up the rusty fire escape to the roof of our four storey apartment building, and with his slingshot and some steak bones that he had fished out of the garbage, tried to teach our neighbour a lesson.

"The guy had it coming, Mumadeus," Zane explained from his hospital bed. "I heard the way he reamed you out last week. *No one* gets away with talking to my mom like that. No one." Zane had shaken his fist dramatically and flashed an infectious lopsided grin, the goofy face he reserved for his purposely clunky puns. "Mr. Gordon needed a friendly neighbourhood reminder to *bone up* on his manners."

After showering Mr. Gordon's car with our dinner scraps, Zane had turned around for the coup de grace. Pants around his ankles, face bent down to his knees, he hung a full moon over Mr. Gordon's house, then lost his balance and fell backward off the roof toward the spiked metal fence below. He fell four storeys. Seven feet above the spot where his skull would have shattered across the pavement, Zane's bagged up jeans snagged on the pointed fence spikes. Neither of us can pass the fence now without shuddering. He fractured his arm that day—lucky number seven in the fracture tally, and lost his roving privileges for two months. I would've come down harder on him if I hadn't found Zane's misguided actions so touching.

I created a scrapbook page of that day—wrote a story called "Steak Bone Warrior," which I laid out on a journaling mat alongside Zane's picture. The photo is a 5x7 of Zane pointing his neon yellow cast at the camera like a weapon, his other hand making the gesture of rock stars: thumb, index finger and pinky finger pointing up, the other two fingers bent into the palm. But it's his face that says it all.

Delicate, beautiful features striving so hard to form sharp edges. His mouth is stretched open, his tongue is out and his eyes are screwed tight in two ecstatic slits. "Come and get me world, I will eat you alive!" is what that face says. Afraid of nothing. Lacking the wisdom to understand the difference between bravery and recklessness. Oblivious to the beast that waits for one distracted moment, that one opportunity as weightless as baby's breath.

A couple of years ago, I edited a piece about a team of Japanese researchers who conducted a study on innate fear in rodents. They genetically altered the DNA of a group of mice so their sense of smell didn't link up with the nerve cells that signaled danger. Normally, the second a mouse gets a whiff of cat, its instincts take over. The genetically modified mice, however, would smell a cat nearby and saunter on over. When I read that, I put my head down on my keyboard and wept. I pictured an alleyway of cats with teeth bared and claws out, and a pocket-sized version of my son smiling up at them stupidly, his sense of danger somehow erased in the womb. Maybe the fear that had tainted every moment of my pregnancy had given him antibodies, made him immune.

It wasn't until I became a parent myself that I was able to understand the boundless feelings a mother has for her child. Something one cannot possibly understand until you've looked into the eyes of a tiny, trusting face that whispers into your neurons, "Protect me or I die." I lay awake for hours each night, my body craving sleep more intensely than any drug, and studied my baby's chest moving up and down, up and down. I would lean into the sunken spot on his crown, drink in his sweet, milky scent, and an ache would burn through my chest. A twinned emotion of overwhelming love, and overwhelming fear for this precious little person.

I devoured baby advice manuals, installed safety latches, sanitized surfaces, banished chokeable objects. Life was a series of calculated risks and it became my job to assess them all and manage accordingly. Few of us know for example, that people are almost four times as likely to die in their homes from falls than they are of being charred to death by fire. One misstep on a freshly mopped floor and we're teetering on the edge of heartbreak. Tragedy lurks behind every dangling curtain cord, hides in every bath tub faucet, waiting for the moment a sleep-deprived parent is distracted by a ringing telephone.

After giving birth to Zane, something else happened. I couldn't stop thinking about my mother, about jealousy, about ugly memories that rippled across the surface of my life in increasingly larger rings. I bet her own children's trusting faces never stopped whispering in her ears either.

A Kawasaki Ninja zips alongside our car just before we reach the bridge, and I feel my pulse quicken. I whip my head around to get a better look at the driver. Female. Maybe this time it will be Rhonda Doyle. I squint at the woman's face as her hair flaps across her cheeks; I catch a glimpse of angular eyes. My heart sinks.

"Still fixated on bikes, eh Madre?" Practically the only words Zane has spoken since we left Toronto. "They're not very safe, you know," he says, parroting my voice brilliantly.

The Escort heaves as it crosses onto the metal flooring of the bridge, sounding like an old-model roller coaster as we clunk and clang across the girders. *You can do this, Marina. Hydrogen, atomic mass 1.008; Helium, 4.003; Lithium, 6.941.* I resist the urge to close my eyes, but even as I blur my focus and summon my harmless chemical elements into ordered rows, in my mind I still see every inch of the landscape surrounding us. The rough, grey waves crashing against the concrete foundation, shattering into

7

white foam that spews up the sides of the squat stone pillars; the deceptively calm waters in the middle of the channel, smaller waves unfurling across the surface. The torn, papery wisps of land in the distance, the jagged outline of the treetops slicing into the white sky and snagging the hapless grey clouds. Thirty-five hundred cubic kilometres of water snapping at the heels of boreal forest. My stomach tightens into a familiar fist as the car convulses along the bridge spanning the cold, dark waters below. *Beryllium 9.012, Boron 10.811.*

My son's first memories of a large body of water are situated in an over-chlorinated pool at the YMCA. I had to breathe into a paper bag in the parking lot before even walking in to the Y to sign up for the Mommy & Me swim classes—my desperate attempt to remove my name from the bad mother list that was the default of teenage moms. I gave up after a few sessions, however. Too many tears—all of them mine. I promised myself that Zane would learn to swim when he was old enough to do it alone. But somehow, a decade and a half rolled by, and we never managed to intersect with the Y pool again.

Odd to think that by contrast, almost every memory I have of my childhood is saturated by freshwater. The other memories, rare day trips to the city, weren't entirely pleasurable. A two-hour drive in to Kentsworth in the back seat of our Ford Country Squire station wagon, prying the backs of our thighs off the hot vinyl to tip our heads out the window so the breeze could cool the sweat prickling our scalps. In the city, the hot pavement, the sensory overload, and the drain of being surrounded by so many strangers took its toll. It was exciting to leave the Island, but it was always a relief to return. To its clean green shadows, to the cool water of the lake. Back when the lake was still a source of comfort.

Despite many hours of therapy in the offices of well-meaning psychologists, my fear of lakes and rivers has not diminished in the past twenty years. I've tried hypnosis, regression sessions, and flooding therapy— a term whose irony was not lost on me—all with little success. But like a tongue to a throbbing tooth, I'm drawn to water. So I study and write about it from a safe distance. Studying water from a chemical perspective, I understand water's uniquely high surface tension. Water is a social being by nature, preferring to clump into drops with other water molecules, rather than spreading out in a thin, lonesome film. Given the abundance of water within our bodies –the human body is almost two-thirds water after all—it is not surprising that we are drawn to oceans, lakes, rivers and streams.

Surrounded by the vast waters of Lake Huron, Mikinaak Island is like an embryo floating in the life-sustaining fluids of its mother. The Island and its inhabitants are rocked to sleep each night by the sound of water on pebbles, the most ancient of lullabies. I guess that's why no one ever leaves.

Except me. I left the Island when I was fourteen and I vowed never to return.

I make it to the middle of the bridge when my hands start shaking and I have to pull my foot off the gas pedal. My pulse races, and my lungs feel as though they are filling with fluid, a vice tightening across my breastbone. *Lake Huron: 6157 kilometres of shoreline; average depth 59 metres; volume of 3540 cubic kilometres of freshwater.*

A blaring horn screams in my ears and it takes me a second to realize I am pressed against the steering wheel. "Zane, you're going to have to drive." I extricate myself from behind the wheel and there is a scrambling of bodies in this too-tight space; a spectacle which may mistakenly appear comical to the drivers behind us. They don't understand the gravity of the situation. I breathe in deeply through my nose. *Focus on the chemical profile of the lake, Marina.* My mind gloms onto an article I edited recently, outlining the pharmaceutical contaminants infiltrating the Great Lakes: Prozac, steroids, perfumes, and antibiotics. I force myself to envision a schematic diagram of the pollution runoff pathways, to mentally draw the arrows from each source of pollutant down to the coastline. The diagram in my head becomes animated, and I am suddenly picturing a long, arrogant chain of toxic molecular compounds, a blocky snake moving in ninety degree turns like an 80s video game. Water molecules, depicted in chemistry textbooks with their large round oxygen heads and two alien hydrogen eyes bulging from each side, have always looked to me like hostile microorganisms. I envision the snake slithering through a pool of these virulent H_2O molecules, zillions of them teeming beneath us. My breath will not come.

Curled in the fetal position in the passenger seat, I direct Zane the rest of the drive with my eyes closed. "Turn right just after the massive red barn with an antique plow and a wooden Lloyd sign at the end of the driveway." I can recall the roads and time-worn homes and farms as though I had driven the route earlier that morning.

The road grows narrower as we pass the outskirts of town. I force myself to sit upright as we bump along past a stretch of birch and deciduous forest, broken up only by a few decaying grey barns, where a cluster of cattle munch on yellow grass in the open field. The road narrows further and then forks, an 'unmaintained road' sign to our right. "Down there." I point to the potholed road, overgrown on each side by thin saplings that stroke the roof of the car. The trees block out the sun overhead, and Zane strains to see the road ahead of us in the gloom. We zigzag down the bumpy road until it opens into a clearing.

A squat log bungalow sits in the center of the clearing. Around its base are the remains of a country garden gone to seed. A tangle of tall weeds, scruffy cedar shrubs, and a mixture of rotting leaves fight for space. The stain on the logs has peeled off in large strips, and the windows are spotted with bug splatters and several seasons' worth of neglect. Thick-stalked thistle have choked out the grass, and an ornate ceramic bird bath lies dead on its side, dried ragweed jutting out all around it.

My chest feels weighted with lead as I stare at my family home. Over the years, a mental blackness has worked backwards in time, seeping through all of my memories like oil spilled over the still frames of our family's past. The mental snapshot of David and me swinging upside down from the maple in the front yard, my brother's hair fanned out like white dandelion fluff; a memory of our family strolling down our gravel driveway, David hoisted high on my father's shoulders; David and I waltzing with Schnapps up on her two hind legs on the front porch—all the happy memories have become tainted black and sticky. Polluted.

Zane walks around the pathway between the forest and the side of the house. I hold my breath and give him time to take all of this in by himself, knowing how furious he must be with me. After a long wait, I walk gingerly along the path to the house's lakeside. I stop as soon as I come around the corner and can see him. He has walked to edge of the lake, and is still, facing the water. The sounds of the waves crash around him. His arms are extended to the sky in a V, his back slightly arched, his face tipped up with his eyes closed. No doubt asking the gods why they allowed me to drag him into such bleakness. I stand and watch my son for several seconds, fighting to keep my focus on him, and not the water behind. Then I sneak away, to allow Zane his privacy.

Eventually he comes back around the house. "A log home in the woods on a gorgeous *lake*? You seriously had to wait so long to bring us here, mom?" A combination of peace and childish excitement flash across his face.

I haven't seen Zane smile like this in such a long time. But I cannot ignore the set of icy fingers laced around my throat. We should never have come back here.

CHAPTER 2

I stand on my mother's porch and stare into the trees. I am not yet ready to set foot or mind inside. A decaying poplar tree sways in the distance, its branches creaking. It is just tall enough to crash into these floorboards, if adequately provoked by the wind that whips up from the lake. *There. I'm thinking about it again.* Even a poplar tree has the power to catapult me back to places my heart is not ready to explore.

There is a photo in my mother's red leatherette scrapbook of a paper bag brimming with mushrooms. I can see it, always, when my mind returns unbidden to this property and the tangled memories that hang from its edges. Beneath the photo, 1971 is written in my mother's obedient handwriting. Every spring, according to locals who knew such things, when the poplar leaves were as big as a mouse's ear, the morel mushrooms would sprout their cone-shaped heads up through the leafy undergrowth of the forest floor. Morel mushrooms were a prized find in the mixed spruce, cedar, and birch forest that ran several miles deep beside our family home.

Morels were ingeniously camouflaged—their brown crinkled caps barely poking through piles of brown leaves like tiny wizards' hats, woods elves in leafy dress ready to preside over the moss and saplings. It was not unusual for a family to go out for an afternoon of morel hunting at just the right time of year, where morels had been found the year before, only to return home with a few lonely mushrooms drooping in the bottom of their brown paper bags.

I was ten years old at the time; David was five. We had scrutinized the poplar trees for days on end, thumbing the leaves to determine if they were the requisite rodent-ear size that signaled the beginning of morel season. It was a Sunday morning when David and I came bursting through the kitchen patio door, announcing to our parents that the morels might finally be out.

My father was sitting at the kitchen table. His hands, thick and callused from ten years spent feeding wood into the insatiable metal mouth at the mill, looked so competent holding the weekly newspaper. He squinted as he read—the mill had slashed benefits a few years back, and dad believed that glasses were for squares anyway—and I thought his squint made him look even cooler, like James Dean in hunting plaid. Dad set down his newspaper and pushed his chair back with a loud scrape across the floor. He clapped his hands together, and slapped a firm palm on each of our backs. "I do declare mates," he said in the fake British drawl that David adored, "if the morels are out, why are we fannying around here with our thumbs up our bleedin' arses?"

"Bleedin arses! Bleedin arses!" David threw his head back and laughed uproariously.

Dad scooped us up under each arm, and whirled us across the kitchen toward our mother. "Kathy, my love, the morel hunting party awaits. And everyone knows that a party isn't a party until Katherine McInnis makes an appearance." He dumped us at her feet as though he had found a more prized treasure, yanked her dish towel from her hands, arranged it on his head like a horn, and charged at her. Mom's laughter was like velvet as she allowed dad to twirl her gracefully around the kitchen. David and I stood transfixed, staring at the woman we believed to be the most exquisite creature in the entire world.

We left the dirty breakfast dishes and the half-drank cups of coffee, and trotted out to the forest, my brother and I lapping up every ounce of this rare opportunity to bask in our parents' undivided attention. No partying, no other adults, just our family of four and our loyal German shepherd Schnapps, traipsing through the woods.

Morel hunting is not for the attention deficit. Hunched over, taking a step and then standing perfectly still, eyes focused on the ground, we passed several intense hours scrutinizing playing card-sized patches of earth. I had to keep rubbing my eyes to focus; I wanted so badly to delight my parents with the first find of the day. At one point, I decided that my best bet was to get down to mushroom level, so I dropped down on all fours and bent my head down, praying that the conical squiggle of brown would appear before my nose. Short twigs cut into my hands as I crawled along, and my face broke through several sticky spider webs, but I came up empty-handed.

Dad had brought along his Canon, and spent the first twenty minutes hunting the best angles to capture the sun emblazoning mom's auburn hair as it cascaded down her shoulders.

As I slipped past them, he said proudly, "Someday you'll be just as beautiful as your mother, Mina." His camera continued clicking away as I hunkered past them.

I already knew this was untrue. The world produced a rare few magnetic people who could destabilize an entire room simply by standing in its corner. I had not inherited this trait. I would always be the type of person who was better at putting the furniture back in its proper place, perfectly aligned, afterwards.

Dad snapped another shot of mom, and for a second I thought of a zookeeper, grinning as he snapped a photo of his prized Bengal tiger.

As usual in the morel hunt, it was David whose skills shone. He channeled some sort of extra-sensory nature perception. He didn't even need to stop and stare at the ground the way the rest of us did—he simply strolled, eyes downcast, and reached his hand down while still walking, to pluck a mushroom that none of us had noticed. Whenever my mother or father crossed paths with David that afternoon in the forest, I heard hearty slaps on the back and, "You have a gift, son," and, "You never cease to amaze me, David." Words that I would have traded a thousand perfect summer beach days to hear directed at me.

Despite his young age, even back then David recognized he was the favorite. He tiptoed over to me when our parents were out of sight, and reached into his paper bag to fish out a handful of his morels, half his day's find. "Shhh. We can pretend *you* found these ones, Meenie," he said, stuffing them into my bag. I'm not sure what made my throat clench up more—David's selflessness, or the fact that he perceived the need to help raise me in our parents' esteem.

As we trudged home from the forest later that day, David stumbled through the high grasses to keep up with me. "Meenie!" He called out, his little voice suddenly terrified. "The *creepers*!" His bag of mushrooms bounced against his thigh as he raced to catch up, his face ashen. My arms reflexively reached out to him— the *creepers* was a feeling that often seized David when he was by himself—but I quickly mashed my hands in my pocket and kept my brisk pace, forcing myself to ignore him for a moment. Part of me longed to coddle him, but part of me felt it wasn't fair that this job always landed on me. I ended up giving in. I hoisted David onto my hip and carried him home, whispering in his ear all the ways I was going to slay the creepers the next time they messed with my little dude.

That evening, our mother sautéed a buttery pan full of the earthy tasting mushrooms, and dad barbecued thick steaks which he made a special trip into town to purchase, in celebration of our successful afternoon in the forest. When we sat around the table, steak and glistening morels heaped on our plates, both my parents beamed up at David. Dad raised his beer bottle, then reached out and ruffled David's hair. "To David, our boy wonder." I raised my milk in a toast to David, part of me happy that he was the recipient of such praise from our father.

I had only the tiniest niggling feeling of something other than appreciation for David. For a fleeting instant, I wished there wasn't a golden child sitting between my parents and me at the dinner table. Maybe then, a stronger ray of affection might beam in my direction. But I sucked that ugly thought back in and trapped it in a screw-top jar in the back of my mind. I loved David so ferociously that I would rip the limbs off anyone who tried to hurt him. Sister bears can protect almost as viciously as mamas.

After dinner, mom wore a lopsided grin from one too many rum & Tabs. I winked at my little brother David from across the table, then led our mother over to her spot on the couch. "You *sure* look like you could use a nice, steaming cup of Tetley," I said, petting her arm.

"Well, Miss Marina, maybe you've got a decent idea rattling around in that head of yours after all." Mom winked and scrubbed her knuckles across the top of my head. I felt a gush of pride.

David sat on the floor at her feet and slipped mom's socks off, starting in on the foot massage. Then, sly as a cat, I maneuvered the steamer trunk in front of our mother, and hopped onto the couch beside her. David lifted open the metal latch of the steamer trunk that held touchingly archived boxes of photographs and bric-a-brac, our mother's scrapbook, and our great-grandparents' most treasured items from their dangerous three-week journey from Glasgow.

The brown leather of the trunk was worn at the corners from being tossed around at sea, jostled on a horse-drawn cart to Owen Sound, and hauled onto the steamship that crossed Lake Huron to Mikinaak Island.

"Tell us again about Great-Grandma & Grandpa Barrett's first year in Canada." David pouted his lips into a puppy face, hands folded in prayer under our mother's nose.

"Oh for Pete's sake—you don't need to hear that one again. You could recite it backwards by now." But her eyes gleamed as she started right in.

Mom painted a vivid picture: April, 1910. A violent battle of metal versus the frozen lake. Two hundred trunks carrying the pared down possessions of ninety Scottish families thumping against the ship's cold metal floor as the ship rammed its way through blocks of ice; livestock kicking and groaning in their pens, their eyes rolled back in terror; mothers fretting over their vomiting children from morning until night; the men keeping helpless watch on the deck, eyes bloodshot from the icy spray, yet afraid to avert their gaze for even a moment lest catastrophe unfold. Everyone knowing too well the number of ships already lining the bottom of Lake Huron.

"The steamer trunk of your Great-Grandmother Barrett had been stuffed to the gills with bags of flour, along with a complete set of Royal Doulton china and several tailored silk gowns. Had she known what a godforsaken life lay ahead of her, she wouldn't have packed so many useless pretty things. Likely broke her heart every time she looked at them.

"Just imagine how Great Grandma and Grandpa Barrett felt, finally standing on the shore of Mikinaak Island after all those weeks at sea, watching that ship turn into a fly speck on the horizon, their brood of kids hungry and bawling. And nothing but dense hardwood forest in every direction. Just imagine!"

"But they managed to clear a small patch of land and build a tidy little cabin, didn't they, mom? And then..."

"And then the fire. Just when they thought they could breathe easy for one minute, that fire wiped out all their winter supplies. And Great Grandpa Barret had only one choice."

"He had to go out on the ice!"

"That's right, Mina. And he knew that only a few homesteaders before him had survived a journey like that, across the channel to Kentsworth. But what else could he do?

"Six days later, he was headed home with a full cart when a blizzard began to rage. He travelled blind—couldn't see so much as his horse's arse. And just like that, the horse's front legs disappeared through a gash in the ice." David and I leaned in when she got to this part.

"Great-Grandpa watched a slow hug of icy water pull down his horse. He looked at the cart, with its winter's worth of food and fuel, and saw the scene for what it was: his family's fate teetering on the edge of that ice.

"And, being a man who believed in things both seen and unseen, he had one final thought. *The lake was hungry for man. But maybe, just maybe, it could also be negotiated with.* 'Please,' he begged. 'I have a family who depends on me. Please, just this one time, spare me.'" Mom paused for effect.

"And that is when the most amazing thing happened."

"The lake spoke back!" David chimed in.

"The lake spoke back. Great-Grandpa Barrett heard a voice which he swore was the lake itself: *'You owe me.'*

"Your great-grandfather flattened himself across the ice, and with hands burning cold inside soaked woolen mittens, he did the unimaginable: he pulled that horse out of the lake.

"He crawled the rest of the way back, leading his shivering mare and the cart with one numb hand. When he finally caught sight of the cabin, that man who didn't shed a tear at his own father's funeral fell down on his knees and sobbed.

"The horse died later that night. Your great-grandfather lost two fingers on his left hand from frostbite.

"Decades later, he would thrust his three-fingered hand before his grandchildren's faces and solemnly recount, 'I thought at the time it was a bargain—trading a horse and two fingers to get off that lake. I hope to God I was right.'"

"Your great-grandfather often reminded us grandkids that many Mikinaak Islanders were not so fortunate when it came to navigating the channel. We had to respect the lake, and accept the cost of living alongside such a temperamental creature. He used to say that when it came to the lake, we needed to understand the nature of the beast."

David's eyes widened. "*Beast?*"

Mom ruffled his blond hair. "No, not really a beast, David. That's just an expression. I think he just wanted to scare all of us kids into being careful, that's all."

But her hand fluttered to her neck, all the same.

In lieu of a physical embrace, our mother knitted words together to create a blanket of stories. She wrapped her children in four generations of ancestral lore, providing us with the warm, fuzzy sense of security that comes with being firmly tied to the past.

As a child I dwelled within my mother's memories as though they were my own. I became a shadowed guest at the lakes and islands that populated her past. While I sat perched at her feet soaking up every syllable, her stories overflowed and stained an indelible mark on me. Like a stamp that indicates ownership of intellectual property, my mother's watermark was imprinted on my own memories.

My mother grew up on Mikinaak Island too, and back then summer island life revolved around the Doyles, a family of inestimable wealth who owned Elsinore, a small island directly across the bay from my family's lot. The Doyle family captured the imaginations of all Mikinaak from early July until Labour Day each year.

"Did the Doyles come from Scotland, like Great-Grandpa Barrett, mom?"

"The Doyles are Irish, sweetie. But mainly they're just thought of as being from Toronto. They own about half of it."

"How did the Doyles get to be so rich, mom?"

"Well, they weren't always that way. The *Record* just published a piece on the Doyles not too long ago, actually. Fascinating family. Wallace Doyle—he would be about the same age as your great-grandpa Barrett—was a farm boy from Kapuskasing. Most boys he grew up with quit school the minute they'd sprouted enough muscles to sling one of those 80-pound hay bales, but Wallace set out for Toronto to find work instead. He worked hard, and was very successful, and a few years later when the Great Depression hit everyone where it hurts, he bought up his competitors left and right and became the largest plate glass manufacturer in Canada."

"Do you think I'll leave this island, and become rich and famous like the Doyles someday, Mommy?"

"That's up to you, I suppose, David. Requires lots of brains and hard work."

"Hmmn. Sounds more like Meenie than me."

Mom ruffled David's hair. "Oh David. Sweet little monkey."

"Tell us about Elsinore Castle again, Mommy."

Mom got a far-off look in her eye whenever we requested a Doyle story. She reached out and stroked David's hair and gave a soft sigh. "Alright. But it's not a castle, sweetie. It's an estate. If you can believe it, Wallace Doyle bought it on a whim, sight unseen, for twenty smackers. Apparently he took a fishing trip up here with some of his Toronto business cronies, and they had such a rip roaring time—much whiskey involved, you can be sure—that he stopped by the Crown Land Department and bought the property on the drive home. Just imagine."

"Oh, I can just picture what it must have been like for all those local Mikinaak men he hired to build the estate. They had to haul every stitch of material by horse and then by boat, and he had over twenty men working around the clock for nine months. I can just imagine those workers, stunned at how one summer home could cost more than any of them could hope to earn in a lifetime."

"I can't believe you got to see Elsinore with your own eyes!"

"Right place at the right time, Monkey. The Doyles always hired a few lucky teenagers to live and work on Elsinore every summer. It was July of '56, and I was fifteen years old, working at the downtown docks when Mr. Wallace Doyle pulls up his yacht for service. Your mom was pretty quick on the draw back then, I'll have you know, and I set my sights on winning over Mr. Doyle before his boat had finished gassing up. Sure as sugar, Mr. Doyle offered me a summer job on the spot. 'See ya, Mac,' I told my boss, and hopped into the Doyle yacht."

"What was it like, mom? Elsinore."

"I remember stepping onto the Elsinore dock: first thing I noticed was the smell. Miles of wild English gardens in full bloom, which I later learned required *two* gardeners working full-time. Just imagine—two full-time gardeners at a summer cottage. Oh, I can still see it all so clearly—the walk along the stepping stone path, winding through sweet-smelling beds of perennials, past a cutting garden bursting with reds and yellows, then past a fountain with a concrete urn spilling water at its center. Beyond the fountain was the main building, Elsinore Estate—a sprawling mansion built like one of those estates from *Gone with the Wind*. I felt like Scarlett O'Hara as I stood staring up at the columns of that majestic white house. And then there were the four guest houses, the tennis courts, the swimming pool, the sauna, the greenhouse, the boathouse. For a gal who pumped boat sewage and cleaned cottages for a living, Elsinore was like something right out of a fairy tale."

I often try to unweave my mother's dark history from that of the Doyles; often ponder what sunny trajectory our lives might be on right now, had my mother not gotten mixed up with the Doyles. I think about how intoxicating the social strata far above her own must have been, and how life back on Mikinaak Island must have seemed unbearably drab.

I picture the society ladies dressed in their delicate silk gloves and floor-length chiffon gowns; mink stoles gracing the shoulders of each well-to-do partygoer; jewel-encrusted headbands arranged across fat curls of hair, the styling of which would have occupied the good part of an afternoon. I can almost hear the swing music floating across the lake as the ladies smoked menthol cigarettes and drank and danced and threw their heads back in laughter.

Many small towns have one well-to-do family that elicits complicated feelings from the locals: fascination with the family's lifestyle, gratitude for the trickle-down of wealth that seeps into the community, but also suspicion of the influence this imbalance of wealth yields. On Mikinaak Island in the mid-seventies, it seemed as though all the families we knew were barely managing to get by. Getting by, from my vista in Northern Ontario, resulted in class photos with kids in first grade wearing oversized Budweiser t-shirts for picture day (promotional giveaway from the Beer Store years earlier). It showed up inside kitchen cupboards, where mason jars substituted for drinking glasses, and a shelf stacked with Kraft Dinner constituted the makings of a family's evening meals. For kids, getting by came in the form of hand-sewing a small tab of red fabric to the thigh seam of our hand-me-down jeans, in an attempt to be part of the off-island culture we didn't understand. It meant working all summer in a local shop or at the marina by the time you were twelve, to afford a few new school clothes for September.

On Mikinaak's Native reserve just a few miles outside of town, getting by had its own set of standards: if your house had functional plumbing, you were one of the fortunate ones.

The words *getting by* did not intersect with the Doyles. "Born a Doyle, were you?" was a comment my father would toss our way if one of us dared to loaf on the couch during daylight hours. My father was born with a Protestant work ethic, even though he was a holidays-and-baptisms-only kind of churchgoer. Loafing was an activity reserved for sundown.

Not that Mr. Wallace Doyle was much of a loafer. While the rest of his family spent the entire summer on Elsinore Island, Wallace managed the glass factory in Toronto during the week, making the trip to join the family on weekends.

Everything about this from-away family fascinated me, even more than stories of my own relatives, and I begged my mother to retell what she knew of them.

"Wallace Doyle built a new cottage on Elsinore for each branch of the family after his kids grew up. Imagine growing up as one of his grandkids, summering on your own private island. He taught every one of his grandkids to swim, too—I learned about this when I lived on Elsinore—using the infamous Wallace Doyle pole method. Mr. Doyle would perch himself on a chair at the end of the dock with a twelve-foot maple pole lodged under his keister, dangling his grandchild off the end of the pole, the poor thing

24

holding on for dear life. He would waggle the pole until the kid fell into the lake, then at the last possible second, dip the pole back into the water to fish the kid back up again. If you were Wallace Doyle's grandchild, you learned how to survive in the lake by the pole method, come hell or high water. Just imagine."

Mom's voice faltered. "It's a shame some of the Doyles forgot those early water safety lessons." Her hand went to her neck. She got up from the couch and walked stiffly to the kitchen. We could hear the crack of a can of soda and the tinkling of ice. David and I closed the lid of the memory trunk and left mom be with her rum & Tabs for the rest of the evening. We knew enough to wait for a better time to ask mom what she meant. I slunk off to my room with that sick feeling in my stomach, like when you remember you've done something horrible, but you can't recall exactly what it was.

CHAPTER 3

It cannot be that every child on Mikinaak Island spent the summer on the water, but through my girlhood eyes it seemed that way. For my little brother David and me, the summer of 1971, like every summer we had ever known, meant endless days swimming off the town docks. From July until early September, we were wild, aquatic little things.

One nippy morning, before the sun had coaxed a breath of warmth into Lake Huron, we set out on my bike for swimming lessons at the public beach three miles away. David sat on the seat while I pumped the pedals standing up, our four hands fanned across my handlebars. He was nervous to ride on his own down the steep hill, and I didn't mind pedaling for two. Our towels flapped against our skinny necks as we flew down the gravel road, the dark green leaves whispering as we passed.

At five years old, David had impressed the swimming instructor enough to be able to join the *big kids* who swam off the docks first thing each morning. We horsed around in the icy water while our instructor sat fully dressed on the splintered grey dock, flicking cigarette ashes into the lake. One sagging end of the dock was an ideal spot to stand and pump our knees up and down, creating a loud sucking noise and huge waves that were perfect for forcing water down the gullet of an unsuspecting fellow swimmer.

Why we needed to propel our feet in that circular, awkward stroke called "treading water" eluded me, but it was accepted knowledge that what we learned in swimming lessons didn't really intersect with the swimming we did off the town docks the rest of the day.

Our skinny bodies provided little in the way of insulation from Lake Huron's chill, but we did our best to keep warm, and followed the instructor's directions. When you are born on an island surrounded by a powerful rip current, you had damned well better learn how to swim.

When our lesson was over, we hauled ourselves onto the dock full of rusty nails that had worked their way out of the wood, their metal heads grazing the undersides of our tender white feet. Shivering, white beads of saliva dotted in the corners of bluish lips, David and I hopped onto my bike the minute the lesson was finished, our terrycloth leisure suits clinging to our wet swimsuits beneath. The first rays of sun were just hinting at warmth by the time I schlepped us back up the dusty gravel hill toward home.

When our lessons progressed from swimming to lifesaving skills a few weeks later, I indulged a little fantasy. I imagined that while boating to one of the nearby islands, our family found an overturned canoe. I pictured jumping up on the bow of our boat, pointing to a stranded swimmer in the lake as my dad squinted ahead of his steering wheel. "I've got this one, dad!" I would yell, and then I would dive off the side of our boat into the frigid water, pushing off hard to make sure I didn't end up being slashed by the motor. Confident front crawl strokes would propel me toward the drowning canoer; an extra life jacket would bob from my hand. My instructor's dramatic words would play in my head, "Never let a drowning victim grab hold of you—they'll snake tight around you and you'll sink like a stone." I would sling the life jacket toward the grateful victim, and she'd patiently hold on as I did a sidestroke to the safety of the boat.

Afterwards, the cold water smell of perch still dripping from my nose, my father and I would shake our heads at the wildness of the waves. "Phewph—that was one hell of a close one. You sure saved the day, Marina," he would say, and I would duck my head as he struck out an arm to ruffle my hair.

That weekend, like every weekend, we went boating on the lake. Mom packed two coolers—one stuffed with store-bought potato salad, packages of hot dogs and buns, a slab of butter folded within a square of tin foil, and squeeze bottles of condiments. The second was jammed with cans of orange Crush soda, cream soda, Tab, and a plastic 40-ounce bottle of rum. It was David and my job to carry these heavy coolers to the car, on tiptoe to prevent scraping the cooler bottoms along the ground.

At the marina, our parents loaded up the boat while David and I passed the time on our bellies on the dock, hunting for rock bass that glided from their shaded nook to warm their fins in the sunlight. We took turns painstakingly inching a stick into the water, seeing whose stick could get closest before the fish shot back under the dock. And then we waited, one eye mashed against the slot in the dock, for another fish to appear.

Tubby McCallister, a boy who most kids gave a wide berth, came up behind us with a net. Tubby was the type of nasty kid you almost had to feel a bit sorry for, despite his well-earned reputation as a criminal and a bully. His bangs hung to his nose, a thick black crescent of dirt lived beneath each of his fingernails, and his face always looked as though the last time it saw a washcloth was several meals back. I got the sense that no one in Tubby's family felt particularly compelled to help him improve these hygiene standards, which was the one thing that kept me from despising him.

Neither David nor I had brought a net down to the dock—we were only playing. When the rock bass reappeared, Tubby shot his net under it, then jerked his arms up. The fish twitched, its fin tips poking out of the net holes. It wasn't until he laid the fish down on the dock that I saw Tubby had picked up a jagged stick. I cringed as he raised the stick high above his head.

"My little fishy!" David screamed.

Tubby brought the stick down hard, jamming it into the fish's eye. The fish flopped on the dock, mouth opening and closing. Gelatinous fish-eye squeezed out along the sides of the stick. "Rock bass ain't good for nothing," he sneered.

David did what I wished I had done. Tubby was squatting over the fish when David charged at him. Tubby grasped at the dock too late to steady himself, then splatted backwards into the weedy lake.

Tubby thrashed around in the water like a hippo, his nostrils flaring as he kicked and howled and tried unsuccessfully to pull his heavy body back up on the dock. "Your brother's a dead man, Mina McInnis!" he yelled.

I scooped David up in my arms. I stared at Tubby struggling in the water, then reached my hand out to him. When he flailed toward me, I flashed him my middle finger. "Stay away from my little brother, Tubby."

I hauled David away under one shaky arm to the safety of our parents' boat a few dock lanes over. David clung to my sweatshirt, his face ashen. He swiveled his head repeatedly in Tubby's direction. David knew he had messed with the wrong kid. I sat David down on our boat's vinyl seat cushion, and placed one hand on each of his shoulders. I rested my forehead on his. "That was dumb," I told

David. "But you're lucky, little buddy. Your own personal knight in shining armor just happened to be nearby." I puffed out my chest and chucked David under the chin. "I will always protect you, Davey."

David's face relaxed at this, and he released his grip on my shirt and snuggled into my neck. "Thanks, Meenie," he said. "You are my best sister in the whole, wide world."

I paid for our transgression with Tubby the next week at school, but the split lip was worth it for the peace I had witnessed settling into my little brother's face as we sat and cuddled on the slick vinyl boat seat.

The following weekend at the marina, David and I were relieved that Tubby McCallister was nowhere in sight. Our family set off for another afternoon of boating. With each slam of the hull against the white-capped waves, my belly would jump in rhythm with the boat, flesh and metal coming together in an anxious song of water travel.

Although he knew it was neither safe nor legal, my father permitted us to ride on the bow of the boat as it lurched toward the beach. Heads tilted to the cloudless sky, throats raw from effort, David and I belted out Kenny Rogers songs we had memorized from our parents' eight-track cassettes, our voices competing with the roar of the motor.

It was common knowledge that five boats on any of the island beaches was too many, and a boater had to keep moving along to the next beach if his first choice was full. When our boat arrived at an available beach, we all climbed down the ladder at the back of the boat and picked our way through the frigid lake, on tiptoe to salvage a couple extra inches of dry clothing, the coolers bobbing alongside.

Once my parents' lawn chairs were dug into the sand next to the other couples with whom they regularly boated, it would have been easier to pry an eyeball from its socket than extract one of those adult butts from its chair. Red Coleman coolers planted between each husband and wife like a lifeline, glass of rum in one hand and cigarette in the other, the parents held a daytime hootenanny that carried over from one Saturday to the next, all summer long.

For the fourth time that afternoon, our mom fought her way out of her nylon beach chair, a Zenlike study in balance. David looked up at her immediately, leaning in toward her as she neared, eyes sparkling, eager to show off his latest sandcastle. But his face went flat as he watched our beautiful mother stumble right past him, wagging her slender hips to the radio, her gleaming hair swaying across her back as she headed to the bush to relieve herself.

"Hey, little buddy. Which room is reserved for me?" I said, turning his deflated face toward his sandcastle. David's eyes brightened, and he jumped into my lap and flung his arms around me, immediately immersed in a thorough explanation of his sandy construction.

Mealtimes on boating days were gloriously kid-friendly, if not exactly nitrate-free. We kids often stood around a fire roasting hot dogs on sticks we had skinned ourselves with a pocket knife. It was usually my job as big sister to pass out the potato chips, one large handful from fingers that had been dusted clean of sand, doled out onto each person's paper plate.

But making sure the children were fed was not our parents' top priority that sweltering afternoon. David was scavenging for food; I had already given him my share of the red licorice and Cheezies, but he was still ravenous. Peeking into our cooler and various beach bags, I couldn't find anything for David. He tugged at our mom's sleeve as she leaned in toward the other mothers, whispering a story about one of our neighbours. David swung himself from her arm like a monkey. "Mommy, I'm *starving*."

Mom swatted him away, spilling her drink. "I think you'll live." She leaned back into her story, and the other wives tilted their chairs in towards her, their faces receptive to mom's every word.

David walked his feet up mom's slender belly, this time holding both of her arms. "Mommy, up!"

Mom shoved his feet away and gave him another swat, this one less gentle. "Mommy's busy, David. You wait until I'm done talking."

David nodded. He crossed his legs and sat down beside her beach chair, the harsh sun beating down on his summer-white head.

Our mother pulled a limitless stream of gossip from her sleeve like a magician. "Oh, the nerve of her, I tell you. Just imagine. And that's not the half of it. You'll be digging your lower jaw out of this sand when I tell you what that McDougall woman did next..."

I whistled for Schnapps, and headed over to the hills to pick blueberries for my brother.

A few hours later, my large dish brimming with berries, I returned to the beach. My stomach heaved when I saw David still sitting there, patient as a monk. His skin was the colour of mom's Solo cup. Just then, mom dropped her drink in the sand. She teetered forward to pick it up, but stopped short, gazing at the sun disappearing below the horizon. She glanced around. "Now how on earth did it suddenly get so late?"

Mom looked over at David, twirling a strand of curls around his finger. Waiting. Her hand flew to her face. "Oh, sweet little Monkey, you're burnt to a crisp!" She reached out to stroke David's neck, then pulled his chin toward hers and gave him a smile that caused my throat to cinch. She scooped David into her lap and smoothed his hair across his forehead in tender strokes, as though the placement of those golden locks was undeniable proof of how much she cared. ""I'm so sorry, Monkey. Mommy will fix your dinner right this instant." She buried her nose in the crown of his head and inhaled deeply. When she looked up, her eyes danced. "Did you know, David, that you are unquestionably my favorite *son*?"

My body stiffened.

I ached to take up David's place in my mother's rum-soaked heart. For a moment, the ache was directed toward my little brother, and it felt like hatred.

The following weekend, the sunburn was forgotten, and our family and three others claimed a different sandy cove for the day, flanked by rocky hills. Playing tag in the rocky outcropping where the blueberries hid—Blueberry Mountain—was something we children did for hours while our parents drank on the beach below. A half-dozen of us scampered up the steep rock, our bare feet stinging from the dried moss that stuck out from the surface and nipped the soles of our feet as we leapt from one rock to another. Our feet learned a cautionary map of the mountainous surface, one that charted crevices and sharp pebbles. We sprinted across these rocks as easily as a gymnasium floor. We had spent hundreds of hours on these mountains, and our feet anticipated each rise and fall of the rock even before our eyes set upon it.

Up on the mountains, we dared the law of physics to spoil our fun. The waves smashed into the craggy boulders at the base of the mountain, white water spewed several feet into the air, and we jumped from boulder to boulder alongside the waves, our bare feet landing on slick wet rock. Sprinting across the mountains, we grew nimbler and more fearless by the hour. Suppose one of us had slipped, cracked a skull, fell unconscious into the churning lake? That didn't seem to be of parental concern, so it wasn't ours either.

After a breakneck game of tag, we all needed a breather. We were bent over filling our plastic dishes with wild blueberries, one small dot of a berry at a time, when I looked up to see my father staggering up the mountain, stopping every thirty seconds or so, hands on his knees and hunched over. "Kids—" he extended his red plastic cup in an arc in front of his chest as if to introduce himself to the mountain, and a splash of brown liquid caught the trim of his shirt, "—how're the blueberries?" He made his way up to us and tipped the last of his drink into his mouth. "Got one heck of a craving for some blueberries. I'm hungry enough to eat the arsehole out of a dead skunk."

I tried not to invite that image into my mind as my father plunked himself down and set into a picking frenzy. He fumbled with the blueberry plants like a blind man, sometimes requiring a second or third go at the berries before dropping them into his plastic cup.

David and I jumped down to flank him; we would take the company of Chuck McInnis in any situation offered. We started picking blueberries alongside him as fast as our little fingers could manage. David popped every blueberry he picked into dad's mouth. The rest of the kids stood around and made sure not to smirk at the hairy slice of butt crevice that had come exposed as our dad assaulted the blueberry bushes.

When he had his fill of berries, our father stood up and began tottering back down to the beach. Two steps in, he stumbled and his body lurched to the jagged rocks, blueberries flying. His plastic cup bounced into the lake. Face planted into the mountain, he lay there for a few seconds. At first, not one of us kids could bring ourselves to help. Caught in an awkward bind between rescuing a revered father and acknowledging the embarrassing scene, we were glued to our spots, none of us daring to reveal any facial expression other than concern. After a painful eternity, David sprang forward.

He brushed pebbles from dad's arm and tried to help pull him up. A trickle of blood sketched a line from dad's eyebrow to his chin. He cleared his throat and bowed deeply. "Ahem. I thank you, my fair lad," he said in his fake British drawl. He ruffled David's hair and then stopped, his hand resting on David's head, staring into his face. David was a miniature version of our father, whereas I took after our mother, and as dad stood staring down at David, they made a pleasing portrait of likeness. "Thank you, son." This time, his voice was genuine and the *son* caught in his throat. He reached up and wiped his eye, then placed his hand on David's shoulder. His emotional bout passed as quickly as it came. "Now—gotta see a man about a horse," he announced, then jumped in the air and clicked his heels together, landing with an impressive wobble. He screwed his ball cap tight on his head, hoisted up his pants by the belt, and jigged back down the mountain to the adults.

I sat hunched over, fiddling with my blueberry dish, an acidic stream rippling in my stomach. If David magically disappeared— just for a summer or something, not for all of eternity—would *I* get a fatherly hand on my shoulder and a choked up "daughter?" I knew it was wrong to think about my brother this way. Still, I did not feel like joining the other kids for the rest of the afternoon.

Later that evening, when Dad took his place at the captain's wheel to drive us home, the unsettled feeling in my tummy returned. I had a hunch that a rum-guzzling marathon under the blazing sun was not on the list of safety protocols.

Windy conditions were tricky, even for veteran boaters. When the waves whipped up taller than the sides of the boat, the safest course was to cut sideways across the waves, like slicing across the grain of a steak. That evening, it was anybody's guess which way was sideways. The wind charged at us and angry waves tossed us off keel. We tumbled over one another, and the lifejackets we should have been wearing scattered across the deck.

The sky darkened, and the lake grew more sinister. David clung to me, his pale fingers wrapped around my neck. We were on the cusp of a tragedy—I could sense it in the pit of my stomach. Eyes bulging, I pleaded with each wave that smashed into our boat, anticipating the terrifying moment when our vessel would capsize in frigid water. A breaker crashed over the bow of the boat, and I burrowed my face into David's hair, cradling his head into my chest as if somehow, my scrawny body was strong enough to shield him. David trembled.

"Remember, little buddy? You're my wee prince and I'm your knight in sparkling armor. I promise I will never let anything bad happen to you. Ever."

When we finally reached the dock, and dad moored the boat, David let out a deep sigh, and his body relaxed. It was not in David's realm of understanding to consider Murphy's Law, or the insidiousness of sibling rivalry.

But for me, the veil had been lifted. One flung cup of blueberries and a hairy ride home, and my juvenile sense of security and immortality buckled. This was my first realization that adults did not, in fact, have everything under control. The consequences surged at me all at once—the risks inherent in being part of a world that had no guarantees, no infallible safeguards. And then the dread came. I suddenly had a feeling that some kind of horrible event awaited us, just around the corner.

CHAPTER 4

Summer was the season that children on Mikinaak Island lived for. And more than anything else, summer meant tourists. When I think back to the tourists that brought our island to life each July, I am tormented by one question: if I hadn't met Rhonda Doyle, how would my life be different today?

A large measure of our island's annual revenue poured in during the summer months, straight from the wallets of our beloved tourists. Many tourists were wealthy families who sailed up from the States and docked their boats downtown. Our postcard-worthy downtown bordered Lake Huron, and in the summer months the entire stretch of docks was flanked by tourists' luxury sailboats and 40-foot yachts. The boaters paid for docking space by the day, their yachts functioning as a floating cottage better appointed than most of the locals' homes.

Because the boaters slept and lived in their boats while they were moored to Mikinaak Island, the dock that their boats were tied to became, by extension, a part of their living space, like a driveway or a front porch. The local children, however, spent the choicest parts of their summer days swimming and horsing around on the docks. The dock was *their* sacred space, which had its own set of rules and codes. The boaters parked their yachts in prime swimming real estate and inevitably broke these unwritten rules of the dock, and the local kids resented them for it. It was a paradoxical resentment, as the tourism dollars from these boaters paid for the swimsuits the local kids pranced around in.

More accurately, local youth resented the *adult* tourists. The tourists' children, however, were the hottest things going, from late June until September. My mother's generation must have been as spellbound by tourists as mine was; she went and named me after one. A pretty American tourist named Marina struck up a conversation with my mom downtown, and my mother thought the woman's name sounded exotic. Never mind that we live on an island with *three marinas*—basically floating parking lots reeking of gasoline and fish—the homonym didn't faze my mother in the slightest.

In the summer of '71, a generous estimate would put Mikinaak Island at least half a decade behind North American cities in all ways significant to young people. Cable TV wasn't available yet. So the few urban trends that worked their way into the closets and hairstyles of Islanders took several years to arrive there. And like the game of broken telephone where a message is warped beyond recognition as it is passed along, by the time a certain snippet of popular culture was ferried to the Island, perhaps via a cousin visiting from the big city, the style that made its way in front of our mirrors was a warped reflection of anything found on the streets of Toronto. So, all young newcomers to Mikinaak were prone to fanatical glorification. When a tourist kid showed up on the Mikinaak docks, they were studied with great interest; they brought the cutting edge of the outside world with them.

Unimaginably wealthy from our perspective, always from places that sounded much more interesting than our own, and with unlimited leisure time on their hands while they vacationed in our town, we met them at our space of shared ownership—the dock—with reverence.

We kept watch as a new yacht pulled up to the town docks, scanning it for signs of kids on board. Small groups of us planted ourselves near the boats that passed our screen test, and we made a boisterous display of Mikinaak spirit: diving; back flipping into the lake; two of us at a time swinging an underdog by the arms and legs, torpedoing him into the water. We performed so well that the young occupant of the yacht simply could not resist coming over to check out the locals. Often a short-term friendship sparked, tempered with the knowledge that once the tourist family's seven or fourteen-day vacation was over, we most likely wouldn't see them again until next year.

Sometimes, families would invite one or two local kids onto their cruise liners. That was thrilling for many of the friends with whom I grew up hanging around the docks, but for me, the constant stream of boaters paled in comparison to one seasonal family: the Doyles.

I did not want to share the Doyle family with the other kids in town. Rhonda Doyle and her family's private island were my greatest treasure, a shiny pearl which I held clenched to my chest until each summer's end.

I met Rhonda Doyle that summer of 1971 when I was ten years old, by an act of boldness that was so out of character for me that the only thing it can be chalked up to is divine intervention.

I was downtown the first time I laid eyes on her. I watched her leap off the yacht her father was docking, then head down Main Street by herself. She carried a scrunched up five-dollar bill in her hand, which I later learned was her allowance for the week, a fortune compared to the twenty-five cents my brother and I earned.

Rhonda stomped her way down Main Street, transistor radio in hand, incomprehensible song lyrics blasting out of her mouth every few seconds. She bobbed her head and strutted in what looked like an angry dance, past the post office and the bank, past our town's only restaurant—Bub's Family Diner, where the locals were welcome to take their time sipping free coffee refills and filling entire ashtrays with cigarette butts, passing the hours catching up with their neighbours about what had happened since they last spoke at length the day before. Rhonda marched her way across the entire commercial offering of Main Street—the small A&P grocery store, Boyer's gift shop, the laundromat, Stedman's, and Smitty's Home Hardware—until she reached the last shop on the strip, Frank's Automotive. She stopped in front of the propped-open auto shop door and stuffed her radio into her backpack. She marched in, as comfortable as if she was walking into her living room. A mechanic with an oil-stained red kerchief secured over his hair and finger-length black curls shooting out the back stopped his wrench, still fastened around a bolt on a tire. Without looking up from the tire, he spat on the concrete floor. "You looking for the gift shop?"

Rhonda took four steps so she was standing directly over the mechanic. "I'm rebuilding the engine of my gutless Honda 125 crotch rocket. I need two CJK spark plugs, a new clutch, and brake pads—and don't bother giving me none of that refurbished crap."

The mechanic's stern eyes moved slowly from Rhonda's black sneakers up to her messy, wind-blown ponytails. Rhonda stood straight, chin out, eyes meeting his. The mechanic stared her down for several seconds, then tipped his head back and roared into laughter and spat once more on the concrete for good measure.

"Young lady, I would be delighted to assist you in the bolstering of your gutless crotch rocket." And he walked away to locate Rhonda's items, shaking his head, his face a large grin.

I know this exchange, because all the way down the street I spied on Rhonda Doyle. I caught a glimpse of her the moment she stepped off the yacht with her father, and I trailed her like a thief every step of the way down the street. I saw something I longed for in myself in the way she swaggered down the sidewalk. Something familiar about the way she looked drew me to her. The moment she left the auto shop, a bag of brand new dirtbike parts swinging from her hand, I mustered every ounce of courage to race ahead of her on the sidewalk, plant my foot down right where she was about to take her next step, and announce, "Hello. My name is Marina McInnis and I would like to be your personal guide to Mikinaak Island."

And that's how it all began. For the next three summers, Rhonda Doyle and I were inseparable from Canada Day weekend until Labour Day, when the Doyles would pull up anchor and return to their urban lives, the glimmer of their presence fading like the wake of a boat in dark water.

CHAPTER 5

That first summer I met Rhonda Doyle, I had a part-time job babysitting all five Miller kids on Tuesdays and Thursdays when their mom went to work. The rest of the week was pure freedom; I spent that freedom on Rhonda.

Every Monday, Wednesday, and Friday morning, I biked into town and down to the municipal docks, propped my bike against a telephone pole, and sat on the dock waiting for my ferry captain to arrive. At ten o'clock sharp one morning, Rhonda's aluminum Lund came skidding across the water toward the docks, closing the distance too quickly, looking as though Rhonda was going to plough headfirst into the dock. Then, just when I was sure I was about to witness my best friend getting pulverized, Rhonda cranked the outboard steering handle as far to the left as she could, and the boat swiveled ninety degrees to become parallel with the dock, coasting the final metre in: flawless dockage. The twenty-something-year-old dock attendant came running over to her, hands planted on hips, eyebrows working overtime. "Miss Doyle, need I remind you *again* that it's against the rules to approach the dock at over 10 miles per hour?"

Rhonda hopped out of the boat and popped the attendant in the arm. "Aw, come on, Gordo. You know as well as I do that my twelve horsepower is not big enough to rock any of these boats. Take a chill pill, chief." She smiled her gap-toothed smile, and Gordon rolled his eyes.

Rhonda drove like a sociopath, but the ride was worth it to spend the day on her island. Elsinore was only two kilometres across the channel, and Rhonda had been driving various models of her father's boats since she was old enough to swim. She had a knack for all things mechanical. I once heard her interrogate a burly repairman down at the marina: "You sure the boat's problem is the *fuel pump*? You checked to see if the coil's pooched?" She thought there was no better use of her time than burning around a private island on a dirt bike, chestnut ponytails flying out the back of her helmet, skinny bare legs riddled with scabs and burns from her bike's exhaust pipe.

When Rhonda pulled her fishing boat up onto shore at Elsinore, we got right down to business. With a shortfall of cash and an ongoing need for candy, I was always trying to devise ways to earn a few extra quarters. I had overheard my uncle telling a story to my parents about how some wealthy American tourists who came to Mikinaak for fishing loved to use frogs for bait, and I suggested to Rhonda that we catch frogs and sell them to the boaters in town. Rhonda jumped at the idea.

There was a shallow bay on the east end of Elsinore Island which we dubbed the frog pond. We squatted for hours along the edge of the pond, nets in hand, indulging the primitive parts of our brains with the thrill of the hunt. From time to time, Doyle cousins wandered over to the pond to ask us if we wanted company.

"How's it hangin, dorks? You two wanna see how it's done?" her cousin Clay asked, peering into the murky green water.

"Thanks, but no thanks, Cheese Weasel."

"Suit yourselves. But don't dork out too hard there, losers."

"The ultimate dickwad," Rhonda said, making a wet farting noise as she tossed a scummy rock in his direction. We giggled as Clay blew his bangs in the air then huffed away.

I turned all my attention back to Rhonda. I had no interest in hanging out with any of the other Doyle kids, but especially not Clay. And for some miraculous reason, Rhonda always chose my company over any of her cousins.

Once we had caught our quota of amphibians for the day, Rhonda and I deposited our writhing green mass into a bucket, and hopped back into her fishing boat with the rest of our business supplies in tow—an old cigar box we had transformed into a cash box; our hand-painted sign: *"Bait for sale: Frogs! Our hoppers will snag you a whopper!!! (50¢ a jar);"* a box of empty mason jars whose lids we had taken a hammer and nails to; and a plastic bag that Rhonda filled with whatever snacks and drinks she could pilfer from the fridge that day—two bottles of root beer and a large bag of dill pickle chips being an ideal haul. We zipped across the channel and set up shop on the town docks, waving around a sample jar of our unfortunate creatures, hollering to every tourist who made the mistake of glancing in our direction, "Frooooooogs! A fisherman's best friend!"

We spent our first week in the live bait business screaming our throats raw and hopping gleefully around the dock without a single customer.

In the second week of business, a windblown man with a stubbly face stepped off a wooden skiff and sauntered over to our sign. "How much for your whole bucket of frogs?" he asked, peering into our swampy pail. A customer wanting to buy all of our stock at once? This was a concept that had not occurred to either of us. Rhonda didn't skip a beat.

"Sorry, partner. Limit of one jar per customer."

The man scratched his beard in slow strokes. "And if I may be so bold as to inquire, just how many customers have you had today, young lady?"

Rhonda polished the sample frog jar with a towel and looked straight up at the man. Her face was composed and serious. "I apologize," she answered, "but that is none of your beeswax."

I blushed and had to look down. The man slapped his thigh so loudly that I jumped, and then he broke into thunderous laughter. "Well, I'll be. It looks like we have two astute young entrepreneurs here. I will take one jar of frogs, and you, young lady, can keep the change." He slapped a five-dollar bill into Rhonda's hand. She handed him the jar of frogs, and he strolled back over to his boat, chuckling to himself as he walked.

We couldn't fathom our good fortune. Rhonda suggested that we celebrate our first sale of the season by closing up shop and walking over to the candy store. The rest of the afternoon was spent lounging under the shade of a weeping willow tree, a colossal bag of malted milk balls and gummy bears nestled between us. We watched the waves rock the boats along the dock and spied on the tourists as they went about their business on their yachts, trying to deduce which families were the good ones, and which ones had the dirtiest, most rotten secrets.

With our workday unexpectedly shortened, Rhonda announced that before she headed back to Elsinore Island for supper, she had enough time to teach me how to drive her Lund. Driving a boat was something I had always been content to leave to others.

"What if you need to come out to my island and get me?" Rhonda reasoned. "You gonna swim?"

Never mind that I didn't have access to a boat. Not in a million years would my dad let me drive his.

"There's no way I can drive your boat. I'm horrible at that type of thing," I said.

Rhonda hopped into her boat and patted the metal bench seat beside her.

"Promise me you won't think I'm pathetic?" I said.

Rhonda stared at me for a long time. My heart pounded. *Please tell me that I don't even realize how amazing I am.*

She shook her pigtails. "No can do, M. I don't make promises. Not even to you."

I struggled to compete against the tossing waves under Rhonda's patient instruction, but every time I steered the boat one way, the waves would tip us the other way. One particularly large wave sent the bow of the boat so high up in the air that I thought we were going to flip completely backwards, and then when the boat slammed back down, the nose sunk so deep that we started taking on water. Rhonda saw my eyes bulging, my white knuckles trembling on the steering handle. She patted me on the knee. "Lesson's over. Good job, skipper," she said, and took over. Rhonda drove us back to the town docks. As I stepped off the boat, I saw a strange look on Rhonda's face that I had never seen before. She looked serious, but also oddly tender, as though she were telling me an embarrassing secret—a rare look for a girl who spat nails. "I'm serious, M," she said, as she revved her motor to head back to Elsinore. "You were brave out there. I think you're pretty cool, in a backwards sort of way." And then she launched a stream of saliva through the gap in her teeth, gave a military salute, and burned out from the dock, breaking the ten miles-per-hour speed limit for the hundredth time.

I could not get enough of Rhonda Doyle.

Rhonda came from a line of people who were comfortable living alongside an army of domestic help. On our walk from the Elsinore dock down the footpath to the cottage, past the wide verandah where Rhonda's mother Victoria was likely to be found, servant bell on the table beside her, through the great room and into the kitchen, we might cross paths with a couple of groundskeepers, the laundry girl, the cook's helper, and the maid. Rhonda's father was the least likely to be seen—he inhabited his office in the north wing of the estate right up until evening cocktail hour, when he would present himself in a silk jacket and meticulously creased pants.

Several of the staff who lived on Elsinore Island during the summers had been employed there since before Rhonda was born. One staff member in particular, Ettie, a robust woman with jowls that lent her a bulldog appearance, took to overseeing Rhonda in the concerned way usually reserved for mothers and close aunts. When Rhonda wasn't behind the estate on the docks, tinkering with a boat motor or rebuilding her dirt bike, she was saddled at the kitchen counter, chatting with Ettie. Ettie was the head cook, and had thrived in her position for over a decade. She lived with the Doyle family in their home in Toronto during the rest of the year as their housekeeper, and took up her post in the Elsinore kitchen each summer.

Ettie's specialty was sauces. She must have been a saucier in one of Paris' finest restaurants in a former life. Her meats were so succulent, always drizzled with a gravy that added an unexpected note, perfectly complementing the dish. Whenever I ate dinner at the Doyle estate, I was underdressed and overfed. It is a wonder that most of the Doyles managed to stay so trim—it was a true testament to their love of outdoor exercise—as Ettie's dishes demanded that everyone at the table ate far beyond their needs.

Every Wednesday, Ettie was responsible for preparing the food for the Doyle family picnic, in which all extended family members piled into a fleet of canoes and rowed over to a nearby uninhabited island. They would spend the afternoon fishing out of the canoes, and then have a fish fry over a campfire, complete with fried potatoes, pork and beans, coleslaw, potato salad, several loaves of Ettie's freshly baked bread, and coffee perked over the fire in a big metal pot. Many a Wednesday found Rhonda and me hanging around Ettie's stove as she prepared for the picnic feast. We drew stories out of her while we feigned helpfulness.

On one such Wednesday, Rhonda sat on a stool yanking off the satin bows her mother had insisted on tying onto her ponytails. Rhonda jammed the bows into the pocket of her overalls.

"Sweetcheeks, don't tell your mom I said this, but I'm not sure you and ribbons were ever meant for one another," Ettie offered, stroking Rhonda lightly under the chin.

Rhonda's mother was bent on sanding down Rhonda's rough edges. Ettie told us that in her younger days, Victoria Doyle had been a promising ballet dancer who was accepted into the National Ballet of Canada. But marriage and motherhood had presented themselves at an inopportune time, and that was the end of her professional dancing career. Less than a year after packing her ballet shoes in a box at the bottom of her closet, she gave birth to a beautiful baby girl and laced her dreams for her daughter in pink satin.

"Did I ever tell you about your fourth birthday party?"

Rhonda rolled her eyes. "Not this one again, Ettie."

"On the day of your party, you made it clear as day that there was no way on God's green earth your mother was going to get you into one of those hand-smocked dresses overflowing from your closet. I seen you tugging at that thing like it was on fire, and you howled until your mother couldn't take it any longer.

"For your present, Mrs. Doyle had custom-ordered a life-sized doll from a doll maker in Paris. Musta cost her a pretty penny, I tell you that. The doll had long, wavy brown hair and moss green eyes—a porcelain version of you. You'd been pacing the house like a dog in heat all morning, asking every two seconds if it was time to open your present. Finally, they set you loose on the gift, wrapped all neat and tidy with a big pink bow on top. You tore off the paper to reveal that lovely porcelain-faced doll. Your mother watched, hands clasped together, longing to see your little face light up.

"You lifted the doll high above your head, and launched that poor thing onto the ceramic tiles. That doll's face shattered into twenty pretty little pieces. You looked up at your mother—I'll never forget—and told her plain and plunk, 'I asked for a train.'"

Rhonda smirked at Ettie.

"Ettie, if you're going to tell us a story, tell us about the ghost of Uncle Teddy. *Pleeease.*"

Ettie shook her head and rolled her eyes at us. "Good Lord, I never seen two girls with such an appetite for ..." Ettie paused to retrieve one of her new words, "...the, ah, *macabre.*"

Ettie was working on refining her vocabulary, and memorized one new word every day. She had been denied an education when she was a little girl, and had grown up knowing that people thought she was stupid. Once she became an adult, Ettie worked her way through literacy classes until she was reading classic romantic literature with ease. She adored Jane Austen, and declared that someday she would speak as eloquently as Emma Woodhouse. But Ettie hadn't lost her fondness for curse words. My ears always perked up at the novelty of hearing Ettie swear, as cursing was one of the few vices my parents strictly opposed.

Rhonda quietly took the dough from Ettie's hands and began to knead it herself. She knew better than to beg. Ettie selected a chef's knife and started chopping celery. I fidgeted quietly on the kitchen stool for a couple of minutes while Rhonda grunted as she worked the bread dough. Then Ettie, without looking up from her cutting board, started talking.

Mikinaak Island was teeming with ghost stories, most likely because everyone had at least a second-degree connection to everyone else's business. Aside from accidents and injuries, our sparsely populated island supplied little in the way of news. But the locals could always count on a handful of annual drownings to satisfy their craving for unsavory tales. Any death that took place within ten feet of the lake somehow ended up as suspicious. You could practically mark a big red x on your calendar: two weeks after someone died, a tale of a new haunting on the lake would be floating around Mikinaak. But I guess that's island life for you.

Teddy Doyle and Rhonda's mother Victoria were siblings— Victoria had kept her powerful maiden name when she married. Victoria adored each of her four siblings, but no one compared to her beloved big brother Teddy. An impossibly handsome young man with a silver tongue and more assets than the net worth of Mikinaak's entire population, Teddy left a stream of fluttering female hearts and clenched male fists in his wake whenever he ventured into town. Shortly after his death, Teddy was immortalized in the form of a supernatural fiction that every Mikinaakian adult and child could recite.

Ettie closed her eyes, then continued.

"Well, if I'm gonna talk about Teddy, it's gotta start with his wedding. From the get-go, there was something not quite right about that day. Started with the weather—worst rain I ever seen, the Elsinore grounds were slipperier n' pigshit. But the sky cleared up at the very last minute, and all of Elsinore's staff were runnin around at a hundred clicks, makin sure every goddamn tree had a silk bow on it and whatnot.

"By the time the bride, Cissy, took her first steps down the path, every flower was hung, every bow was tied. It was...ah, *sublime*, I tell you.

"But then Teddy stepped into view, and all the guests sucked in their breath. It was his eyes. I ain't never seen a man looking so... ah, *tormented*.

"Well, the ceremony goes on fine enough, but the whole time, I just can't keep my eyes off Teddy. Something was not right with that man. Then, as I'm headin back to the main cottage to grab more trays of food, that's when I seen him, lurking around."

"Saw who, Ettie?"

Ettie slid the celery into a plastic bowl. She dumped a bag of dirt-encrusted potatoes next to the sink and started scrubbing them. We knew enough not to prompt her—that would only result in her pausing even longer, to teach us to mind our manners.

Ettie lifted the clean potatoes onto a cutting board. One rolled toward the edge but Rhonda snatched it up and put it back.

"Lenny 2-Pints. Didn't know his real name at the time—Teddy'd dubbed him that, thought it was funny. Lenny was this Native guy who delivered pints of milk and groceries by boat here almost every day. I remember thinking, 'Now what in God's name is 2-Pints doin here this late in the afternoon, and on Teddy's wedding day to boot?' Teddy couldn't stand Lenny—just the week before, Teddy'd given him a shiner.

"Well, I keep my eye on Lenny, and I'm gettin the uneasy feeling that I'm watchin something very bad unfold. At first, I think Lenny's spyin on the wedding guests through the trees; then I figure it out—he's got his eye on Teddy. Watchin him like a hawk. It gave me the chills, I tell you. So, I'm just about to go ask the guy what the hell he's up to, when I seen him head down toward Teddy's boathouse. By now I've got a real sick feeling in my belly about whatever is goin on, and I decide I'd better go get Teddy.

"Well, soon enough after I talk to Teddy, I hear fightin and screamin, and I go runnin down to the boathouse, in time to see Teddy beating Lenny to a pulp. And there's your mother Katherine, on the ground, cryin, her hair every which way. Teddy'd got there just in time, from the looks of it, thank Jesus. So I'm helping Katherine out of there, and I turn around for one last look at those men, and I'll never forget what I seen. Lenny is glarin at Teddy, and the look in his eyes—the only way I can describe it is that they were burnin with pure evil. I tell you, those eyes lit up like a man possessed. Then Lenny got real quiet and his voice took on this....ah, *ominous* sound. Made my skin crawl. He whispered, 'You messed with the wrong guy. You're a dead man, Teddy Doyle.'

"Now, someone could just chalk words like that up to nothin, especially considering Teddy was a racist son of a bitch—I'm sorry to say that he *was* that. But there was somethin about that warning that I just couldn't shake. I tell you, I'll never forget the look in that man's eyes that night, or the chilling sound of his voice as long as I live." Ettie paused. "I've never been able to shake the suspicion that Lenny had something to do with Teddy's death."

"Seriously, Ettie? You honestly think this 2-Pints dude had something to do with Uncle Teddy's drowning?"

Ettie scowled at Rhonda. "It'd serve you well to shut your yap, Rhonda Doyle. If you'd seen that man's eyes, and then later learned more about him, you'd think it, too."

Ettie waited until the kitchen was completely silent for several seconds. "Several years later, I seen his face on the front page of the *Record*. It was him, all right—Lenny 2-Pints. The Bearwalker case they called it. He was killed while attempting murder." Ettie's eyes watered as she told this last detail. She shivered, and swallowed hard before speaking again. "Said he had some sort of shape-shifting powers."

The air around us seemed to dip several degrees colder.

Ettie lowered her head, and began slicing the clean potatoes into uniform discs. She sliced away, silently daring either Rhonda or me to disrupt the pacing of her story.

The Bearwalker. I got tingles thinking that man had crossed paths with my mother on Elsinore Island. My mom had a *Record* article about the Bearwalker case tucked behind a photo in her scrapbook, and I liked to sneak it out and look at it when she wasn't home. I always just thought my mom was interested in creepy, mysterious things the same way us kids were, but that she kept her curiosity hidden, as adults do.

Ettie continued working her knife in silence. Finally, Rhonda lost what little patience came naturally to her. "But what about the *ghost*, Ettie?"

Ettie sliced quietly for a few more minutes and then looked up at Rhonda with narrowed eyes. "The ghost. I thank you for that unnecessary reminder, Honeybunch." She paused again. "A few days after Teddy's wedding, he was out at his favorite fishing hole over by Hay Bay when a bad storm swept up. Who knows? Maybe it was the rough waves that overturned Teddy's fishing boat—no one will ever know for sure. All we know is that Teddy never made it home." Ettie swiped at her face with shaky fingers, pushing away an invisible lock of hair.

"Ever since then, on stormy nights when a fierce wind is thrashin across the lake the same way it did the night Teddy drowned, many fishermen say they seen a man bobbin in the lake, waving his arms. As the fisherman steers his boat toward the drowning man to help, the man's head disappears beneath the waves, and suddenly reappears right in front of the boat. The fisherman has no time to swerve to avoid the man, and feels a sickening thump, as his boat slices into the man's skull. And then the boat makes a second heave, and the boat's prop mows through the man." Ettie checked our faces to gauge our reaction, then continued full steam. "Blood and flesh spray out from the prop, warm chunks go splatterin across the fisherman's face. And then suddenly, the blood, the bits of skull, the shredded clothing—they all evaporate into thin air, and the fisherman is left with a poundin heart and the memory forever burned into his skull of those few god-awful seconds when he was responsible for the gruesome mangling of another man."

Rhonda gurgled an ugly noise.

Ettie shook her head. "Teddy—that poor, stupid son of a bitch—I think maybe he picked the wrong man to mess with. May have gotten *both* your families cursed in the process."

I felt cold beads of sweat prickling my armpits. "What do you mean, Ettie?"

Ettie's face grew uneasy. She drew her lips together as though she shouldn't have let those last words slip. She shifted her attention to her potatoes, eyes glued to the cutting board in front of her. Rhonda and I quietly excused ourselves, and snuck into her aunt's cottage to snoop through the closet full of Teddy's old things that Aunt Cissy could not bring herself to get rid of. We knew Ettie was not going to say another word on the subject of Teddy Doyle that day.

CHAPTER 6

Rhonda took all the sparkle with her when she returned to her Toronto life that September. I had my school friends who I had known my entire life, but it took me a while to regain my taste for them after a summer with Rhonda Doyle.

Jeannie Baker had been in my class all the way through public school. A chubby girl who relished her role as ringleader in our lunchroom games, "Raise your hand if you think Sally Miller's story about Teddy Doyle's ghost is a big fat lie!" Jeannie had a knack for pinpointing the soft spots of the weaker kids in our class, and exposing them for all to take a kick at.

Nobody knew their way around flour, butter, and sugar like the Baker women. When we had church picnics, all of the kids used to crowd around Jeannie Baker, bidding to get her to point out which pie on the long stretch of plastic-covered tables came from her family. One time, my offer of a bag of apples from the best crab apple tree in our forest interested Jeannie, and she whispered in my ear, "Fourth pie up from the Jell-O salad." My brother and I would have been happy to climb our crab apple tree and pick a whole barrel of apples for a slice of Baker family pie.

Jeannie had a different homemade cupcake, frosted with all manner of pink swirls and icing rosebuds, in her lunch pail every single day. I would gaze at the fabulous cupcakes in Jeannie's lunchbox, and saliva would pool in my mouth.

It did not go unnoticed by Jeannie Baker that some school lunches spoke a very different dialect. Following deer hunting season, a third of the kids in my class, most of them Native, would come to school with venison or moose-meat sandwiches. At that time, none of us kids suffered from the modern childhood problem of being disconnected from our food sources, of imagining that hamburgers were plucked whole from tree branches. The walk to school was a brisk forty minutes down our country road, past the Miller farm and into the town proper. On the walk through town, we were greeted with the information, whether we wanted it or not, about whose fathers in town were enjoying a productive hunting season. Sad, almond eyes pleaded with me from where the animals hung, hooked to the garage door frame of each successful hunter. Back limbs splayed and tethered with nylon rope, tongue hanging lopsided toward the ground as though trying to lick one last speck of salt from the pebbles on the driveway, those deer haunted me.

As my brother David and I walked to school, I would keep my eyes squinted so that each deer was a blurry abstract. But in the end I always had to look. As though, if I stared hard enough at the animal's pain, I would somehow be able to stretch my mind over to the animal and salve its wounds.

A third of the children in my class were from the Big River Ojibwe Native reserve. The reserve spanned only two miles—inland territory that government officials had not thought of as particularly valuable at the time the Natives were forced to give up their hunting lifestyle and become farmers on unarable crown land several generations back. Natives were permitted to hunt large game outside of hunting season, and their children would often come to school with sandwiches featuring the hunting bounty. When a Native kid in class held up a moose-meat sandwich, smiling broadly, I knew that despite the slight repulsion I felt, I must not show disdain. When a kid peeled back the pasty white bread of their sandwich to show the dark, wild meat, what they also saw was a father who had spent hours waiting silently in the cold bush, suppressing coughs and sneezes, scarcely breathing as he awaited the thousand–pound creature. They saw the expert shot of the gun or arrow, ensuring that the stomach lining or inner organs were not nicked, tainting the meat with the flavour of acid and bile. These children also knew that shot moose don't just fall over and die. That is what one might picture, if they bothered to envision the sequence from moose meat sandwich backwards to the moment bullet met flesh. A moose will soldier on for several miles, leaving a trail of blood painted on pine branches that the hunter must track until it leads either to an animal or to nothingness. In the case of a dead end, the hunter must use a combination of intuition and hunter wisdom to determine which way the moose staggered. The Native children understood, better than any of us white kids, that the meat of the hunted animal was to be proffered respect.

Jeannie Baker felt differently. Even though I had no part in it, my light skin burned with an accomplice's shame just from having witnessed what happened. Bird Manaabeh was a Native boy for whom a packed lunch was something of a rare event. At school, while the rest of us were eating our lunch, Bird usually sat quietly, thin hands folded in his lap, staring intently at the crude etchings from a former occupant of his Formica-topped desk.

One remarkable day, Bird—whose real name was Brian, although only the teachers called him that—brought a lunch to school. He tenderly unrolled the large brown grocery bag that was repurposed as his lunch sack. His back straightened and he held his chin high as he pulled out an unwrapped sandwich. The sandwich had thick chunks of grey moose meat poking out the sides. Bird lifted the sandwich, and just before he took his first bite, Jeannie Baker pointed to his sandwich and let out a squeamish *ewww*. She screwed up her face and jammed a finger down her throat. "Ever sick!" She dragged the last syllable of 'ever' up to a loud, high note. "Bird's got a road kill sandwich! Get that raunchy thing away from me!" Jeannie dragged her desk a few inches away from Bird's, then pitched her head forward and made vomiting noises.

Several other children laughed at the drama. The pride bled from Bird's face, his dark amber eyes ducked down to the familiar spot on his desk, and he placed the sandwich down on the finished plywood. As Jeannie continued to dry retch, Bird slowly peeled the upper layer of soft, white bread from his uneaten sandwich. He summoned a rattling mouthful from the back of his throat, and, neck bent down, released a long, yellow-green wad of spit from his mouth that dangled before it made a soft landing into the center of the grey moose meat. He then carefully placed the sandwich back in the paper grocery bag, walked across the classroom to the metal garbage can, and dropped his sandwich in. This by the thin boy who barely whispered an answer when the teacher asked him a question, the boy who had probably not eaten a proper sandwich since the previous moose hunt.

That cherished meal hitting the metal can made a sickening clunk; a one-note song of deprivation and intolerance that made my heart ache whenever I let down my guard and allowed myself to think about such heavy things. I sensed there was something that implicated me as guilty along with Jeannie, even if I was still too young to comprehend precisely what.

That night, with Schnapps at my feet waiting for every dropped morsel, I toiled in the kitchen over a batch of monster cookies. Chock full of peanuts, chocolate chips, and Smarties, they were the tastiest treat I knew of. I brought the entire batch of cookies to school in a paper bag the next morning, and slipped it into Bird's locker along with the note, "Sorry it's not moose meat" and a smiley face. I knew my father wouldn't approve of me making something for a boy from the reserve, but I didn't care. I didn't fully grasp the reasons behind the guilty ache I felt in my stomach when I thought about Bird—his lean body, his dark amber eyes, his tan beige skin—but I had a general sense that life was far harder for him and the people who made up his community on the reserve, than it was for me and the people who made up the community I occupied a few miles down the road. I intuited that, even if not because of anything I had done to him specifically, there were reparations to be made, and it was partially my duty to make them.

I cherished watching Bird eat those cookies at lunch every day that week, and the following weekend, I spent my allowance on more chocolate chips and Smarties. Somehow, Bird figured out it was me. He inched up to me at recess, and then stood there, shifting from food to foot, eyes averted. Finally, he brought his eyes up to meet mine. His voice was barely a whisper. "Thank you, Marina."

That winter, the McInnis children's school lunches resembled those of the Native kids. Our father was getting fewer hours at the mill; we ate a lot of trout sandwiches. Dad didn't have a taste for shooting large game animals—a deer had once looked him in the eye for one second too long, and that had been the end of his hunting career— but he lived for ice fishing. Usually dad preferred to fish alone, but one bright February Sunday, he smiled up at David and me over his eggs. "You kids wanna join me out at the shack today?" You would think he had offered to take us to Disneyland.

The concept of a house built on *ice* did not sit right with me, but I pasted on my most enthusiastic grin and lugged as much as I could carry across the ice alongside my dad. David was at ease out on the ice, and his eyes shone as he helped our father crank the auger to bore a hole in the ice. I tried not to think about the fact that we were half a mile from shore, standing under the hot sun with only a layer of ice separating us from the frigid lake.

Dad set up rods for both David and me, and within minutes, David's line was jerking. Of course it would be *David's* line. He squealed with delight, and dad was immediately at his side with the gaff hook, hollering encouragements.

David yanked his rod and pleaded with the fishy, and dad waited on standby with the gaff, and after a few moments of an underwater tussle, David reeled the fish to the surface and dad hooked the gaff through its jaw.

"Attaboy!" Dad ruffled David's hair and let out a loud whistle. "Some catch, son!" David clapped his hands and danced around the fishing hole, until he caught a glimpse of me. He stopped clapping and patted me on the back. "You'll get the next one, Meenie!"

I suddenly *needed* to show my father that I could catch a fish. *Had to.* I held the fishing line in my hand and prayed secretly. "*Please*, lake. Please give me a fish. I'll do *anything* you ask for just one big fish." I plopped the line into the hole.

I held my breath and studied the lake's gentle tug on my line. "Please lake. I'll do *anything.*"

Suddenly, my fishing pole was nearly wrenched from my hand. The rod was bent so deeply it looked like it would snap. Adrenaline and joy shot through me. I jumped back, my hands shaking, and screamed for my father to grab the gaff.

"Can't!" Dad yelled from the ice shack. "Gotta see a man about a horse."

"David! Grab the gaff!"

David tripped over his own feet as he raced to get the gaff. He scrambled over to the hole. My rod was being yanked so hard I feared it would slip from my hands. Certainly the line would break at any second. My heart was pounding. "Dad! Hurry up! *Please, please hurry!* I think this is the biggest fish any of us have *ever* caught!"

I started to reel the line in, and the fish's head surfaced. My mouth fell open.

"You caught Jaws!" David's eyes bulged.

"Dad! Quick! You won't believe this!"

My reel jammed. I clicked the handle back and forth desperately, but it wouldn't turn the spool. "Dad! Hurry!"

David faltered with the gaff.

"*Jesus,* David!"

David plunged his gaff into the hole again and again, and misjudged the fish's trajectory every time. The end of the rod was bent down in a deep arc, submerged. I tried to hoist the rod up, but the end just bent deeper down into the water. I cringed, waiting for the horrible snapping sound.

"For crying out loud, David, get it right! The line won't hold much longer!" My arm muscles were already aching from exertion at such an unusual angle. "Daaaaaad!"

David scrambled to the opposite side of the hole and lunged with the gaff hook. I felt an instant release as my rod sprang back.

David's eyes widened. He dropped the gaff, and his hands flew to his cheeks. "Meenie, I'm so sorry."

Suddenly I was overcome with rage. I hurled my rod across the ice. "You idiot! You had *one job* to do!"

David's chin began to tremble. His eyes glistened with tears. I had never spoken harshly to him before. I looked up, and our father stood behind me with his hands on his hips. He shook his head and looked from David to me.

"I think you owe your brother an apology," he said. The disappointment in his voice burned my ears.

I stomped off to the shack, instantly feeling sick for losing my temper with David, but feeling even worse that I had displeased my father. I sulked in the shack and consoled myself with the thought that the school year was more than halfway over. Only four months left until the return of Rhonda Doyle.

CHAPTER 7

A pandemic plagued Mikinaak Elementary School that spring: we had the supernatural on the brain. Every kid on the playground was obsessed with out of body experiences, telekinesis, séances, Ouija boards—anything to transport our minds out of our insulated town. One of the kids in our class had access to the entire twelve-volume *Extraordinary Phenomena* hardcover series, each volume exploring a different paranormal phenomenon in great detail. This kid thanked his lucky stars for the day his parents phoned in the order after seeing it on a TV commercial. Those books made him the recess king. We would all huddle around *Out of Body Travel* or *Phantom Encounters*, our bodies spread out in the grass in a tight circle, every neck straining for a glimpse at the book in the center.

Teddy Doyle's ghost was another headliner for the kids in my class. We had our pick of several homegrown ghost stories to amuse ourselves, but Teddy Doyle, with all his glamour and gore, was our hands-down favorite.

There were two popular activities we would do to summon Teddy Doyle's ghost, either of which could land us in the office for the strap. One involved a kid bear-hugging another kid who held his breath. A ring of kids would encircle the suffocating boy, chanting,

Charming Teddy Doyle, Lake Huron got your nose
Show us, Teddy Doyle, what the dark lake knows

over and over as the kid had the consciousness squeezed out of him. The kid's head would eventually flop forward, and he would be laid down on the ground, where he would supposedly see a vision of what really happened the night Teddy Doyle had his face chewed to shreds and drowned.

There were many variations of the Teddy Doyle summoning, and I longed to try one of them. But I was loathe to risk earning a teacher's disapproval. If I so much as got scolded by my teacher for turning in incomplete homework, I would lay awake at night mulling over my teacher's words, chastising myself for having compromised my status as the perfect student. So, I saved my dabbling into the mystical realm of Teddy Doyle for home turf.

But I needed an assistant. David was the type of kid who whimpered during scary movies, and frightening scenes in books. He was convinced that the *creepers* were out to get him whenever he was alone. I knew he was going to be a hard sell. But David would crawl to the edge of the earth if his big sis suggested it.

"David, do you want to try a magic trick in the bathroom?"

I filled our bathtub with water, and turned out the lights. Grasping one another's hands, we leaned over the bathwater and closed our eyes. I led us in the chant, "*Charming Teddy Doyle, Lake Huron got your nose—*"

Suddenly, David's hands recoiled from mine. He let out a scream that flooded my veins with adrenaline. I opened my eyes, and turned to see my little brother covering his wide eyes with one hand, and pointing with his other hand toward the bathwater. I saw nothing.

Our mom came rushing upstairs, and when David was finally able to stop the horrible noise blaring from his mouth, all that he would say over and over again through tears was, "Teddy Doyle..."

Mom's face grew visibly pale. "You have no idea what you are messing with." She rung her hands, undecided whether to smack me or pull David close. "I don't *ever* want to hear of you tampering with Teddy Doyle again. Never! Do you hear me?"

Our mother was a superstitious woman who always chose to take a wide detour around anyone gossiping about the local ghosts that were part of the fabric of Mikinaak life. I had once made the mistake when I was much younger of bringing home a schoolyard story about Teddy Doyle, and I remember how distressed she was then, too. "Have you no respect, Marina McInnis?" she had yelled, her voice an odd pitch. "Did you forget that I worked for that man's family? That I knew the Doyles personally? Let the poor man rest in peace." I sensed from the way her voice faltered that she had good reason to believe in the ghost of Teddy Doyle, despite her protests to the contrary.

Mom gave me the silent treatment for the next two weeks. But the thing I felt far worse about was that whatever David had seen in the bathtub began to give him terrible nightmares. The first time he woke up screaming, mom marched David into my bedroom where I was deep asleep, yanked back my covers, and handed David over to me. "You created this problem. You deal with it," she said, then walked out and slammed my bedroom door. I was used to having David come scuttling into my bed in the middle of the night whenever his dreams were haunted by the *creepers*, but he would always fall right back to sleep as soon as he was snuggled against me. But David was not able to sleep peacefully now. Whatever he thought he saw in the bathwater that day was creeping into his thoughts when he lay down at night. He found no peace in my logical explanations about how these types of things are just make-believe stories crafted to tickle children with fear. For the next month, my little brother became my restless bed companion, and the set of dark circles beneath both of our eyes grew darker with every passing day.

CHAPTER 8

I learned about the animal spirits from Bird Manaabeh, the Native boy in my class whose lunch bag had not deigned to carry moose meat sandwiches ever since Jeannie Baker humiliated him. Bird's mother cleaned our house twice a month, and sometimes she would bring Bird and a few of his younger siblings along. It was understood that my father preferred the cleaning lady's brood to stay outside while their mother cleaned. "It's okay to be *school friends* with them, but just...know your place, Mina," he instructed me about the Native kids. My mother shook her head at him, muttering under her breath.

I felt like a traitor to Bird as I nodded obediently. I wondered where this invisible ranking system came from, and promised myself that when I was an adult, I would disobey it.

The younger kids would play by themselves with their bums planted in the gravel at the end of our driveway, content to toss stones. Bird was too old to be entertained this way, so he sat in the car and watched the birds fly from one leafy branch to the next, not seeming to mind the heat of the sweltering car.

It wasn't often that the opportunity for a playmate my age presented itself on my driveway. I strode over to the car and stated the obvious. "Hi, Bird. So—you came with your mom."

He continued to watch the birds. "No shit, Sherlock." His voice was quiet, and I couldn't tell if he was embarrassed or being mean.

I kicked at the gravel, sending it skipping under his mother's sedan. My fingers drew swirly patterns in the dust on the car door.

"Want to explore the forest?" he asked, still staring at the birds.

I shrugged, conscious of my face beginning to heat up. "Nothing better to do, I guess."

And with that, he jumped out of the car and dashed into the thick line of trees, and I hurried to catch up.

Bird began to consistently accompany his mom on cleaning days. Each time he would wait in the car until I walked over to greet him, as though on any given day our friendship could expire without warning and he would no longer be invited to come out of the stifling car. Bird and I roamed the forest, and each time he became a little freer with his words.

Our first excursion started out as a silent affair—we stomped around between the birch and the cedars, and Bird pointed out interesting bugs on leaves, then picked the leaves to dangle in front of my nose. As he grew comfortable, he began to name the wild flowers, weeds, and berries, classifying them with a two-word description of their healing properties. I listened, wide-eyed, trying to make a mental note of each of the plants as he presented them to me.

"For sleeping," he said, as he pointed to a wispy flower I did not recognize.

I was fascinated. "Bird, you know so much about this kind of thing."

Bird suddenly fell to the ground.

"Bird! Are you okay?"

Bird rolled around, laughing hysterically.

"What's so funny, Bird?"

"Man, you should see your face!" He fluttered his eyelashes. "*Ohhh Bi-iiird, you wise young Native healer!*" He sat up. "I don't know shit about flowers and herbs, Mina!"

I stared at him, my face growing hot.

Later that day, he pointed to some poison ivy leaves clustered in a sunny clearing. "Aha! Itchius Scratchius Leaf," he said, laughing and lightly tickling my arm. Bird's fingertips set off a cosmos of excited cells radiating across my skin. I slapped his hand away.

One day Bird presented me with a pale yellow flower held intact in his fist. "Hey man, check it out. One flower I actually know. It's a *prim*rose," he said. "Like you. Yellow hair, and..." he smirked.

"All prim and proper?"

He reddened, and a shy smile crept onto his face. "I didn't mean it as a bad thing. Honest."

He sat down, then motioned with his chin for me to do the same. Sitting on the ground, he grew in confidence. "Hey man, do you want to hear something my auntie told me about this forest?"

"More made-up stuff, right?"

Bird's face grew solemn. "Nope. The real deal this time. Scout's honour." He raised his hand in the Vulcan salute, squinting one eye, a cockeyed grin across his face.

I smacked him in the shoulder.

"But seriously, Primrose. I'm not making this stuff up. Here goes. My auntie told me that my people believe there are...what would you call them?...spirits, I guess, that live around here. They're called *Pa'iinsak*, or something like that. My Ojibwe kind of sucks."

He searched my face for a reason to stop talking, and when he found none, he continued to talk. "It ever happen to you, that you're walking along through the woods, just minding your own beeswax, when suddenly you hear a noise that sounds a little like... a bird, but...weirder?"

"Um, I guess. Maybe."

"That's the *Pa'iinsak,* or whatever they're called—the little people." Bird looked over his shoulder, then scooched closer to me. "They're these teeny, ugly people who live in the forest. They'll try to trick you by luring you with their singing." His voice got even quieter. "My auntie thinks my cousin was taken by the little people."

"Come on, Bird. You're making this up. Stop it."

"Am not." Bird paused, and I scrutinized his face for signs of joking.

"My cousin went partridge hunting behind his house, and—" Bird snapped his fingers and I recoiled. "—gone. Never found him."

I looked around, suddenly suspicious of birdsong that filtered through the trees.

"Primrose, man, promise me if you ever hear a weird singing voice in the forest, you won't go over to check it out."

Bird's unease was contagious. Part of me wanted to joke about how following a strange voice through the woods was the *last* thing you'd ever catch Marina McInnis doing, but instead, I gazed toward the forest in the same direction as Bird, and nodded solemnly. "I promise."

Bird went on to tell me of encounters his relatives had had with these forest-and-lake-dwelling spirits. How a pouch of tobacco was once stolen from his uncle's pack while he dozed by a tree; and about a brush with death when the little people overturned his grandpa's canoe. He said more words that afternoon than the sum total of all the words he had ever spoken in my presence.

The next time Bird came to visit, he sat with me on our shore while his mother scrubbed our toilets. He pointed to a spot far out on the horizon. "Hey man. You wanna hear my auntie's story about another creature who lives in this lake?" He pitched a flat rock the size of his palm onto the surface of the lake.

Bird was a master of skipping rocks, and it was my job to act as rock skipping secretary, diligently counting the number of times a rock touched down, and calling out the total when the rock finally lost momentum and sank. It was nothing for Bird to skip a rock fifteen times. Despite his patient instruction, I was not able to achieve the necessary angles to make a rock perform this water dance. So he skipped the rocks and talked, and I tallied the rock results.

Bird's rock skimmed the top of the lake, skipped a few inches in the air, then touched down for an instant before ascending again. "You know sometimes when you're swimming out deep, and suddenly you get the feeling that something awful is right underneath you?" Bird cleared his throat and looked far off where the lake met the horizon.

I nodded. I knew exactly what he was talking about.

"It's not always your imagination, man. Sometimes, it's *Mishi-ginebig*." Bird paused and scrutinized my face, deciding whether he should reveal more.

"*Mishi-ginebig* is an evil serpent who lives in this lake. He has sharp horns growing out of his head and thick, ugly black scales. His tail is so strong it can sink a boat. This Mishi-ginebig, he can't get enough of the taste of human meat. And..." Bird smacked his lips, "...the more sweet and innocent the human is—like you, Primrose—the more delicious it tastes to him!"

"Cut it out, Bird!"

"Sorry, sorry. Anyways, Mishi-ginebig likes to wait until a swimmer or a fisherman is all by himself out on the lake, and then— whoosh! He pulls them under. And man, is he sly—he makes it seem like the person drowned, or he attacks when it's stormy so people blame the sunken boat on the weather."

Bird lobbed another stone toward the lake and we watched as it hopped across the surface.

"Eleven skips," I said. "Does anyone ever manage to escape from this...*gishi-binig* creature?"

"Mishi-ginebig. Get it right."

Bird launched another stone into the water.

"Thirteen."

"Hardly ever. But if someone *was* lucky enough to escape, *Mishi-ginebig* would get sooo mad, man. Once he gets a taste of someone, his hunger for that person grows to the size of the lake."

I tried to assume Bird's quiet poise when I retold his stories of the spirits in the forests and the lakes to David. I embellished the parts I knew would thrill him—the wolf gamboling with a human like a brother in a time before man and wolf became enemies; the trickster *Nanabush* chucking his eyeballs into the sky, never to retrieve them; a small ball of earth placed on a turtle's back as it rested in Lake Huron, expanding to become Mikinaak island.

Bird had told me other stories too, including a little bit about the *Bearwalker*. I tried not to appear too eager as he spoke. It was common knowledge on the Island that Bird's father was serving a life sentence in prison for killing his uncle, who he believed had been using black magic to transform himself into a bear and stalk members of their tribe at night. Bird dug beneath the surface of the story, explaining how the Bearwalker was viewed as a grave threat on the reserve; in killing it Bird's father had done his duty to the tribe. I didn't tell David that story. I knew that if I divulged the gory details of the Bearwalker, it would haunt his dreams too.

The story that brought a squeal of delight, and which David begged me to repeat until he could mouth the words as I spoke them, was the Ojibwe story about a mystical place in the lake. This was a story that Bird had heard many times from his elders, as the flames of a campfire licked the toes of those gathered for a healing retreat.

"Bird's people know about a sacred place hiding way down deep in Lake Huron," I began, "where the great spirits can heal a troubled person's heart. The place is surrounded by *mbaanaabe-kwe*—I'm pretty sure I've got that word right—creatures who have human bodies and fish tails. Native mermaids, basically. The *mbaanaabe-kwe* are lovely, magical creatures who want to help humans who are in trouble. A person can send out a request with his mind, kind of like an underwater telegram, asking the *mbaanaabe-kwe* mermaids to guide him to this sacred healing cave at the bottom of the lake. Bird's elders named this sacred healing place *bagoneyaa wenji-bimaadiziing*—Bird decided a good English translation would be something like 'Broken Man's Grotto'. Anyway, if a person enters Broken Man's Grotto, powerful healing energy zooms through him, until his heart is healed. Then the person can return to the world above to use his healed heart to help others in some way."

"*Mbaanaabe-kwe*," David whispered, spellbound.

Despite me culling the scary parts from Bird's stories when I put David to bed at night, his night terrors continued. Shortly after he drifted off to sleep, stuck to my side like a leech, David's feet would begin to twitch. Then the moaning: "...no! Nooooo! NOOO!" And then the screaming.

David was in a liminal zone in those screaming moments in the middle of the night. He looked awake: his eyes were open, his mouth was a gaping hole. But when I tried to soothe him, I realized he wasn't quite there. He just kept on screaming, not hearing the comforting words I tried to force into his ears.

These screaming sessions had my pulse racing for more than one reason. Whenever David's night terrors went on long enough to wake up my parents, my mother was furious with me. *This was my fault.* Fortunately for me, my parents were devoted to their evening cocktails, and slept like the dead. But there were nights when David's howling managed to cut through the fog of their sleep and the blare of the late night test pattern on their bedroom TV.

I was terrified of waking my parents. Finally one night, out of sheer desperation as David's screams filled the air, I clapped my hand over his mouth and hurried him out of the bedroom and down the hall past the rip of Dad's snore. Downstairs, I knelt to slip David's shoes on, opened the front door and took him outside, still howling. Thank goodness that our closest neighbours were several acres away.

The crisp night air that surrounded us outside was therapeutic for David. His howling tapered down to a whimper as I guided him toward the beach, and then the familiar flicker came back into his eyes. David looked around, puzzled to find himself on the beach in his jammies in the moonlight. Then his little head made sense of the incongruent pieces of information available. He clapped with delight. "Ooh! We're playing a nighttime game, Meenie?"

In a flash of inspiration, a new late-night ritual was born. "Yes, David. A nighttime game. I'll explain how it works."

Several nights earlier, when I had told David the story of the mermaids and the sacred Ojibwe underwater healing place, he had clapped his hands together and sang out the words *Broken Man's Grotto* every time he glanced out the window at the lake. The idea of a helpful sprite frolicking in our lake captivated him. David had a special affinity for water—he had no qualms about charging straight into the frigid water of the lake in early June, when it felt as though the lake's icy rind had only just slipped away. David could spend all day splashing and swimming around in the lake behind our house, oblivious to his body's need for warmth or nourishment. More than once he had come into the house as the sun was setting, begging for food because he hadn't eaten a bite all day, his swimsuit dripping a pool of water on the floor around him, lips purplish blue, teeth chattering uncontrollably.

So I hit my mark when I introduced the nighttime game of seeking the *mbaanaabe-kwe* mermaids in the lake. David forgot all about his nighttime fears.

When Bird had told me about the *mbaanaabe-kwe*, he had not specifically spoken about seeking them out at night—that was my interpretation. But it felt right to me: if we were to find something so outside the realm of the ordinary, it could not happen in our sunlit lake. David and I knew the landscape of every inch of our lake's rock bed, knew precisely where the weed beds started without glancing down as we swam, knew exactly where to plunge our hands into the lake bottom to retrieve fistfuls of oozing clay. But in the dark, the lake transformed into a bottomless pool whose depths held unknown secrets; a liquid mystery. And beyond all logic, I sensed there was *something* we were always just on the verge of meeting in the water.

CHAPTER 9

Night took on a new purpose for David and me. Instead of struggling to cope with David's night terrors, we played *memory lane* under the covers until we heard our father's loud snores over the drone of the small black and white TV our parents fell asleep watching each night while sipping their nightcaps and smoking in bed. Memory lane was a game David had invented, for long car rides and rainy Saturday afternoons. His memory was much sharper than mine, and he was always able to add more layers of detail to the family stories.

Once our parents were asleep, we would sneak outside into the pitch blackness. Schnapps trotted along behind us, our fearless protector against *creepers* that prowled in the dark, and David and I would slip into the lake as quiet as eels.

Thinking back to those nights, I have come to understand a certain transcendence that was possible when swimming at night in the dark. David and I would wade into the dark waves, neither one of us wanting to disrupt the tranquility with words. The blackness, gliding in fluid, echoed our fetal origins. In our first nine months of life David and I were fish, sloshing around in the water and electrolytes in our mother's plasma. For nine months we inhaled our mother's waters into our lungs, and we never entirely lost the memory.

Much later in my chemistry studies I learned that approximately sixty percent of the human body is comprised of water. Some organs are waterier than others, but if we focus on the two organs that poets and philosophers do—the brain and the heart—these organs are almost seventy-five percent water.

Electrolytes float within the fluid of human bodies just as they float within large bodies of water. They work as microscopic ferrymen, transmitting packets of energy from place to place across water. Freshwater lakes are a teeming pool of these invisible circuits of energy. At night, if each of those ferrymen were to turn on their high beams, the lake would look like a circus of a million Ferris wheels, lit up and spinning wildly through the waters, flickering a million white fractals across a submerged countryside. It is no wonder David and I felt at home in the lake; the liquid within us and the lake water were the same.

The silence of the lake at night was not actually silence at all; layers of sound were muffled by the layers of sound above them: the lapping of waves on shore, the chirp of crickets, the rustling of leaves.

When David slipped into the water, it was as though his young skin absorbed the wisdom of the lake; he was transformed before my eyes each night. When he swam beside me in the darkness, he was not my younger brother, not the little prince I needed to protect from all things jagged. David became an old soul when he passed through the moonlit ripples, and his awareness seemed to grow keener the deeper he swam.

When we had swum out just over our heads—deep enough that the lake felt bottomless, but safe enough to return to where David's feet could touch bottom if he lost confidence—we would begin our ritual.

The first time we went night-swimming, I had no clear plan in place for what we would do once we got out on the lake. I had promised David a game, and I figured an idea would wash over me in the moment. What I hadn't anticipated was that David would assume the role of leader. He was in his element, out on the water in the darkness, floating above a world of unseen creatures.

"Guess what, Meenie. We're going to call the *mbaanaabe-kwe* mermaids," he said, his eyes sparkling. "We'll swim underwater— you go that way, I'll go over here," David pointed in the direction of Elsinore Island. "We'll use our minds to call out, 'Heeere *mbaanaabe-kwe*, come heeere.'"

An uneasiness came over me. What if we were to actually make contact with *something*? *Something sinister*? I reflexively looked down; of course I couldn't see anything in the inky water. I tried not to think about the various creatures that could be lurking beneath us. I pushed past these thoughts, and humoured my brother.

We pointed our chins to the sky, and filled our lungs with air. Then we plunged under the water, heading off in opposite directions. David's childish call to the *mbaanaabe-kwe* mermaids echoed in my brain. Even if I had wanted to try to communicate more eloquently with the spirits that dwelled underwater, my mind chanted David's singsong mantra, "Heeeeeeere, *mbaanaabe-kwe...*" over and over as my limbs pulled my body through the dark waves. Part of me was sure that nothing out of the ordinary was going to happen. Yet sometimes as I plunged underwater, I found my mind leaking thoughts of the dark, horrible creature that Bird's people believe dwelled within the grey water. David and I would be splashing and giggling, and suddenly a terrified thought of *Mishi-ginebig* would radio out from my mind. I feared that, just as a shark can detect one drop of blood half a mile away, *Mishi-ginebig* could sense these thoughts.

I could tell by the eagerness with which he approached the water that my brother felt differently. David was certain that something extraordinary and wonderful was going to happen; it was only a matter of time.

David loved the nights when the weather was wild, when the winds blew in 30-knot gales, and the waves swelled so high that even if he perched on my shoulders, they would still crash over his head. The power of those waves terrified me and exhilarated David. He would dive blindly into a thunderous collision of waves breaking on shore while I stood hugging my arms around my chest.

I preferred the safety and tranquility of the nights when the water was a mirror, the moon reflecting crisp white rays across a flat expanse of black. These opposite preferences summed up the McInnis siblings: one an intense wave of passion, one a placid pool. Our parents also preferred the thrill of a wild storm over a calm, monotonous vista—I was the anomaly in our family of four.

The moon waxed from a sliver to a gibbous bulb overhead as David and I returned to the lake each June night. As the nights passed, I began to forget about the stories of water-spirits that Bird had told me, and embrace the physical thrill of entering a cold lake each night. David, however, sustained his belief that we were always just on the verge of encountering something beautiful and inexplicable.

One mild night the clouds drifted away, and the moon stamped its image onto the water's surface. David and I were diving like porpoises, silently plunging over and over into deeper water. David was probably also telepathically calling out, 'Heeeeeeere *mbaanaabe-kwe*' to the spirits he hoped were listening. I was simply enjoying the feeling of near weightlessness as I soared underwater, and the secure feeling of water compressing my flesh.

The sound of low, cautious growling sounded from shore. I could barely make out Schnapps' silhouette. Her haunches were bent low to the ground, and her back was humped up, making her look larger than she was. She crouched motionless, her head tipped up slightly and her jaws open. Every muscle in my body tensed; a shudder coursed up my spine.

Schnapps went tearing into the forest, and I let out a relieved breath. She was probably just treeing a small animal.

David pointed to an odd swirl on the lake's surface ahead, and he began swimming toward it. I watched his arms cutting through the water, the distance closing between his body and the place where the water spun like a weak current. "David—don't go toward that," I said to him in my mind. For some reason, my mouth remained closed as I watched him swim toward the patch of moving water.

Suddenly, my right ear picked up on a high frequency metal-on-metal screeching noise, a kind of barely detectable radio feedback whine. The whine grew deafeningly loud in my ear, expanding down my ear canal and into my spine, where it alerted each of my synapses that something horrible was happening. A feeling of dread rose in my gut, and the noise in my right ear continued to drone unbearably. The metallic whine filled my head, where the sound waves transformed into an image I could somehow sense: *a sharpened blade slicing through scalp, then skull, then soft matter; the smell of smoking marrow; the metallic scent of blood.*

David reached the patch and dove straight down. His feet kicked upwards, and bubbles swelled in expanding rings around him. The bubbles eventually stopped rising to the surface, and the concentric rings from his kicking thinned out to calm. I watched and waited.

And waited. There was no movement on the surface where he had gone down. Not even air bubbles. The metallic whine pounded its warning in my right ear, and sickness flooded my belly. David was able to hold his breath longer than someone with such a little pair of lungs should be able to, but he had been submerged far too long.

I cut through the lake, arms plowing through like a propeller, choking on water that snuck in in place of air. I got to where David had dived under, and plunged downwards, kicking my feet hard to get down deep. My heart was racing so fast it felt like it was about to explode out of my chest. The moon bathed the lake in soft light, but its rays did not reach my eyes deep under the water. My eyelids were open, but it was like the circuit between my eyes and my brain was jammed. I blinked again and again into the blackness. Nothing. I swept my arms maniacally in every direction, lunging forward and then to the side, turning and sweeping, growing more disoriented and terrified with each lunge. I shouted David's name underwater, but it came out as a burbled scream trapped in a bubble. My lungs could not allow me to stay below the surface any longer, and I clawed my way up, sucking air the second my face broke through into the cold night.

I screamed David's name, and the sound soared across the lake. I caught a glimpse of a dark shape in a white streak of moonlight, several hundred metres out—much farther out than David and I had ever felt comfortable venturing. I screamed his name.

No response. I jetted through the water like a shark. Up until that moment, I was not aware that my body was capable of such athleticism; I kept my eyes fixed on the dark shape that could possibly be David's head, and just when I got within throwing distance, it sunk under and disappeared. A tsunami of panic crashed through me, yet I kept swimming. When I got to the place where the object had been, I dove down once again.

"Go down to the very bottom," something told me. I obeyed. My arms hauled me downwards, deeper and deeper, using every ounce of strength I had to force myself down. I had never swum down so deep before, and had no frame of reference for how far down I might be. My arms carved a V in front of me, and I kicked with all my strength, but the pressure grew so strong that my ear canals felt as though they were swelling to the point of eruption, as though my brain was expanding to take up more room than my skull could accommodate.

I sent out the silent call we had reserved for the *mbaanaabe-kwe* mermaids, pleading with the lake to courier a message to David and back. Nothing. "David? Where are you?" I had to ascend; my body had run out of oxygen. Just as I reached the surface, my fingertips brushed something solid. I clutched at it, and my hands grasped onto clothing, then the heavy solidness of a body. I yanked it closer and patted along it, frantically feeling for a face. My fingers found the soft clumps of hair before my eyes could discern what was before me. I pulled the face close to mine. David's face peered back at me, eyes wide, lips contorted in a silent scream. He was not moving.

In the distance, out of the corner of my eye, a smear of black snaked through the surface of the water for a second, then was gone. Every hair on the back of my neck stood stiff.

I swung my attention back to David. Three summers' worth of lifesaving training fluttered out of my brain like skittish birds: I grabbed both of David's shoulders and shook the living daylights out of him. Treading water, I continued to shake him, screaming his name and sobbing. My arms were losing the strength to keep me afloat. Then a muscle in my foot seized up, and suddenly a different tone of alarm blared through my brain. Pain scorched up my leg and into my spine.

I struggled with my one good foot to thrust myself up high enough to keep my mouth above the surface, but I was starting to sink. Water rushed into my lungs each time I gasped for air. Choking, I kicked with all of my might with one foot, desperate to keep my head above water.

I am drowning. David is dead. And I am entirely to blame.

And then David blinked, and that one flutter of eyelashes aroused the brute force I needed to propel us, foot cramp and all, back to the safety of shore.

David was in shock. But his heart was beating—I jammed my ear to his chest and heard it thumping steadily, incompatible with the pale blank face connected to it. I repeated the same maneuver I had done out on the water, again incapable of accessing the countless hours of CPR training my swimming instructor had drilled into my brain. I grabbed him by both shoulders and shook him hard, my voice blasting into his face, "David! Wake up!"

Unbelievably, it worked. David blinked several times, and then he flapped his head back and forth like a dog just out of the water. His eyes looked as though they had aged a few decades in the minutes he had been underwater, and his mouth was a quivering hole. He wrapped his arms around himself and arched back, as if to protect his body from something unseen.

I cocooned David in a soft beach towel, and cradled him on my lap like a baby. Eventually, he stopped shivering and his body relaxed a bit.

"What happened out there, David? Did you get a muscle cramp?"

David couldn't speak. He shook his head repeatedly and opened his mouth, but no words came out. His jaw worked away silently at his thoughts for several moments, and finally, three words tumbled out of his mouth.

"Very bad thing."

He turned away from me and buried his chin in his chest, his whole body stiff and shaking.

CHAPTER 10

Every time I allowed myself to think about David and his encounter under the water, the story of *Mishi-ginebig* clawed its way to the surface of my mind. I teetered through the next several days on weakened knees, my mind conjuring horrific images of what *very bad thing* could have dragged David under the water.

I tried to carry on our normal activities each evening. I read David a chapter from his favorite book, *Two Against the North*, although he didn't seem to pay attention. And I gave him his usual *telling story*. The telling story had been part of our bedtime routine ever since David was a toddler. I would read a storybook to him, his *reading story*, followed by a story that I made up on the fly, his *telling story*. But instead of him bursting with ideas about what the night's telling story should be about—"Tonight I want a story about a magic bunny who hurt his paw,"—David would just shrug his shoulders and mumble, "You pick, Meenie."

One night, after David's reading story, his telling story, and his ten-minute snuggle in bed, my curiosity outweighed my desire to grant him his privacy. I propped myself up on one arm and turned sideways to face him.

"David, what did you see that night on the lake?"

David chewed on his knuckle, a new habit. His face twitched. He would not speak. I waited to see if he would change his mind, but he just lay there gnawing the skin from his knuckle, so eventually I slumped down beside him and closed my eyes. Just as I was drifting off to sleep, David's arm made its way around my neck, and he nestled his little face into my shoulder. His voice was barely audible. "Promise you'll believe me if I tell you?"

"Course, David."

"Need to hear you say it."

"I promise I'll believe you."

David took a deep breath then let the words rush out. "When I was underwater, I think something attacked me. A...creature."

"A creature? What did it look like?" I tried to keep my voice casual.

"I couldn't really see it. But it felt long, and kind of...slippery." He looked at me imploringly.

"Maybe you got tangled in the weeds and they pulled you down?"

He shook his head. "That's not what it felt like."

"Maybe you panicked and went under?"

David shook his head. "No, Meenie. Something dragged me. Down deep." David grabbed my arm and squeezed too tight, his little hand shaking. "My fingers banged into something that felt like sharp teeth. I think it...I think it was going to eat me. But the *mbaanaabe-kwe* saved me."

I forced my face to remain neutral. "A mermaid saved you?"

David nodded, his eyes begging me to understand. "I called the *mbaanaabe-kwe* with my mind, and one came." He started to shake again. "But what if the *mbaanaabe-kwe* hadn't come in time?"

I lay beside David, quiet for a long time. David had always had an active imagination; I should never have planted ideas about Native mythological creatures in his fertile mind.

So, despite David being the most sincere person I know, and because I am a horrible sister, I patted David on the head and I told a half-truth. "I believe you, David."

My reassurance gave David temporary relief. He let out a long sigh, rolled onto his side, and closed his eyes, drifting, I hoped, away from the monster that now resided in the waterscape of his dreams. I never told David the Native legend of the lake serpent—the story of *Mishi-ginebig*. That is the part that gnawed at me.

We learned in school that myths and oral legends were created hundreds and thousands of years ago, in the absence of a scientific understanding of the world around us. Boats sank in stormy waters because they lost their buoyancy after too much water intake. Swimmers had their strength sapped by the massive force of water currents. Centuries ago, the Natives had created stories to make sense of the inexplicable things that happened around them. Without scientific tools to scrutinize the natural world, they had looked inwards and asked their higher spirit to show them the truth. And in their mind's eye they were delivered vibrant stories of snakes and turtles and bears enacting the dramas of creation and death amongst the rocks, lakes, and forests. Stories that begged to be painted with bold, curved black outlines and vivid primary colours. A worldview born of dreams and intuition. But intuition was not my style.

I have always preferred the safety of black and white answers to the ambiguousness of grey zones. I was born with a brain wired for binary; for me, the elusive world of things believed yet unproven did not compute. In actions as well as beliefs, I clung to established safe havens. These characteristics must have rained down upon me at birth, because I was the only person in my family whose mind worked in this way. By contrast, David was wildly imaginative, and both my parents held firm beliefs in the benefits of approaching a moment with reckless abandon, and would concur that a year of magical thinking was a year well spent.

The more my burgeoning scientific mind contemplated the legend of the ravenous snake that trolled the waters seeking to gorge on fingertips and eyeballs, the more I needed to figure out what might have attacked my brother in the lake that night. I checked books out of the library, detailing the marine life of the Great Lakes. I learned about a vicious local fish named the muskellunge, or *muskie*. Muskie could be up to six feet long and had rows of teeth like tiny daggers. These demon fish were known to bite the toes off young swimmers. Perhaps there was a particularly aggressive or mutated muskie prowling around the lake. Or maybe David had encountered one of the metre-long lamprey eels that called Lake Huron home.

I consumed books about creatures that inhabited the lake, obsessing over assigning a name to David's lake creature. I pored over a book entitled *In the Domain of Lake Monsters* that outlined over thirty documented sightings of a massive snake-like creature thrashing around in the Great Lakes. One entire ship crew, along with their captain, swore an oath before a magistrate that they had been attacked by a snake-like creature that was thirty feet long and as wide as the captain's wheel. The budding scientist in me was fascinated by these firsthand accounts of an unidentified creature, but I needed proof. Every time I looked at David, his nervous little face propelled me to search for information that could demystify whatever had attacked him.

I was walking down the hallway at school when a poster from a recent Ojibwe theatre production caught my eye. *The play!*

Maybe that was it. Earlier that month, every kid in our school had been invited to come down to the gym to watch an Ojibwe theatre company play. It was an attempt to foster awareness and appreciation of the local Native culture, as over a third of the students at our school were Ojibwe Natives. A theatre production at school, even a small-scale one, was a rare treat, and we were all captivated. The play was called *How the Mermaids Lost their Legs*, and told a colourful tale that entwined several Native legends featuring kindly mermaids, and turtles that expanded to become entire islands. The villain of the play was a gargantuan black snake, portrayed by a costume overlaid with hundreds of black shining discs. The costume was so long that it required one actor to stand in the head of the snake, and one actor to trail several feet behind, his body concealed within the snake's tail. Although the snake was referred to as "The Great Horned Serpent," I recognized him from Bird's stories: *Mishi-ginebig*. Some of the smaller children were frightened at the appearance of this large serpent character, and I had sought out David's shock of white-blond hair in the audience. When I located him, I saw his face grow pale as he stared wide-eyed at the serpent on stage. The grimace on his face may simply have arisen from fear of a character in a scary costume, but it looked like a deeper fear, like there was something more to it. A nagging thought from deep within me suddenly wondered: could that terrified look on David's face have been a *premonition*?

Whatever happened out on the lake, something continued to plague David. His shoulders had taken on a slump, as though he was carrying an invisible backpack that required unbearable effort with each step. He trudged through our home like a defeated soldier who had witnessed unspeakable horrors. He would not speak another word about what had happened to him in the lake, but I could see that the incident scraped away at the edges of his mind all day long. I owed David a better explanation than the one his imagination had conjured. It was my duty as his protector to heal the damage that our night in the lake had caused.

After I had exhausted the literature on lake creatures, an unexpected insight came to me. It whispered straight into my brain, and made so much sense that I didn't pause to question where it came from. *If I went back out to the lake, I would get the concrete answers I needed.* There were no sharks in Lake Huron—whatever was out there, how bad could it be?

Once David was deep asleep in the bed beside me, I edged along the mattress as quiet as a ghost, grabbed dad's waterproof flashlight, slipped a fileting knife from the kitchen drawer, and set out toward the lake, my heart pounding.

Fear is a gaseous substance: it expands to fill the confines of whatever contains it. When I stood alone before the dark water, the unease within my chest swelled. It pulsed through the flesh of my legs and arms, and pounded against my fingertips curled against the filet knife. Nervous energy threatened to burst through my skin in an explosion of white hot terror. I exercised every ounce of my mental strength to suck the fear back in. Every fiber of my being wanted to turn around and head back into the house, but for once in my life, I needed to be brave. For David. There was nothing left to do but wade into the cold black lake, without a soul knowing I was out there.

My arms sliced through the water, the blade pointed away from my body. My legs kicked in powerful arcs until I was out so deep that the light of my flashlight could not make its way to the rocks and undulating life below. I aimed my body downward and hauled myself against the pressure into the dim expanse.

I pushed past the terror and swam down into the murky depths of the lake, where the water was several degrees colder, my nerves taut to breaking. *Something* was down there with me. I could sense it. The seconds spread into slow motion, and I knew I was on the verge of discovering what the *something* was. My heartbeat pounded in my throat, my tongue felt too thick for my mouth. But nothing came to me, and I was forced to surface, disappointed and relieved in equal measure.

Several consecutive nights I stole outside, suppressing my fears and plunging into the waters that had darkened the light in my brother's eyes. And later each night I slid, shivering, back into the bed I shared with David, panic still tightly encased in my chest, my body still prickling with the dread of not knowing what I might have encountered beneath the lake's surface. Most nights sleep did not come to me; I lay in bed guiltily relieved, yet feeling a gambler's certainty that the next night's quest in the lake would finally provide me with the answers I needed to quell the fear in my brother's heart.

CHAPTER 11

Rhonda Doyle arrived that July like a summer storm, clearing the cloud of dread that had settled in my chest and made breathing feel difficult. On July 1st I heard the thrum of a dirtbike in our driveway, and my heart began to race. *Rhonda Rhonda Rhonda Rhonda Rhonda Rhonda Rhonda Rhonda Rhonda Rhonda Rhonda!* I flew out the door and across the gravel driveway in my bare feet, excitement bubbling inside me, feeling as though it might burst right through my skin. My concerns about David and the lake flew from me as my world shifted its course to orbit around Rhonda once again.

But as the summer unfolded, it was impossible not to notice that David was becoming even more withdrawn. Whatever was eating away at his mind began to show signs of feeding on his body as well. His round cherub face lost its padding of baby fat, his cheekbones became apparent for the first time and his eyes took on a sunken look. I often caught my mother staring at David, her eyebrows drawn, her hand worrying the skin at her neck.

David still slept in my bed, but he had lost interest in hearing a telling story or playing memory lane. After he fell asleep I gained insight into the troubled landscape that was painted on his face throughout the day. His dreams tumbled out in ragged words. And the word that came out of his mouth most often was *snake*.

"No...snake...no!" David would jerk his body from side to side as he slept, pleading for the *mbaanaabe-kwe* to save him. Guilt poured into my stomach as I lay beside him, yet each night I let him battle his demons alone. I knew that whatever was stalking my brother in his dreams was connected to the incident that night in the lake, and I knew I was directly responsible for putting him in harm's way, but I could not bring myself to deal with it.

Each night I promised myself that in the morning, I would sit David down, we would talk about what was haunting him, and I would help him to slay his demons. But each morning my thoughts zoomed to Rhonda Doyle. I would scarf down a quick bite and head out on my bike to the town docks, awaiting the familiar drone of Rhonda's outboard motor. I vowed daily that tomorrow, I would have a long talk with my little brother. But somehow, tomorrow stretched its way across each July day, and my brother drifted farther away from any possible safeguards onshore.

Rhonda and I decided we were going to venture into the newsletter business that summer, in addition to our jarred frog operation. The lifeblood of the *Mikinaak Howler* would be stories with a superstitious bent—ideas I mined mainly from the stories that kids swapped on the Mikinaak Elementary playground all year long. Each week we would chronicle a different supernatural tale, complete with interviews and hand-sketched illustrations.

We designated ourselves as chief marketing officers as well. We knocked on Rhonda's father's office door, something we knew better than to do without good reason. We dove into a sales pitch centering on the offer of a hand-drawn ad that would take up prime real estate on the front page of our newsletter, sure to catch customers' eyes.

Rhonda's dad held our mock-up ad at arm's length, smiling and shaking his head as he studied the details. "The things you girls come up with when you're together. You two were meant for each other."

He pulled his wallet out from his back pocket and slid out a one-dollar bill, then held each end between his thumb and index finger, snapping it loudly. He had a gleam in his eye as he gave Rhonda a hearty slap on the back, and then me. The pride beneath his touch buoyed me for the rest of the afternoon.

Rhonda's mother was harder to read. I would often catch Mrs. Doyle staring fondly out at Rhonda and me from her sitting room window, eyes glassy as though she had gone to a place far away in her mind. But then she would come outside, and her annoyance would surface. Mrs. Doyle was particularly displeased whenever she found us lying on our bellies along the edge of the frog pond. Rhonda's shoes were always dripping wet from accidental slips as she lunged for a catch, her overalls caked in mud. "Rhonda, how is it that the two of you have been doing the same activity, yet only one of you is filthy from head to toe?" she would say with a deep sigh, hands on hips, already walking away.

For our newsletter, Rhonda took on the role of illustrator, and I was the journalist. The idea for the *Mikinaak Howler*'s first story came from a playground rhyme that every child from our school could recite. It was called "Bearwalker". I wrote out the rhyme in large, scrolling penmanship –on top of my journalist duties, I was also the official scribe for our newspaper, as Rhonda's writing was the type of chicken scratching that typically trailed out of the pencils of six-year old boys. The rhyme went like this:

Black magic, fireball, burning hot and bright,
Turn into a Bearwalker, slash you in the night.
Jordie killed his uncle, cuz uncle was a bear

Sent to rot for thirty years, the judge don't care.

Beside the chant, Rhonda drew a picture of a bear standing on its hind legs, a fountain of blood spouting from its decapitated neck. Next to the bear, a man stood holding a knife in one hand, the bear's dripping head in the other.

"Rhonda, the Bearwalker guy died of stab wounds to his chest."

"Yep. And this looks a thousand times more interesting."

The article beneath Rhonda's illustration was an interview we had conducted with Angela Manaabeh. Angela was Bird's cousin, and with the help of two quarters and much begging, we were able to convince her to talk about her uncle, Bird's father, who was in jail after the notorious Bearwalker killing.

Bird would have found our prying worse than unforgiveable, but we swore Angela to secrecy and persevered. "I don't feel right about this, Rhonda," I said, wanting to cancel our meeting with Angela at the last minute.

"Do it for the Howler, M. A *murder* story—how friggin cool is that?"

"It just—it seems like maybe something we shouldn't be writing about."

"You wanna be a writer someday, don't you?"

"Um, yeah, I think so."

"Then get over it, M."

Rhonda envisioned thrill and intrigue with the piece, but Angela had not met us on these terms. She chose her words carefully, her face grave, as she spoke about the Bearwalker, and her tone caused me to squirm in my chair as I held the tape recorder on my lap.

An amazing talk with a Bearwalker's niece
An interview with: Angela Manaabeh
Reported by: Marina McInnis and Rhonda Doyle

Reporter: "Angela, can you explain what a Bearwalker is?"

Angela: "A Bearwalker is a medicine man who learns bad magic, and can use his powers to change himself into a dangerous creature, like a ball of fire, or a bear. Then he comes at night to hunt down someone who has made him angry."

Reporter: "Is it true that you have a connection to a Bearwalker?"

Angela: "My uncle was haunted by an elderly relative on the reserve, who knew bad medicine and became a Bearwalker. One night, the old man grew his stinking fur and fangs, and walked on all fours into my uncle's bedroom. Just about everyone on the reserve could hear the shrieks and howls of the attack that night, and it sure wasn't the sound of two men fighting. My uncle ended up killing the Bearwalker. He was sent to jail for life for it."

Reporter: "Do you believe this story, Angela?"

Angela: "It's not a story. It is what the people on my reserve saw with their own eyes."

Reporter: "Oh. Okay."

The End

Rhonda was thrilled to have recorded a real, live interview. The nervousness Angela had shown when she talked about the Bearwalker made me feel even more uncomfortable about including any of it in our newsletter, but in the end, Rhonda's enthusiasm won me over.

We figured that our Bearwalker interview was the main meat that our newsletter required, but for extra measure, we threw in a few more articles of local intrigue—including a story about my neighbour's cat who had gone missing for over a month, then returned with a mysterious wound on her paw and part of her ear missing. We had some space remaining on the back of our newsletter, and in what we considered a stroke of pure genius, we added our own classified ad.

WANTED: We would like to interview several lucky people for thrilling future editions of the Mikinaak Howler. Have you ever seen the ghost of TEDDY DOYLE??? Do you have any secret information into the mysterious death of TEDDY DOYLE???? You could become Mikinaak Island's next celebrity! Please contact Marina McInnis or Rhonda Doyle for more information.

Once a few final embellishments were sketched onto our newsletter, Rhonda's dad agreed to let us use the Ditto machine in his office. We pranced and giggled as we cranked the heavy handle of the machine, the ink's alcohol scent lending a feeling of professionalism to the process. We churned out thirty copies of our newsletter, and dashed down to Rhonda's boat, the pages still warm in our hands.

We barked out to every person who set foot across the town docks, then later headed over to the residential part of the street and began knocking on doors.

One woman who answered her door found us far less darling than we anticipated. She had long, glossy chestnut-coloured hair like many women from the reserve, and wore red lipstick on an otherwise naked face. "What you got here, then?" she asked, yanking the newsletter from my hand and scanning it with the tip of a light brown finger. "So. You think the Bearwalker is amusing, do you? Think Ojibwe beliefs are something you kids should be mucking around in, eh?" She sucked her teeth and stepped toward us, then kicked at the toes of our shoes, causing us both to stumble backwards. She then slammed the door in our faces. My ears burned red. I had to hold Rhonda back from knocking again and asking for the ten cents she owed us for the newsletter.

Fortunately, business chugged along steadily after that, with many gracious adults expressing keen interest in our one-page newspaper. Four hours after we began, we had sold our entire stack, and were dancing our way to the treat store. Paper bag of candy in hand, Rhonda and I stretched out under our favorite willow tree by the docks and watched the clouds transform from the shape of one animal to another. "You and me, we make a perfect team," I said, as I dangled a gummy worm into my mouth.

For a moment, Rhonda's face was a troubled sky. Then she leaned over and punched my arm, hard. "Yeah. You and me, M." We lay there like that for what seemed like hours, two sisters warming themselves under the sun.

The following morning, when I swung open our front door to let Schnapps out for her morning business, I caught a glimpse of a red-streaked page resting on our porch. Our family lived too far outside of town for anyone to bother delivering flyers to our house, and the weekly local paper, the *Mikinaak Record*, only came on Tuesdays.

I tiptoed across the cold concrete in my bare feet, and leaned down to pick it up. At first I didn't recognize the page, because of the red lettering scribbled across it. It took a minute for my eyes to decipher the scratchy words written across *the Howler* in lipstick. "*STAY AWAY. This is not your story to tell.*"

A panicked feeling rose up inside of me, along with a flashback to the nervous look on Bird's cousin Angela's face when we had interviewed her. I had experienced a moment of realization then, when I shoved my black tape recorder into her face and asked for her story, that I was trespassing on Ojibwe property. But I had tossed the feeling aside, and pushed to get Angela to tell the snippets of her family's story, eager to record her words and make them mine.

I tucked the *Howler* inside my nightgown and rushed upstairs to my bedroom. My first instinct was to phone Rhonda. But I knew what she would say. "Just some crackpot, M. *Seriously*—you're actually giving this a second thought?"

And I would feel stupid for even mentioning it.

I turned the page from one side to another, trying to discern the person behind the handwriting. Probably just a prank from one of the kids in town. I chucked it into the waste bin. Nothing was going to come between Rhonda and me and our summer fun.

My days of selling the *Howler* on the docks blurred into one long stream of glorious afternoons spent with Rhonda. I continued to receive warnings on the occasional morning, each time a copy of the *Howler* defaced with the same angry red lipstick. And each time, I dropped it into the trash and disregarded the unsettled feeling in my stomach.

One morning, I went out to the porch to check if my secret correspondent had paid me another visit. There sat another copy of our newsletter, covered in more red scrawls. My arms prickled with gooseflesh and my insides squirmed as I read the terse message: "You were warned."

Just some stupid kid, I told myself.

But my stomach twisted as I crumpled the page into a crude bird and sent it flying.

Our mother wasn't the quickest when it came to noting small changes in her children. She loved us, but that love did not necessarily translate into attentiveness. As the summer progressed, however, I could see the concern in her eyes whenever she looked at David.

By mid-summer, David could barely force himself to push one mouthful of food past his lips at mealtimes. He spent most of his time in his bed, hunched over a notebook. I couldn't even entice him out with an invitation to come hiking with me in the woods. Each time I looked at our injured little sparrow, a sick feeling rose to my throat. But always, I was able to push the feeling down and continue on with my day.

Rhonda and I had become inseparable. I couldn't guzzle down my Froot Loops fast enough in the mornings, I was so excited to hop on my bike and speed into town to the docks. From there, we would either stay in town, or climb into her boat and zip over to Elsinore Island for a day spent romping around the pond, the woods, or diving off the pock-marked rocks that sloped gracefully into the lake in front of the Doyle summer estate.

Rhonda had her own reasons for wanting to be in my company. The atmosphere on Elsinore Island had grown increasingly tense. We often heard snippets of angry shouts between her parents, from our perch on the lawn below her father's office window.

"And I suppose you're okay with the direction she's heading? Are you going to be happy when your daughter grows up to be a—a grease monkey? Or *worse?*"

"Drop it, Victoria!" Mr. Doyle's voice bellowed overhead.

"This is just like you, Boris, refusing to deal with anything until it's too bloody late!"

Rhonda spat through the gap in her front teeth. "Let's haul ass outta here," she said, punching me in the arm, then jumping up and heading toward her boat without waiting for a response.

She gunned the motor, and our troubles grew distant until they were just an insignificant speck on the horizon.

I came home from another afternoon of selling frogs and newsletters on the docks with Rhonda, and knew instantly that something was wrong. Typically, my mother spent summer afternoons in her room recovering from a late night, or tanning in the back yard drinking her Tab & rums. But she was standing waiting for me in our front hall, hand on her neck. Another red flag went up when I saw my father in the living room, standing too still and looking uncharacteristically serious. David was sitting on the couch, head hanging down, eyes fixed on the floor.

"Marina. Your mother and I need to have a talk with you," my father said, motioning with one hand for me to have a seat. My pulse quickened, and the guilty nausea swelled through my insides. Sit-down talks with my parents were rare, and almost always associated with horrible feelings. I sat on the chair opposite David, wanting to distance myself from the source of my guilt. "We've noticed that your brother has been acting very strange lately. Withdrawn. Your mother felt she had no choice but to read his diary."

I thought back to David hunched over on his bed with his notebook. His *diary*.

"David has told us some things we find very concerning."

By now, the guilt and anxiety were making me so dizzy I needed to steady myself with my hand on the armrest.

My mom took over. "We know what went on around here after that stunt you pulled in the bathroom with David—trying to contact the ghost of Teddy Doyle. And now David's told us about the swimming in the dark, night after night. And that he was attacked by something in the water." She fidgeted with her gold necklace as she spoke, and her face was pale. "I warned you once already about the dangers of dabbling in the supernatural, missy. There are powerful, dangerous things out there that you know nothing about." Mom glanced behind her, out the window that overlooked the lake. "I think part of the problem is that Doyle girl's influence on you. That girl is wild."

My father stood silently with his arms crossed. He opened his mouth, then changed his mind and closed it. Then he opened it again. "You're grounded for the next three weeks. And from now on, no more hanging around with Rhonda Doyle."

I wailed. "This has nothing to do with her! You can't do this! Rhonda Doyle is my best friend! She's my LIFE!"

"Enough!" my father boomed, in a volume I had never heard him use before. He turned and walked upstairs to his room.

Just like that, my parents had served my summer a death sentence. And I hated them for it.

Later that night, I phoned Rhonda to tell her in tearful bursts about my fate. At first I heard only silence on the other end of the line. But when I strained my ears, I made out a faint sniffle. "Your family sucks the big one," she finally said, her voice unsteady.

Rhonda had barely flinched the day she dropped an anchor on her finger and her nailbed turned black. She had not shed a single tear when her mother smacked her across the face so hard it left a red handprint for three days. But that evening, Rhonda Doyle cried on the other end of the phone line.

Then her voice got all tough. "Your parents are going to regret the day they messed with Rhonda Doyle."

Her words hung between us for a moment.

"What do you mean by that?"

"Nothing. Forget I said it."

CHAPTER 12

David and I dragged ourselves through the final days of summer, deflated by the hot August sun. The school year lurched toward us. We slunk into our places in our respective grades, each of us resistant to the buzz of students sifting themselves into the social hierarchy of the school yard. David and I ended up near the bottom of the pile. We each had our reasons, but our parents blamed me.

Everything about David had become flat. The students who boasted sharp edges received the support they needed at school, but my brother slid under the radar. I was uninterested in the company of anyone other than my best friend. Compared to Rhonda, all other available playmates seemed tedious. Rhonda and I had bonded even closer over the summer, and I was not about to jeopardize our bond by inviting anyone else in.

My mother received a free milk calendar from the grocery store that she let me have, and I became fixated on it. I transformed it into my countdown to summer calendar, which, more accurately, was my countdown to Rhonda calendar. I figured the deception necessary to sneak around with Rhonda the following summer would be manageable. With the heavy social agenda our parents kept in the summer months, David and I could basically run around like wild dogs.

I kept up with new editions of the *Howler* as a tribute to our friendship, although without Rhonda's participation, most of the enjoyment drained out of the process.

The Native legends that Bird shared with me on our afternoons spent wandering the forest had taken hold of my imagination. I had plenty of other mystical subject matter that I could have chosen to write about for the *Howler*, as there were a handful of different cold-case mysteries that had accumulated on Mikinaak Island over the decades: stories about fishermen who were lost at sea, a few missing persons cases that had remained unsolved, and a smattering of classic ghost stories that floated around the Island.

But it was the Native legends that captured my thoughts. The Native reserve was just outside of town, although it felt more like a neighbouring foreign country. The Ojibwe on Mikinaak had strong spiritual beliefs that were anchored tightly to the earth. The Native stories I spent most of my time thinking about, however, were the ones about the *Bearwalker* and *Mishi-ginebig*. I craved more information about how these dark threads were woven into the fabric of life on the reserve.

Bird and I did not really spend time together at school. We said hello if we passed each other in the hall, but at recess, the Native children generally played with other Native children, and the white kids played with other white kids. Whenever Bird's mother came over to clean our house, those rules were set aside. I surprised myself when I realized that I had begun counting the days until his next visit. Although his guarded manner prohibited him from talking directly about his feelings, Bird must have enjoyed his time on our property as well, because I could almost always count on seeing his face in the passenger side of his mother's sedan whenever she came over to clean.

Bird told me how his relatives and neighbours on the reserve often got together around a kitchen table—what would have been a campfire in a more traditional time—and the adults would tell stories. Bird held me as a captive audience when he relayed the words of his elders. He was happy to regale me with stories about Nanabush, a youthful trickster spirit who often learned life lessons the hard way. I was intrigued by the organic ways in which Nanabush was punished for his bad choices. Once, Nanabush skirted his chores and joined in an eyeball-tossing game with some ducks in which he didn't follow the rules. Nanabush was punished with natural consequences for his disobedience. I loved the stark magical realism of that tale. He didn't just lose his vision—Nanabush lost his eyeballs.

When I pushed Bird to tell me more about the Bearwalker, however, he clamped right up. "Man, Primrose, why would you want to hear about bad medicine?" he said, his voice a sharp blade.

"I don't know. It's really.....interesting," I cringed at my trite choice of words.

Bird lifted his eyes up to look directly into mine, which I knew was a rude gesture according to the teachings of his culture. "Listen to me, Primrose," he said. I had never seen him speak so urgently. "That shit is seriously dark. It's dangerous. More dangerous than you know. Don't even let yourself *think* about the Bearwalker, Prim. I mean it."

Bird's words made me suspect that he'd seen our first *Howler* interview about his dad and the Bearwalker. I had to look away from him then, but my eyes had already betrayed my guilt.

"Primrose, I wanna hear you say it. Promise me that you'll forget about the Bearwalker."

"I promise," I said, eyes still fixed to the forest floor. I was becoming practiced at making promises I could not keep.

I was disciplined at sending biweekly letters to Rhonda, counting down the days until she returned to the Island. Winter turned to spring, and still I kept writing, despite no response. Finally, a letter arrived from Rhonda. She apologized for being such a shitty friend when it came to letter writing, and bemoaned the fact that she had flunked out of Finishing School, and would be staying in Toronto for more than half the summer to attend summer school. With the receipt of that letter, the hope that was fueling me toward summer vacation evaporated. I couldn't possibly imagine making it all the way to the July 1st finish line, knowing that Rhonda was not going to jump off her father's boat and on to the dock to greet me. I checked out of life in general after that.

Eventually, after a generous serving of self-pity, I looked around my abyss of despair and noticed that I wasn't alone—David had sunk even further below me. I had pushed David out of my mind for so long that I had stopped worrying about him. One evening, I stepped into the living room and took a good look at my brother, languishing on the couch. It snapped me out of my self-absorption: David desperately needed my help.

He had grown even thinner, which was painful to look at on his already slight frame. Mom eventually took David to see Doc Miller, who suspected that David had mono. He advised that David take it easy until the virus ran its course. Mom let David stay home from school for two weeks. He lolled on the couch watching soaps, poor kid—we only had two channels. This only seemed to increase his lethargy.

My medical opinion differed from Doc Miller's. I suspected David's illness was not viral, but *waterborne*. And I knew I was the only person who could help.

At first, David was unreachable. I began my wooing under the impression that a week of concentrated attention would have him blossoming into the sweet flower he had once been. For seven straight days I planted myself next to my brother, telling tales of heroic mermaids, offering to read his favorite books to him, giving him back scratches, attempting to engage him in perky conversation from morning until night. But I underestimated the strength of whatever was pulling David under. He didn't want to communicate, and certainly did not want to bend his mouth into a smile.

I was forced to bring out the big guns. "Hey David," I said, rapping on his bedroom door, *The Flora and Fauna of Northern Ontario* tucked under my arm. "How about you and I go see if we can identify some wicked cool flowers?" David was stretched out on his bed staring up at the ceiling, still in his fire truck pajamas even though it was past noon.

"No thanks," he said, not bothering to look away from the ceiling.

I brought out my only other piece of artillery. "I caught a glimpse of some hairy willow herb in the forest the other day. Thought you might like to check it out." I stood there silently willing him to say yes, afraid to move for fear of disturbing the vibes of optimism I was beaming his way. David lay motionless on his bed, still inspecting the ceiling tiles. A quiet minute passed, and I feared I really had lost all connection with my brother. Then he rolled toward me, and looked me in the eyes for the first time in months.

"I'll get my shoes." His face was still troubled, but I rejoiced inside. *Operation David* was gaining traction.

David and I spent the afternoon traipsing through the forest behind our house. For the first hour or so, David trudged along behind me, wordless. He had agreed to come, but he hadn't agreed to enjoy it.

We walked to a marshy pond and I got down on my hands and knees. My eyes zoomed in to the pond water, scanning for black dots on green. If Rhonda were here she could catch David a frog with her eyes closed. I said a quiet prayer and plunged my hands in at the first sight of movement under the pond surface. I was astonished to feel the springing legs of a creature trapped in my cupped palms. I stood up and swung my hands around to David's face, and made a peep hole between my thumbs.

"I caught you a froggy, David! Do you want to name him?"

David glanced at my hands and then kicked at the grass. "Yeah, sure. Call him Frog." He took a few steps away from me. "I think you should give him back to nature."

I sighed and released the frog back into the pond.

We continued walking, and the sounds of our feet crunching twigs amplified in my ears. It was the sound of lost words between my brother and I, and each snap of wood caused an ache in my chest.

I decided to give it one last try. "Wanna play *memory lane*?" I said, waggling my eyebrows. "How about the time when mom and dad boated home and accidentally left you behind on Blueberry Mountain?" That story—which our mom always told in a way that had us roaring, but which always made me feel anxious when I thought about it for too long, was a McInnis classic.

David looked up, and for a split second, I caught a flash of the old David in his face. And then it was gone. We walked and walked in silence, and I lost hope in bringing my little brother back under my wing.

Just as I was about to turn around and take us home, David piped up. "Well? Are we playing memory lane or not?"

I jabbered nonstop for the rest of the afternoon, weaving in reminders of all of the ways David was cherished by our family. I didn't let up until the sun began to set, and we both sported scratched up legs from walking so long in the brush.

As we walked through the forest trail back to our house, David draped his arm around my waist, and my heart felt as though it was going to explode. He smiled up at me, his pure little heart beaming through his face with a look so innocent it made me want to weep.

"I love you, little buddy," I said, as I laced my fingers in his.

"Love you too, Meenie," he said. He reached up to tickle his finger against my silver teardrop earring, my treasured heirloom from Great-Grandma Barrett's steamer trunk, David's favorite of all my jewelry to touch.

With one sun-dappled afternoon in the woods, our world was whole again. My sweet-tempered, beautiful brother was mine once more to cherish. It seemed possible that everything might just work out all right. I had reclaimed my role as David's keeper, his big sis who loved him to the bottom of the deep grey lake and back.

CHAPTER 13

David and I welcomed the summer of '73 together, and I replaced my heartache over Rhonda Doyle's absence with a newfound zeal for working on the *Mikinaak Howler*. I brought David on as support staff, and he knocked it out of the park. We toiled away on a new edition of our newsletter, this one featuring a riveting account from Billy McDonald, a scruffy fifth-grader who swore that on a stormy night, his dad's boat had started acting up over by Hay Bay where Teddy Doyle's own boat had gone down. Billy told of how he and his father were heading home from their fishing hole when they spotted a drowning figure in the water; he described in gory detail the horror of passing over the man's face with the motor, leaving both Billy and his father howling like babies out on the lake.

Billy McDonald's story was followed by our other dazzling scoop, an account by a tough sixth-grader named Suzy Gagne who had, one infamous evening, apparently witnessed the ghost of Teddy Doyle hovering over the lake while canoeing at her family's camp.

David and I biked up to the town docks together three afternoons a week, and peddled our newsletters just as Rhonda and I had done. The sales job drew out the old David. He danced a graceful jig around our cardboard box-cum-newsstand, waving a copy of the *Howler* in each hand and flapping his arms like a crazed bird, completely unselfconscious in a way I envied. I laughed until I was rolling around on the dock, watching David cavort so freely with the tourists. And he sold a lot of copies. We depleted our stack of thirty newsletters in record time, and I had to admit, I was having almost as much fun with David as I had had slinging newsletters on the dock with Rhonda.

Rhonda returned to Mikinaak in August with neither a phone call nor a letter in advance. She pulled up unexpectedly to the town docks, and we pounced on each other the second she got out of her boat. We tumbled around on the dock like two rambunctious puppies.

"Thought I'd find you here," Rhonda said, punching me lightly on the arm. She eyed David at our newsstand.

"David and I have been doing really well with the *Howler*," I mumbled, feeling as though I had somehow betrayed Rhonda.

"Well, I'm back now, so he doesn't have to keep you company anymore." Rhonda walked over to David and patted him on the head. "Hey little man—isn't that McCallister boy over there on the docks your age? Why don't you go see what he's up to?" She picked up a newsletter, and started calling out to tourists alongside David. He seemed to shrink a few inches. He stood still, not sure whether to obey Rhonda or not. He looked up at me, hope in his eyes.

"Why don't we all play together?" I chirped. David's face perked up.

"Three's a crowd, M," Rhonda said. "Go on, Davey. I bet that McCallister boy is tons o-fun."

I looked from Rhonda to David and back to Rhonda, torn between my two loyalties. I forced enthusiasm into my voice. "Little buddy? Why don't you go over there and just see if Tubby wants to play."

David tilted his chin down to his chest. His shoulders slumped. "Okay Meenie," he said, in a sad little voice, and trudged away.

"Where were we?" said Rhonda, and threw her arms around me again, more affectionate than I had ever known her to be. But I couldn't stop following David with my eyes as he walked down the docks, alone.

I juggled David and Rhonda for the next few weeks. Each time I tried to suggest that David join us, Rhonda came up with a reason why it would be better if it were just the two of us. The less time I spent with David, the more he began withdrawing back into himself. It would have been so easy for him to win this tug-of-war, by telling our parents that I was hanging out with Rhonda Doyle again. But he kept my secret. It pained me to measure the strength of David's loyalty against my own. Rhonda Doyle was the most intoxicating element I had ever experienced, and I guiltily chose her over my brother every chance I got.

Our parents took us out boating to a nearby island one day in mid-August with four other families. It was horribly hot, even more so for us hardy northern Ontarians who spend six months of the year in winter's brutal grip. It was a fierce sun for parents to leave their children baking beneath for six hours straight, and for once, we kids were eager to escape the beach. By the time the late afternoon sun was dipping toward the tree-lined mountains to the west, none of the four sets of parents were taking notice of their children's discomfort, or anything much, aside from the contents of their red plastic cups.

Aside from the extraordinary heat, there was another outstanding thing on the beach that day: Rhonda Doyle. She had been invited by the Baker family to join their daughter Jeannie, the cow who never missed an opportunity to prey on someone else's weakness.

My mother fumed when she saw Rhonda on shore; she flashed me a look that told me, "Watch it, Mina, if you know what's good for you."

The four families' boats were anchored side by side, far enough out to protect their motors from slamming against the hard sandy bottom with the rocking of the waves. Each set of kids made its way onto their family's boat, to escape the heat and also to send a subliminal plea to our parents that it was time to get things rolling.

David and I were stretched out in the cool reprieve of our boat's cuddy cabin, playing Old Maid, our cards sliding across the woven cushions with the motion of each wave. The smell of coconut suntan oil mixed with the mildewed scent of the tweed upholstery, and a hint of fishy smell from a successful catch a few days earlier.

There was a rustling above on the deck of the boat. Rhonda popped her head into our cabin, her shoulders hunched down to peer into the tiny space.

"How's it hangin' M? Want some company?" She winked, as though letting me in on a private joke. Rhonda had ignored me the entire day on the beach, playing up my parents' ban on our friendship a little too heavily, in my opinion. I had been surprised to feel sharp pangs of jealousy as I watched *my friend* frolicking in the water all afternoon with Jeannie Baker, of all people. Unbeknownst to the parents on shore, Rhonda and Jeannie had been improvising a rambunctious séance in the lake, sending out calls for Teddy Doyle's spirit in between synchronized swimming twirls. I had never seen Rhonda fooling around like that with anyone other than me, and it gave me an ugly feeling inside.

But now, Rhonda had snuck over to *our* boat; she had come to *me*. I wanted to jump up and down and hug her. I was overwhelmed with relief to have Rhonda back by my side. Mine.

David sat up and wiggled his face a couple of inches from Rhonda's chest, trying to read her t-shirt. He began poking the silkscreened faces on the Bobby Orr trading cards that fanned across Rhonda's shirt, naming them as he went along. "Slappy, Happy, Speedy, Skatey…"

Rhonda shifted away from David's finger. "It felt really gross not being able to talk to you all afternoon, when we're on the same freaking beach," she said. She reached out and touched my arm. "Do you have any idea what you mean to me, M?"

Heat crept up my cheeks.

"Fasty, Pucky…" David had inched his way around to Rhonda's side, poking his finger into the face of each hockey mask on her t-shirt.

"Ouch, little man—take it easy there, dude." Rhonda scowled and shoved David's finger away. A second later, her face softened and she patted David on the head.

Rhonda leaned in to me, and placed her hand on my arm again. "I really need to show you something, M. *Alone.*"

I opened the door to the cuddy cabin, and we both jumped in. I slammed the slatted wooden door closed and latched the lock.

Rhonda sat down. She unzipped her backpack and pulled out a mason jar of amber liquid. "That séance Jeannie and I did this afternoon in the lake was Mickey Mouse." She shook the jar. "Wanna do the real deal? "

" What do you mean? What is that stuff?"

"Teddy Doyle firewater. Ever heard of a summoning tincture?"

I shook my head.

"I swiped one of Teddy's hairs from a sweater in his old closet. Hair, scotch, lake water, a frog's eye, and the light of the full moon."

She swirled the jar slowly, staring intently as the wave of liquid lapped the sides of the jar. I averted my eyes from the cloudy mass settled on the bottom. "This brew should be ready to work its magic."

Rhonda gestured for me to sit down beside her. "First we drink, then we summon."

She unscrewed the jar lid, tipped back her head, and chugged three giant gulps. Her eyes squeezed tight and her whole body shook in a coughing fit.

David banged on the cuddy cabin door. "Meenie, what are you two doing in there?"

Rhonda brought a finger to her lips.

"Just give us a sec, Davey."

Rhonda slugged back another two inches from the jar, then winked at me and handed it over. "Down the hatch, M. This is gonna be bitchin."

I put my hand over Rhonda's on the jar, and we tipped it to my lips together. The alcohol was like burning acid, singeing its way down my throat. Fumes filled my nostrils, and tears sprung to my eyes. I pushed all thoughts of my mother's disapproval out of my mind and swallowed the remains of the jar for Rhonda. Vomit threatened in my throat, but I swallowed hard and handed the empty jar back to her. A pleasant heat filled my belly.

David banged his little fists on the door again. "Let me in, or I'll tell mom, Meenie!"

Rhonda swung her face towards the slats in the door, starting to yell something back at David, and bashed her head on the light above the cabin door. She rolled her eyes up in her head, making her face into a woozy grin that made her look like a cartoon character who was seeing stars. She brought her hand up to the sore spot on her head. Her fingers came away with a smear of blood, and she smiled another dopey smile that sent us both into hysterics. "I

almost forgot. Blood is a key ingredient for a summoning tincture."
She stuck one red fingertip into her mouth, then reached toward
my mouth with the other blood-smeared finger. The cabin began
to feel spinny.

David banged on the door again, his voice hysterical. "Let me
in, Meenie! Let me in!"

"Blood sisters," Rhonda said, and although the cabin continued
to spin, my mother's voice in my head was clear: *never, ever, touch
someone else's blood.* But another part of me wanted to do anything
Rhonda Doyle asked of me. I opened my mouth, and she slid her
finger in.

Rhonda leaned in to me, and placed her hand on my arm again.
I felt a confusing warmth running up my skin, radiating from
beneath her hand. She stuck out her chin in David's direction.
"How bout you find something to keep him busy."

The floor reeled beneath my feet as I lurched out of the cabin.
Without thinking about what I was going to say, I opened my
mouth, and the poison just rolled out, dipped in honey. "Da-vid," I
said, in my I've-got-a-surprise-for-you voice, "wanna play a game?"

David shrugged, then let his shoulders droop. He hung his head
down to hide the hurt look on his face. I reached up to my ear
and unhooked the curved back of my silver drop earring from my
earlobe. I held it in front of David's face, and jingled it like a parent
brandishing keys to a new Mercedes. David always loved to brush
his finger against these earrings when I wore them; he would coo as
the cluster of silver teardrops made a delicate tinkling sound when
they swayed from my ear.

"Okay, David. The game is simple: you dive in and bring me
back this earring. When you do, you'll get an amazing prize."

David's face brightened instantly. He didn't even ask what
kind of prize. He jumped up, clapping his hands; an eager smile
stretched across his face. He tore off his Sesame Street t-shirt, ready

for the challenge. I stepped to the side of the boat, then drew my arm back in a wide arc and tossed the slender silver earring into the air, meaning for it to go farther than it did. The cluster of silver teardrops collided with the wind, and the earring spiraled down, glistening as it spun in the sun, landing too close to the boat.

A beautiful, shimmering lure sinking slowly into the sand.

David jumped into the water. He dove down, and scoped from side to side like a seal hunting a fish.

I lurched back into the cuddy cabin, my steps unsteady. Was the lake getting wavier all of a sudden?

Rhonda took my hand. "Okay, M. Think as hard as you can about Teddy Doyle, and repeat after me: *Spirit in the lake draw near; spirit show us you are here.*"

I repeated the chant, then Rhonda said it again more forcefully. Each word felt electric with possibility as it slid off my tongue. My head swam as we continued to chant the words together, louder and louder. Rhonda's voice got stronger, until she was preaching the chant at full volume, and I was chanting right along with her, every cell in my body focused on commanding, *begging* the spirit of Teddy Doyle to make its way to us through the water.

Rhonda jumped out of the cabin, into the middle of the deck. "Now spin!" she yelled. She began whirling, still chanting, her arms pointed to the sky, her head thrown back. I joined her, spinning and stumbling and chanting. *Is this a good idea?* I thought. And just as quickly, the idea dissolved into a cloud of dizzy pieces and floated into the swirling air around my head.

My body began to buzz with the heat of a hundred bee stings, and I tingled everywhere. I thought again, *should we really be doing this?* and at the same time, *this is what it feels like to be joyously, wondrously alive.* We continued whirling and chanting, chanting and whirling, my brain feeling like I actually might be making contact with some thrilling other entity, my heart feeling like it might explode out of my chest. I spun so fast that my feet got tangled. I tripped and fell down hard, and a loud *thump* sounded beneath me. But it almost sounded as though it came a split second *after* I hit the deck. I paused for a moment; my mind dipped into the lake surrounding us, as though there was a question that needed answering. Then Rhonda and I looked at each other, and the thought slipped from my grasp. She grabbed my hand, and we lay on the deck together, staring up at the clouds, their movements making my head swim. I lay perfectly still until the buzzing in my head turned into a hot screeching metal sound whining in my right ear, just like that other time on the lake.

I bolted upright.

I looked over the boat's rail. Waves lapped against the side; my brother was nowhere to be seen.

I called David's name but there was no answer.

And there never would be.

PART TWO

CHAPTER 14

Oh, how I am suspicious of my role in David's death. *Thump*. The sound rattles around my skull, in sleep or awake. *Thump*. The seconds surrounding the *thump* have raked at my brain for the past twenty years, but a gossamer veil shrouds my thoughts from that moment. Had some part of me, however small, known what that sound was? Whenever I wrench my mind back to the place where my little brother's spirit was shucked from its tender shell, I try to plant myself in the background, dig my feet in the damp sand, and scrutinize the events for hidden detail. But I see nothing.

In the darkest hours of the night, my mind twists even deeper: had Rhonda and I summoned something wicked in the lake? No matter how many times I spin these blunted memories around in my head, I can't pin down the truth. How much blame to apportion to myself? I fear the worst.

And then there is the worry of what came next. In my memory of the day the horror seeped in, I strain for a glimpse of David's spirit travelling onwards, but see nothing. The only certainty was that my sweet little man who radiated joy in whatever direction he looked, who was the light of my family and the answer to the question *what is purity, what is beauty*—my little brother David was dead. I am seeking nobler answers.

My mother didn't explicitly say that I was responsible for the death of my little brother that day at the beach. In the scene of mayhem, adults stumbling around the shore, desperate to fix what they knew was irreparably broken, not one person permitted themselves to address the suspicion that might have been riding alongside the horror. The blame came later, in ways far less pleasant than finger pointing.

I have reason to believe that David's spirit never made it to a peaceful afterlife. For the past two decades this thought has left me thrashing around at night beneath sweat-soaked sheets, reciting the periodic table like a Zen chant. The ghost of my brother haunts me nightly, tugging at my heart like an insistent child, forcing me to revisit my sins that day on the lake. When I close my eyes at night, I am hauled through the barbed tunnel of our family past. My brother always awaits me at the other end, his mouth twisted into a plea for my help. Upon waking, it is impossible to tease out whether this was a dream, or whether David's terrified spirit has come to me, lingering near the one person he thought he could trust.

The nightmares take different forms, but there is one particular version that renders me red-eyed for days. The dream is set in an oil painting called 'The Tree of Life,' a work by a local Ojibwe artist recognizable to almost everyone who lives here on Mikinaak Island. The painting depicts a tree furred with animals, two narrow branches forming a long altar, a naked man splayed across the branches in a familiar pose.

In this dream, I cover my face with my hands as I realize it is David who is pinned to the tree. He looks up at me, and I am struck by something odd about his face. It is the wrong colour. A dusky blue that will never recover from one fatal lapse in judgement.

"Why have you forsaken me, Meenie?"

David's face leaks sadness. He grapples against the oily outline of the tree, grunting and sweating as he arches his back and braces his feet against the trunk, trying to wrench something free from the palm of one hand. I squint and see a shiny object has impaled my brother's palm, wedding him to the bark of the tree, and he is bawling as he bashes his head against the rough trunk. I am unable to discern the finer details of the silver object, but I don't need to.

It is my silver earring.

I don't wear jewelry anymore.

For two decades I have worried over David's last moments like a finger at a scab. I have tried innumerable times to send the memory up into the sky, have begged it to fly far away and set me free. But the weight of that one horrible moment is anchored to my legs. It drags me below the surface, down into the cold, dark water. Down to where David's pale and slender body sank, unresponsive.

I was the one who found him, settled on the sandy bottom beneath the boat. The adults spread him out on the beach and tried their best to pound life back into his frail little chest, but that only served to further insult his lifeless body.

They told me I finally stopped screaming once we reached the hospital. Throughout the panicked boat ride home, David's little body wrapped in a tatty beach towel in my mother's arms, I shrieked into my parents' ears like a terrified animal. I have no memory of my parents' faces on that ride home, although I imagine that screams were exploding out of their own throats as well.

Rhonda and I did not share one word for the rest of the summer. I didn't want to imagine what I would see in Rhonda's face if I looked too deeply into it.

Sleep became my enemy. I fought drowsiness as best I could at night, tried with all my willpower to avoid going to that place where I was forced to witness what I feared most. But grief exacted a heavy toll on my resolve, and as I lay awake each night repenting, my eyelids grew unbearably heavy.

The lake water is always dimly lit in my dreams, and the silver hull of the boat bobs gracefully to the rhythm of the waves. Each downward thrust of the boat makes a phlegmy sucking sound that reverberates through the water. I can see David swimming along the sandy lake bottom, his neck craned downwards. Looking for something. Suddenly David squeals with delight, and the sound makes its way in distorted bubbles, across to where Rhonda and I are swimming underwater. David thrusts his hand into the sand, and his fingers clench around something slender, shiny. A silver earring. And then, as though he has forgotten that he is in six feet of water directly beneath a metal boat, he plants his feet on the lake bottom, bends his knees, about to spring straight upwards. I am swimming as fast as I can toward him, swimming and screaming for him to stop, trying to warn him that he is going to bash his skull on the boat's hull. But all that comes out of my mouth are white noise bubbles that burst in front of my face. My heart is hammering in my throat and my arms are slashing through the water to get to David in time, but it is too late. He launches himself straight upwards, and a sickening thump echoes through the water. I keep swimming frantically toward the boat, toward David, but the distance between us increases. Suddenly my right ear is reverberating with the metallic whine and I realize with the slow certainty of dreams that this sound is not coming from within. Something is with us in the lake.

I turn my head to look up at the boat bottom, and what I see turns my muscles to stone, my jaw wrenched open in a silent scream. The boat is gone, and in its place is a warty black serpent with cancerous skin and dark cesspools for eyes. The serpent twists its massive head toward me and I see horns like rotting tree trunks jutting out of its forehead. The serpent is clenching my brother's limp body in its jaw. It focuses its beady eyes on me. "You were warned," it hisses.

Mishi-ginebig.

My nightgown was always soaked to my skin when I awoke. My mind would go to Great-Grandpa Barrett, almost drowning a hundred years before. And then I would think of Ettie's words about Teddy Doyle being cursed.

And how my family was too.

The day before David's funeral, Bird Manaabeh and his mother pulled up in our driveway. For three days we had a steady stream of visitors dropping off lasagnas and ham platters, community members acknowledging our family's pain in the compassionate way that even the most distant of acquaintances take the time to do on Mikinaak. Bird's mother carried a foil-covered casserole pan into the house, and I was surprised to see that her face was puffy, and red rings circled her eyes.

It hadn't occurred to me that David's death had impacted so many people on our island. It wasn't until years later, when I became a mother myself, that I understood how the death of someone else's child mirrors the potential death of one's own child. A mother empathizes with another mother in her loss, while simultaneously grieving with the realization that her own heart could also, at any second, be slashed to shreds.

While Bird's mother was holding my mother in a strong embrace, now openly sobbing, Bird caught my eye and jerked his head to the side, motioning for me to slip outside with him. I joined him on our driveway. He stood, kicking gravel into the yard. He held his hand up toward me, balled into a fist. "I made this for you."

He spread open his fingers to reveal a leather pouch the size of a walnut shell, hanging from a leather cord. "When my baby cousin died, my Auntie made a little doll out of his hair and carried it around with her. It's called a sorrow doll." Bird rubbed the soft leather of the pouch and pushed his fingertip into the opening. "Anyways, I thought maybe you might want to, I don't know, carry some of David's hair in this. If you want."

"Thanks," I said curtly. I snatched the pouch from Bird's hand, and strode back into the house, letting the screen door slam behind me.

Bird's sympathy for me was too pure, too freely given. If he knew the truth about my role in David's death, he would be sickened. The pouch, however, I could accept without misgivings. The Ojibwe carried their sorrow dolls; I would wear a guilt pouch.

On the day of the funeral, angry thunderclouds rolled in. As the preacher eulogized my little brother, claps of thunder punctuated the ends of his sentences at precisely the right moments. God himself was showing his personal disapproval of what I had done.

"...but Jesus said, 'Let the little children come to me and do not hinder them, for to such belongs the kingdom of heaven.'" BOOM.

"...for this child I prayed, and the Lord has granted me my petition that I made to him. Therefore I have lent him to the Lord." BOOM.

I looked at my parents. Their faces were both impermeable masks of grief. Looking at them, I realized they did not hear a single word the preacher spoke. I found slight relief in knowing they were unaware of this sign from above; a sign that my sins were duly noted and would be dealt with accordingly.

After the service, we were allowed one final goodbye to David before the casket was folded into the earth. I had stolen a tiny pair of scissors from my mother's sewing kit, and held them in my pocket like a concealed weapon. This was my chance. First, my parents made their way up to the casket. My father eventually had to pry my mother's hand from David's cheek. "Kathy. You have to let him go." My mother was a tantrum-stricken child in my father's arms as he dragged her away from David's body.

Then it was my turn. My heart was pounding. I recognized the taboo in what I was about to do. I imagined the horrified shrieks coming from my mother if she were to turn around and see me wielding scissors above the forehead of my dead brother. But I had to have that hair. The face in the casket looked like a doll, sculpted by a craftsman in flawless imitation of David. I leaned down and begged, "Please, David, can you ever forgive me?" The doll face ignored me. I smoothed a lock of hair between my fingers, gave a quick snip, then jammed my fingers into my pocket. And then the funeral parlor was spinning, and a metallic taste rose into my mouth. Suddenly the walls switched places with the ceiling; concerned voices garbled in my ears.

Later that day, after dirt had been tossed on the grave, I gently tucked the lock of David's hair into the leather pouch, and fastened the cord around my neck. From that day forward I wore my sins around my neck: an albatross crafted of leather, hair, and fathomless remorse.

"David, I promise," I whispered as I cupped the pouch in my palm like a small bird's egg, "somehow I will earn your forgiveness."

CHAPTER 15

In an ocean of grief after the funeral, rum became my parents' life raft. My mother's brand of drunk was a roller coaster in a dark tunnel. I could never anticipate when we were going to plummet straight down. She made no effort to cloak her suspicion that I was at least partially to blame for David's death. "And just *what* were you doing on that boat with that Doyle tomboy? I have a feeling I know. I hope it was worth it." Then tears would course down her cheeks, and she would stumble to her room.

My father could not look me in the eye. Whereas mom brandished her grief like a weapon, dad's grief was a puncture wound. He sat at the kitchen table, his head resting in his hands, and tried to cry his son back into existence. He grieved at that table for five straight weeks, bottle of rum by his hand. The guys at the mill had the decency not to call and ask when he was planning on showing up for work.

And then early one morning, my father came to a resolution. I picture the taut lines around his eyes relaxing, his face smoothing over. I picture him staggering into the spruce forest with his hunting rifle, putting an end to his waiting with one clean bullet to the head.

I was in my bedroom when the blast rang out. I knew immediately what the sound meant. It wasn't a hunting rifle. It was his Datsun pickup, backfiring on its very last exit out of our driveway. After that, I heard from my father every few months, and then every season, and eventually only at Christmas and birthdays, often through remorseful handwritten letters with sentences too slipshod to match the dad I remembered. In a way, the hunting rifle seemed as though it may have hurt less.

Rum couldn't flush out the ache that throbbed in my mother's chest from the moment she crawled out of her sour-smelling sheets in the morning until she fumbled back in between them each night. She had lost her favorite child and her husband, and she spent the rest of her moments praying for time to cease so she wouldn't have to live in their absence.

The welfare cheque and the baby bonus became our only source of income; mom managed to spend the majority of those at the liquor store. She bought Kraft Dinner by the case, and at first I was welcome to make my own if I wanted something to eat—mixing it with water and margarine when there was margarine in the fridge, and just water when there wasn't. I didn't dare ask my mother what was for dinner; she spent all her time in her bedroom, and made it clear I was not to bother her.

Without stability or support, my entrance into seventh grade was overwhelming. But my bigger worries arose when I came home from school each day. I assessed the situation through clues I found in the living room and kitchen. New dirty dishes in the sink: good day. New photo of David masking-taped to the kitchen wall: Look out.

One afternoon, I walked into the house and slung my school bag down in the front hall, then tiptoed into the kitchen to determine whether today was the type of day I should hang out in the yard with Schnapps until dark. Thank god for the steadfast love of my loyal hound.

A saucepan of congealed orange macaroni sat on the stove. I breathed a sigh of relief.

"Marina? Is that you?" Mom's throat sounded raw.

I climbed the stairs to her closed bedroom door. Squeezing my eyes tight, I gave the door a soft rap.

"Come in, honey."

After so many weeks of negligence, that one word of affection brought moisture to my eyes. I swung the door open and bounded over to my mother's bedside. She coaxed a weary half-smile onto her face, and patted the comforter. I leapt onto her bed before she could change her mind, then nuzzled my head into her lap. A pooch of flab bulged beneath my head. My mother had worked hard to keep so slender before; I liked this new softness. She began to comb her swollen fingers through my hair, and I closed my eyes and arched my neck toward her middle. Finally. I had my mother back.

"Mom? Tell me about the time you worked on Elsinore Island?" I gambled that an Elsinore story was my best chance at sustaining the moment.

Mom looked up at the ceiling for several seconds. Her hand went to her neck and massaged the sides of it. I had set her off in the wrong direction.

"Hmmn. That might be just what the doctor ordered."

I sighed with relief and snuggled deeper into her belly.

As she spoke, her face brightened, and for a few magical moments, she seemed to forget that her husband was gone and her son was sown into the land.

Mom continued to stroke my hair after she finished the story. I kept my eyes closed, trying not to breathe, not to create any movement that might derail the moment.

"Marina, honey?"

I bit my lower lip. "Yes?"

"Could you please tell mommy exactly what happened that day at the beach?"

The question was a lump of sand in my throat. I swallowed. "I already told you. I don't know what happened. I was in the cuddy cabin."

My mother removed her fingers from my hair. She shifted her body to the side, and my head slipped from her lap. Her face was no longer gentle. "Marina. Please. I need to know. What happened that day?"

I looked up at her, my eyes wide. I slowly raised my shoulders an inch.

"Marina. Answer me!" Her voice was a restrained shout.

"I told you already." My words folded in on themselves and barely made it out of my mouth. "I don't know."

Patches of red blossomed across my mother's face. "I swear I just turned my back on the two of you for a minute..." she muttered to herself, cradling her head in her hands. She snapped her head back up at me. "I need to know how my son died!" She tore at the comforter, yanking it out from under me, then scrunched it into a tangled ball.

I looked down at my hands.

"Get out! Now! Get out of my effing room, and don't come back until you're ready to tell me what happened!" She was panting.

I nodded my head tearfully, then scurried away.

The more depressed my mom became, the more complicated my school life was. Mom couldn't bring herself to leave her room to shop or cook for either of us, and I had no money to buy groceries on my own. I salivated during lunch time when the other children popped open their plastic lunch pails and pulled out sandwiches, apples, and cookies. At first I tried to conceal my situation by packing a fake lunch consisting of Tupperware stuffed with garbage. I would pull out my plastic container at lunch time and peek under the lid, then roll my eyes. "Good lord. Tuna casserole again. Our cook should be shot," I would say, jamming the container back into my lunch pail. "I'd rather starve."

I thought this was working for the first few days, until Jeannie Baker rolled her eyes and announced, "Can it, Mina. Everyone knows your mom doesn't pack you anything." A few kids snickered. The shame stung worse than the hunger pains, as I officially joined the ranks of the lunchless kids who pretended to be absorbed in homework while the others ate their lunches.

As the weeks passed, I got to the point where I was obsessed with finding food. I scavenged crab apples and even rooted through school garbage cans when I thought no one was looking, and on days when mom was well enough to make herself some lunch while I was at school, I ate every mouthful of congealed macaroni that clung to the pan. But it was never enough. My clothes from the previous year began to puddle over my thin frame. Surely, I thought, if mom takes a good look at me, she will snap out of it. Surely she will remember that mothers are supposed to take care of their children.

One day, I resolved that when I got home from school, I would work up the nerve to knock on my mother's bedroom door and give her another chance to mother me, to show compassion. I envisioned standing there, and her cold face softening as she took a long look at the pathetic ragamuffin her daughter had become. She would open her arms, her face full of remorse, and croon, "My word! How could I let this happen? Come here, Marina honey.

Mommy's going to make everything all right." I would melt into her arms, and we would somehow pull ourselves out of our downward spiral.

When I got home from school, my courage fled. Legs shaking, I mounted the steps to her bedroom and knocked.

"What do you want?" My mother's voice sounded so weary.

"Mom?" I opened her door wide enough to step inside her room, and was met by the smell of soiled laundry and body odor. I stood straight, so that she could get a good look at me in all my pathetic glory. "Mom? I was wondering if maybe you might, um, come out of here and join me? Maybe we could go buy some, uh, food? I'm really hungry, Mom." My words sounded so absurd.

And then, as though imagining it had made it so, the hard angles of my mother's face turned to butter. She scanned me from top to bottom, and her eyes glistened.

"Oh, honey. Look at you. How could I let my baby get like this?" She patted the comforter, and I leapt over to the bed. Just as I was about to climb on, something shifted in her face. Her arm sprang up like a barricade across my chest. "You've decided to tell mommy what happened?"

My eyes fell to my feet. I exhaled a long, quiet breath, then shook my head almost imperceptibly. Millimeter by millimeter, I raised my eyes to hers. A dejected set of eyes stared back at me.

She sighed, her stringy hair falling over her puffy face. A face that ached for relief from her own nagging guilt about that day on the beach. "I am very sorry, Marina. But the minute I learn what happened on the beach is the minute I will get up out of this bed and start taking care of both of us." Her face went blank and her hand found its way to her neck. "Now get out of my room."

A sliver of pity for her bore into my chest as I trudged out of her room and closed the door with a muffled click.

I was going to have to figure out a way to fend for myself.

CHAPTER 16

My seventh grade teacher that year, Mrs. Haggerty, was a kind-hearted woman whose soft rolls swung from the undersides of her arms when she pointed, and who the other children called 'Mrs. Saggerty' behind her back. Sometimes I dreamed that she would scoop me up in those soft, fleshy arms and take me home to live with her.

Several times since the start of the school year, I caught Mrs. Haggerty staring at me when she thought I wasn't looking, her brow knitted in concern. Once, when I was reading alone at a library carrel, she came to stand near me. She smelled of rose perfume. I looked at her sideways, and contemplated her crisp, squiggly hair, the consequence of a perm and a liberal dose of hairspray. *Was this what a good mother smelled like?* Mrs. Haggerty touched her hand to my shoulder. I looked into her face, and was surprised to see tears well up in her eyes. She was quiet for several seconds, and I squirmed uncomfortably. For a millisecond, a bolt of hope shot through my chest: maybe Mrs. Haggerty would ask if something was wrong at home.

She patted my shoulder and finally said, "We all mourn for your family's loss."

Acid churned in my stomach. I had been caught focusing on my own needs and not the death of my brother and the absence of my father. I resolved from that moment on, I would not allow self-pity to take the place of the remorse I must carry. I had a death to repent for. I would manage to survive because it was my duty to find a way to make amends.

I began stealing that same day. Theft went against the way I was raised and my own inherent fondness for rules, but I told myself I had no choice. I had to eat.

Mrs. Haggerty kept some money in her desk drawer—I had seen a two-dollar bill beside the small plastic dish of gold stars she often gave me despite my lackluster schoolwork. *Where has my brilliant young Marina gone?* she would write, with a happy face drawn beside.

I plotted at my desk all afternoon, waiting for the lunch bell with a sick feeling in my stomach, sweat making my pencil slippery between my fingers. Once lunch break was underway, I darted down the hallway toward our classroom. My heart was pounding as I peeked my head into Mrs. Haggerty's room. No sign of her. I dashed over to her desk and pulled open the top drawer, and there it was—my ticket to a satisfied stomach and a new identity as a thief. I stared at the two-dollar bill, unable to reach down to steal money from my beloved teacher.

I heard footsteps clicking down the hallway and I stood frozen, my hand on my teacher's open desk drawer. I could feel my pulse in my ears. Just as the footsteps approached Mrs. Haggerty's classroom door, I heard an adult voice say, "Oh, shoot. I left my copies in the staffroom," and the clicking of dress shoes departed in the opposite direction. I exhaled, grabbed the money, and speed-walked out to the school grounds, where I sat stunned under a tree, sweating adrenaline, contemplating the unimaginable thing I had just done.

That evening, I spooned an abundance of fat and calories into my hungry body. I had sold a small corner of my troubled soul for one economy-sized jar of peanut butter.

Mrs. Haggerty kept replenishing her two-dollar bills, and the thievery got easier each time, right up until the day our principal caught me in the act. That day I received five sharp licks from Mr. Maller's leather enforcer, *the strap*, on the palm of my left hand, and a stern lecture about what happens to young girls who are untrustworthy. Mr. Maller spoke about how communities work together to help one another out, and how this kinship is built on trust for one another. There was no place for a liar or a thief in a tight-woven community like Mikinaak. "You do want to be part of this community, don't you, Miss McInnis?"

Mr. Maller mistook my silence for impudence and gave me another five lashes. There is no place in this community for someone with secrets like mine, Mr. Maller.

Mr. Maller instructed me to hand over the money I had taken from Mrs. Haggerty's desk, and as I peeled the two-dollar bill out of my pocket, a small piece of paper slipped out. I slid the paper back into my pocket, and handed over the money. "One last thing," Mr. Maller added, as I stood up to return to class. "I tried to call your mother." He coughed, embarrassed. "I trust that you will bring this letter back to me, signed."

I made the walk home from school that day like a virgin shuffling toward a volcano. Pale and shaking, I forced my leaden legs to make the final steps to our front porch. My mother was sitting on the living room sofa, legs crossed, forehead resting in her hands. She lifted her chin to me. Intense grief and unremitting rum consumption made for an unforgiving skin tonic; her face had aged a decade since the day she lost her preferred child.

I handed over the letter and time came to a stop.

Mom read it very slowly. "So now you're a thief, too." She dropped her head to her knees. "I can't take another day of this! The *whole town's* going to be talking about this by noon tomorrow." Her voice hardened. "But I guess that's nothing compared to what everyone already knows you did to your brother."

I felt the bile rise in my throat. People knew about what I did to my brother?

A sick feeling flooded over me.

Mom's arms fell limply to her sides, and the letter fell to the floor. "Marina, I need you to tell me what happened that day on the beach. Do you think I want to be like this? It doesn't have to be this way, Marina. I just need to know about my son's final moments. I'm begging you. Can you please, please give your mother that much?" She slouched forward and grabbed onto the couch arm, and her shoulders began to shake.

The burr lodged itself in my throat again. I tried to swallow; my hand went to the leather pouch around my neck.

"Marina—did anything *unusual* happen, before David dove into the water?"

I stared at the floor for a full minute.

Mom snapped her head forward. Her nostrils flared. "You stubborn little bitch!"

She charged over to me, and her hands flew toward my neck. She throttled me, jerking my whole body forward and back, and then her hands flew to the sides of my head and she yanked fistfuls of my hair as she shook me. Fire burned across my scalp. "I need to know the effing truth," she screamed, her face a twisted mess. "What happened to my son, why HIM?"

A waft of alcohol breath hit my face. "Mom—don't! Please!"

She threw me down on the couch, but one of her hands did not release its grasp on my hair in time. Mom looked down at the clump of hair in her fist and gasped. She stared at her hand for a long time, contemplating it as though it was not her own.

When she finally spoke, her voice was sad and hollow. "Let me know when you feel like talking about that day on the beach. Until then, don't bother coming to me for anything."

She turned and walked toward the stairs, then paused at the bottom step. She turned to face me; all the poison had drained from her face. She looked so feeble. I suddenly wanted to run to her and throw my arms around her. If only I was brave enough, there might be a chance I could cut through the despair with a bold gesture of love. But I couldn't force my legs to move.

I stood still, willing myself to call out to her, to tell her whatever she wanted to hear.

"Marina—there's something else I need to tell you. Schnapps is missing. I called and called but she hasn't come." She flinched at the word 'missing,' and a look of horror darkened her face. She hung her head, and her next words were so quiet I could barely hear them. "The last I saw her, she was down at the lake. I searched for her all afternoon. I loved that dog almost as much as you did. I'm sorry, Marina." Then she trudged up the stairs and slunk back to her bedroom.

That night, after combing the forest and the shore, I lay stiff on my bed and tried not to think about the way my beloved Schnapps may have met her end. I knew my mom didn't have anything to do with it—she was sick and confused, but there was no way she would ever lay a hand on Schnapps. I massaged the sore spot on my scalp, noting the yellowed bruises on my arm from a few days earlier. My chest ached. It felt like a fresh scab had been split open, and all of the grief for David and my father that festered inside me came oozing out. I truly was on my own now. And most of this was my fault. I hugged my arms around myself and rubbed them up and down. I felt so cold, so numb.

My hand rubbed across my pocket, and I remembered the slip of paper from Mrs. Haggerty's two-dollar bill. I pulled it out, and read the neat script: "Let me help you."

I examined the note for several minutes. What relief I would feel, to be held tight in Mrs. Haggerty's generous arms.

I scrunched the note up and threw it to the floor. Other people's pity could not bring my father or David back. I would weather my family's downward spiral alone.

The following week, I spied a furry lump far down the shoreline. My stomach twisted as I watched the waves wash over it and then retreat. *Mishi-ginebig.* My brain scrambled to find an alternative explanation: *maybe the rip current got her. But Schnapps was such a strong swimmer.* I ran to confirm my fears.

I buried Schnapps in the forest that afternoon.

I found out that the Doyles had moved back to Elsinore Island the same day as every other kid in seventh grade. We were standing for "O Canada" when the classroom door swung open and in waltzed Rhonda Doyle, as casual as if she had always been part of our class.

"Class, we have a new student I would like you to welcome," Mrs. Haggerty said, after the morning announcements were through. "I believe that some of you already know Rhonda Doyle. Her family is now living on their island, and Rhonda will be joining us for the rest of the year."

If Mrs. Haggerty was aware of the reason for Rhonda's family to have moved from Toronto, her cheery smile did not betray it. "Rhonda, would you like to say a few words to introduce yourself to your new classmates?" Mrs. Haggerty swept her arms in front of her, soft wings of flesh swinging beyond her short sleeves as she motioned for Rhonda to take center stage. Rhonda walked to the front of the classroom and stood tall, her face taking on the solemnity of a politician. She clasped her hands at her navel. "Fellow classmates, my name is Rhonda Doyle, and I believe it will be an honour and a privilege to work amongst you at Mikinaak Elementary School." Mrs. Haggarty raised an eyebrow. "I thank you in advance for your small-town kindness and generosity." She gave the class a companionable smile, then stepped backwards to her desk. Mrs. Haggarty let out an audible breath.

"One more thing." Rhonda raised one finger in the air and gave Mrs. Haggarty the eye. "I regret to inform anyone in a position of power at M.E.S. that SCHOOL CAN SUCK MY LEFT NUT!"

With that, Rhonda jumped high into the air with her legs splayed, punched her fist toward the ceiling, and then spun around and did a karate kick in our teacher's general direction. The students howled in adoration of their newest hero.

Rhonda scanned the classroom, and our eyes met for the first time. She winced.

"To the office, Miss Doyle. Now." Mrs. Haggerty said, and spent the next thirty minutes trying to reign in her electrified students.

Waiting for the lunch bell felt like an eternity. I dreaded talking to Rhonda, but also longed for the comfort of a best friend. Finally, we were released. Rhonda and I both walked silently to the farthest corner of the school grounds, our heads down.

"I heard about your dad. That's just so incredibly shitty." Rhonda said, pulling blades of grass from the scraggy ground in my hideout behind the baseball diamond. I nodded and squinted up at some seagulls that were circling, scavenging for cheesies that some kid had snuck outside and then spilled all over the ball field.

"And... I'm sorry about...what happened to David."

I nodded again, fixated on the gulls plummeting and then soaring back up toward the clouds; all that grace and effort for a scrap of junk food. "I don't ever want to talk about what happened that day. Ever."

Rhonda nodded, then was quiet for several minutes, which was unusual for her.

Finally, she touched me lightly on the arm. "You let me in when you're ready, M," she said.

It was the 'M' that did it. It brought me straight back to the freedom and innocence of our last summer messing around on the docks and exploring every crevice of Elsinore Island together. I crisscrossed my legs and bent my head down, then spoke into the yellowed grass. I told Rhonda everything that was happening with my father, my mother, the alcohol, the neglect.

But I told her nothing of the eerie presence I had sensed in the lake with David. She knew our part in David's death; she didn't need to know more. When I was finally through spilling the awful words I looked up at Rhonda. Her eyes glistened.

"I can help you, M," she said, taking my hand. "I have an idea."

CHAPTER 17

Victoria Doyle showed up at our doorstep early the next morning. I was distracting myself from my hunger by watching Saturday morning cartoons—thank goodness the two television channels available to Mikinaakians were free, or my television watching would have gone the way of the phone line and the hot water. My mother was upstairs, likely passed out from a big night of pounding back the rums in her bedroom. From the number of empty pop cans riddled across the kitchen counter, it looked like she would be unconscious for many hours to come.

Crab apple season was over, and with it went one of my reliable sources of food. I was studying a library book called *Edible Plants of Northern Ontario*. Foraging was my new thing—I had an empty stomach to fill.

Although, I hadn't gone completely hungry lately. A few days after Schnapps went missing, I had come home to find a cake box with a neon pink *reduced for clearance* sticker on top. Inside the box was a blue frosted Winnie the Pooh cake. Beside the cake sat a five-dollar bill, and an envelope with my mother's handwriting on the back: *Mina, I can't live with myself and the way I've treated you.*

Please go to town and buy yourself something nice. I could hear the heartfelt apology beneath her words.

I had immediately biked into town, and blew half the money on a huge slice of peach pie and a hot turkey platter smothered with gravy at Bub's Diner, smiling to myself as I shoveled hot French fries into my mouth. The rest of the money bought me a stash of chips, chocolate bars, and a large bag of carrots. I had summoned my courage and knocked on my mother's bedroom door when I got home. Her face was puffy and her eyes were ringed with red, but she broke into a weak smile when she saw me.

I was invited once again to snuggle my mother in bed, and she didn't have to ask twice. Soon the bed shook with her sobs. I felt drops of moisture patting my neck and I held my breath and prayed that she wouldn't ask about David. She stroked my hair, and wept quietly, and my chest felt as though it was not big enough to contain my heart. All she had to say at that moment were the words *I'm sorry* and I would have forgiven her anything, everything.

Finally, she curled her body beside mine under the duvet, and wrapped her arms around me so tight it was difficult to breathe. I lay there, enveloped in my mother's trembling arms, until a rattling snore rose from behind me with each of her breaths. I stayed snuggled against her chest for a long time, longing to stay in her arms, yet afraid to still be there when she awoke.

The following day, the tenderness vanished. My mother ate the remains of the cake—out of bleakness, not spite, I would like to believe—then spent the rest of the day locked in her room.

When Rhonda's mother knocked on the door, it took my brain several takes to connect the pretty face on our doorstep with the Doyle family. Mrs. Doyle knocked a second time, and I bolted to open the door before she knocked again and woke up my mother.

Mrs. Doyle straightened the hem of her skirt, then stepped into our front hallway and looked around at our living room. If pressed to choose one, this room was the most presentable in the house— no stack of dirty dishes sitting in a pool of scummy grey dishwater in the sink; no obvious traces of bodily functions—but as I looked around at the room through Mrs. Doyle's eyes, I was horrified. My mother's full ashtrays, empty chip bags, macaroni boxes, and tabloid newspapers were scattered on the floor; rumpled socks and pants sat atop the furniture; greasy fingerprints covered every inch of the lacquered coffee table. My mother and I were living like trolls.

Mrs. Doyle politely refrained from looking around at the mess. She approached me with both pity and restraint, the way you might a wounded animal. "Rhonda has come to me with some rather unsettling information." She surprised me by reaching out to stroke my hair; her face took on the sad, distant look I had often seen when she watched Rhonda and me from afar.

"Mina," she said, her voice kind. "I know what it's like to lose a brother. I would have followed my big brother Teddy to the ends of the earth. After he died, I would have given away every last thing I owned for one more day with him."

I stared at her, uncertain of what I was supposed to say.

"Mina, how would you feel about not living here," she swept her arm in the direction of a mound of garbage beside the couch, "any longer?"

I blinked, confused. Where else would I live? I didn't see that I had any other options other than running away—an option which I had considered and rejected after picturing myself hungry and shivering on a sidewalk in the rain at night.

"Mina," Mrs. Doyle stepped over a pair of underwear to come one step closer. She stood with her feet neatly together, her hands clasped behind her back. "I am wondering if you would like to come live with Rhonda and me on Elsinore Island." Despite her calm voice, I could see that her neck was marbled with blotchy red patches, and her cheeks were flushed. Mrs. Doyle stood still, reading the reluctance on my face. "You'll have your own bedroom, which you can decorate however you want, and Rhonda would be happy to share all of her things with you."

"My mom would never let me," I said flatly, biting my lip to hold back the tears. I felt a pain in my chest when I allowed myself to think about how much I would love to let Rhonda's mother whisk me away. I ran my finger along the page of the book I was still holding, trying to blink back the tears and focus on the leaves in the picture, pulling my mind away from a haven that was Rhonda Doyle's birthright, not mine.

Mrs. Doyle bent down and gently closed the book in my hands. "Parents can't treat their children this way, Mina. Deep down, your mother knows this. Let me talk to her."

I looked down at my feet, and didn't budge.

"Go on, Mina. Get your things together. I'll deal with your mother."

I didn't want to insult her, but I still didn't move.

"Go on. It will be all right. I promise."

Unconvinced, I tiptoed upstairs and threw my paltry possessions into a worn red Budweiser duffel bag. My books were my prized possession, and I made a second trip to carry an armful of them down. Mrs. Doyle insisted on carrying my things to the car, and then gestured for me to make myself comfortable on the maroon velvet upholstery in the front seat. Then she straightened herself and strode back inside the house to face my mother.

Fifteen minutes later, Mrs. Doyle scrambled from the house, my mother yanking violently at her arm. My mother was in a ratty housecoat. Her wild hair looked as though she had just emerged from a cave. "You're not going anywhere with my daughter!" she screamed.

Mrs. Doyle stunned me by walloping my mother in the belly. My mom went down hard, and I sat frozen in the car, my jaw unhinged. My mother jumped up and pounced on Mrs. Doyle, then wrestled her to the ground. Her bathrobe came loose in the scrimmage, and ended up tenting Mrs. Doyle's head. To my horror, my mother's puckered expanse of bare white ass flashed in my direction. I cringed, both fascinated and terrified, as the two women rolled around on our front porch.

Mrs. Doyle gained the upper hand, and straddled my mother. Her face and neck were a map of red blotches. "Tell me what happened to my brother out on the lake!" she screamed into my mother's face.

My mother, now completely free of her bathrobe, squirmed from beneath Mrs. Doyle. She bronco-bucked her hips, and Mrs. Doyle was launched into the air like a doll. "Your piss-drunk brother fell out of his boat and drowned!"

Mrs. Doyle fanned her arms across the porch, grasping for anything she could hit my mother with. The only thing on the porch besides a black trash bag was a roll of newspaper flyers. She began beating my mother over the head with it. I sat transfixed, unable to move a muscle. I suspected that if I so much as breathed too loud, I would disrupt the alternate universe we had somehow entered. Mrs. Doyle whacked my mother in the forehead with the newspaper roll. "Liar!"

My mother clenched her fist and cocked it back. My hands flew to my eyes; I couldn't bear to see Mrs. Doyle's lovely teeth knocked loose. My shoulders crowded my ears, trying to block out the noise of my mother's fist, but the sound never came. I peeped over my hands to see my mother just standing there, fist clenched at her side. She stared at Mrs. Doyle for an eternity, and then relaxed her fist. "Take the girl, for all I care," she said, and walked back into the house. My throat felt as though it might close over. My last glimpse of my mother was those cheese-curded ass cheeks, juddering as the screen door bounced off them.

Mrs. Doyle slid into the car seat, panting. "I'm sorry you had to see that, Mina." She reached out and stroked one of my curls. "Don't worry, sweetheart. Your mother made the right choice."

CHAPTER 18

All the exhilaration I felt as Mrs. Doyle shuttled me away from my mother seeped out as we made the journey toward Elsinore Island. Mrs. Doyle made for an elegant captain, confident at the helm from a lifetime spent around boats, the picture of glamour in her ankle-length striped cotton dress. But by the time I was seated in the Bayliner, my hands were shaking so badly I had to sit on them.

Rhonda was overjoyed to see that her mother had succeeded in whisking me away. She leaped up from her cross-legged pose on the Elsinore dock the second our boat came into view, waving her arms and calling us in to shore. She yanked at the boat ropes once we reached the dock, jerking the boat and its cargo into a secure hold on Elsinore.

The Doyles had saved me.

Yet I couldn't bring myself to even look up at Rhonda, let alone reciprocate her fierce thumping on my back, or her howl of delight as she hoisted me up and spun me around.

Mrs. Doyle grabbed Rhonda's arm and pulled her off me as I stood there like a statue, arms pinned to my sides. "Let's give Mina some space," she said. The three of us made our way up the path to the estate which we all needed to adjust to call *home*. Mrs. Doyle showed me which room would be mine, and I quietly thanked her, then stepped inside and closed the door on whatever plans Rhonda had for us.

I had deserted the home where the memories of my father and little brother remained—had fled to the home of someone complicit in David's death. I needed to make up for this latest betrayal. In my bedroom was a white desk with pink roses on the handles; I set myself up there and opened a lined notebook I had brought amongst my stack of books. One way I could memorialize my brother was through stories—stories had always been the oil that kept our family memories burning brightly. *Speaking* about David was not something I felt inclined to do, but crafting stories in his honour came naturally to me.

I sat myself down and began to write my first of many short stories about a magical young boy with a tuft of white-blonde hair who taught everyone around him lessons about goodness and unconditional love. I called it *The Legends of David*.

It seemed that Rhonda Doyle dealt with her guilt by focusing on my healing. Each morning she requested Ettie to whip up a hot breakfast fit for a spa. The first morning, Rhonda showed up at my bedroom door struggling to hold up a silver tray laden with French toast, a plate of sliced strawberries and orange segments lovingly arranged to resemble the petals of a flower, and freshly squeezed orange juice.

I thanked Rhonda politely, then set the tray down on the floor and slouched back over to my bed. My body was famished, and the food looked like a meal I might have conjured in my dreams; however, I could not bring myself to touch it.

To satiate myself would be one final disloyalty to my mother. Despite the anguish she had caused me, there was still a part of me that wanted to clutch on to any available threads connected to her. Even in her dark days after the accident, I still accepted one strand of my mother's tangled logic: I deserved to be punished for what happened to David.

I set a waiting period of one hour, before permitting myself to go near the tray of food. It took all the restraint I could muster, but sixty minutes ticked away as I tried to distract myself with a book, salivating. When the hour was up, I took two nibbles of the French toast, and one sliver of strawberry. It filled my mouth with such pleasure, so impossibly sweet compared to crab apples. Once I finished my three bites, I forced myself to pick the tray up and carry it back to the kitchen, warning my fingers with each step that they were not permitted to snatch an extra morsel. And then I headed back to my room, where all I really felt like doing was writing stories about David.

For lunch, Rhonda thought up a menu more tantalizing than the last. She had Ettie prepare baked macaroni and cheese, the crust golden and crisp atop creamy noodles nestled in gooey cheese. The pungent smell of baked cheddar filled my bedroom. I decided that maybe it would be okay to permit myself six bites instead of three, and decreased the waiting period down to a strict five minutes, not a second less.

Rhonda and Ettie wooed me with a lineup of classic comfort foods for dinner: roasted chicken drizzled with gravy, buttery mashed potatoes, a soft homemade dinner roll glazed with butter and sugar, and strawberry shortcake on freshly baked tea biscuit. My stomach ignored my directives completely, and began stirring in anticipation of the feast before my eyes.

Not one molecule of gravy escaped my dinner roll. I carried the tray of empty plates down to the kitchen, my head hanging low. Ettie did not look up from her sinkful of dirty dishes as I set the tray down beside her. I turned to leave, and Ettie ran her finger across my shining plate. "Figured I might have to sign myself up for classes at the Cordon Bleu," she winked, and her face broke into a wide smile. I looked down at the floor and a tiny grin crept onto my face. "Welcome back, Sugarpie," she said, as I walked out of the kitchen and back to my room, where, for the first time in months, I felt wisps of happiness brushing against the empty shell of my chest.

Rhonda, Mrs. Doyle, and Ettie saw to it that my cheeks grew plump and cherubic. Ettie cooked extravagant meals each night, as though adding flesh to my frame had become her driving force. She asked me to make a list of my favorite foods, and I sat blinking in disbelief each evening as she treated us to a royal spread, each night's menu showcasing a dish from my list.

Mrs. Doyle gave me the Sears catalogue to order clothes that fit, and took me to get my hair cut so my eyes were once again visible beneath my bangs. My frizzy snarl of hair was transformed into curls that bounced and shone.

Mrs. Doyle beamed when I tried on one of the dresses that arrived from the catalogue order. Rhonda continued her stubborn rejection of dresses and frills, so it was a treat for Mrs. Doyle to help tie the silky bow at the back of my dress, and braid my hair into neat French braids ending in pink ribbons that she cut especially for me. I overlooked that the braids were on the childish side for a girl my age, and lapped up the attention, following Mrs. Doyle around the house like a puppy. Whenever I tried to broach the subject of my mother, however, Mrs. Doyle's face would drain of all its tenderness. Whatever had happened between them was to remain their private business.

Mrs. Doyle's face had looked pinched and drawn when we first arrived on Elsinore. The McInnis family was not the only family to suffer severe injuries in 1973. The Doyles were getting divorced.

Divorce was a rare event on Mikinaak Island at that time, and pre-nuptial agreements were unheard of. But in the circles that the Doyle family ran in, both of these things had become standard. And Rhonda's mother Victoria found herself at the financial mercy of both.

At the time she was married, Victoria Doyle's dowry had consisted solely of a powerful family name—so powerful, in fact, that her father had encouraged her to keep it, and advised her fiancé Boris that if he enjoyed getting ahead in the business world, he would be smart to consider adopting the influential moniker as well. So, upon marriage, Victoria's fiancé Boris Smith became Boris Doyle, and as promised, a legion of business allies spread their arms around him in a nepotistic embrace.

The pre-nuptial agreement had been drawn up at the insistence of Victoria's father, to protect the Doyle family estate. What had been overlooked, however, was interim money for Victoria in the event of a bitter parting of ways. Upon Victoria's discovery of her husband's new love interest, Boris had bled their accounts dry. Abetted by painfully slow legal proceedings, Boris had taken all of Victoria's assets hostage. Victoria would eventually get what was rightfully hers, that much was certain. But in the meantime, Victoria needed money.

Even before the dust settled from the divorce proceedings, one thing that Victoria owned without question was the sprawling family estate on Elsinore Island.

While she waited for the lawyers and judge to hash out the divorce settlement, Victoria decided that the best place for her and Rhonda was at their summer home. No need to struggle over paying Toronto rent or undergo the daunting task of buying a downsized home in the city as a single mother. Ettie, bless her soul, had agreed to accompany them, and Fat Joe, who was actually rather trim, and who had been Elsinore's caretaker for as long as Victoria could remember, lived in the staff quarters on Elsinore Island year-round to look after the property. Fat Joe could be counted on to provide wood and trek over to the mainland and generally help hold down the fort in whatever way was required. Also, the entire Doyle clan would migrate back to Elsinore once summer arrived, and Victoria would then be buoyed by a band of relatives.

Elsinore Island had been a part of Victoria's life since her earliest memories—it had witnessed her learning to swim amidst a brood of cousins when she was three; it caught a glimpse of her first kiss under the broad oak tree when she was fifteen at a box social that her parents had hosted; it had overheard her declaring wedding vows to a man she genuinely believed would love and cherish her until death did them part. But Boris Doyle had found a supple new subject for his loving and cherishing, and Victoria needed a familiar place to fall.

But now Mrs. Doyle was beginning to fill out her dresses again, her girlish curves reappearing. Rhonda also began to resemble a younger version of herself, one I had seen in a photograph on the living room wall: she was around six years old, standing barefoot and proudly holding a frog up for the camera, a wide grin ending in two pink apple cheeks. My rejuvenation, it seemed, was contagious.

Those first few weeks of being in the care of three kind females was like being wrapped in a downy cocoon. I spent many hours each day sitting in the English garden that bloomed on the east side of the estate. The crisp autumn air carried the earthy scent of gold, red, and orange chrysanthemums, and black-eyed Susans fluttered delicately around me as I sat cross-legged on a mossy stone, thinking. On chillier days, Ettie appeared with a floral quilt over her arm, carrying a tray of herbal tea and honey. She would wrap the quilt around my shoulders, set the tray down beside me, and leave me be. Mrs. Doyle decided it wouldn't hurt Rhonda or me too much to miss a bit of school. My only job, as Mrs. Doyle put it, was to "rest and allow time to sprout my colourful wings." Rhonda was patient with me on my moody and sullen days, which were frequent at first. One day, I would be capable of a small smile as I helped Ettie prepare supper in the kitchen, and the next, I could not think of a decent reason to leave the solitude of the English garden. Some days I soaked my cheeks in hot tears from the time I woke in the morning until the moment I drifted back off to sleep in the early evening, my body dehydrated and too emotionally drained to hold onto consciousness.

As the days passed, my down days became fewer. The resilience of a young person is miraculous: happiness eventually eclipsed my darker emotions. I was thoroughly cared for, and that was almost enough. But just when I found myself starting to feel better, a faint voice hissed in my ear: *stay away*.

Living on a small private island posed many logistical challenges. Once the lake got too icy to safely boat across, our two primary challenges were securing food and education. After the ice hardened, we would be able to drive the snow machines across the ice, but the month of November would see us stranded.

Mrs. Doyle fretted for days about bringing the proper supplies over before we became marooned on the island. Rhonda and I plotted breathlessly for the day when the ice started forming.

Mrs. Doyle made arrangements with the school for Rhonda and me to do correspondence courses during the weeks we would be unable to make the trip across the lake. This type of seasonal absence was not new to our school—there was a cluster of farming families who lived on the far west side of Mikinaak Island whose children also did their studies at home during the winter months, when the icy country roads were just too risky for the school bus to pick them up.

Ettie was given her second hat to wear, as headmistress. Rhonda and I worked with her on our correspondence packets each morning, as Ettie flitted between the kitchen and the sun room where we had set up two card tables as school desks. The correspondence work was dull, but if we worked diligently we were able to finish it in about three hours, which meant we had the entire glorious afternoon all to ourselves.

When it came to school work, Rhonda aimed for completion above all else. She scribbled her way through the pages, punctuation and penmanship be damned. "Rhonda," I asked her one morning, looking over her work, "how is someone even going to be able to *read* this?"

"They can't read it, they can eat shit. Last I checked, a mechanic don't need to know about the meter of a sonnet."

It annoyed me that Rhonda used poor grammar sometimes; I believed she knew better.

"You're so smart, M," she said, as she stared at the mainly blank page where her English essay belonged.

"*Books*mart," I corrected her.

"It took me about one day at our school to figure out you're the smartest person in our whole class, and you're barely trying. I bet you're the smartest person in the whole school. Someday, M, you're going to be a famous...journalist. Or a university professor. Or whatever you want. You're going to become some famous person I used to know, and I'll still be here on Elsinore, tinkering away on my boatercycle."

Rhonda had drafted plans for the world's first-ever hybrid boat/motorcycle, and so far had dismantled two boat engines and one motorcycle in the process of building it. Basically, she dreamed of cruising around the lake on her motorbike, and was hell-bent on figuring out a way to engineer this dream into a reality.

"You know what I want to be, Rhonda? I want to be happy."

Rhonda looked at me as though I had just told her I wanted to learn how to breathe. She shook her head and sighed. "Happiness is a choice, M. How is it that you're so smart, but you don't get that? You have to find a way to let all of the bad stuff go."

I was quiet. It rubbed me the wrong way when Rhonda told me what to do.

Never one to allow solemn words to linger, Rhonda sent a jet of spit sailing through the gap in her front teeth, which landed on her school work. She broke into a wide grin as the dot of saliva landed right at the end of the only sentence she had written. "*There's* some punctuation for you. "Now hurry up so we can hit Mount Elsinore."

Mount Elsinore was more of a hill than a mountain. It consisted of hard-packed dirt peppered with scrubby saplings that would never amount to mature trees, and thick, woody weeds that made excellent handholds for climbing. Once the frost had set in, the hill was just icy enough to make for a challenging race course. Rhonda and I had invented a game we dubbed *Bazookers*.

Rhonda yanked at my ankle as I tried to scramble up the hill, digging my fingertips into the unforgiving earth. "Bazookers!" she howled, socking me in the back with a dirt clump the size of an apple. I screamed out in glee as I kicked my leg free and scurried a few steps above her head. I yanked a doozy of a rock out of the ground and hurled it at her leg, striking my target with surprising accuracy.

"Bazookers yourself!" I hollered back, laughing so hard that I had to stabilize myself with both hands in the frosty dirt while I caught my breath. Rhonda seized the opportunity, wrenching a sapling, roots and all, from the ground and whacking me across the ankles with it.

"Bazookers-til-the-sun-goes-down," she crooned, marking each consonant with a good smack.

I grabbed a fistful of muck and smeared it all over Rhonda's face. "One kick in the butt, coming right up!" she yelled, a blob of dirt falling off her face as she spoke.

"Totally worth it, dirtmouth!" I said, as Rhonda held my arms to my sides and gave me a good boot to the rump. I sat out my five-second penalty, and Rhonda scrambled to the top of the hill.

"Winner! Triumphant once more!" Rhonda arched her back, fists clenched and pointing to the sky. "And now for your dare." She sat down on the top of the hill and scratched her head theatrically, a smirk across her dirt-streaked face. "Mina McInnis," she paused for dramatic effect, "I dare you to become part of our family for the rest of your life."

The smile vanished from my face, and I felt my stomach do that nauseous flip which I had not felt in several weeks.

"You belong with us," Rhonda said, her smile failing to mirror the anguish that must have shown on my own face. "The Doyles are your family now."

CHAPTER 19

The channel converted its last remaining black waves into a sheet of dense, white ice. Although there were sections of Lake Huron that never froze over completely in the winter, the channel between Elsinore Island and Mikinaak was reasonably safe for travel between December and March each year. For Rhonda and me, this signaled an end to our afternoons spent romping over the icy hills of Elsinore. Fat Joe had tested the ice all the way to the mainland the previous day, and it held firmly. It was time to return to school.

Rhonda was given free reign of Fat Joe's snowmobile for travel to and from school. We roared off across the ice, clouds of gasoline-scented snow spraying out the back of our Skidoo. I gripped Rhonda's waist with the urgency of the dying; Rhonda howled with elation. Every so often we would encounter an ice boulder, and she would crank the handlebars at the very last second to veer around it, with me nearly sliding off the seat, my winter boot dragging in the snow for balance. "Jeeee-ust flippin' givin'er!" Rhonda would screech into the barren expanse each time she righted our machine after a dicey swerve. I wrapped my arms around her parka and focused on the horizon ahead of us, and forced a stiff grin every time Rhonda craned her head around to see if I was as thrilled as she was.

Rhonda parked the snowmobile in the teachers' parking lot at our school. I felt like an Arctic dignitary as I swung my leg over the back of the snowmobile to dismount, then sloshed across the parking lot to the school playground, shiny black snowmobile helmet tucked under my arm. Kids swarmed around us as we walked through the metal gates of the playground. "Take me for a spin after school?" a chorus of voices begged Rhonda. She had won friends effortlessly at our school from day one—this attention was nothing new to her.

Rhonda chucked the snowmobile keys high in the air, and held out her hand so they dropped neatly into her palm. "Nah. The only person going near this sled is Mina McInnis." Rhonda walked past the throng of eager classmates. Everyone turned to stare at the unlikely recipient of Rhonda's esteem. I straightened up, clutched my helmet proudly, and marched to catch up with Rhonda.

The scent of gasoline on our clothing permeated our classroom that month, as though we were publicizing our return with our own brand of perfume—the aroma of freedom and self-reliance. No other kids in seventh grade were driving themselves across the lake to school on a snowmobile, that much was certain. Rhonda and I were instant playground royalty, our helmets our crowns. I knew all the attention was solely because of my association with Rhonda, but I basked in the warm glow of popularity for my first time ever at school. It took my mind off my family.

"Piss on the attention," Rhonda said at recess, as we gathered snow to replenish our stockpile of snowballs. "It's fickle." I blushed a little as she said that, her words pinpointing the key difference between her and me. Rhonda was a complete person; she produced her own feelings of goodness from within. It's why so many of our classmates were naturally drawn to her. But me on the other hand—

ever since my father leaving and David's drowning, I had a hole somewhere inside of me. The good feelings that the safe haven of Elsinore helped build just started to leak out, drop after continuous drop: all the attention in the world wouldn't be enough to fill me up.

All week, loads of classmates were keen to hang out with both Rhonda and me at recess. Rhonda was used to the attention, but I lapped it up. A gaggle of girls approached us—their eyes aimed more at Rhonda, I couldn't help noticing—to ask us if we wanted to join them in a game of snowball tag. Rhonda was super-fast on her feet, and had an arm like a man. All the girls quickly started gunning for her, and she took her place as queen bee.

As I ran across the schoolyard, I glimpsed a cluster of kids hunched over in a circle, rocking gently. I felt the skin on my arms tighten into gooseflesh. Something was not right. As I approached them, I could hear the singsong lilt of a chant coming from within the ring of snowsuit-clad bodies, and even though I couldn't make out the words, I felt a cold wave of dread wash over my insides. I stepped closer to the circle, and poked my head through a gap under someone's arm. Inside lay a thin boy, face-down in the snow. He wasn't moving. The chanting suddenly trumpeted in my ear, but the words sounded warped, as though they were snaking backwards out of the kids' mouths. My throat tightened. My lungs suddenly forgot how to breathe. Only two words were recognizable in the chant: *David McInnis.*

Hearing my brother's name brought all of the guilt and the pain rushing up, rupturing the delicate membrane of my peace of mind. I turned and ran away, my ankles unsteady through the deep snow. I ran straight to Rhonda and crumpled in a heap.

Rhonda picked up a snowball and lobbed it toward the circle of kids. It fell in a perfect arc and exploded directly in the center of their circle. "I see you just found out about Mikinaak's latest ghost story."

Rhonda wouldn't tell me what she knew until we were home. Finally back on Elsinore, we sat in our snow fort, our breath warming the air around us.

Rhonda began: "The story goes like this...M, you sure you want to hear this horse shit?"

I nodded, a heavy weight settling in my chest.

"They say it started happening to kids in mid-August. It freaked so many kids out, half of Mikinaak youth stopped going in the water. Now some kids won't even set foot on the *docks*.

I shifted in the snow, my stomach a tight coil. "*What* was happening?

Rhonda took a few deep breaths. "It always happened when someone was alone in the water. Not necessarily entirely alone—just out of reach of their friends. Far enough away that the others couldn't see what was happening under the water.

"So, a kid brushes up against something under the water. He figures it might be a fish, and dives under to take a look." Rhonda swallowed twice. Her face was pale.

"At first, he doesn't see anything down there. And then suddenly, his mouth is full of this totally skeeve taste—like rotting meat mixed with shit or something—and without knowing why, the kid feels every nerve in his body wired up, totally terrified. But he can't swim up to the surface. His arms feel like lead, and the rank taste in his mouth is now growing *inside of him* until it feels like it's *under his skin*.

"And that's when David shows up underwater. The closer David swims, the stronger that sick taste gets. And then—here's the part that has kids screaming at night—they get a closer look at David's face. It's his eyes: they are very, very wrong. One look into those hideous eyes and the swimmer is gasping for air underwater, choking, sure he is going to die.

"And then David finally swims away," Rhonda paused and seemed reluctant to finish her sentence. "And stretching out behind him is a thick, scaly black tail of a snake."

I shuddered; my flesh had turned icy cold. Pain throbbed in my chest as I pictured David's wretched little spirit trapped in the lake, his white-blond hair swirling in the water, his little hands flailing helplessly.

CHAPTER 20

The following week at school, Rhonda didn't hesitate to pummel any kid who mentioned the ghost of David McInnis.

What neither Rhonda nor I realized was that, right beneath Rhonda's watchful eye, the embers of the David ghost story were smoldering. I sensed that a shift was taking place in the zeitgeist of the school; the pitied looks I previously received were taking on a more accusatory flavour, as though kids were confirming to one another, "That's the girl. She's the one," whenever I walked past.

In the tranquility of the school bathroom stall, I took deep breaths, trying to rid my lungs of the viscous blackness that choked up the spaces where air should be. If only I were as resilient as Rhonda.

I heard two girls enter the washroom, and I gingerly lifted my feet up onto the rim of the toilet. I heard the girls whispering, and recognized the voice of one of Jeannie Baker's underlings.

"...she was always so jealous of David. She was always looking at him funny. Like she wanted him dead."

"Yeah. And I know *exactly* what happened—straight from Jeannie Baker. Jeannie was *there* that day on the beach. Mina confessed to her that she held her brother underwater. Crazy jealous of how everybody liked David so much better."

My heart pounded in my throat.

I heard a squeaking sound, like a balloon being rubbed with a moist finger.

"Let's get out of here before Rhonda comes to her rescue. I don't get it—Rhonda could be best friends with anyone in the school. Why *her*?"

"Maybe she feels sorry for her. Her parents being total deadbeats and all that jazz."

I heard shoes scuttling out of the room.

I sat staring at the floor, feet up on the toilet rim, until my legs started to prickle. Eventually, I climbed out of the stall. Written across the bathroom mirror in red magic marker were the words: "Mina McInnis is a murderer."

Rhonda made a painful example out of Jeannie Baker. Only once have I heard a more sickening sound than the wet thumping noise of Rhonda's fist making contact with Jeannie's nose. The pounding served as a cautionary reminder to the rest of the kids that they had best find a new way to entertain themselves.

I couldn't make eye contact with Rhonda after she pummeled Jeannie. Rhonda was suspended from school for two weeks for that fight. Mrs. Doyle grew quiet around Rhonda during that time, the exact opposite of what I expected a mother's reaction to be. "I knew you were a lot of things, Rhonda Doyle, but I never imagined that a bully was one of them." Mrs. Doyle said little else the night she found out about Jeannie Baker's broken nose. This was the hardest reaction for Rhonda to handle. Rhonda knew all there was to know about *tough*, but she didn't know what to do when faced with her mother's soft, nebulous disappointment.

Rhonda also couldn't bear the uneasiness that lingered in the air between us once again. She knocked on my door as I was getting ready for school. "M, can I come in?"

I opened the door and focused my eyes on a shaft of light across the carpet.

"M, I'm ashamed about what I did to Jeannie. I swear I didn't mean to hurt her so bad. I just short-circuited. But I want you to know that I did it for you."

I nodded my head, and bit my lip to prevent my disapproval from escaping. But it seeped into my eyes, and Rhonda recognized it instantly. She tilted her head, and stared into my face until it felt as though her eyes were scanning past all my protective layers, burrowing right into the putrid parts only I had access to.

"I wouldn't be so quick to judge if I were you," she said, her eyes fixed on mine. She walked out of my room, and I felt the cold slice of another wedge driving between us.

As time passed on Elsinore Island, Rhonda's mother revealed surprising facets of her personality that I had not understood during the summers spent hanging around with Rhonda. In summers past, the main interaction I had with Mrs. Doyle was hearing her shrill disapproval of Rhonda, and I assumed by extension, of me. Rhonda and I were always too noisy, too dirt-caked, too rambunctious. Mrs. Doyle wanted to parent the rough and tumble right out of Rhonda, and as the years went on, she met this challenge with a frustrated determination that sounded, to the unsympathetic ear, quite a lot like nagging.

But as I spent more time living on Elsinore, I began to notice ways I had misinterpreted Mrs. Doyle. What could easily be misjudged upon first impression of Victoria Doyle as her sense of entitlement—bred of an upbringing steeped in the refined tastes of Toronto's business elite—was actually sheer childlike appreciation for beauty. I noticed how she lit up when Fat Joe brought in his delivery of goods from town, at the sight of the fresh cut flowers she had coaxed into her budget. Mrs. Doyle would gracefully unwrap the flowers and fuss over the placement of each stem, arranging and rearranging until there was a composition of varying flower heights and leaves poking at odd angles, singing from the crystal vase: *Behold—fleeting beauty in all its messy imperfection.*

One of the objects of beauty which Mrs. Doyle chose to adore caught me by surprise: my hair. At first, her attentions were common enough. I was writing away at my *Legends of David* on the couch one day while Rhonda was in the kitchen pestering Ettie. Mrs. Doyle sat down beside me, Ettie's worn copy of *Pride and Prejudice* in her hand. Instead of opening her book, Mrs. Doyle slid her hand down my hair, the way she might pet a long-haired cat from head to tail in one long stroke. "I used to have beautiful blonde curls just like yours when I was your age, you know."

I looked up from my notebook. I was never quite sure what to say around Mrs. Doyle.

She continued, lost in thought. "All my siblings had bouncy blond curls too. My mother used to say that when Teddy and my sisters and I ran around together we looked like a field of golden daisies bobbing in the breeze." Mrs. Doyle stared off in space for some time, absentmindedly twisting one of my curls around her finger. She finally snapped back into focus. "Mina, could I French braid your hair?"

The braided hair of my classmates had always mystified me as a child. It seemed unimaginable to me that there could be someone on hand at these girls' homes who had both the patience and desire to weave hair into the intricate pattern. "Might want to do something about that rat's nest," my mother would say, plucking a dripping Cheerio from her cereal bowl and making a blast-off noise as she lobbed it at my hair, which always made David howl with laughter.

I nodded to Mrs. Doyle, feeling suddenly shy.

Mrs. Doyle gathered all of the hair from one side of my head, gently parted it into sections, and tenderly passed strand over strand, inching her way down the back of my scalp. She began humming a melody that I recognized from the *Bach Goldberg Variations* album, her favorite record to slide onto her antique Victrola before sitting down to the dining table; music to feed our souls while we dined each night.

Rhonda walked in just then, a sandwich in each hand. "Ettie says dinner's gonna be late tonight, so I managed to swipe us these..." her voice trailed off as she saw her mother nestled beside me on the couch, her fingers entwined in my hair. For several seconds, Rhonda's face betrayed a bitter place in her heart. As quickly as it came, the look was gone. Rhonda set the plate on the coffee table in front of me and punched me lightly on the shoulder. "Mom finally got the daughter she always wanted," she said, and sauntered out of the room with a nonchalance that was almost convincing.

The hair-braiding became a fixture in my morning routine. As soon as Mrs. Doyle heard me lumbering around in my room, she would knock on my door. "Would you like me to French braid your hair this morning?" she would ask; and each time, despite the pangs of betrayal I felt as I invited her in, I savored every second under the doting hands of Mrs. Doyle. Next time, I always promised myself as I pictured Rhonda's pained face, I will turn her away.

While Rhonda served her detention at home, I was left without a snowmobile driver to chauffeur me to school. "Now just remember," Fat Joe said, as he pushed a bulbous black knob on the snowmobile's front panel, "you want to hold down on the choke for just a few seconds—don't go floodin' the gears—then give the gas here a good rip and..." Fat Joe saw the panicked look on my face and rubbed his stubbly chin like he was lathering it. "Come to think of it, we could use a few more gallons of gasoline out here. How's about I drive you to school on my way in to pick up a few supplies?"

I let out a huge breath. God bless Fat Joe.

"Now get yer arse in the house and grab your things before I change my mind." Joe winked at me.

I ran back into the house and passed Rhonda seated at the breakfast table. She had a pencil in her hand, and was sketching onto a yellow notepad. She looked up at me, and there was a tiny hesitation before she gave me a nod. "Knock 'em dead today at school, M," she said, and then winced at her own words.

"Um, bye," I said, then headed back out to Fat Joe and the snowmobile. The entire cold, slushy ride into school, I agonized over the dead space that was expanding between me and my best friend.

Fat Joe dropped me off in the school parking lot. "Yer prince in shining skidoo gear will await you here at three P.M., m'lady," he said. He brought his hand to his waist, and bowed low over the side of the snowmobile. Then he snapped the visor down over his helmet, the clear plastic shield fogging up as he turned the keys in the ignition. He revved the engine twice with his free hand and raised his eyebrows in concert with each of the engine's deep growls. Fat Joe tore out of the school parking lot, one arm extended straight up, hand curled into a fist. I was left to face the school without the support of my sole defender.

When I walked to the staff parking lot after school, Fat Joe was not there to meet me. In his place stood Mrs. Doyle, clad in a one-piece black snowsuit that reminded me of a panther. Only Victoria Doyle could pull off such elegance on a snowmobile.

"What are you doing here?" I asked.

"I have a surprise for you. Climb on." Mrs. Doyle smiled a broad smile, her eyes dancing with a secret.

She drove the snowmobile with the same confidence that flowed through Rhonda. It was an example of the raw Doyle power—the same power that reassured Mrs. Doyle that she would do just fine moving to an isolated island without the support of a husband, and that also led her to take on the guardianship of another woman's neglected child. Victoria Doyle took to challenges with an adeptness as natural and refined as silk.

Mrs. Doyle steered the snowmobile into a parking spot downtown. She pulled off her helmet and smoothed her hair until it lay obediently in one glossy strip, then ironed her hands from her hips to just above her knees, as if to decrease the bulk of the black nylon one-piece snowsuit.

She's taking me shopping, I thought. I had never been on a mother-daughter shopping trip, and I tried not to picture Rhonda's hurt face if she caught us fawning over a sweater in Stedman's. But instead of leading me toward one of the two stores that might possibly stock clothing for a thirteen-year old girl, Mrs. Doyle headed for the double doors of the bank.

"You could use a little more security in your life, young lady," Mrs. Doyle said as she stroked my hair in one long sweep, the same way she had smoothed hers a minute earlier. "And if there is one gift that Victoria Doyle can offer you, it's financial security." She touched the tip of my nose and smiled, revealing a row of strong, flawless teeth.

I knew that her financial situation was worse than she was insinuating. A few nights earlier I had overheard fragments of her phone conversation with her lawyer, as well as a particularly ugly argument she had gotten into with Rhonda's father. I had crouched at the top of the stairs, where I could catch a glimpse of the lower half of Mrs. Doyle's body as she stood facing the parlor wall where the phone hung.

"Don't you give a damn about providing for your own daughter?" I had heard her growl into the phone, trying to yell and keep her voice down at the same time.

After a long pause, Mrs. Doyle responded again to her husband, "How can you do this to us, you heartless bastard!" Her voice was inflamed. She slammed the phone onto the receiver, and then I heard a heavy *thunk* on the floor, and a strange, childlike wail, and I felt sick as I realized that Mrs. Doyle was indeed capable of being crushed.

When we reached the front of the line at the bank, a teller I didn't recognize greeted us with a bright smile. "And how can I help you two lovely ladies?"

"I would like to open a chequing account for this young lady," Mrs. Doyle said, smiling down at me as she placed her hand on my shoulder.

"Oh, how wonderful. It's never too early for your daughter to learn about finances, is it?"

Mrs. Doyle gave my shoulder a squeeze, her kind, brown eyes warming my face. "Money makes an excellent sword," Mrs. Doyle answered.

The teller looked at her sideways for a second, surprised by the comment. "Yes, I suppose it does. It makes a pretty handy shield too," the teller replied, and looked up into Mrs. Doyle's eyes, two women complicit in their own discrete battles.

Mrs. Doyle filled out the paperwork while I stood beside her. If I squinted and used my imagination, I could almost resemble her daughter. Her hair was a darker version of mine, and I had tight corkscrew curls, whereas her hair was more like a soft swirl, but still, a resemblance was within the reach of my imagination. I dreamed up a photograph of just the two of us, me sitting proudly on Mrs. Doyle's lap, her chin resting on my head, a goofy grin plastered across my face. But then, as I zoomed in on the blurry background of my imagined photo, Rhonda's face came into focus. And something else caught my mind's eye.

I strained my imagination to get a better look, and visualized a ragged black silhouette lurking in Rhonda's shadow. My mind leapt back to the unsettling *thing* I had intuited in the lake with David, and my ear recalled the metallic whine of propeller blades. Whatever the *thing* was, I feared it wasn't finished with me or my loved ones.

But maybe this time I could do something to prevent it.

Rhonda used her detention time as an opportunity for two weeks of wood- and metal-working lessons under the resistant tutelage of Fat Joe. She headed out into his workshop in the mornings before I had even left for school, and came back in when Ettie rang the dinner bell, her sweatpants coated in a golden fur of sawdust. "What are you making out there?" I asked her one morning, as I nibbled my toast alone at the breakfast table in my hooded sweatshirt.

"Just fine-tuning my skills for building my boatercycle," she answered, and headed out the door, hollering in the direction of Fat Joe's quarters. "Get your lazy arse out of bed!" We all knew Fat Joe rose every morning before dawn.

Once Rhonda left, I pulled my hood down to rest on my shoulders, and awaited Mrs. Doyle. I chewed my toast as slowly as possible, so there would still be some left, something I could focus my attention on when Mrs. Doyle entered the room. Eventually I heard her footsteps patting toward the kitchen, and I took a deep breath.

"Good morning, dear Mina," she sang as she waltzed into the room. She stepped toward the table and looked at my head, and all the joy left her face. She just stood there, hand to her lips, staring at me. I could not look at her, so I focused on my toast and chewed, the small bite growing doughy and large in my mouth.

"I see," was all she finally said as she turned and left the kitchen, the long hem of her sea-foam nightgown trailing on the floor as she walked away.

I had not meant for the haircut to resemble mange quite as much as it did. I had aimed for a very short haircut, and erred on the side of baldness. Standing in the bathroom and staring at my shorn head in the mirror, I felt a surreal disconnect from the person I had always thought of as being *me*. This person staring back at me looked strange, but also strong and in control; the kind of person who didn't need much in the way of help from others.

School that day was rough, but I was bolstered by my brush cut. With my scissors, I had succeeded in cutting away the tangled, emotional parts of me. I walked around school as a young woman who drew her strength from colder, harder parts of herself. I felt an otherness from my peers, as though a new rational way of thinking had freed me from caring what they thought of me. I felt like a warrior.

At home that evening, Rhonda knocked on my bedroom door. I put aside my *Legends of David*, which now filled the pages of four coil-bound notebooks.

"I have something for you," Rhonda said as she walked in, her hands clasped behind her back. She looked at me seated at my desk, and her eyes widened when she saw my scalp. Then she spat through the space in her teeth, and a tiny wet missile landed on my carpet. She walked over and slapped me hard on the back. "Looks good on ya, M," she said. Then she produced the object she was hiding behind her back. It was a long, wooden stick with one pointed end, and a metal handle on the other end constructed out of what looked like recycled bicycle parts. The edge of the wooden shaft was carefully planed up its length, and there was an M.M. branded into it.

"You made me a walking stick?"

"It's a sword, M. You know, to fight your own battles?" she smirked, then shoved the wooden rod into my hands. I studied the sword, running my finger along the intricate trim work that must have taken hours, the chunky metal pieces she must have painstakingly soldered into a smooth handle. "Judging from the buzz cut, looks like I'm giving it to the right person." She turned and left me alone, and I felt a tension escaping my body. I rolled the word *sister* around in my head the rest of the afternoon, and tried not to picture David's face as I allowed Rhonda's words to echo through my mind. "The Doyles are your family now."

CHAPTER 21

The spring thaw would bring a new round of correspondence courses for Rhonda and me, completed under Ettie's distracted eye. From early March onwards, every morning Fat Joe tested the ice that connected our island to Mikinaak, using long boards which he slid several hundred feet across the lake. He would then come back to our cottage and pronounce whether the ice was still safe to voyage across. Each morning, Rhonda and I said silent prayers that the ice was starting to give.

One morning, Fat Joe gave the verdict that Rhonda and I had been waiting for. We hugged and did a dance of joy around the kitchen table, then got right to our lessons—the sooner we finished, the more time we had to ourselves.

"Just stay off that ice, you hear?" Ettie warned us, elbow deep in a gigantic stockpot simmering on the stove.

Rhonda headed straight for the ice once we were out of sight of the adults. "Are you sure we should be doing this?" I asked, as Rhonda coaxed me to join her several feet offshore on the snowy lake. "I'm pretty sure the reason we're not in school right now is because this ice *is not safe*."

"Aw, don't get your gitch in a knot, M," Rhonda called over her shoulder, as she got down on her belly and swept the snow off with her arm. She peered down into the ice. "See? The ice isn't even dark. We've still got at least four inches of ice here. Go grab your new sword."

I couldn't think of any argument that would persuade Rhonda to choose a more sensible activity, so I headed inside. I had placed the sword close to my pillow in hopes that some Rhonda-style clout might work its way into my hands as I tried each night to pull David out from under the boat just as he slipped away. But even in my dreams I was powerless.

I grabbed the sword and headed back outside to the lake. When I got to the shore, I stood and watched Rhonda on the ice for a moment. She was lying on her back, her face basking in the sun, her eyes closed. She swept her arms and legs in and out, painting slow-motion snow angels on the ice, completely absorbed in the moment.

I picked my way across the ice, distrustful of the four inches of frozen water. I looked back up at Rhonda and forced my limbs to relax a little. Just let it be, Marina. *Que sera sera*. Go with the flow.

I walked out to join Rhonda, and she explained the rules of *Sliders*, a game she had devised one minute earlier. "Don't worry, M—your weight will be distributed across the sword, so the ice isn't going to break."

I reluctantly agreed to play Sliders. Ten minutes in, we were both drenched in slush. On Rhonda's turn at the sword, I nailed her right in the face with a drippy snowball; her squeal had me bent over laughing so hard I started coughing uncontrollably. Rhonda was right—I needed to let myself *just be* in the moment and enjoy life.

When it was my turn to walk across the sword, Rhonda said, "Hold on a minute," and slid the sword several feet further out, onto ice of unknown strength. "You're up!" she said, clapping her hands together, her wet nylon mitts producing a sharp slapping sound that reverberated across the lake. I walked out to where the sword rested on the ice, then carefully placed one foot in front of the other, inching across the sword. "High-yah!" Rhonda yelled, as she creamed me in the back of the neck. Giggling, but still able to maintain my focus enough to stay on the narrow wooden shaft, I took another step, and felt an explosion at the back of my head. "Take that, M!" Rhonda cried. I jumped off the end of the sword and Rhonda did a series of karate chops in my direction.

"Be very afraid!" I yelled back, giddy as I grasped the sword and gave it a good heave away from me. It slid farther out than I had anticipated, skidding to a stop about ten feet ahead of us. Rhonda looked at me with hesitation for a second, and then shrugged. "What the hell. I'm going for it!" she shouted, and skated her boots across the ice. When she reached the sword, she stretched her arms out to each side like a tightrope walker, and began smooth, easy steps across the narrow wood. I formed a dripping ball of slush and threw it at her, but the snowball disintegrated into bits that fell to the ground well before they reached their mark. I packed another handful of slush together as best I could, and pumped it at her with all of my strength. The snowball connected with the side of her face with stunning accuracy, and Rhonda let out a shriek.

Then the boom came.

So loud, so wide-ranging that it sounded like the entire lake was one gigantic drum being pounded upon. The sound reached my ears from every direction at once. A series of slow cracking noises followed the echoing drum blast. "Rhonda!" I called out, as the cracking noises coursed along their invisible tracks.

Rhonda's feet were surrounded by a thicket of jagged white lines. Suddenly she plummeted straight downwards into a dark hole where solid ice had been a split-second earlier. Rhonda thrashed in the hole and then she was gone; all I could see was a dark pool of water surrounded by sharp edges of ice.

I lunged onto my belly and slid across the ice, screaming Rhonda's name. The loud cracking noises continued right underneath my torso as I frogged my way toward the hole in the ice. I stared with all my power at the hole as I wiggled toward it, willing Rhonda's head to surface. I continued to scream for help as the ice cracked louder all around me. When I reached the hole, I pushed my head and shoulders past its edge and lowered my face until it almost touched the dark, icy water. I opened my eyes as wide as I could, trying to blink the ice and snow off my eyelashes so I could see into the water. It was like looking into a bowl of black ink. "Rhonda!" I screamed again, and then I heard a sound both sickening and hopeful: a thump directly beneath my chest on the ice. Rhonda was trying to find the hole to the surface.

The wooden sword was on the other side of hole; I shimmied a few inches to reach for it. The ice beneath my chest began separating in crackling branches, and cold water bubbled up, drenching my snowsuit. I gasped as the cold stung my skin, but I forced my arm to stretch a little longer to reach the only tool within sight. I managed to graze the sword with my fingertips, and pulled it closer. I plunged my arm in the icy water, flailing the sword underneath the ice like a swordfighter.

I poked the sword as far as I could to one side of the hole, then the other. Then I swung it blindly around in a wide ring beneath the edges of the hole, prodding into the icy water, my fingers beginning to numb. I repeated this underwater sweep again and again, my arm submersed up to my shoulder in the bitterly cold water. My grasp was loosening.

And then I felt a tug. My arm was yanked further down into the hole, and suddenly my face was underwater and I felt the ice give beneath my chest. I wiggled my lower body backwards and pushed back with my one free arm, and managed to hold my ground for a few seconds, my arm with the sword still taut under the water. And then there was a rasping gasp, as Rhonda's head surfaced. She opened her mouth wide and sucked in quick breaths, one breath on top of the next, not giving her lungs enough time to utilize the air they so desperately needed. Her eyes bulged; her face was contorted in fear like an animal caught in a trap. I pulled on the sword to try to propel her upwards, but the ice supporting my arms broke beneath my weight. I shimmied backwards and tried once more to heave Rhonda toward me, and again the ridge of ice between us split in one clean line and sunk, a line of bubbles belching to the surface where the ice had sat seconds before. Each time the ice broke, Rhonda slipped back beneath the water for several seconds, and then resurfaced again, inhaling water as she gasped loudly for air. Again and again, I tried to hoist Rhonda up, and each time, more ice broke and she slipped beneath the water.

I had to change tactics. I placed Rhonda's arms across the lip of ice surrounding the hole, and shouted into her face, "Kick your feet. Hard." And then I wriggled away, until I could stand and run back to shore, my lungs scorched by the icy air, my legs two frozen stumps that I somehow willed into a sprint. I raced all the way across the ice and up the path to the house, screaming. I tripped on the bottom step leading up to the house and came down hard on my hand, my palm bent upward to break the fall. I felt a bolt of pain slice through my wrist, and I found I could not use that arm to push myself back up as I half ran, half crawled up the stairs. When I got into the house, I tipped back my head and screamed the names of all the occupants of Elsinore Island. Nothing. "Mrs. Doyle! Ettie! Fat Joe! Help! Please help," I screamed over and over as I ran through the house, knocking into furniture.

I raced out of the house and headed around back to the staff quarters. I called out Fat Joe's name, cradling my dangling wrist as

I ran toward his door. I turned the doorknob and it stopped in my hand. Locked. I pounded my fists against his door, screaming his name. Where the hell was everyone? And then my eye passed over Joe's workshop. I sprinted to it and threw the door open. All of his tools were neatly hung along the walls, his bandsaw in the middle of the room, sawdust carpeting the floor. No Joe. My mind spun around and around the same panicked loop, unable to think my way toward a solution. And then a word flashed into my head as though someone spoke it directly into my ear.

Rope.

I raced around Fat Joe's workshop, my eyes scanning the shelves of woodworking tools, farm implements, shovels, rakes. *Where does he keep the effing rope?* I searched shelf after shelf, blinded by snot and tears as I rushed from one side of the workshop to the other. "God, would you please, please just give me some effing rope," I wailed. At the far end of the workshop, my eyes met a yellow coil of nylon rope.

I grabbed the rope and surged out the door, terrified of what I was going to find when I got back to the lake. I squinted as I ran toward where I thought the hole was. The wind had blown away all traces of our footprints. I moved my head back and forth, skimming my eyes across the horizon for a dash of colour, movement, anything. I saw only white ice and gusts of wind whipping up the last traces of winter's snow. I ran across the ice, screaming Rhonda's name, my body filled with a dread so overwhelming that I felt like just lying down on the ice and giving up.

I ran further ahead and as I got past a hilly drift of snow, I saw a black mass upon the ice, several feet from where I thought the hole had been. I raced toward it, setting each foot down as gingerly as possible while still running. As I got closer, the black mass came into focus as a pair of arms and legs, a head and a body lying motionless, face down on the ice. How could she have possibly pulled herself out?

"Rhonda!" I raced to her and grabbed her ankles, not even bothering to flip her to face upwards. I concentrated solely on getting both of us away from the thin patch. I dragged Rhonda's limp body along the ice with one arm, my other wrist hanging at an unnatural angle. When we finally got close enough to the shore that I felt safe to pause, I flipped her body over. Her face was like a red and white lily—red streaks ran from her throat to her forehead from being pulled along the ice, and yet the rest of her face was petal white. I dragged her the rest of the way to the house, my arm burning with exhaustion by the time we reached the verandah steps. Somehow I managed to hoist her body up over my back, and I crawled up the stairs hunched over, with her torso dangling precariously across my back, her legs bumping each step as I climbed toward the door.

I managed to turn the doorknob with my dangling hand, and rolled Rhonda off my back onto the hardwood floor. Her head thumped the floor despite my efforts to set her down gently, and her eyes flickered. "Rhonda! It's M. You're going to be okay. Just keep your eyes open." I rubbed her face as gently as I could, my fingers stiff and cronish from the cold water. Rhonda's face was a sickening colour, and becoming even paler as she lay there. I pulled one eyelid up, and this worked to coax her other eye open again. She pressed her lips together to try to speak, but a weak hissing sound like air slowly leaking from a tire was all that came out. She tried again.

"Ghost..." she whispered, and then sucked for air, inhaling in wet, rattling gasps. Her breathing got quicker and quicker, until the breaths ran together into one long ragged indraw. And then she stopped breathing altogether and I ran screaming to the phone to call for help.

The paramedic talked me through the first aid treatment for hypothermia over the phone. He instructed me to take Rhonda's pulse and listen to her heart, and quickly determined that Rhonda was in cardiac arrest. A medical helicopter was dispatched, and the paramedic guided me through CPR while we waited. It would be an agonizing wait, as there were only two medical helicopters in all of Northern Ontario, and the closest one was located over 100 miles south of us. The whole time that I was breathing into Rhonda's mouth and pumping her chest, I kept calling out for Mrs. Doyle, Fat Joe, Ettie. *Where was everyone?*

I prodded Rhonda's heart to pump blood through her body and inflated her lungs every ninety seconds, and begged her not to leave me. I kept checking my watch to hurry the helicopter along, but the time dragged on and on. I just kept pumping and breathing and crying, and no one came. I was soaked to the skin and freezing, but there was no time to think about that. My arms became so tired that I started getting sloppy, and my hands kept slipping off Rhonda's chest as I tried to pump life into her. Splinters of pain seared through my wrist with each pump. Rhonda just lay there, cold, white, and unresponsive.

I don't know how long I laboured there in my wet clothes. I watched the story of our friendship pass before me as I pumped mechanically on her chest. Two girls sprawled on their bellies at the frog pond, the tips of our hair dipping in the cool water; waggling mason jars of frogs at tourists along the town docks; combing local lore for the next newsworthy scoop; cruising Lake Huron in Rhonda's Lund. Rhonda had rescued me from neglect at home and loneliness at school. She had the fire that I lacked. My best friend who confronted life fully aware of its hurdles, determined to trample them.

I pumped away at her chest, my face stinging with tears and mucus, until the sweetest sound reached my ears: the huffing of the helicopter's propeller.

The chopper landed on the Elsinore tennis court, and paramedics rushed in and swarmed around Rhonda. I answered all of their questions in as few words as possible, then kept out of the way. I did not want to draw their focus away from helping Rhonda.

Within minutes she was being shuttled across the sky to a tertiary hospital in Kentsworth. One paramedic stayed behind with me. She tended to my arm as I lay in front of the woodstove, hiding my head in the muffled safety of a woolen blanket. I closed my eyes and allowed the fire to coax warmth back into my body.

Mrs. Doyle, Fat Joe and Ettie burst in through the front door. "What in heaven's name is going on?" Mrs. Doyle asked, out of breath. All three of them rushed to my side. I looked up and saw that Ettie's front was covered in sawdust. A chainsaw hung from Fat Joe's hand.

The paramedic recounted what she knew. I tried to interject, but my mind was so fatigued that I couldn't seem to muster the energy to explain it properly.

"Sliders...the sword on the ice...*Where were all of you*? I called and called and called, and none of you came..."

Mrs. Doyle's face was ashen. "Fat Joe was teaching us how to cut wood for the stove," she said, and then dashed over to the telephone.

For six days Rhonda lay in her hospital bed, her chest rising and falling to the clicking rhythm of a ventilator. The doctor explained that her heart had basically shut down with the shock of the cold water, and that the lack of oxygen to her brain during the several minutes when her heart was not pumping may have caused brain damage. There was no guarantee that Rhonda would even awaken from the coma. Mrs. Doyle stroked Rhonda's hair tenderly, her tears making a soft tapping sound as they landed onto the plastic tubes that sprouted in all directions from Rhonda's body.

I kept returning to the scene in my mind of Rhonda stretched out on the ice, her black snowsuit shining wet. She must have managed to pull herself out of the water by sheer Doyle power. I sat by Rhonda's side day after day, willing the fighter that was within her to rise up and take command of her still body. On the seventh day, Rhonda's eyelids flitted open, and her eyes made a slow, concerted sweep across the room, taking in the IV pole, the ventilator hose that snaked from her face, her mother at the head of her bed, and me. She had a pained look on her face which may have been confusion about her whereabouts, or may have been anxiety as she recalled her struggle in the icy water.

Rhonda was taken off the ventilator when she was able to breathe on her own. When we were allowed to return to her bedside, Rhonda's eyes opened wide. She strained to lift her head, but was unable. She worked her eyebrows instead of moving her head, and pumped them in my direction. She opened her mouth to try to speak, but did not seem to be able to control the muscles in her throat. A thin, raspy sound was barely audible when she moved her lips. Rhonda kept trying to say something, over and over, mouthing the same undecipherable sentence.

Finally, she pulled a deep breath in and used brute force to form sounds that came out as comprehensible words: "David. Saved. My. Life."

The intensive care physician explained that, when Rhonda was submerged in the icy water, the cold water leeched her body heat at an alarming rate. As her body became colder, her organs began shutting down as a protective mechanism, shutting the power plant down so it didn't require more energy. The lower her body temperature, the lower her brain function, ultimately reaching the point of becoming comatose. Hallucinations and confusion were the classic signs of severe hypothermia, of the brain starting to pull its own power handle down before going completely offline. It made sense that Rhonda's hallucinatory brain would grasp onto an image of my brother. The myths of David's ghost in the lake had painted a colourful image linked with fear and water, and that was the first image that drifted through her mind as her brain started to fail; an image which a sluggish neuron had reached out and seized. That's what I told myself, anyway.

Over the next several weeks, Rhonda's recovery in the hospital gave us opportunity for small celebrations. Muscles that are completely immobile for even a week lose their strength with astonishing speed. Rhonda had to retrain her body to do even the simplest tasks. We were her cheerleaders as she attempted arm curls with the miniature Kleenex boxes from her bedside table. We sang the tune of the can-can: "Da-da, dooty-dooty, da-da, dooty-dooty" as she worked with all her strength to lift her feet a few inches from the bed.

The ventilator tube had gouged her throat on its way in, and each time Rhonda swallowed or tried to speak, pain flashed across her face. But she was not to be kept down, and as the weeks passed, her arms became stronger, and her face regained a hint of its brash confidence. Aside from horrible seizures which overtook her body at least once a day and terrified all of us, Rhonda seemed to be recovering at an encouraging rate.

One day, I sat on her narrow bed, the plastic protective sheet crinkling whenever I shifted, while Rhonda grunted through her daily arm exercises. Mid-lift of the can—she had graduated to weightlifting soup cans— she hurled it across the room, where it slammed against the pale yellow concrete wall with a loud *clack*. "I'm outta here," she said, and made a long, drawn-out farting noise with her mouth as she yanked the IV needle from her wrist, then threw the needle toward the IV pole.

Against his better opinion, the doctor reluctantly agreed to allow Mrs. Doyle to take Rhonda home later that day, with several pages of physiotherapy exercises and a long list of rules which Mrs. Doyle promised to make Rhonda abide by.

"I want to warn you that you may notice changes in her personality, things that may become more apparent once she's back in a familiar environment," the doctor told Mrs. Doyle as she signed the hospital release forms. "The brain is responsible for self-control and social awareness; you may find Rhonda doing things that are inappropriate—things she wouldn't have done before."

That showed how little he understood about Rhonda Doyle.

The doctor continued, "Sometimes, behavioural problems are exacerbated when a brain injury patient returns home and expects her life to return to normal. The oxygen deprivation did a number on the memory center of her brain, and with these cases, we just don't know how long her cognitive function will be impaired; we can't predict what gains she will continue to make. Take her false memory, for example—Rhonda is very confused about the events that led up to her getting out of the icy water. She continues to insist that the spirit of a young boy assisted her out of the water that day. This is a textbook symptom of oxygen deprivation to the brain. Rhonda is confusing imagination with memory."

I shuddered as the implications of the doctor's words sank in.

Paperwork in hand, we were free to return to our lives back on Elsinore Island. During the four weeks that Rhonda had been hospitalized, Mother Nature had erased all signs of the traumatic scene on the ice. A series of bright afternoons had transformed the frozen stretch back to frigid lakewater. The occasional ice floe bobbed like wreckage through the lake, but the route from Mikinaak to Elsinore was now navigable by boat.

Fat Joe met us at the town docks with the Doyle family Bayliner, and scooped Rhonda up in his arms, his chin tucked over her head like a protective wing. Once he had Rhonda nestled comfortably on the boat seat, cocooned in blankets, Fat Joe reached out his hand toward me. I was standing on the dock beside the boat. "Come on, love, let old Joe help you in," he said, extending his hand a little closer to me. I stood frozen on the dock, my heart thumping in my chest, knowing suddenly that there was no way I was going to take Joe's hand, no way that anyone was going to get me into that boat. Fat Joe kept his hand out, good-natured and calm, giving me the time I needed to move forward of my own volition. He was unbearably patient, but in the end, he dropped his hand to his side and nodded, his eyes closed. "Looks like we have a bit of a problem here," Fat Joe said to the air just above his head.

He was right.

CHAPTER 22

Fat Joe eventually managed to wrestle me onto the boat. He improvised a straitjacket with a blanket, and held me on his lap with one iron arm while he steered the boat with the other. I screamed and thrashed and lost my mind. By the time we reached the Elsinore docks, it was clear to everyone on the Bayliner that I was terrified of the lake.

It was Mrs. Doyle who puzzled over my extreme behaviour until she came across a word that fit my condition. *Limnophobia.* It sounded almost glamorous, the way Mrs. Doyle drew out the word, but the mouth-frothing and muscle spasms that proceeded from the condition quickly clarified that point. Limnophobia: an abnormal fear of lakes. The definition sounded judgmental and misinformed. To me, the lake was death in liquid form. It was no wonder that myths came rolling off the lake, reeking dank and fishy. It had worked its claws into the lungs of the two people I cared most about, wringing out the air in each alveoli sac with its greedy hands.

Once back on Elsinore Island, Mrs. Doyle accepted that for the time being, my feet would stay firmly planted in the security of densely packed earth.

Rhonda was facing her own challenges. Her recovery required a regime of physiotherapy exercises and mental gymnastics that left her pounding her fists against the wall. And the seizures weren't relenting. "Screw the memory games. I just need to get back into Joe's workshop to sort myself out—a little boatercycle therapy," she said, her words a little slurred and louder than necessary now, making her sound slightly drunk at all times.

Eventually, Rhonda wore Fat Joe down and he conceded to let her swing a hammer alongside him in the workshop. "But absolutely no power tools, you hear me?" Joe said.

We heard the bandsaw humming half an hour later. Rhonda emerged from the shop that evening carrying an oar she had carved with the bandsaw. The oar had a slight asymmetry to it, and the edge along one side had clumsy grooves where the bandsaw had fits of stopping and starting, but it was a workable piece of gear nonetheless. Joe trailed into the house behind Rhonda, shaking his head. "I'd sooner wrestle a grizzly bear than go toe-to-toe with Rhonda Doyle," he said, the corners of a guilty smile visible on his downturned face.

Rhonda carefully placed the oar against the wall, took one step away, and then turned back around and karate-kicked it. The oar fell to the floor with a crack. Rhonda looked at the crooked oar with its childish woodworking, and shot a thin spray of spit at it through the gap in her front teeth. "Piss on it," she said, as she walked across the room toward the hallway. "Time to ship me off with the other retards at the Ray of No Hope." She shuffled toward her room and slammed the door so hard I could feel the vibration on the floor beneath my feet.

With two young women captive on Elsinore Island, Mrs. Doyle instructed Ettie to dive right back into her role as our correspondence teacher. It could not have been an enjoyable position, with 50 percent of Ettie's student body a nervous basket case, and the other 50 percent a belligerent brain injury victim. But Ettie took our fragile mental health in stride and humoured our requests for stories.

"Ettie, you've spent as much time on Elsinore as anyone. Have you ever actually seen the ghost of my uncle Teddy with your own eyes?" Rhonda asked, as she grabbed a soup can out of the cupboard and began doing curls with it.

Ettie's face got all pinched up, the way it always did when we asked her about Teddy Doyle. "Honeybunch, there are plenty of things I enjoy discussin, but Teddy Doyle's face lurkin around the lake on a stormy night isn't one of them." Ettie removed the soup can from Rhonda's hand and flicked her eyes over to the window, indicating the path she predicted the soup can would take if Rhonda was to continue this particular physiotherapy regime.

I jumped in with a request I had made a dozen times before. "Ettie, *pleeease* tell us what it was like when my mother worked here." Ettie looked at me with an uncomfortable expression, as though I had just asked her to describe her most unusual sexual encounter in explicit detail.

She picked up a large potato and began rotating it beneath her paring knife, the peel loosening in one long, satisfying strand. She finally sighed. "Alright."

"Katherine—your mother—must have only been about fifteen the first summer she came to work in the kitchen here at Elsinore. I'd just been promoted to head cook, and I can tell you, I wasn't about to screw it up. The Doyles were wild about entertainin in the summertime—every last one of the Doyle clan invited their own crew to stay for weeks at a time. This island was always crawlin with so many new faces it was hard to keep track of who was comin and who was goin. And on the week leading up to the regatta—I remember it clear as a bell —in walks this new girl who didn't know a spatula from a hole in her ass.

"Now, you have to understand, most local teenagers would have given their eye teeth to live on Elsinore for the summer. So I'm cursin Bunny Doyle for sending me a new girl who is sure to cause me grief more than anything else. Then Katherine says to me, not a hint of *irony* in her voice—that's one of my new words this week, *irony*—anyways, she says to me, 'Don't get me wrong, I plan to earn my keep here like everyone else. But I'd prefer if it didn't involve touching *other people's food*.' She was a piece of work, that Katherine. Lucky for her, there was just somethin about her that made you want to put up with her whims. But I hadn't figured that out yet.

"Anyways, we got started on the wrong foot, you could say. And it went from bad to worse real quick, cuz I had more work than I knew what to do with to get ready for the regatta, and the Doyles couldn't seem to resist invitin all of Toronto to come stay with them here on Elsinore.

"But you don't mess around when it comes to the regatta weekend. The Doyles have been hosting the Doyle Summer Regatta ever since I been here—it was an idea your granddaddy Doyle cooked up one summer as a way to get to know the locals. The highlight of the summer for many locals—some families spend weeks gettin their canoes decorated for the event. God forbid something goes wrong on regatta day, I tell you.

"Well, the day of the regatta comes, and there musta been a hundred people on this island, eatin my handmade tidbits and drinkin champagne and Scotch like it was their callin.

"Then suddenly, the sky turns the colour of coal, and a fierce wind whips up. Lemonade pitchers go crashin to the ground, napkins are flyin every which way, and I think I seen just about every pair of them pretty ladies' panties as the wind got ahold of their long summer dresses.

"We quickly shooed all the guests and the bagpipe band under big white tents, and within minutes we got the party roarin again. But the actual regatta could not be held in that...ah, *tempestuous* weather. Out on the lake, waves the height of hydro poles were slammin into one another. Folks' canoes would get tossed around like spit in the wind.

"Well, the look on the faces of the Doyle family members was plain as day, I tell you. Heartbreaking disappointment." Ettie began chopping her potatoes into small cubes, and sliding them off the end of her knife into a massive Tupperware bowl.

"At one point, Mr. Doyle staggered over to the canoes smackin against the shore. He stood there for a long time, sippin his drink, watchin the waves chuck the canoes around. Then he teetered back toward the wedding tent, his head hangin low. Now, Mr. Doyle was a man who was accustomed to gettin exactly what he wanted. The kind of man you didn't want to disappoint.

"Katherine, my so-called kitchen assistant, she seen that look on Mr. Doyle's face too. But she just set her platter of dainty sandwiches down on the buffet table, then turned and left. I was keen to give her a piece of my mind, I tell you. I stood there watchin her go, wonderin how quickly I could convince Bunny Doyle to give this little piece of work the ol heave-ho.

"A few minutes later, out Katherine prances. But instead of her staff uniform, she's wearin an apple red bathing cap and a matching one-piece swimming suit that might as well have been a corset. She raised an eyebrow or two, let me tell you.

"Katherine walked right up to the party tent, and I thought, 'Good lord in heaven, what does this child think she is doin? Bunny Doyle is gonna have my hide.' I panicked as she headed straight through the crowd, each guests' head turnin as she worked her way toward Mr. Doyle in that getup.

"I watched her speak, her eyes never leavin Mr. Doyle's face, and then he looked over at the waves crashin against the shore, and scratched his chin. He stood that way for quite some time, starin at the water and rubbin his face. What on God's green earth did that girl say to Mr. Doyle? And then Mr. Doyle nodded slowly. He leaned over and whispered somethin to the band leader, and the music ended. Mr. Doyle raised his champagne glass in the air and clinked it with a fork—not that he needed to get anyone's attention, with that apple red swimsuit standin there, I tell you.

"'Ladies and gentlemen, dear friends,' he announced, 'it is with great disappointment that I must cancel today's regatta.' The guests nodded in support, but the disappointment on their faces was plain as day.

'However,' he continued, 'in the spirit of the regatta, we are going to hold a different type of race, for those who are daring enough to entertain the idea. We may not be able to *canoe* in these waves, but I challenge the bold among us to try to *swim* to the finish line.'

"Well, a roar went up among those guests somethin fierce. Mr. Doyle clinked his glass once more, and nearly lost his balance. "By the way—" he added, "—this feisty young lady here claims to be the fastest swimmer on the Island. She's issued a challenge to all of the guests, to try to beat her in this race. And—I've just at this very moment decided to add a little incentive to sweeten the pot. If any one of you can beat my little...' he'd had to pause to lean down and ask your mother her name, and nearly lost his balance in the process, '...beat my little Katherine here, you will be the proud new owner of...' Mr. Doyle had craned his neck around and stumbled. Then his eyes settled on his yacht. '...the proud new owner of this sailboat right here!'

"The crowd thundered again and my stomach clenched. *His yacht!* Mr. Doyle got up early every morning and buffed the silver railings of his beloved seventy-foot yacht himself. A man of his word, I knew that Mr. Doyle would follow through with this offer, no matter how liquored up he was when he made it. I was fit to be tied, I tell you.

"Well, men started yankin off their shirts and hopping around on one foot pulling shoes off, and everyone seemed tickled pink at the idea of headin into those... ah, *colossal* waves, and at the possibility of winning that *ludicrous* prize.

"About sixty swimmers entered the race, all men and teenage boys except for Katherine. Mr. Doyle blew a whistle, and the swimmers dove into that wild water, their arms flailin as they tried to reach over the gigantic waves and keep their mouths above water. They looked like a swarm of beetles, clawin at each other in a bucket of sloshin water. The waves slammed the swimmers into one another, and on several occasions I held my breath as a swimmer went under for what seemed like far too long. Each time one of these swimmers finally got their heads above water again, I would breathe a sigh of relief then curse the foolish girl who proposed this race.

"But as I looked around, it dawned on me that I was the only one who seemed to have any sense. Wives and daughters were cheerin themselves hoarse, and men who didn't have the balls to get wet were salutin the swimmers with shots of tequila. Mr. Doyle stood on a massive rock and screamed out a play-by-play of the race, taking a swig from his glass with every new turn.

"My heart nearly stopped when I seen that Katherine was not outracing the men swimmers. Good Lord, Mr. Doyle was going to lose his yacht.

"There was a group of five swimmers who were leading the pack, and Katherine was in that group, but she could not find the strength to break ahead. The swimmers made it out to the red buoy, circled past it, then continued powerin back to shore, getting pummeled with each new wave.

"It was becomin obvious that Katherine was beginning to wane. Her arm strokes were gettin sloppy, and she was collapsin into the water like dead weight after each stroke. The leading four men slowly distanced themselves from her. With about fifty feet to go, your mother had lost all steam.

"And then it happened." Ettie stopped her paring knife mid-slice.

"Katherine slipped under the water. With all of the din and the booze and the cheerin, it was hard to tell if anyone else seen Katherine go under. I tried to push my way to the shore, but people were hootin and hollerin and flingin themselves every which way. I tried to keep my eyes on the spot where Katherine had gone under, as I stumbled over people to get to the shore. *Please dear God in heaven, let that foolish girl come back up.* I reached the shore and grabbed the arm of a man dressed in a full suit—I don't swim a stroke myself—and I pointed to the place where Katherine had gone under. I begged that man to dive in and save her.

"But there was a new layer of cheering, even louder than before, and the man just kept pointin to his ear and shruggin his shoulders. I shifted my gaze toward the shore, where the leading swimmers had almost arrived at the finish line.

"Katherine's red bathing cap surfaced at the finish line like a rising sun. My heart nearly stopped, I tell you. That clever little thing, bless her soul. Katherine saved the day. She'd taken an underwater shortcut and outfoxed them all.

"Well, despite my best intentions, I was not able to dislike your mother for long after that. Even though she became the boss's pet after the regatta, none of us staff were able to hold it against her. And let me tell you, that says somethin about Katherine, if you knew some of the petty housekeeping gals we had working with us that summer. The sun shone out of that girl's ass for the next three summers here on Elsinore. Right up until the summer when Teddy Doyle's death haunted her right off this island..." Ettie winced, and a crescent of blood appeared across her finger. She put down her paring knife and brought the sliced part of her finger to her mouth, sucking it clean.

"What do you mean, 'Teddy Doyle's death haunted her off this island'?" I asked, trying to avert my eyes from Ettie's finger-sucking. A shudder went through me, and my hand went to the pouch around my neck.

Ettie removed her finger from her mouth and gave me a tight smile. "I don't mean nothing, Sugarpie. After his death, Teddy haunted all of us in different ways," she said. "Now I think it's time you girls skedaddled out of here and got some fresh air." And she swatted us away, looking a little more cheerful than the moment called for. Looking a lot like she was lying.

CHAPTER 23

The summer of '74 arrived, and brought with it the extended Doyle clan and their holiday moods. Similar to Mikinaak Island, summer days on Elsinore were measured in swims rather than hours. Doyle cousins greeted the early morning steam rising from the lake, as the first rays of sun drew out the previous night's chill. The Doyle morning dare was unchanging: cousins competed each dawn to be the first to jump off the dock into water so cold that it pulled their skin into tight, itchy gooseflesh.

The gaggle of Doyle cousins ranged in age from four to thirteen, the eldest cousin Clay being only a few months younger than me. Clay was Teddy Doyle's son, although he was just a tadpole in Cissy Doyle's belly when his father drowned. He was under the impression that his direct descendence from the legendary Teddy Doyle lent him a status of morbid coolness, and he was not opposed to inserting his father's specter into conversations that had veered in unfavorable directions. And whenever grey storm clouds rolled in on the horizon, Clay was the first to suggest going out to the shore to watch for his father's ghost.

Rhonda couldn't stand to be near her cousin the Cheese Weasel.

Clay was almost unrecognizable from the previous summer when his family had holidayed on Elsinore for a few weeks; his shoulders had thickened and his face had taken on a hardened shape that made him seem slightly dangerous. He had also shot up a good four inches since the last time I had seen him, yet he looked as though he was only comfortable claiming two of those inches; the other two inches he concealed in a slumped posture that added to his body language's general warning: keep your distance.

Clay wore his bangs in a long, stiff swoosh that covered one eye like a patch, and which likely required a sizeable investment in hair products. He was also the only young person, other than me, who was not part of the lake's summer ecosystem. I secretly wondered whether the upkeep of his bangs played a large role in his avoidance of the lake, and, as each day passed and presented me with opportunities to hang around Clay, I said a silent prayer of thanks for those crisp tendrils of teenage angst that saved me from complete loneliness. Just as long as Rhonda didn't see me talking to him.

Clay was not the kind of person who was interested in the give-and-take dance of conversation. But he warmed up to talk show mode, with me as host, mining each of his sentences for something interesting, holding up each fascinating tidbit so we could both get a better look at what came out of his mouth.

I preferred not to talk about myself anyway. Once, in a rare moment of interest outside of himself, Clay said to me, "Hey—I heard your little brother drowned in the lake. How, like, grody did his body look when you found him? That's why you're so afraid of the water, isn't it?"

I fingered the pouch at my neck.

Rhonda divided her time between working on her boatercycle in Fat Joe's workshop, and swimming with her cousins. Each time she emerged from the shop, she looked as though it was sucking the juice right out of her: her face was haggard, her gait took on a more pronounced droop. Despite the physio and cognitive therapies, her brain was still refusing to fully cooperate with the rest of her body. Every time I watched her awkward shuffle, I felt a pang of guilt in my belly and had to look away. Somehow, I had brought the evil in the lake to Elsinore.

But for Rhonda, the lake was an elixir. I spied from high up on the lawn as she struggled to remove her shoes, kicking her heels into the sand and cursing her laces for being so difficult to untie. After a painstaking strip down to her bathing suit beneath her clothes, Rhonda would do her awkward shuffle across the dock and then dive into the lake. Once she was in the lake, however, she became her old self: fearless, capable, fluid. Rhonda swam and splashed her cousins and laughed as though everything was as it should be.

One afternoon, Rhonda saw me sitting on the lawn as she made her way back to Joe's workshop. She shuffled over to me in her drunken gait, then stood looking down at me, water dripping from the ends of her hair. The brightness in her eyes from the swim clouded over. "I miss you, M," she said.

I looked up at her. "I haven't gone anywhere," I replied, a little more curtly than I meant to.

"Ever since my accident—you don't want to talk about what happened on the ice, you don't want to hang out with me at the lake—it's like you're...not here anymore," Rhonda said to the crown of my downturned head.

The stain of my ruined family was a tattoo more visible to some people than others. The person who had the keenest eye for these sorts of things, who could see right through the skin, muscle, and bone to the rotted parts inside was Cissy Doyle. A humourless woman who constantly eyed me as though I was just about to commit a petty crime, Cissy was the one person on Elsinore whose path I tried not to cross. She was Clay's mother, and had remained a committed member of the Doyle family despite losing her betrothed only days after she and Teddy Doyle were married. Watching the Doyle clan interact from a distance, it was difficult to classify the role Cissy played on the Doyle stage. Hands on her hips, she always seemed to hover just offstage of rollicking Doyle family fun.

Her most severe looks were reserved for me. Sometimes when I sat at the edge of the massive yard, pen in hand and the nearly full *Legends of David* notebook spread across my lap, I had the self-conscious feeling that someone was watching me. When I looked up, there would be Clay's mother Cissy, standing far off in the yard, quickly busying herself with an untied shoelace or pulling a weed from the lawn. Judging me from afar.

"How is that mother of yours doing these days?" Cissy once asked me, in a tone that made clear she was not inquiring about my mother at all. What lay unspoken beneath her words was a reminder that I came from an inferior breed of people, and did not belong on Elsinore with the good, upstanding Doyles.

I didn't need a reminder of the shamefulness that came before my time on Elsinore. I wore it on a leather band, a half-inch too tight around my neck. My guilt pouch. And I despised Cissy for her recognition of the truth.

One afternoon, the sun burned in an ultramarine sky, baking the smooth rocks along the shore. The sun coaxed all of the Doyle cousins to postpone lunch and linger in the cool lake. All of the cousins but one, whose coiffed bangs required constant vigilance against watersport.

I would have given my left eye to be able to toss my shoes off and charge into the water, pouncing on Rhonda, splashing and laughing along with her. But each time I came within my shadow's reach of the lake, my insides churned and a panic tightened my chest until I couldn't breathe. The lake had come between us.

I sat on the grass and wrote as the Doyles swam, when suddenly the metallic whine began to swell in my right ear. The Doyle cousins' yelling and horsing around had changed to complete silence. A cold shiver raked my skin. Something *wicked* was in the lake; I just knew it. I put down my notebook, stood up, and scanned the lakefront, my hand shading my eyes. None of the Doyle kids were visible in the water. I sprinted down to the lake.

My heart battered in my throat as I approached the shore, sweeping the lake frantically with my eyes. The deafening whining noise in my ear pressed out all other sounds. I called out their names. No one responded. The closer I stepped toward the shore, the faster my insides churned. Although it was impossible to see beneath the dark water, I could sense, beyond any doubt, that something sinister was lurking there. *Mishi-ginebig* had followed me here. My chest became a cage of raw terror. I screamed Rhonda's name as I stood frozen helplessly on the shore, begging her to end this stupid farce. But deep down, I knew that something horrible was happening. On those dark nights when I swam in the lake with David, calling out for the spirits to join us, I had invoked something terrible and unspeakable in the lake.

Suddenly, I glimpsed a series of bubbles rolling to the surface of the lake, several hundred metres from shore. Farther out than I had ever seen any of the kids swim. I held my breath and prayed to see a head emerge from beneath the bubbles. I gasped, as the surface of the lake was broken by a slick black curl. It slithered back into the water as quickly as it had emerged. I opened my mouth wide, but was incapable of screaming.

Rhonda came to the surface of the water a moment later. Her face was a mask of fear. A hundred metres away, her cousins all surfaced at the same time.

For days I pleaded with all of them to tell me what had happened under the water, but no one would utter a word. "Good one, Doyle family. You really had me going for a minute there," I would say, and give Rhonda a thump on the arm. Rhonda's pale face was her only response.

For weeks afterward, I spent most of my time staring out at the lake from my bedroom window, watching. Like the heightened senses of the blind, my awareness of the dark *thing* hovering just beneath the surface intensified.

Whether this dark *thing* is what I feared most, or whether I felt unworthy of the love that was being offered to me, I will never know. Whenever I attempt to disentangle the strands of my storyline, I worry over this knotted logic endlessly. I can never pinpoint the *why* exactly—the reason I felt compelled to cleave myself from the Doyle family. All I know is that I soon found a *how*.

While the Doyle cousins reveled in the sensuality of water on skin, I sat in the shade, tucked within the outskirts of the forest surrounding the west side of Elsinore. I had taken to doing my writing in the seclusion of the poplar and birch trees, to avoid the disapproving gaze of Cissy Doyle. I sat, notebook perched on my lap, and wrote about the heroic young David, who in this particular tale was learning a lesson about kindness from an encounter with a den of sympathetic wolves.

A rustling of leaves jerked me from my reverie, and I looked up to see Clay. "Hey Mina." He blew his bangs up away from his eyes in a puff of air with his lower lip extended out, then the crisp strands of hair came to rest once again over his eyes like fingers dangling down his forehead. My mind went to the lake where his cousins swam, its dangerous contents. Now was my chance.

"Clay. Perfect timing. There's something I want to show you." I nodded my head toward the trail.

There was nothing in the woods I wanted Clay to see.

Although part of me was repulsed by his vanity and self-centeredness, another part of me was feeling hot and prickly with an excitement I couldn't have predicted. I stood up, and led Clay through the thick maze of mature trees, until we were far from the periphery of the forest, far from prying eyes. I stopped in front of a shaggy maple tree, a thick rivulet of sticky sap frozen mid-flow down its bark. Clay stared at me for a second, a bemused look on his face, then placed his hands around my waist like an old-fashioned dancer, and guided me up hard against the tree's rough trunk. I felt my hair catch in the glop of sap, and thought about how annoying it was going to be to strip the sticky residue out afterwards, and how fortunate it was that I had hacked off my long curls.

Clay's mouth was on me, hot and wet and far more distracting than I could have imagined, and suddenly I was reeling with the awareness of how good it felt, and also how absolutely forbidden. *I am an honourary member of the Doyle family, which makes Clay my honourary cousin.* But that became less and less central to my thoughts as his warm mouth continued and embers flashed in sequence up my spine.

The slap across my face felt like fire.

For a split second I thought my body was exploding from intense pleasure. By the second strike across my cheek, my eyes were open; I saw the poplar switch shaking in Cissy Doyle's fist and Clay's stunned reaction.

"You despicable piece of trash," she growled, baring her teeth. "How dare you defile my son." She lunged toward me and struck a third time, scalding the skin across my other cheek. "You have *no business* being on this island! Victoria practically adopted you. Treated you like family," she screamed, baring her teeth. "You've crossed an uncrossable line!" She lunged toward me and struck a fourth time, scalding the skin across my other cheek. "You have more of your mother in you than I thought. Stay away from our family!"

She knew. I could hear it beneath the venom in her words. Maybe she hadn't intuited the full extent of my horrible secret, but somehow, Cissy Doyle sensed that deep down at my core lay something putrid and black. She couldn't know that this blackness also trailed me like an invisible tail, attracting its dark equal in the lake. Regardless, Cissy didn't want her family infected with whatever it was the McInnises carried.

Although she couldn't have guessed that the real reason had little to do with her son, Cissy was right—I had to leave. I couldn't bear to bring more harm to the Doyles. I had to get away; far away.

I gathered myself together and ran. Through the forest, across the yard, into the cottage. Cissy let me go. I headed straight for my bedroom, where I crammed only the bare essentials into my red Budweiser bag. Then I bolted into the bathroom, flung open the mirrored panel of the medicine cabinet, and grabbed the bottle of pills that Mrs. Doyle's doctor had prescribed to calm her nerves throughout the anguish of her divorce. I had no choice but to shake a mouthful of the small white pills onto my tongue. Then I darted to the parlor, grabbed the crystal decanter of scotch from the bar shelf, and gulped burning mouthfuls, willing myself not to retch it back up, the scotch dribbling down my t-shirt.

My next stop was Mrs. Doyle's purse. I pulled it from the front hall closet. I paused, cursing myself, then pocketed a thick wad of twenties from her wallet. I kicked open the screen door so hard that my foot tore the screen from the frame.

I stormed over to Clay's cottage and threw open the front door, prepared for a confrontation if necessary. Clay had already returned there, alone. I made my demands. Clay was bewildered, but to his credit, within minutes he was unfastening the ropes that held Rhonda's Lund to the dock. He ferried me to Mikinaak, where a bus would shuttle me to Toronto, away from the two islands that had become contaminated by my poisonous secret.

PART THREE

CHAPTER 24

Mikinaak, April 1994

When Zane and I step inside my mother's house, I see that its condition is both better and worse than I had imagined—better only because my imagination has a tendency to careen off at extreme angles. When envisioning the decay and disrepair of a house that had been lived in for over two decades by a depressive alcoholic, I had pictured entire rooms brimming with garbage, twenty years' accumulated stench of rotting food and underclothes. I expected toothless stairway railings, dingy carpets, sad holes where broken fixtures had come loose and never been replaced, doors and handles missing from sagging kitchen cupboards, a yellowed toilet rooted in a water-damaged ring of peeling linoleum. I also pictured fist holes punctuating the walls of every room. I'm not sure why my mind conjured up these wall holes, as my mother's anger was more subtle than a punch: she would gnash anger in her mouth for days until it became a poisonous dart, spat from her mouth in the form of words.

But of course, the cleaning crew had removed all the rotting and stinking things they encountered. "Burn everything but the furniture," had been my reply when the cleaning lady had asked what to do with the thirty-odd garbage bags she had collected, "... or donate it. It's your call."

After the cleaning crew had done their part, the realtor had offered a staging service. The decorator had her work cut out for her. She bought pretty vases of silk flowers for tabletops, a centerpiece arrangement of pillar candles in tall glass hurricane vases for the kitchen table, and placed framed prints of foliage throughout the house to add a touch of elegance. The result was a house that looked shabby but hopeful; like a withered old lady limping around in a faded floral dress and scarlet lipstick.

Shards of painful memories launch themselves from the objects left behind: the couch that accommodated our lounging bodies, the heavy green curtains that blocked out the sun, the orange shag carpet David and I stretched out on to watch our favorite TV shows.

And there, in the corner of the living room, is the heavy brown steamer trunk that had served for over a century as a compact museum of McInnis family history. When my eyes touch upon it, I am transported back to nights when my mother told us her stories, to the safe, happy feelings that I had forgotten entirely.

"Zaner honey, I'd like you to leave this steamer trunk and the small blue bedroom alone." I had closed the door to David's bedroom earlier, his posters of dolphins still tacked to the wall. "Can you do that for me?"

"Whatever you say, Marines."

Since the day Zane was born I poured my energy into planning, organizing, structuring, safeguarding our space. And my child stayed safe and healthy. Because accidents aren't really accidents. But then the outside world started exerting more influence.

When Zane was eleven years old, he forgot his lunch bag at home one day, and I drove it to school for him. I strode alongside the school playground, and was buoyed by the sight of young children monkeying on the bars, playing tag, the older children playing soccer in the field. I scanned the school yard, eager to see my son at play.

Zane was sitting slouched on the raised edge of the playground sidewalk, carving lines into his bare leg with a pebble. He looked up to steal a glance at the boys playing soccer, and his eyes were dull and wet. I was panicked that he would see me, but I was unable to look away. I stood clenching my fists and watching him for several minutes, a lump forming in my throat. I wanted to storm onto the soccer field and seize whichever player was closest at hand, rake his face through the mud, and insist that he try harder—*try harder damn it*—to include my sweet, sensitive Zaner. I stomped back to my car and wept, holding Zane safe in my gaze until the recess bell rang and the children filed back into the school.

I waited out Zane's early teenage years like a nervous stage mom, watching for symptoms of my past to start showing up in him—looking for strategic marks across his arms, under-dilated pupils, any sign indicating that the thing I buried deep within myself had infected the psyche of my son.

But in these last few years, safeguarding his existence had become even more complicated. I closed my eyes for a second and my bubble-wrapped toddler transformed into a remote, vulnerable teenager. As each day passed I lost more of my grip on the world Zane inhabited; I longed to return to the dangers of uncut grapes and unpasteurized honey.

Now at sixteen, it seemed my fears were coming true. Zane had always struggled to find his pack, and I thought he'd been content to be a lone wolf – some children are. But in the past several months, something cancerous had wormed its way into the den.

One month before we left Toronto, Zane had come home from school several hours late. When I asked him where he had been, his head jerked back for a split second, and he covered his mouth with his hand before he stammered, "I was at the library. On the sixth floor." Zane had always been a horrible liar, and detested dishonesty in himself even more than he did in others.

"I see. Where are your books?"

"That's the great thing about libraries," he had answered with forced gusto, unable to look me in the eye. "They let you use theirs."

Oh God, here it comes, I thought, my stomach rolling. *My son is sneaking around doing drugs.*

Zane barely talked anymore. We had a tacit understanding that I could ask him for three pieces of information about his day at dinner, and he would provide three answers—no more, and no follow up questions. But his answers lately all consisted of one word. I felt I had no choice but to seek other portals into his mind.

Library books coated every surface in Zane's bedroom, like a layer of moss. *Organic Small Container Gardening* bookmarked at a page about wasabi horseradish plants; *Transcendental Meditation for Everyone*; his collection of Phillip Marlowe pulp detective novels; *The Anarchist Cookbook*.

Zane had developed a taste for horror, too: Edgar Allen Poe and Clive Barker hardcovers mingled with worn Stephen King novels on the floor beside his bed. I was attracted to these same kind of writers when I was a teenager, and remembered how they heightened my awareness of the evil skulking just beneath the surface. I couldn't help but view Zane through the lens of my own shadowed history, and I imagined the worst.

One afternoon as I lugged a basket of folded laundry into his room, I saw the corner of a floppy disk peeking out from beneath the cover of a book. The handwritten label on the disk made my stomach churn.

I grabbed the disk, my heart pounding. I looked for some kind of clue as to why this little rectangular question to the universe would be lying amongst my son's possessions. I rifled through his desk drawer, looking for any other signs of Zane's interest in this subject that brought bile creeping up my throat. And I found the thing I had dreaded finding all these years.

The printout from *Ancestry InfoBase* was dog-eared and had obviously been thumbed beneath eager eyes countless times. One of the names on the genealogy tree was circled in red pen. On the final page of the printout, Zane had scrawled the words *Chuck McInnis, Unit 530-261 Jane-Finch Towers.* Jane and Finch—the murder capital of Toronto.

A brain functions differently when its neurons have been infused with guilt for two decades. The guilt is like a serum that cultivates a special new ability—the deciphering of codes hidden within ordinary events. The codes of the dead are whispered within sentences that sound banal to the average person. They murmur from beneath the lyrics of songs that play on the radio, or in the way a bird cocks its head and screeches directly at you. The message that came whispering through the printout beneath Zane's scrawled handwriting was this: *your past is catching up with you.*

The pages fell from my hand as I lurched forward and vomited on Zane's bedroom floor.

Hydrogen, atomic mass 1.008; Helium, 4.003; Lithium, 6.941. When the sleep wouldn't come that night, I cycled through the soothing data and tried to push away thoughts of what exactly Zane might find out if he succeeded in seeking out my father, and what that might do to him.

Zane had called the following day after school to let me know he was going to be studying late at the library again, and the hitch in his voice partway through was his tell. I hung up the phone, threw on my jacket, and headed out to the Escort.

The elevator in the lobby of Jane-Finch Towers had a yellowed, handwritten Out of Order sign taped to it that looked like it had been there a while. My heart pounded in my chest and a sick feeling lurched in my stomach as I yanked open the stairwell door, which was slashed with deep scars and covered in black marks, as though someone had taken an axe to it. What the hell goes on in places like this? I took the chipped concrete stairs two at a time to the fifth floor, the smell of curry spices and mildewed carpet assaulting my nostrils. A fat cockroach skittered away from my foot as I reached the top of the stairwell. This was a building of shattered dreams.

Zane cannot speak to my father. He must not find out about my past. I flung open the stairwell door to the fifth floor, and stepped into the hallway. My eyes scanned the yellowed industrial carpet to the far end of the hallway. At the end of the hall, Zane was on the floor against the wall, slumped forward in a heap. My heart hammered in my chest. Had he been shot? Overdosed on drugs? Anything was possible in this neighbourhood.

"Zane! Are you alright?"

He lifted his head slowly, as though he was expecting me. His face was pale.

"Chuck McInnis died last Sunday. Shot himself in the head with a hunting rifle." Zane tried to blink away the tears, and quickly looked away.

A physical shot hit me in the chest, and a swell of tears rushed to my eyes. I knelt beside my son and tried to wrap my arms around him. He shrugged me off.

212

"I'll never get the chance to meet my only grandfather." His voice broke. "Why did you let me believe he was dead all these years?"

"Zaner, I'm sorry I never told you about my father. Please believe that I have only wanted to protect you from certain ugly truths." I looked away.

Zane swiped his sleeve across his eyes. "Sorry doesn't cut it anymore, Madre." He looked down at his hands. "Guess I'll add Chuck McInnis to the growing list of chapters in the McInnis family history I'm not allowed to read. You know—like the chapter about who my dad is. Shit like that. Gotta hand it to you, Marines. You dangled that fat fuck of a whopper in front of me all these years, and it didn't occur to me to question it. My father didn't die when I was a baby either, did he? What else haven't you told me?"

I stared Zane in the eyes; blood pounded between my temples. "He did die, Zane." I pressed my palms into my eyes and took a deep breath. I hated lying to my son. "I'm trying to do the best I can with you, Zane. Really trying. And it's been a long time since I've felt any sort of reciprocation." I was trying not to think of my father; trying to hold back the tears.

"I need a name. What was my father's name?"

Zane's eyes carried a hopefulness that bore a hole straight through my chest. It would be so easy to toss him a generic name right now, a name that would satisfy him in the moment, and only lead to dead-end searches. I could say *Michael Smith*, and Zane might be mine again. I opened my mouth and Zane leaned in expectantly.

I shook my head slightly.

Zane grimaced and cocked his open palm. For a second, he looked capable of seriously hurting me. His hand shot through the air and slapped hard; a red handprint blossomed across the skin of his cheek. This was a move he had devised a few years ago, a passive-aggressive knife to my heart.

"Stop that, Zane! Listen, I know this is hard for you to accept, but some family histories are poison."

I felt sick about the drivel about to come out of my mouth. "Zane, I've given you the gift of a blank canvas. You want to imagine that Martin Luther King is your father? Or Che Guevera? Go for it. Dream big, Zane. Emulate your highest standard, but don't waste your time looking for ghosts."

A vein bulged in Zane's neck. "Eloquent bullshit, Madre. You're robbing me of my *roots*, and you know it. I've spent my entire life feeling like fucking tumbleweed."

I took a deep breath. "Zane, can we both just call a truce?" I reached my hand out to brush the hair from Zane's eyes, and he wrenched his neck backwards. "I've just found out that my father has died."

His face darkened with shame. "I'm genuinely sorry for your loss, mom." He gathered himself up from the floor. "But you'd better figure out a way to deal with whatever you're hiding from before it's too late."

Zane was conceived when I was eighteen, during one of my darkest periods: a gin-soaked phase when I opened the floodgates and invited alcohol to wash away the bad feelings that kept me thrashing alone in bed each night. The alcohol carried away with it my love of rules, of structure, my need for a wide berth of personal space with men I hardly knew. Any number of dirt bags could have gotten me pregnant that year, but the man whose DNA Zane shared was the worst of them all; an alcoholic loser by even the most charitable standards. Behind him snaked a mile-long trail of horrible choices. But he was also big-hearted and generous, and had the rowdiest, best laugh I had ever heard. I could see the potential for a good man, lost behind all those wrong turns.

In my pregnancy, I continued to let him in whenever he stopped by, banging on my door, slurring his words, his clothes reeking of stale cigarettes.

"The baby's yours," I whispered to him hopefully, the first time he acknowledged my swollen belly.

He had snorted and turned away, but hung around long enough to get laid.

By the time Zane was two months old, the resemblance was stunning—Zane had his father's steel grey eyes, the same feminine cupid's bow lips, his quiet, serious nature. Looking at Zane, the miniature version of the man who fell so short of the man we both deserved, I felt raw shame. I had tethered my innocent son to this man with chains forged in blood. Zane's father wasn't an evil man—in fact, despite his self-destructive lifestyle, his hopeless addictions, the downward spiral of his adult life, I could envision the kind, loyal person he had the potential to be. It was *that* shadow of a good man I wrapped my hopes around when I called him over to my apartment and presented him with his son.

I held my breath as I tilted my beautiful baby boy towards him, Zane's head scrubbed shiny clean and smelling of sweet milk and baby powder.

"He's your spit," I said, touching my finger to Zane's cupid lips, and then reaching out to touch his father's same delicate mouth. He yanked his face away from my hand and stared past Zane's ear, refusing to look at his son's face.

"Don't look anything like me."

I tried not to let baby Zane see me blinking hard, or feel my arms shaking as I strode to the door. "You're right." I swung the door open. "Get out."

He would leave no further mark on our lives other than a blurry genetic fingerprint.

CHAPTER 25

Zane's initial openness to my mother's house wears thin within a day. The artful touches of the interior decorator could only do so much to mask the sadness and anger that has infiltrated every molecule of paint, every fiber of carpet in the house.

Emptying our U-Haul trailer is a pathetically quick process. Zane and I have moved from one dismal apartment so many times over the years that we have both become proficient at the "bring one object into your home, take one out" minimalist tenet.

There is so much purging to do. The cleaning crew I had hired after my mother's death removed the obvious junk, but there are still closets and drawers and a basement crammed with remnants of my past.

I resort to bribery to bring Zane onboard. "Why don't you use those computer skills of yours to see if there's any way to sell used stuff on that World Wide Web? You can sell anything you find around the house and the garage, and keep all the profit." It goes without saying that our strict budget cannot accommodate luxuries such as internet access, and that Zane will have to use the internet at the tiny public library.

"I doubt anyone would want to buy any of this crud." He slumps onto the tattered couch. "Remind me again why you dragged me here?"

"Come on, Zaner. You know why. This house is rent-free. I figure that if we live frugally, we can survive for several months on my credit cards. And if we devote ourselves to fixing up this house, we can attract a buyer and make a decent amount of money. Money that would mean freedom in a lot of ways for you and me, Zane."

It never takes Zane long to dive to the complicated part. "Now—here's a dilly of a pickle, Momsidius: what if we don't sell this place before we run out of money? What's your plan B?"

I look down at my hands. "I'll figure something out, Zane. I always do."

Zane's eyes search me from top to bottom, as if the key to understanding his mother can be found there. "I get that you're trying. I really do. It's just..." he rakes his fingers through his hair, "...it would literally *kill* you to provide me with a stable freaking upbringing, wouldn't it?" He stalks to his new room, where he lets out an exasperated groan, then slams the door.

The last time I felt this kind of helplessness with Zane, I was huddled in the back of an ambulance en route to a Toronto emergency room. The paramedics were working frantically on the lifeless body of my beautiful son. It took three minutes for Zane to reclaim his body and the dark emotional palette that had been passed down from mother to son like a birthright.

He had downed an entire bottle of vodka the night after I had found him in the hallway of my father's apartment building at Jane and Finch. He nearly died of alcohol poisoning—his blood alcohol level was five times the legal limit. I had soaked the hospital room in tears for two solid days, until it felt like there was nothing left of me but a papery husk. When Zane and I returned from the

217

hospital, neither one of us could muster the energy to even remove our shoes. I can only imagine how depleted Zane must have felt, his blood deprived of dozens of oxygen-delivering breaths, his system offline for those minutes. My intensely private boy couldn't meet my eyes for days, after I had witnessed such a disturbing scene—the empty bottle, the room sprayed with vomit.

"I don't have, like, a *drinking problem*, mom," Zane had said, as I stood beside his hospital bed choking back tears. I had asked him to explain how the drinking had begun.

"I've only ever gotten buzzed like, three times."

"I see."

"It was stupid. I was just feeling completely bummed, and I wanted to be numb for a night. I wasn't thinking about consequences." Zane paused. "I swear nothing like this will ever happen again." He turned his head up to extend his ocean grey eyes across the hospital room, directly into mine. The look had sealed it. I believed him. Zane was reckless, but he was also honest.

"You know I'll be seeing you to therapy for the next twenty years."

Zane nodded, his mouth sewn into a thin line. "Marina McInnis wouldn't have it any other way."

Hydrogen, atomic mass 1.008; Helium, 4.003; Lithium, 6.941. When the sleep wouldn't come at night while Zane was in the hospital, I cycled through the soothing data and tried to push away calculations of how much of this was my fault.

I give Zane a few days to sulk over his new surroundings before his big adjustment to Mikinaak Secondary School. He is crazy intelligent, and I know he can make the adjustment into his classes easily enough, but socially, this is going to make Zane's brain froth. He has always been a loner, and I believe the anonymity of urban life suits his personality. His comfort zone involves shuffling within a large group of interesting people, none of whom he knows on a first name basis. I think back to my own school days on Mikinaak, and how intimately everyone was aware of everyone else's backstory. I could probably rhyme off the names of the dogs owned by eighty percent of my classmates' *grandparents*. I fear the social transparency of living on such a small island is going to feel like a direct assault to Zane, and will supply him with yet another stone to pile upon the wall of discontent he is constructing.

"Do you have any idea how fortunate you are," I hear myself saying one too many times, "to have a parent who cares for your well-being above all else?" But I may as well be telling him how lucky he is to have a functioning set of lungs—always there, labouring reliably just beneath the level of awareness, fundamental to survival yet not eliciting a moment's consideration. Zane has had the luxury of being deeply loved his entire life. Not appreciating the value of the gift I laboured to give him since the day he was born, Zane would undoubtedly trade a significant portion of my dedicated parental love for a boost in material wealth. He disapproves of the difference between what I can afford to give him and what he sees in the lives of the classmates who inhabit the financial upper echelons, and as Zane grows older, the wealthier parents continue to raise the stakes in ways I can't possibly keep pace with.

It is hard to measure which one of us has been dreading Zane's first day of school more. When Zane comes out of his bedroom the morning of, I try to conceal my disapproval. He looks like a vagabond farmer. His dark hair droops over his eyes, and he is wearing black jeans that are ripped in all the wrong places, accompanied by a faded black t-shirt that has only specks of colour left where a silkscreened image had once been, and whose neckline has separated at the seams and ruffles outwards like a frayed necklace. Layered on top of his t-shirt is a long-sleeved red and black checkered flannel shirt that brings pinpricks to my eyes—my father's hunting shirt. I had paid for new shoes before we left Toronto—Zane picked them out of course, as we were years past him allowing me any input into his clothing selection, but he has chosen instead to wear sagging boots that he must have fished out of the same stash as the hunting shirt, the creases in the boot leather so worn and dusty that they appear to have been shipped straight from the trenches of combat.

"Interesting choice of ensemble, sweetie."

"Don't want the Islanders to stereotype me as an urban peacock."

"Looks like you've averted that landmine brilliantly." I pull a chair out for him at the table. "Zaner honey, how many slices of my famous French toast do you want for breakfast?"

Zane swerves around the chair I hold out for him, tips his head sideways under the faucet at the kitchen sink, and gulps. "Not hungry."

I force myself to look away so he can't see the exasperation on my face. "Okay, then. Your lunch is in the fridge. Hope you like..."

"I'll buy my lunch," Zane says, the screen door already banging in my ear.

Our first Saturday night in my family's old home finds me stripping wallpaper alone in the living room, and Zane in his bedroom with the door closed. Zane had been edgy all day, and had spent most of his time outside in the backyard with work gloves and a shovel, digging up the cold, overgrown land where my mother had half-heartedly attempted to grow peas and tomatoes three decades earlier.

I had watched him all afternoon from the living room window, thrashing the hard earth with his shovel. I could see all of the anger and frustration he had for me, discharging into the ground with every smack of metal against soil. His hairline was soaked, and his face pink with exertion when he finally came into the house and went straight up to his bedroom, closing the door firmly. I said a silent thank-you that this time the earth was what he was choosing to turn his anger towards. For now, at least. There was a small mercy in that.

The house is dark by the time I peel off my rubber gloves and pad to the bay window. I strain to see all the way to the shore, but can only make out the jagged outline of the trees on either side of the beach. I pull my jacket from the closet, then exit into the cold night.

Standing a safe distance from shore, I squint to see the island two kilometres across the lake, where some of my most conflicted memories live. My chest aches as my thoughts go to Rhonda Doyle, and then immediately to my father, to David, and all that was lost.

My entire adult life, I have mourned both David and Rhonda. A flash of my wild-haired friend comes to me every time I see a gap-toothed smile. Yet I have never been able to bring myself to try to locate her. She was too enmeshed in the guilt of my Mikinaak life. But I ached to know now—whatever became of Rhonda Doyle?

I shift my gaze to the black water. My eyes cannot make out Elsinore Island across the channel. A bitter wind flings my hair across my face. "Da—vid," I whisper to the lake. "Are you out there?" A ripple curls across the surface of the water, and I envision a scaly black tail lurking just beneath.

An owl screeches, and I jump, my heart banging in my chest. Real or imagined, this island holds too many ghosts.

Aside from a grocery run, I barely leave the house for the next week. I clean, cull, and read up on DIY home renovation projects from an armful of books I borrowed from the library. By Friday night I have a severe case of cabin fever. After checking twice with Zane to make sure he is okay with me leaving him home alone, I grab the keys to the Escort and head down to the town watering hole. I loathed the thought of running into someone I knew from childhood, but I needed to see if I could find out anything about Rhonda Doyle.

The Captain's Wheel was an establishment that had plunked its sagging ass onto Main Street several generations back. It was an entrepreneurial dream—not a single dollar was needed for advertising: aside from the veteran's legion, it was the only place in town to wet your whistle.

The Wheel is the kind of bar peculiar to isolated small towns—a bar that takes little offense to sweatpants or missing front teeth; to spells of vomiting under the table before buying one last round; to 11 A.M. regulars drinking away their unemployment checks while their toddlers watched a third consecutive hour of TV at home alone. My parents used to tell us about big nights out they would have with their friends there, where a motley cross-section of the population could be found on the pub's makeshift dance floor. I could picture a nineteen-year old girl with expertly applied eyeliner do-si-do-ing her heart out in a hybrid of hip-hop and line dance moves, with her arm laced through that of a peg-legged veteran.

I walk in to The Wheel and quietly make my way to the only empty stool by the bar. It takes all of my emotional strength to do it—I am a table-in-the-back-corner kind of patron by nature. Having the bodies of strangers seated within the boundaries of my comfort zone makes me want to reach into my purse for the small blue pill my doctor has prescribed for precisely this type of occasion.

I am not a drinker anymore, for many obvious reasons. And I prefer to be in control at all times. Life is safer that way.

Seated at the bar, I draw stares from Farmer Bob on my left and Painter Pete on my right. My clothes speak with a Toronto accent—a dialect which I'm guessing has a knack for stirring up trouble in a place like this. I curse myself for thinking that coming to The Wheel was a good idea.

"What'll it be?" the bartender asks.

The two men on either side keep their eyes on me. Farmer Bob disguises his surveillance of me with a determined search for a message beneath his beer bottle label with blackened, swollen fingers that remind me of overripe bananas. Painter Pete tends to his ear hygiene using the pointed tip of a car key while glancing sideways at me. I simply cannot bring myself to order a diet Coke.

"I'll have what they're having," I say. "And bring another round for my two friends here."

Farmer Bob thanks me with a nod and a half-grunt when his beer arrives, and Painter Pete lifts his bottle in the air and tips it in front of me in an imaginary clink with my bottle. I urge myself to seize the opportunity with these two local yokels before it disappears. Without knowing exactly what I am going to say, I open my mouth: "So, you guys from around here?"

Despite my graceless entry into their evening, Farmer Bob—whose name is actually Bert Martin—turns out to be a former large-scale chicken farmer who had grown disillusioned with the push toward industrial farming and its inhumane practices. Speaking in an animated voice, he explains how he has redesigned his entire farm as a self-sustained ecosystem modelled after nature.

I find myself humbled. Why had I assumed, because this man sat at the bar in dirt-smothered overalls and an orange sun bleached John Deere cap, that he was somehow less complex than I?

Bert Martin had figured out how to work with nature rather than against it, to go with the flow. It strikes me that I have spent the past several decades doing the opposite: fighting against the natural flow of things. With my focus so narrowed on safeguarding Zane and myself against potential risks, perhaps I was missing the bigger picture, not allowing life to flow through us in all its chaotic beauty as life intends to do.

Painter Pete, whose name is actually Clare, is a soft-spoken man who started his own painting company, which provides full-time employment for twelve other people in town. Shame on me.

I listen to the fascinating stories that both of these men tell of their lives on Mikinaak, and they each in turn order us another round of beer. Out of a desire to make private amends for the way I mentally dismissed them on sight, as well as not wanting the evening to come to an end before I have my chance to ask what I came to ask, I accept a second beer, and then a third. And soon enough, their beers need refreshing once more. Technically, it was my turn to order us another round. I didn't know what else to do other than nod at the bartender and draw a big invisible lasso around our three empty beer bottles.

As the night goes on, it feels necessary to talk louder and louder to be heard over the music, until my voice grows hoarse. The bar stools are slipperier than I remembered them being when I first entered, and Clare graciously guides me back up to my stool each time I slide to the floor. "I think it's time you headed home, ma'am," Bert says to me as he hooks his arm in mine and helps Clare hoist me back up.

"No, I'm fine," I say loudly over the music, dusting off my jeans. *Keep it together, Marina.* I give my head a good shake, then order myself a coffee.

I watch nervously as Bert drains the last dregs of his beer, and Clare rubs his eyes and stifles a yawn. Bert reaches for his keys and starts to slide his bar stool back. "Time to call 'er a night."

"Wait," I say, jumping up off my stool, the country music blaring so loud in my ears that I need to yell. "I was hoping to find out... um, do either of you know..." My words are catching in my mouth like cotton balls, and I suddenly feel so dizzy that I have to sit back down. "Look, I'll be honest with you. I'm not actually from Toronto. I'm from the Island—well, I lived here a long time ago—

and there is someone I used to know...someone I want to find out about."

Bert sits back down and looks over at Clare; he gives him a slight nod.

"Thought you looked familiar. You're Katherine McInnis' daughter, aren't you? I went to school with Katherine—you're the spitting image of her." Bert lifts his cap and ruffles his hair vigorously from back to front, then works the cap back onto his head. "I was very sorry to hear about her passing. She was a good woman."

I let out a snort. "A good woman—maybe you're a less honest person than I thought," I say, poking him hard in the chest with one finger, which costs me a precarious wobble to the edge of my stool. Bert looks down at his hands and chooses not to comment.

"But yes, I'm Marina McInnis. I came back here to settle some... family business." I am having trouble wrangling coherent words from my foggy brain.

"You're David McInnis' sister." Clare cuts in, in a tone that states the jig is up. His eyes narrow. "You're the girl the kids sing about, aren't you? *Mina McInnis.* I've heard my daughter chanting your name out on the driveway with her skipping rope. The jealous sister who killed her little brother."

What the—

"That's enough, Clare," Bert says loudly, his face solemn. "Those damn rhymes are nothing but kids poking fun at a tragedy." Bert pushes his barstool into the bar then looks at Clare and jerks his chin toward the door. "I think it's time you found your way home, Miss McInnis."

How dare these guys tell me what to do. I slap my hand down on the bar more forcefully than I mean to, and the bartender wrenches his head toward me.

"Home? Find my way home? Ha! Home! And just what would you know about my home, anyway, Clare-n-Bert?" My voice has gotten loud. The people at the pool table beside us set down their pool cues. One gnarled cowboy continues two-stepping by himself with his eyes closed on the dance floor.

"Easy for you to say, isn't it, pardner, as you rassel up your cattle and head home to your lovely farm wife and your cozy roast beef & potato dinner. I've got news for you, Claresy. Finding your way home isn't always such a warm and fuzzy experience..."

I point dramatically in Clare's direction, and that sends me sliding off the bar stool. I land on my tailbone with a hard thump, my feet tangled in the legs of the bar stool. The scent of vomit and stale beer rises from the floor. I close my eyes and lay still. *Please let me be anywhere but here.*

Suddenly, a familiar voice is whispering into the crown of my head.

"Man! Grade-A homecoming, Primrose."

My mind is sent to long days spent hunched over a path carpeted in dry pine needles, and my hand goes to the leather mourning pouch tied around my neck; the pouch that has helped me carry my remorse since the day Bird Manaabeh placed it in my outstretched palm some twenty years earlier.

CHAPTER 26

I awaken with a brain hammered to a pulp by a ruthless combination of regret and alcohol toxicity. Even my little blue pill is ineffective against the emotional bile that snakes through my veins as I lie in bed and warily flip through blurry mental images from the night before.

A torn piece of paper sits on my nightstand, with a phone number and *Call me, Primrose.*

A wave of panic rushes over me. I throw back the covers and peer down at my legs, then breathe a deep sigh of relief. I am still wearing last night's jeans and tall leather boots.

After cleaning up a pool of vomit that I discovered on the floor beside the bed—retching into the bucket in between swipes of my cloth—I make my way to the kitchen, hunched over because the room spins less from a horizontal position.

"Big night on the town, Mamatello?" Zane studies me, an amused look on his face. "But, um, can I ask? Who was that dude who brought you home, anyway?" He is still smiling, but his voice betrays a note of anxiety that catches me off guard.

"Just an old friend, Zaner." I straighten myself up for Zane's benefit, despite a wave of nausea.

"I'm genuinely happy for you, mom—you could really use an 'old friend.'" He makes air quotes around the words, and the suggestive look on his face makes me blush. He lowers his voice. "I just really hope this 'old friend' isn't someone who ends up charming you into wanting to stay permanently on this remote mound of shit. Please mom, I'm begging you. Don't keep us here. Please." His voice cracks, and I feel the fracture like the shifting of tectonic plates in my chest.

I busy myself all day with the monumental task of sterilizing my mother's house of its misery. My stomach, always attuned to the stresses of my external world, twists painfully as I try to cram down my worries about Zane and concentrate on transforming the house into something marketable. I cannot imagine wanting to live in a home that bows under the weight of so many painful memories, but Zane and I will muscle through until it sells, or until I run out of money—whichever comes first.

As the vinegar and water droplets spray across the grimy backboards, I rifle through old data in my mind to locate the molecular formula of vinegar. It should be an easy one, one of the first compounds we learned in first year organic chem. It comes to me in a few seconds. Acetic acid: $C_2H_4O_2$. I imagine the acidic molecules zapping the dirt particles with their slow-moving electrical charge. The charged dirt particles become instantly attracted to the charges in the water molecules. Strong intermolecular forces pull the dirt into the water, which I then easily wipe away with my rag.

The house has already started worming its way into my consciousness; my dreams of David weeping, trying to claw his way to safety, are now occurring nightly. But I will do whatever it takes to get the house sold and hopefully be able to provide a lifestyle closer approaching what Zane feels he needs. Maybe then the tension between us will dissipate.

The other worry that looms incessantly over my head is how I am going to pay for Zane's post-secondary education. He is incredibly bright, and it would be a tragedy not to be able to send him to university. But once all of the bills are paid at the end of each month, there is never anything left over to invest in Zane's education. Whenever I stand in line at the bank and glance up at glossy advertisements for RESPs, I feel dizzy with guilt. As a single parent, a twenty-four hour day does not permit enough time or earning potential to give my son greater opportunities.

Selling this house is my one chance.

Overwhelmed by the amount of purging that still needs to be done, I decide to tackle it one square foot at a time, beginning with the most innocuous storage space—the hall closet. My hand touches on a bin of Schnapps' old chew toys and leashes. I pick up a squeaky toy shaped like a hamburger and give it a squeeze. The squeal that rushes out of it rouses an image of my loyal pet in her final moments, her bug-eyed face washed up on the shore.

I cannot catch my breath.

The hallway begins to reel. I grow dizzier, the harder I try to suck in air. I get down on my hands and knees, which helps a little, then crawl across the carpet, away from the memories. *Hydrogen, atomic mass 1.008; Helium, 4.003.* I fumble for my purse and fish inside for relief in the form of a tiny blue anxiolytic. *Lithium, 6.941; Beryllium 9.012.*

The following day, I brew myself a cup of tea then sit down in front of the brown leather steamer trunk that had been central to my family's history. How I long to be transported to a moment snuggled beside David on our family couch, listening to my mother's stories.

I take a deep breath, and my hands shake as I unhinge the brass clip and pull open the heavy lid. A fusty smell wafts out. My stomach flip-flops as I look inside.

Blankets. The trunk bulges with mildewed blankets. I pull blanket after blanket out, unwilling to believe there is nothing left of the several generations' worth of McInnis memorabilia. I pull the last worn blanket out and stare at the trunk's bare leather bottom. Empty.

I seize the trunk's lid, then slam it closed, a loud cracking noise resonating through the living room. Then I wrench it open and slam it again. And again. I jerk the lid up and struggle with all my force to rip it from its hinges. I wrestle with the lid until a sharp jolt shoots through my back, then I kick the trunk so hard that a bullet of pain tears through my big toe. I sit down on the floor, cradling my broken toe, bawling. Eventually I am able to compose myself enough to hobble to my purse in search of chemical relief.

The last physical traces to my heritage were no longer in existence. Gone. My family had washed away like the tide, leaving only a watermark along the shore indicating where it had once been. All that remained were shards of broken shells and a furrowed swathe across the shifting sands.

But I must remind myself: it was I who chose to leave everyone behind so long ago. It was a miracle that I made it out of town in one piece the day I fled the Doyles and life on Mikinaak. I had been reeling from my chemical cocktail as Clay ferried me across the channel to Mikinaak, yet I was deeply numb in a way that didn't change once the drugs and alcohol wore off. Over the course of two days I made my way to Toronto, and began an early second act of my life. The theme was survival. I owed it to David to make something of my life in exchange for the life I tore from him.

I had called my father from the Toronto Greyhound station pay phone and told him I needed a place to live, and he had obliged. The booze had taken front seat in his life by then—he was certainly in no state to be a father figure—but he provided food and a roof over my head, and for that at least, I was grateful. After a while, I followed his lead and started partying hard with his riffraff friends. I don't like to think about the night I came home and told him I was pregnant, and that the father was one of his wino buddies. In retrospect, it was probably more guilt than disgust that drove him to say what he said to me. That was the last I ever spoke to Chuck McInnis.

One person kept my life from turning out the way my father's did. The year my classmates were preparing to head off to college and I was sterilizing baby bottles in a low-income apartment, an astonishing sum of money materialized in the bank account Victoria Doyle had opened for me. More than enough to cover tuition fees at Humber College. For four years, Mrs. Doyle provided me with the luxury of creating a secure future for myself—something which would have been impossible otherwise. Juggling little Zane on one hip with a textbook in hand, I clawed my way through a Bachelor of Science, then ended up getting my first big break as an editorial assistant for my chemistry professor who was the editor of an academic journal. Science copywriting was a satisfying fit for me, combining my love of objective facts with my love of writing, and the industry provided security for Zane and me for a good decade. But the past few years had seen the once abundant freelance jobs in my field dry up.

I toiled harder than any of my colleagues to make a life for Zane and me in homage to Victoria Doyle, and as an apology to David. My stomach had clenched every time I opened a receipt for tuition fees and thought about my graceless exit from the Doyle circle of trust. My adult life has been guided by the hope that someday I would be strong enough to make amends for the mistakes of my youth.

Thinking about Mrs. Doyle and the tuition fees that were magically financed in those early Toronto years, my thoughts shift to a familiar worry—how am I going to pull a magic financial stunt of my own? So far, despite our realtor's renewed efforts, there is little interest in the house. The stress of moving back into my mother's house and uprooting Zane from his Toronto life is eroding my ability to stick to a task, and each time I convince myself I need to work on another room of the house, I feel compelled to trot into the kitchen and make a fresh pot of tea, give the sink one more good scrubbing, fold laundry. My attention span scurries in all directions except toward the house renovations.

I grant myself permission to spend half of each day organizing and restoring the house. The tasks prove painful in different ways. As I sift through the decay of my mother's final years in the house, a closed off part of my heart begins aching like a rotted tooth. I had fled Northern Ontario with guilt and anger slung alongside my frayed Budweiser duffel bag, and had carried those emotions across my shoulders for many years. As an adult, I had worked on trying to let go of some of that heavy anger, racking up credit card bills in painful attempts at unpacking some of the blame I held for my mother with the help of a family addictions counsellor. I had learned to talk the talk—knew that I had to someday accept that my mother's depression and addiction to alcohol had rendered her mentally ill. But still, deep down I felt that many of her actions were unforgiveable. My therapist had gently told me I still had a long way to go.

Over the years, the molten hatred I once felt for my mother cooled and hardened into a pointed stone wedged firmly in my throat. I felt it during the holidays, and always during the changing colours of the fall leaves, the season when I'm most vividly aware of death and loneliness. It reminded me of that first autumn which I spent as a frightened pregnant teenage girl in Toronto, heart aching with loneliness as the world all around drained of colour and warmth.

As my fingers touch my mother's dainty antique porcelain figurines, her velvet-lined box of silver cutlery, her treasured collection of country music records still neatly arranged in the glass-fronted cabinet beneath the old record player—as I allow myself to physically connect with these objects, an unfamiliar emotion rips through me, causing a streak of physical pain across my sternum. For a brief moment, I am a little girl again, gazing adoringly up at my mother as she glides her hand down a lock of my hair and tells me a story about a distant relative's fantastical life many generations ago. I am a little girl darting around the house, desperately seeking ways to earn one more radiant smile; a little girl whose world revolves around the bright, beautiful planet that is my mother.

My heart aches so sharply as I think about how much was lost; it is all I can do to crawl into bed and pray for the mercy of sleep. Deep down, I know Zane is right—it's time I figure out a way to deal with my past. But how?

CHAPTER 27

I wait several days before working up the nerve to call Bird. When I finally find the courage, his words are kind and easy. I feel immense relief just speaking to someone who I knew from a time before life had become so difficult. Bird invites me to his home, and I accept.

Bird still lives on the reserve. I drive past the vast stretches of farmland which separate the town from the reserve, past a few clusters of horses and cows huddled together to fend off the cold wind that blows across fields still recovering from the winter's frost. The houses on the reserve are smaller than in town, the exterior paint more colourful. Several dogs view my passing vehicle as a challenge to a road race.

I pull up into the driveway beside Bird's house. It is an unassuming rectangular block with one window in the front, four concrete steps above an exposed cinderblock foundation, and a salmon-coloured door. A satellite dish perches on the roof, incongruous amongst the modest properties.

Bird opens the door and I am greeted by a strong, radiant version of the boy I once knew. His thin face has acquired a layer of padding that complements his bone structure, and his tan beige skin, although brushed with fine lines, glows. My face flushes as he smiles and welcomes me in.

I step inside and stop short, struck by the contrast between the exterior and the interior. It is like walking into a contemporary art gallery. Velvety jazz hums through the room, and the walls are a textured burnt amber that infuses the space with warmth. Hanging upon every wall and displayed from wooden easels in each corner are vibrant paintings. Each piece of art glows under accent lights that shine from the ceiling and walls.

"You run an art gallery?" I ask, confused, because there is no sign out front indicating a business.

Bird laughs and looks away in modesty. "Nah. Not many of my buyers come here in person. I'm lucky to have amazing gallery representation in Toronto. It's been a busy couple of years for me with exhibitions down south. But I *am* thinking about starting my own gallery in the next year or two—looking into using the World Wide Web to reach out to buyers." He sees my eyes widen and he gestures toward a box snaking with cords beside his giant beige desktop computer. "AOL." His face breaks into a sly grin. "One of the first houses on the Island with internet is on the *rez*."

"Wow."

Bird's eyes sparkle. "I've been very blessed." He reaches out to straighten one of his paintings. "But these paintings here—these are the rejects that didn't make the cut in T.O. I mainly hang these here just in case I start thinking I'm hot shit." He laughs, and a faint wisp of warmth rises in my chest.

I take a closer look at the oil paintings that cover the walls of Bird's living room. I recognize the mythical figures from the elders' tales that Bird used to tell me—Nanabush, the turtle spirits, the wolf spirit, the Earth Mother. I stare at a vivid painting of a tiny, hairy-faced person peeking from behind a rock in the forest, a nefarious plan written across the features of his ugly face. Bird's stories of the *Pa'iinsak* little people come flooding back. I am stunned that a person can depict so many powerful stories using the wordless medium of paint and brush.

Bird serves me jasmine tea at a hand-hewn harvest table large enough to seat twelve. He tells me about his life as an artist, his life as a single dad, his Native rights work with the band office.

Eventually Bird finishes filling me in on the major landmarks of his life, and our conversation comes to a quiet point, resting politely at a crossroads that he will not traverse without my assent.

I lay my palms flat on the table and tell Bird about trying to sell my mother's house.

"So, you came here to say goodbye to the past?"

"Basically, yes." I glance quickly at Bird, then look away.

Bird is silent for a moment, allowing my half-truth to sit unclaimed between us.

I clear my throat. "I've been thinking about the Ojibwe myths you used to tell me."

Bird winces at the word *myths*, but says nothing. He interlaces his fingers, and stares at his open palms. Eventually he stands up and motions for me to join him. "There's something I want to show you." He leads me into a den, walks over to a painting at the far side of the room, and stops to gaze at it. I join him, and look up to see a depiction of an underwater cavern, radiating honey-coloured light in concentric rings. A woman with a pained expression on her face is being led toward the cavern, swimming hand in hand with a man whose lower half bears the shimmering aquamarine fins of a fish. The merman's peaceful face reminds me of the gold-flaked religious icons of Archangel Gabriel with his promise of good news for a troubled soul.

I think of my night swims so many years ago with David, of calling out for the Native mermaids. "*Heeee-rrrre mbaanaabe-kwe.*" I feel the prickle of sweat snaking along my back.

"Broken Man's Grotto," I whisper, recalling every detail of the story Bird had told me of the underwater healing place where the *mbaanaabe-kwe* mermaids led troubled people to heal their souls.

"Actually, this one is 'Broken *Woman's* Grotto,'" he laughs, and the sound transports me back to our days of romping through the forest. Bird turns to me and touches one finger to the leather pouch around my neck. The skin around his eyes tightens, and he suddenly looks much older. "I see it's been a while since you went necklace shopping," he says, his face growing serious.

My hand instinctively shoots to the pouch.

"Broken Man's Grotto exists, Primrose."

I look from the painting to Bird's face to scrutinize it for signs of storytelling. He looks serious. "I think we both know that there is no such thing as a mythical spiritual healing cave," I say too loudly. I have to turn my eyes away from the painting, as the thought of swimming underwater, *of seeking a mythical creature underwater,* is causing my throat to clench up.

Bird closes his eyes and nods silently.

"It was a mistake to come here," I say. "I packed up my childish beliefs a long time ago." My purse slides into the crook of my elbow as I reach for the front door, and Bird puts his hand on the edge of the door to prevent it from opening.

"I see." Bird pauses. "I must have missed that part when you flinched at the sight of these paintings."

I throw him an angry look.

"Broken Man's Grotto exists, and I can take you there," he says, and then lets his hand drop.

I scuttle into my car, fishing for the pill case in my purse before I have even settled into my seat. Quick, shallow breaths come in succession; my heart pounding its way up my throat. I fight to stem the panic that is flooding over me. As I drive home, sucking purposeful breaths through clenched teeth, my fingers shake with anger. It isn't until I get home that I hold my emotions up to the light of logic and discover that it isn't anger at all. It's fear.

CHAPTER 28

As April draws to a close, I push Broken Man's Grotto from my mind by busying myself renovating the house. The realtor is advertising an Open House that is just a few weeks away, and I have my work cut out for me.

Zane has grown to dislike our new living arrangements more with each passing day, and makes sure to broadcast it in a litany of creative non-verbal ways: dramatically slumped posture; a disdain for personal hygiene that results in dark, oily strands of hair shrouding his scowling eyes; a newly acquired footfall that is heavy and laboured, as though his shoes are made of lead; and my personal favorite—a frequent need to draw forth long, wet loogers from the depths of his throat, and hork them loudly into whichever receptacle is the closest, the kitchen sink not exempt from this honour.

If he isn't in his room with the door locked, he is hammering away at the garden with his shovel, savagely tilling the hard, weedy ground until it bleeds dark soil and earthworms. I am under no illusions about where all this anger is coming from.

I bite my tongue and roll with it the best I can. And I believe I've earned a bit of street credit with Zane in the process, as each day goes by and I withhold my judgement. He seems to have softened a bit, since it has become clear I'm not going to impede his right to express himself through vulgarity; we've even enjoyed a stretch of nearly civilized evening meals together this week.

And then, this afternoon Zane comes home from school and throws the door open so hard it bounces off the rubber doorstopper and swings back toward him, nearly slamming him in the face. "Who the fuck is David McInnis?" he shouts, panting, his hands on his knees as though he has run all the way from the bus stop.

Oh no. No no no no no.

I take a few steps toward Zane, and have to steady myself at the table. I try to remain composed as I explain to him about the brother who drowned when I was young.

"You dragged me here because of him, didn't you? Your constant hovering, the secrecy, —it's all because of him, isn't it? You're terrified of every single move I make because you're running from your own personal fucking ghost story, isn't that right, Madre?"

Zane takes several deep breaths. He shakes his head slowly. "You know what's got me plum-fucking bamboozled? How someone who has zero. Fucking. Life—no offense—can have such an intriguing past. Couldn't you have saved a bit of the fucking sparkle for the Zane years?"

I open my mouth to defend my choices, and close it again.

Zane's voice softens. "Your lake phobia. I finally get it." He looks up at me with those clear grey eyes that seem to peer right into my soul, and the last traces of anger drain from his face. His voice becomes choked with tears. "I'm sorry, mom" he says quietly. "I really am. I had no idea there was so much going on beneath the surface with you. I just wish you'd let me in. I can't take it anymore." He closes his eyes and drops his chin to his chest. The next part comes out as a whisper. "But mom, if you can't figure out a way to deal with your issues, I don't think I can live with you anymore."

After everything I've sacrificed for him, he threatens to leave me.

A hot wave of fury roars through my body. Zane's ultimatum wrenches something loose inside of me, an inherited venom which I had kept securely contained in all my years as a responsible parent. I do something I swore as a mother that I would never allow myself to do: I lose control.

My hand springs like a cobra and smacks him across the face so hard he is knocked backward. That is it. Zane throws down his backpack and tears out the door. But the look on his face as he flings open the door tells me that I have crossed a line, and that there will be consequences.

I take Zane's ultimatum to heart. I knew the next terrifying step I needed to take, for both our sakes. My entire life I have dreamed of sitting down and writing a book. Now was the time.

I have always been a closet scribbler—creative writing late at night in my room is my form of psychic surgery to heal my childhood wounds. I have never told anyone about the fervent writing I did in my youth, creating the collection of stories about the heroic young nature-lover, the *Legends of David*. Over the years, I thought constantly of returning to it and transforming the sophomoric writing into something that could be passed on in some way, allowing David's memory to live on through the stories. Since Zane's birth, the *Legends of David* has rested securely tucked away in a bin.

I come to a decision late that night: I am going to face my demons in a productive way by writing a book about local Mikinaak folklore. I would retell the ghost stories, superstitions, and legends that have floated around Mikinaak Island for generations. And—here is the hard part—I would investigate into the supernatural fog surrounding my brother's death. For the first time since I left Mikinaak Island as a teenager, I am prepared to dig deeper into the circumstances that haunted the McInnis family; to answer the questions that clawed through the canvas of my dreams at night. I needed to atone for whatever mistakes I have made.

I divide the next few weeks between working on the house and writing an outline for my book. It will require a fair amount of interviews and research, and the local newspaper office, *the Mikinaak Record*, is a trove of useful information. But it takes hours of sifting through archives to turn up the nuggets of folklore that will be the cornerstones of my book. This book will be a very public undertaking and completely out of my comfort zone, but I am ready to push myself to do it, for Zane's and my sake.

But every time I sit down at my computer to write, I freeze. I begin to doubt whether I am emotionally prepared to face the stories of David's ghost. Yet I *need* to find out if there is anything to them. The images that continue to haunt my dreams—of my brother unable to find rest in the afterlife, drifting forlorn in a world which he no longer inhabits but cannot escape—these images are destroying me. Just as my mother had ached for the truth about the events leading up to David's death, I needed to know the truth about the *presence* in the lake. And if David really has been lingering in a spiritual liminal zone, I would have to find a way to free him so he could finally rest in peace.

It takes Zane these two full weeks to settle on a punishment for me. One that he thinks is fair and steeped in irony—that necessary ingredient in his teenage acts of rebellion. In the meantime, I plod along on my book and the house. I slough away more ugly wallpaper, paint several rooms a comforting butter yellow, and hold an unfruitful open house. During all of this, I keep on alert for any war signals from Zane.

News of Zane's insurrection comes on a Saturday afternoon. I had left for town an hour earlier to buy groceries, and when I pulled out of the driveway, Zane was furiously shoveling in the garden. Now, a message from Zane greets me in the kitchen, in the form of a yellow life jacket. The life jacket is arranged over the back of a kitchen chair as though the chair is wearing it, the buckle pulled across the chair's chest and secured. My pulse starts to race. *What in God's name is he up to?*

I call through the house for Zane, and when he doesn't answer, I run outside. I race down to the shore, tripping in the sand, already able to guess what I am going to find. My face and neck are flushed, my blood flowing furiously by the time I get to the sandy strip that meets the water's edge. The smell of gasoline is sharp in the air, and a wide path is cut out of the sand, heading into the grey waves.

I force my eyes to look out across the rolling grey and white lake, searching for an anomaly on the horizon. A tiny black dot inches its way across the skyline, and I reel with nausea as I train my eyes on it. Every fiber of my body urges me to look away from the water; panic rising up inside me. Looking at the lake is only marginally less terrifying than being on the lake. I seem to stand there for an eternity. Cold beads of sweat surface on my face and body, and soon my clothes are damp with dread. I fear I will never see my son again. The rip current. *Mishi-ginebig.*

I stand on the shore for almost an hour, pleading with the lake to return my son to me, too afraid to move a muscle in fear it might weaken the power of my prayers, the wind slapping tears across my cheeks. But I do not permit myself to look away from the capricious expanse that carries my son. A wind whips a chill through my damp cotton shirt, and I realize my teeth are chattering violently. In painfully slow motion, the dot on the horizon grows larger, until it transforms from a dot to a rectangle, and eventually to the shape of a small fishing boat. The boat inches its way across the rough waves, until I can make out the silhouette of my son seated at the back of the boat, his hand resting on the tiller of the outboard motor. He wears a blue hoodie instead of a yellow life jacket.

I collapse in the sand, my knees shaking. Thank you, thank you, thank you. I send a kiss out to the lake, quivering with respect at what it has chosen to forego.

I later learn that Zane bought the boat with money he had gleaned from selling a truckload of my father's tools and equipment, as well as furniture from the garage. He had made a personal connection with Jib, a teenager who worked part-time at the marina; Jib had facilitated the purchase of the small aluminum fishing boat and taught Zane how to drive it.

Soon after, Jib invites Zane to join him on a series of fishing excursions, where he shows him some of the best fishing holes on the lake. Apparently, Jib will make an avid fisherman out of Zane in no time. He even offers to teach Zane the basics of swimming. I am filled with remorse at the memory of how the YMCA pool had lorded itself over me when Zane was a toddler. And now my son was becoming a boater who barely knew how to swim.

And just like that, my city boy who has never set foot on a boat in his life is suddenly taken by the world of sport fishing. Zane begins spending all of his free time hanging out on the docks at the marina, and soon meets other boys his age who also own boats, which on Mikinaak is almost as common as a Toronto teenager owning a bus pass. Zane comes home at dinnertime, hands smelling of the mossy earth from the worms he has been handling, his cheeks pink and wind-chapped, his eyes bright. He still punishes me. Refuses to engage in any sort of conversation with me, still holds his words as ransom for all the years I refused to tell him about his family's past, which he is now learning about from the gossip mill at school. But his slumped posture straightens itself out, and his hair resumes its relationship with the shampoo bottle. For the first time in many seasons, my son looks almost happy.

Zane is a model student under Jib's nautical instruction, and before long, I am hearing snippets of conversations on the phone that sound like Zane has been raised an Islander. His words even take on a hint of the maritime twang that stretches out the vowels of the locals' words and make a plain sentence sound like a punchline. *Just* has morphed into *jeeust*; *doing it* has become *doin'er*. He brings hunting and fishing magazines home from the library, and pores over them at the table during meals. Magazines eventually make way for thick diagrammed manuals, and I discover after much prodding that Zane is studying for his hunting license.

I manage to maintain a calm face as I picture my son trudging through the woods in camouflage, other men in the same woods eagerly cocking their guns at the sound of a twig cracking under Zane's foot.

I come home from the library late one afternoon in early May to a smell that transports me alongside my mother in the same kitchen, thirty years earlier. Fish fillets are popping in browned butter, and Zane's laughter mingles with the voice of another boy.

"Serious knife to the heart, man! I trusted you with all our hard-earned bass, Zed-dog!"

Zed-dog?

I walk into the kitchen to see a husky, round-cheeked boy standing at my stove, holding a plate of blackened fillets in two hands. Zane stands beside him, a warped plastic spatula in hand.

"Zed! Flip it *now*! We've got this one, bro!"

Zane dives for the fillet, and after several attempts with the spatula, manages to flip the fillet in the pan. The plastic spatula is melting at the edges, and the butter in the pan emits wisps of black smoke.

"Zaner, are you going to introduce me to your friend?"

Zane looks almost chivalrous as he reaches out and gestures to his friend, and then extends his arm toward me. "Mompadre, Morgan. Morgan, this is my mom." He blushes, and I see how hard he is trying to conceal the pride he feels in this new friend. I fight the urge to wrap my arms around both of them.

I set the table for three and steal extra minutes smoothing out the tablecloth, spying. Zane and Morgan are still at the stove, bent over the plate of fish, laughing so hard that a line of drool comes running out of Morgan's mouth. "Dude! These bass don't need any of your *special sauce*!" Zane gives Morgan a light shove, and a thread of saliva hits the edge of the plate, sending the boys into hysterics.

Throughout dinner, I hide my swelling heart. Watching Zane and Morgan razz each other over plates of inedible fish they are extremely proud of, I realize how long it has been since I have seen my son look this comfortable in his own skin. I feel giddy as I sip my water and inhale every second of this rare opportunity to witness Zane so radiant.

"So, Zed-dog, you in on the hunt next fall? There's room for one more in our hunt camp, and the bed's got your name on it. But speak now, because my uncles are always trying to pack the place full of their friends."

Zane's eyes shine. "Been dreaming of tagging a huge buck lately."

I grimace and Zane sees, which I regret instantly. A shot of pain flashes across his face. He puts his fork down and speaks quietly. "But it might not happen, man. Not sure if we'll still be here by then."

The evening's joy quietly seeps away. We finish our meal with awkward small talk, then Zane dutifully clears the table, and Morgan thanks me politely and follows Zane out of the kitchen.

I make many attempts to reconnect with Zane in the days that follow. One afternoon, I approach Zane as he sits on the couch, flipping through a hunting magazine. A searing image of my father and his hunting rifle make my eyes water. I take a deep breath.

"I hear that wild game is very healthy," I offer, a slight upturn of my lips the best that I can manage.

Zane perks right up. "Yes, it is! It's lean, and has no added antibiotics or hormones. And it's humane if you do it right. Plus it's free!" Zane's eyes sparkle. "Hey—ever heard of smelts, mom?"

Zane's question fills me with shame about how little I have imparted to him about my life growing up on Mikinaak. "Of course I've heard of smelts, Zaner. I grew up here."

Although not officially noted on calendars, there is a season that occurs in Northern Ontario which turns the riverbanks into a festive outdoor hall in the dark hours of the night. It comes in mid-spring, its exact date to be announced each year by the enthusiastic souls who make their way out to the river at night, flashlights swinging a ribbon of silver through the dark, tumbling water. They report their findings back to the rest of the town: the smelts are finally running.

Smelt season is a spring ritual ingrained into the mental almanacs of every Mikinaak Islander. Memories of the surreal nights slogging in hip waders through the river in the pitch dark, neighbours wading alongside—these memories stand out in my mind more vividly than Halloween or even Christmas. The incongruity of half the Island's children sloshing around in the river, a gazillion hours past our bedtimes, was what gave smelt fishing the mystical feeling of being so *out of place,* so disconnected from the reality of our everyday lives.

Smelt fishing was an event that drew more fathers than mothers, which also added to the unlikeliness of it all—kids swarming around with flashlights in rapid-moving icy water which, if one were to trip on a slippery rock, might fill up a child's tall rubber boots and whisk him along the bottom of the river, tumbling him away like a small stone. And this dangerous activity taking place under the unwatchful eyes of *our fathers*, of all people. We were all warned about the boots-filling-with-heavy-water danger; I had such a fear of falling over and getting pulled away down the jet black river that I felt a little queasy every time I laid eyes on my set of tall rubber boots in the closet. But for most children, the danger made it all the more exhilarating. And the fathers bolstered their sense of occasion with the assistance of six packs of beer, kept propped in the frigid water along the shore's edge—nature's beer cooler.

By the age of seven, my brother David was already a natural born smelt fisher, despite being barely tall enough for the top of his boots to clear the surface of the river. Unlike some of the other kids mucking around with their flashlights, David knew that he couldn't shine his light into the river if he wanted the fish to stick around. He would wade to an unoccupied stretch, and stand alone under the veiled light of the moon. He would wait until he *sensed* it was the right time to scoop his net into the water, revealing a shimmering, wriggling mass, each smelt the size of a finger. The fresh cucumber scent of smelt would trail in front of David as he struggled to hold his arms high in the air, his net a heavy, writhing trophy. I would watch with a mixture of jealousy and pride as my brother emptied his net into our plastic smelt bucket, as other adults shone their flashlights up at his net and whistled in admiration of the hefty haul such a little guy had managed. David would tip netful after netful into our smelt bucket, while some families left the river with only a meager handful of smelts circling inside their pails.

I remember one smelting night, Doc Miller was standing in the river, talking to my father. A beer was resting against his hip waders, and a cigarette dangled from his lip as he spoke. He reached over to rustle my brother's hair as David approached our bucket with another heavy net. "Your son here is about the luckiest damn smelt fisherman I've ever seen," he said, and shook the remaining drops of beer from his bottle into the river.

I watched my father shake his head. "Nah. Just beginner's luck," he said, a proud grin plastered across his face. "Isn't that right, David?"

David. Always David.

"Earth to Madre..." Zane's voice brings me back. "Morgan and Jib and a couple other guys from school have invited me to go smelt fishing tonight. Thousands of these tiny fish make their way here for only a few nights a year, and it's, like, a major island event to go fishing for them in the dark."

"I'm glad you're making the most of the local culture *before we leave*," I say, and scrutinize his face for a response.

Zane scuffs his boot across the floor, leaving a row of black marks that I will be annoyed to clean up later. He picks up his hunting manual. "Right. Before we leave," he says, and his voice makes it clear that leaving Mikinaak Island is not the urgent matter it once was.

I am going to have to sit him down and talk about this. Maybe tomorrow.

Zane heads out right after dinner, clad in multiple layers of sweaters which bulge under his heavy jacket. He is going to Morgan's house to hang out until around ten P.M., the time when the smelts will be good and running. A small group of friends will then make the drive together down the unlit backcountry roads to the river.

I am concerned that Zane and his friends, or someone else on the road, will be drinking and driving. Sitting around with a drink in hand used to be the number one pastime on Mikinaak Island, a sport which many young Islanders put in years of dedicated training for, before the Ontario government gave them the nod to do so. And growing up with no local taxi service and little traffic save for the occasional raccoon or deer, it was common knowledge that after a night of parents drinking around someone else's kitchen table, everyone would make it home in one piece as long as the dads all drove slowly.

At least, that had been the attitude when I last lived here. I pray that this attitude has shifted since the days of my parents' shindigs. I had recently noted a few public service ad boards denouncing drinking and driving on the island, but I suspected these gravel roads still saw their fair share of two A.M. drivers hugging the middle of the road, the palm of one hand covering an eye to prevent double vision as they inched their vehicles home from a kitchen party.

My other concern brings me right back to my nights of swimming in the lake with David. I envision Zane wading in the frigid river, and getting separated from his friends—just out of sight of anyone. I picture a swirl of dark water gathering around Zane's thighs, and a rising metallic whine swelling in his ear. I shudder as my mind conjures dark, ugly endings to this scene.

I pull my mind away from Zane and force myself to do some writing. Lately, it has been a struggle to direct my anxious flurry of thoughts into graceful prose. Something has been persistently abrading my thoughts ever since the afternoon I made my trip to the reserve to visit Bird. My mind keeps catching on one thought, slippery as stone, that tumbles along my stream of consciousness. Each time my mind reaches to grasp the thought, an image of a haloed grotto appears for a moment, and then just as quickly, the grotto dissolves into the surrounding waves.

I had never really thought of Bird Manaabeh as a close friend when we were young. He was a boy from the reserve who came over to our house with his mom, and with whom I shared afternoons exploring the intricacies of the forest. At school, we kept to our own clans. All that time we spent together as kids, we never really talked about much, other than the forest and the Ojibwe stories of his elders. Maybe that is why I want so badly to reconnect with him now. I long for the days when we shared a singular focus on things of wonder; when we were innocent. Bird is a link to a time when peace of mind was a possibility. But something holds me back from picking up the phone and calling him again.

After several hours of unfocused writing, I close the file, open a scrapbooking file, and shift my worrying back to Zane. I park myself in our faux leather La-Z-Boy in the living room, eyes fixed on the window to the driveway. *Zane is a strong swimmer, and the river will be full of parents and kids.* I rearrange dainty digital flowers across the scrapbook page. *And the probability of a car collision on such barren roads is remote.* I change the title of the journal piece I have matted alongside the photo, from 'Amazing Zane' to 'There's No One Like Zane'. *Statistically, the annual smelt fish is completely safe.*

Two A.M. comes, and my nerves are taut.

Three A.M., and still no sign of Zane.

By three-thirty, I have worn a path across the living room carpet. *Hydrogen, atomic mass 1.008; Helium, 4.003; Lithium, 6.941...*

Shortly after four A.M., a ribbon of light sweeps across the living room, and I hear gravel popping beneath the wheels of a vehicle. All the panic that had intensified as the clock's hour hand crept toward dawn turns to anger. I hold my palms against my temples. *Calm down, Marina.*

Zane steps into the house, tiptoeing in exaggerated high steps like a burglar in a cartoon, his face drooping in a slack grin. He doesn't notice me sitting in the chair, waiting. *Careful, mama bear.*

Yet before I can think of something calm and composed to say, my words burst out in a shrill pitch. "*Where. Have. You. Been?*"

Zane jerks his head in my direction. "Whoooa Momphetamine," he shakes his hands high in the air, as though he is in a hold-up. "You could do some serious emotional damage, sneaking up on a person all unannounced and shit."

"Do you have any idea how worried I was about you? Do you realize how late it is?" I can feel the heat rising to my face.

Zane fumbles with the cuff of his jacket, trying to get a look at his watch. Each time he pulls the cuff clear of the watch, he draws his arm up to look at the watch and the cuff slides back over the watch. "I was down at the river with the guys. Smelt fishing. I told you that's where I was going—mom, you have *no idea* how awesome the whole scene was—forty people hanging out. *In a river!* So fucking surreal—scooping up nets squirming with these tiny silver fish—there must have been hundreds of them in my net each time I brought it up, and everyone laughing and fishing and wading around the river under the moonlight..." Zane steadies himself with one hand on the wall.

"Look at you." I shake my head. "What do you think you're doing, being out in a river in the state you're in? You could have been *killed*, David."

My hand flies to my mouth.

Zane freezes. His face slowly changes from that of a sweet, bumbling drunk to that of a sad little boy. His shoulders slump forward. Slowly, he slides down the wall and rests his head in his arms.

"David. You see him every time you look at me, don't you?"

He raises his head and stares past me, his eyes unfocused. "There was a *miniscule possibility* that I could've gotten hurt. I was in a shallow fucking river—three feet of running water that for some fucked up reason is just too fucking scary for you to handle. But

I'm not David, and I'm *certainly not you*, mom. I'm not terrified to step out into the fucking world and actually live." He shakes his head and smiles bitterly. "Do you know that I cannot think back to a single fucking time that I've ever heard you laugh? You know how fucked up that is?" His voice goes flat. "Do you know that I can barely fucking breathe, the way you've hovered over me my entire life?"

"Enough, Zane."

"No, it's not enough. I've got miles of this shit backlogged." Zane staggers back to his feet. "You are so trapped in whatever happened in your fucked up family in the past, and you're trying to drag me down with you. Like how you dragged me here—to chase some fucking ghost. But I've got news for you. I like it here. And I'm *staying*."

I stare at Zane, speechless.

"Bet you didn't figure that into your plan. Of course you didn't, because it never occurs to you to think about what I want. Did it ever occur to you that by keeping me safe from every fucking little thing, you're fucking *killing me*?" He makes a fist, then slams his hand through the wall beside me.

Drywall dust flies into my eyes. I stand frozen, staring at the gaping hole in our living room wall as Zane storms up the stairs to his room.

CHAPTER 29

Zane and I settle into a cold war that causes my breath to hitch in my chest every time I walk past his closed bedroom door. Several evenings, I try bribing him out with popcorn and a movie, but each time, I get a brusque rejection from the other side of the plywood.

It is Friday evening, and I am home alone. Zane is with Morgan and Jib at their friend Eddy's place, as usual. Every time I sit down and try to write, the words "Broken Man's Grotto" work their way to the surface of my thoughts. I need to speak to Bird again.

It takes all my strength of character to dial Bird's number, and I don't even allow myself the mental cushion of rehearsing what I will say when he answers, for fear I will lose my nerve.

It turns out that my anxiety was wasted on Bird. "Primrose!" His voice warms the phone line. "You caved a little early. I had you pegged for a six-week fumer."

I mention that, among other things, I have a business proposal for him, and Bird agrees to come over to talk. "I'll meet you at the edge of your driveway. I'll be wearing my finest camo." I can hear him smiling across the phone line.

As I hang up, I realize how badly I long for adult conversation, how large a void of connection to other adults I have allowed to span over the last few years.

It hurts both my pride and my heart to acknowledge that I have no real adult friends who I can call in a pinch, no band of sassy girlfriends to pull together to celebrate my birthday or invite over for a glass of wine to commiserate a terrible day. I have conserved my emotional energy for being a good mother, period.

The evenings feel especially barren on Mikinaak; at least in Toronto, there was the comfort of being in close approximation to large numbers of people. In my mother's house on Mikinaak, we have no neighbours within shouting distance; the tall poplar trees are the only living things that would hear my cries of distress if something untoward were to happen to Zane or me.

But I can't fool myself. There is more to it than just a need for adult conversation with Bird; a pleasant shiver zips through my spine as I picture him standing in my doorway.

Bird is all business when he shows up. He only has a few minutes, he says. He has to pick up his daughter from his ex-wife's house. I try to focus on the notes laid out on the kitchen table; try not to let him see the disappointment in my eyes.

I explain an idea I've been toying with for my book. "What do you think about collaborating with me, Bird—my writing, your artwork? It could make a beautiful coffee table book. I've looked into it, and I think it's the kind of project that Georgian Publishing would eat right up."

Bird rubs his hand up and down the back of his neck. "Hmmn."

"A lot of the legends I'm writing about, you've already done paintings of. It could be great publicity for you."

"You mean you're retelling Ojibwe stories?"

"Um. A few. Is that bad?"

"Hmmn. Let me get this straight. You, a white woman, want to publish, for profit, *my* artwork—artwork that is already commercially successful I might add—along with stories you've taken from *my* culture?"

I cringe. "Oh, god, Bird. I'm sorry. When you put it that way it sounds like a horrible—"

Bird shoots me a smile. "Relax, Primrose. I'm fucking with you. If done respectfully, I think it could be a really cool project. Let me think about it."

Bird calls the next day, and agrees to work together. "I've always wanted to do a collaborative project."

I hope there is more to it than that.

"But I've got two conditions. I want us to go to a council of Ojibwe Elders for guidance with the project—make sure they don't think it's offensive or exploitative or anything like that."

"That sounds good. What's the other condition?"

"We not be seen together too often. Don't want everyone on the rez thinking I've sold out and am sleeping with a white woman." He laughs, but I can hear the ten percent truth that lies beneath every joke.

I go to Bird's home that afternoon to start our work together. As I flip through canvas after canvas of works he has stacked against a wall, I am astounded to be reliving all the stories he had entrusted in me when we were kids. I brush my fingertips against the stippled colour, and warmth swells within my chest.

I flip past a canvas of Nanabush throwing his eyeballs in the air. The next painting in the stack is shaded in greys and blacks. It is a horned serpent slithering through the dark lake, with a limp human body flowing out along the sides of its mouth like a mustache. I quickly flip to the next canvas, but Bird sees me flinch.

"A book about Mikinaak spirits won't be complete without *Mishi-ginebig*," he says, eyeing my face for a reaction.

I grip the canvas frame; my knuckles blanch. "Of course."

Bird and I spend three afternoons that week going over art and story ideas. He has insisted on meeting at the library each time. "You don't need to be on the rez, Primrose," he says. "All those wild dogs—wouldn't want you to get bitten." He pinches me playfully on the arm.

My heart dips unexpectedly in my chest. I don't push the issue.

It feels so good to be reconnecting with Bird, revisiting memories of exploring the forest behind my house so many years ago. I remember how he would lean forward and brush the petals of a wild flower across my cheek as he spoke. The firm muscles of his smooth, tattooed bicep peeking out from under his white t-shirt sleeve. How I would hold my breath, my nerve endings tingling, my mind praying for that hand to work its way a little lower. But—wait. Bird had been a slim kid with wiry arms. And I hadn't felt that way about him back then. My breath quickens as I realize the tattoo, the white t-shirt are images from today. It takes a while for my body to cool down and for my mind to concentrate on work again. An hour later, still at the library, my bare arm brushes up against Bird's as I reach for a book. He inhales sharply, then his tan skin turns a pinker shade. Again, it takes several minutes before the heat dissipates from my skin.

I delve into more research for the book all week, seeking any source of information I can find pertaining to local legends and myths.

The Bearwalker is one story I can't leave alone, but it is thorny territory. I feel deeply connected to the story after having written about it so many years ago, but don't think Bird would approve of me writing about it. That Bird's father is in prison for his role in the Bearwalker murder makes me intensely, guiltily curious. Did their people truly believe in shape-shifters stalking our Island, bloodthirsty and seeking vengeance? Part of me worries that I have no right to appropriate stories from a culture to which I do not belong, but I assuage my uneasy feelings by reminding myself that despite the stories' origins, over time they have reached the ears of both the Native and non-Native population of Mikinaak, and are now part of a collective mythology we all share. Still, I would have to get Bird's blessing.

I bring it up with him as we are leaving the library one evening.

"Bird, there's another legend I'm hoping to include in our book."

"Don't keep me in suspense."

"I want to write about the Bearwalker."

"Don't even dream of it, Primrose."

I see a discomfort in his face that tells me not to press matters further.

"Got it."

The Council of Elders agrees to hear our proposal the following week. "I'm so incredibly nervous," I whisper to Bird, as we walk into the Band Office board room where about twenty men and women sit around a conference table.

"Relax, Prim. They don't bite." He gives me a light squeeze on my side, and my nerves tingle where his fingers graze me.

Bird had thought it best that I present to the elders. When it is my turn to speak, I introduce myself and outline the book proposal, my voice trembling.

"So, basically you're hoping to seek our endorsement of your book, is that it?" A heavyset man who goes by the name of Flip asks me.

"Yes, I guess you could say that."

He crosses his arms. "Well, you've come to the wrong place, Miss McInnis. The Mikinaak Council of Elders certainly doesn't *endorse* books in the name of Mikinaak Ojibwe. You think eighteen Elders could possibly act as some kind of unified voice for our entire community?"

Heat spreads across my face. "I—I'm sorry. I didn't mean to insinuate that. I—"

Flip uncrosses his arms. A mischievous smile spreads across his face. "Relax, Marina. I'm messing with you. You looked like you could use an icebreaker."

Bird breaks into laughter.

"But seriously, we don't endorse things. Not even close. What we can do is work with you to ensure your book comes from a place of respect."

I let out a huge breath and feel my nervousness fading away. "That sounds great. Would you and the other council members like to hear more about the book, Flip?"

"Very much so."

The meeting is a very positive experience. The Elders seem genuinely interested, but just as Flip had explained, they are certainly not a unified voice. Some of them like the book proposal, others feel it is a bad idea, and many others want to hold off on an opinion until we have more to show them. "We welcome you to come back and consult with us when the project is further along," Flip says to me at the end of the meeting, giving me a hug with a hearty backslap. "We're not a one-and-done kind of operation." He squeezes my hand and smiles. I assure Flip we'll be back.

Spring melts into early summer as I continue to work feverishly on the book and the house. If nothing else, the solitude of my domestic life benefits my writing life.

The interviews I had envisioned conducting were proving more difficult to obtain than I had imagined. I had anticipated compiling a variety of anecdotal material, much of which might read a lot like fictitious yarns, the progeny of islanders' boredom and imagination.

But I suspect there might be a few interviewees who remain adamant that their brush with the supernatural was true. I am counting on *these* vivid, wide-eyed accounts to make the book soar. I think back to how my mother's hands would fly to her neck at the mention of Teddy Doyle's ghost. Obviously, *she* had found reason to fear something supernatural on our island.

The crown jewels of my book would be the ghost of Teddy Doyle, and the ghost of my brother. I felt a combination of nausea and anticipation whenever I thought about uttering my brother's name in an interview: "Is it true you had an encounter with the ghost of David McInnis?" I shudder, thinking about David from the perspective of someone telling a dramatic ghost story, the storyteller not recognizing that the character being floated around for entertainment is a beloved family member with a backstory of tragic loss. A thought nags at my conscience: in writing this book, could I be accused of the same cavalier offence?

I dust off my elementary school yearbook, and compile a list of over a dozen names. List in hand, I solicit the help of the local librarian who has an impressive mental genealogical map of the people in town. She eagerly supplies me with the whereabouts of most people on my list.

The first person I am able to arrange an interview with is Billy McDonald, a boy I had interviewed a lifetime ago for the *Howler*. I picture the crusty shimmer that was always caked below Billy's nostrils when he was young, and wonder if his scruffy appearance has carried over into adulthood. When we were kids, Billy had told an emotional story about how he and his father had come across a drowning man near Hay Bay, and how they had ended up in a grisly situation involving their boat's propeller and Teddy Doyle's face.

Billy agrees to let me interview him in his home, and as I make my way across town, I stare at the familiar houses. I had been living back on Mikinaak Island now for three months, and aside from going to the grocery store and my one knockout night at the Wheel, I hadn't wanted to revisit the town at all. Too many painful memories were paved into these streets: David and I doubling on my bike; walking with Rhonda to the candy store. I knew this town so well I could sketch a topographical map of the entire thing.

I pull into Billy, now Bill, McDonald's driveway, then stall for a moment in my car, psyching myself up. A fit, clean-shaven man comes to the front door, and I scramble out of the car to greet him.

We are seated at his kitchen table when I segue into the tougher part of the conversation. "Bill, I know it was decades ago, and you were quite young, but do you remember a story that you told many of us kids, about a fishing trip gone wrong with your father, and how you experienced something...something unusual?"

Bill gives me a blank look. "You mean in—what would that be—*fifth grade*? When I bragged to all the kids at school that dad and I saw the ghost of Teddy Doyle?"

"That's exactly what I'm talking about. Can you tell me more about what happened, that day on the lake with your father?"

Bill tilts his head and examines my face as though I have sprouted a horn from my forehead. "Lady, I don't know what you're getting at."

"What you saw, that day on the lake." By now, a defensive tone has crept into my voice. *Get it together, Marina. The businesslike composure of a professional writer—the demeanor you practiced at home in front of the mirror all morning.*

"You've gotta be kidding me. You made your way back to the Island to ask me about some inane ghost story I made up when I was eleven years old? Seriously? Is this what you're writing your book about?"

The hostility that edges into the conversation catches me off guard. It sounded so foolish, the way he put it. For a second, the fragile version of myself, the one who existed before I moved to Toronto, wants to withdraw and apologize for wasting his time, for being ridiculous. But the tougher version, carved by the hand of impoverished single parenthood in the city—that woman holds up her chin.

"It is obvious that pursuing this conversation any longer would be a pointless waste of both your and my time." I clap my notebook closed and carefully place it and my handheld recorder back in my bag. I leave, closing the door behind me with precisely enough force so that it does not slam, and hold my shoulders back and my head up as I walk back to the car.

Hands trembling, I place one small blue pill onto my tongue and dry-swallow before I have even pulled out of the driveway.

It takes me a whole week to feel emotionally prepared to attempt another interview. In the meantime, I devote myself to working on the book with Bird. Zane is barely home these days. He goes straight over to either Eddy, Jib, or Morgan's house after school—two of these friends I have yet to even meet—and he doesn't come home most nights until the sky is black and I am already in my pajamas. I resign myself not to push him on this one, and make great pains to hold my tongue as he saunters in the front door at night.

"Zaner honey, why don't you invite Eddy over here for dinner one night this week?" I ask him one evening. "It'll be fun." Zane looks at me as though I have just suggested we go naked horseback riding together down Main Street.

"Going to have to pass on that one, Madre."

I make sure my face shows no signs of hurt feelings. "Please, Zaner. I would absolutely love to meet more of your friends. I promise I will keep the embarrassing stories to a bare minimum."

No response.

"Okay, then. Whenever you're ready."

I had set a daily writing quota of four pages, every single day. But with the house being so quiet, and Zane either off with friends or outside thrashing the earth with his shovel, I am able to ratchet my output up to seven pages of writing per day. Never before has my writing life been so productive.

For the most part, I am disconnected from the outside world as I work, cloistered behind a mountain of books I have borrowed from the library and purchased from the local newspaper office. The research necessary for my book has taken me far down a stream I had only intended to dip my toe into. I have become fascinated by the history of Mikinaak Island and its culture several generations back, from which many of the local myths were born.

Also, the more I research and write about Ojibwe stories, the more uneasy I feel about being an interloper, even with Bird on board. Back to the Elder Council I go, to consult with them about what I have written so far—this time, I feel comfortable enough to go without Bird. The meeting is educational, although its outcome is difficult to accept. Several of the Elders disapprove of the way I have framed the Ojibwe stories. They advise me to rewrite all of them from a Native narrator's point of view. But then a few other Elders bristle at this, and argue against me appropriating a Native voice. The lack of consensus leaves me feeling disillusioned about the project, but we agree to meet again in a few weeks. I walk out of the room unsure of how I am going to tackle the rewrites at all.

Scanning through microfiche of old *Mikinaak Record* articles at the library one afternoon, a headline catches my eye: *Fourth Mikinaak drowning fatality in two years.* I scan the article, feeling an uneasy sense of being about to learn something I won't be able to forget later. The piece outlines how a young man went out for his usual morning swim and never came back, and that his body had still not been found. It mentions the names of three other drowning victims who had also succumbed to tragic fates on the water a short time before. I comb through the microfiche archives to find these stories as well. A few hours later, I click off the microfilm reader and sit rooted in the library chair. I cannot shake the image of a young fisherman's body washed up on shore, his face and limbs mangled. Or how in each of the four separate cases, the circumstances surrounding the drowning made little sense. My mind rushes to pinpoint a logical explanation for each of the drownings stories— *maybe the rip current got them.* But a soft voice whispers a question just beneath the drone of rational thought: *was it possible that the Ojibwe's covetous lake creature was real?* I bolt from the library, my legs feeling heavy and unstable.

Days of researching and writing pass, and my unease increases whenever I think about the drownings. As I write about local ghost stories and mysterious accounts of missing people—a statistically significant number, relative to the island's population size—a nagging suspicion pokes at me. Could there actually be a connection between the two?

I push on nervously. I hope that once I finish weaving together the history of the community, portraits of the deceased, and the mythologies that surround them, I will have created something worthy of those who had passed.

Worthy of David.

My mind goes to the honey-coloured cave in Bird's painting, and his words: "Broken Man's Grotto exists, Primrose. I can take you there." Even just thinking of the lake, my chest tightens and the pounding in my ears begins.

No, I could never hope for that sort of absolution. I don't deserve it. Long ago I had accepted that a slight release was the most I could hope for.

One week after my first interview, I force myself to contact the next person on my list. A woman named Suzy Gagne, who had been a ringleader in all things related to the ghost of Teddy Doyle when we were kids. I knew it was a longshot, but something told me there might be *something* to her stories. I recalled how Suzy's eyes would fill with tears when she solemnly relayed the details to our eager group at school about the fateful night she had witnessed Teddy Doyle's ghost.

I learned my lesson from my previous interview. I planned to ask a few preliminary questions over the phone with Suzy to determine if it was a good idea to meet her in person. I dial her number, my fingers shaking as I push the buttons. I take a deep breath when a woman answers the phone, and I break into my rehearsed introduction. I explain who I am, and that I am hoping to interview her for a book about local legends.

"First off, no one's called me Suzy in twenty years. Name's Sue."

"My apologies, Sue."

"Second, I remember who you are. Mina McInnis. You're the girl who drowned her little brother. You hung out with Crazy Rhonnie. Guess she won't be hammerin' on people no more now, will she?" She lets out a loud snort. "At least Crazy Rhonnie was good for the tourism all those years. Don't know what those boaters would've done to entertain themselves all summer long if it weren't for Crazy Rhonnie whizzing around the lake every day in her bathrobe on that lunatic water-motorbike thing of hers. It's damn near a cryin shame she ain't showin her face around here no more."

I flinch at her words, speechless. *Crazy Rhonnie?*

Sue snorts in amusement, then makes convulsing *ack ack ack* sounds, as though her tongue is too large for her mouth. I picture her on the other end of the phone line, one eye squinted shut, her tongue lolling out of her mouth in imitation of a spastic convulsion.

She goes on, "I don't know what you're nosin around for, but you got no business calling me up and involving me in whatever it is you're up to. I wouldn't touch nothing to do with the McInnis family with a ten-foot pole."

I hear a click and imagine the loud slam of the phone in Sue's hand. I stand there, dead phone in my hand. A series of morbid questions about Rhonda Doyle gnaws at my chest.

Days pass, and I continue to wrestle with the phone conversation I had with Sue Gagne. Early one grey morning, after another long night of distressing dreams, I walk to my bay window and peer out across the lake, straining to see across the few kilometres that separate me from Elsinore Island. My stomach twists into a ball as I think once more about the hellian blur of pigtails and gasoline that was my childhood best friend. A question surfaces for the millionth time since I was a teenager: whatever happened to Rhonda Doyle?

The sunny, warm days of July arrive, and give me the positive boost I need to move forward—I call seven other people from my interview list. I force myself to ask about the ghost of David McInnis as well, although I am terrified. Six times I come away from the conversation with knowledge that the supernatural stories these people told as children were entirely fabricated. The seventh interviewee, however, urges me to come to her house to speak in person. Maureen Smythe had been a few grades above me in school, and I didn't know her very well, but she reaches for my hand and chokes back tears as she recalls in vivid detail the most horrifying evening of her young life. She swears that she has no reason, at her age, to hold onto a story like this other than the fact that it still rocked her to the core whenever she thought about it. "I can still remember exactly how I felt out there on the lake: my ears had suddenly filled with a high-pitched whine like the sound of an electric saw. The sound was so loud I could almost *feel* the saw blade—" she reaches up and grips her head, "—feel it running across my scalp."

I know that feeling intimately. This interview fills me with both hope and dread.

CHAPTER 30

Bird is coming over to discuss the book. I run around gathering stray objects from the living room and kitchen and flinging them into my bedroom. Zane and I have accomplished much over the past months in our efforts to organize and redecorate the house, and in the forgiving evening light, with the flames from the pillar candles on the coffee table casting a warm yellow glow, the living room and kitchen almost pass for inviting.

Bird knocks on the door and I stumble over the carpet on my way to let him in. Then I bumble my way through a greeting and whisk him into the living room and am rambling on and on before I realize I have not even let him squeeze two words in. "I apologize. I don't entertain often," I say, wiping my clammy palms on the front of my skirt. "Can I get you a glass of wine?"

"I'll have tea if you don't mind making it." He pauses. "I don't hit the hard stuff anymore." His eyes shift away and tell me it's best not to pry.

Bird and I sit down on the living room sofa, the flame from the candles tossing shadows across his face. I make small talk, and he reciprocates, and I begin to think that it was a mistake to have him over. I feel like a teenager on a first date—everything that comes out of my mouth sounds awkward.

I put my teacup down on the coffee table, and am just about to feign a migraine when Bird puts his hand on my arm.

"I can empathize with how you feel, Primrose," he says.

I squint at him, confused.

"I know that you carry the guilt of David's death, and I understand how that feels," he says, his eyes revealing flecks of amber that bring to mind neat rows of mason jars at my uncle's sugar shack in the woods. Thoughts of the woods shift to memories of Bird and me sitting on the pine needle-covered ground, legs stretched out in front of us, our backs resting against the reassuring strength of a maple trunk. My mind goes to Bird's story of the evil serpent that roams the lake.

Suddenly, I am spilling out the hidden, murky details of my brother's death. Unleashing ideas that I have not allowed myself to think about in decades. Thoughts that only resurface in nightmares.

I feel light-headed as I tell Bird absolutely everything: the night swimming, *Mishi-ginebig*, Rhonda and my role in David's drowning, my fears surrounding Zane, my worries about David's spirit. "I've reached a point," I say, "where the guilt has drained me of everything. I don't know a way out—I can't let go of what happened, and I can't move on."

The release of this poison, verbalizing for the first time in over twenty years the albatross that hangs around my neck—brings a sea of relief flooding over me. My neck grows moist from fat tears that stream off my chin and down my blouse. I can taste the saltwater as the tears drip down my lips.

Bird walks over to the bay window and pushes aside the gauzy white curtain. He peers out toward the lake, even though there are no lights of any kind. He squints into the absolute blackness. "It would make things easy if I could say that the Elders' stories I grew up listening to were only colourful yarns spun around a campfire to entertain us kids." He tilts his head as though he is watching the path of something out on the lake. "But unfortunately, I can't. These are stories that my people pass on because they believe them, because their elders before them saw these things with their own eyes. And the stories that have haunted your waking life, Primrose, like the story of *Mishi-ginebig*—these are stories that we believe to be true. I'm sorry I can't say they're fairy tales." Bird lets the curtain fall back to its place, and returns to stand in front of me, looking down to where I sit. "But dark spirits are not the only ones who inhabit our world. I told you before; there is a place where good spirits can perform powerful spiritual healing. Broken Man's Grotto."

I try to imagine what peace of mind would feel like, how light and free my soul would dance if I weren't obliged to drag a boulder of guilt along with every step.

Then I picture myself swimming in the murky lake, and I feel my chest constrict with fear. I have not set foot in a lake in more than two decades. Cannot think about deep expanses of water without feeling my heart staccato, my throat clamp up, cold sweat springing up across my palms. Even if a mythical underwater place of healing does exist, and I am fortunate enough to have a guide willing to take me, journeying to such a place would be impossible.

"I think you need to push yourself harder to look at your fears, Primrose."

Bird's right. Until I face the truth—whatever it is about *Mishi-ginebig*, the lake serpent will continue to haunt my dreams and drive a wedge of fear between Zane and me. I owe it to both David and Zane to exorcise this ghost.

But there is no way I am going in that lake.

Bird's face tightens. "The last time I went to Broken Man's Grotto, I was seeking healing along with my son, Jib,"

I jerk my head in his direction at the name *Jib*. Zane's friend Jib, whose brother had died in an accident.

"I know about dark days, Primrose. That's why I want to help you. Part of my own healing journey for the rest of my life will involve helping others to heal."

"My son and Jib are friends," I tell him.

Bird nods. Of course he already knew this. How could I know so little about my son's life?

"Zane told me that Jib's brother was killed in an accident. I am so sorry. I had no idea he was your son."

Bird looks away from me for several seconds. When he turns his face back to me, it is ashen. "Took my son ice fishing with me for the first time when he was five years old. At that point in my life, ice fishing involved a lot more whiskey than it did fish. I preferred to get liquored right up for just about every activity back then. Especially enjoyed pairing booze with climbing out of bed.

"My little guy and I spent a long afternoon out on the ice. I remember how happy he was, itchin to get back and show his mother his first-ever winter catch. I was blind drunk by the time we climbed on my snowmobile and headed home. I gunned the motor, told him we were going to *fly* all the way home so he could show his mom his big fish." Bird pauses.

"My snowmobile hit an ice ridge, and my son flew forty feet. Killed on impact. Killed by his stinking drunk father."

Bird openly wipes away a tear. "I owe my own peace of spirit to this cave beneath the waters, and I am willing to take you there, Primrose."

I rise and step toward Bird, then hold out my arms. He hesitates, then pulls me into his chest. I smell the spicy bite of aftershave on his neck, feel the strength of his biceps as his arms wrap around me. His fingers press firm, healing circles down my back. I feel a hot tear drop onto my neck. Bird holds me for longer than a hug, then longer still, and I realize how badly I long for him to take my face in his hands and draw my mouth to his. Realize how every cell is focused on what might happen next between his body and mine.

"Primrose, I have wanted to hold you like this since the second I saw you standing on that barstool..."

I close my eyes, ready to either freefall into ecstasy or crash hard. My body is warm in all the places where it touches Bird's.

"...but the tears, the guilt—this isn't the way I want this to happen."

I pull my head back to look him in the eyes, and nod, trying to keep the disappointment from my face. Wanting even more to taste every inch of him.

Bird shakes his head. "Then again, what am I afraid of?"

I pull his head toward mine. Our lips collide hungrily, frantically.

Thank God Zane is not home.

CHAPTER 31

I stare at the flattened whorl on the living room carpet, evidence from the night before. It practically narrates the delicious scenes that took place across its fibers. *I should fluff up the carpet before Zane notices.* Better get the vacuum. But all I really want to do is pound down every strand of the living room carpet, the hallway, the bedroom carpet with Bird again—luscious rugburn on my back, my neck, my legs. It is all I can think about.

Yet I have work to do. That morning I had heard back from Georgian Publishing about the book outline and sample artwork I had sent them. They were enthusiastic—it looks like our book has actual publishing potential. There is just one more person on my interview list.

The name Jeannie Baker fills me with dread. Jeannie is forever linked to that day on the beach. She is also my last hope that the stories about David's ghost contain a grain of truth. If David's spirit still lingered on Mikinaak, maybe it would be possible for me to contact him. To find out if *Mishi-ginebig* had something to do with his death. And to ask David's forgiveness and help him along to his final resting place. But I know that this final interview is a long shot.

Jeannie was the childhood classmate who had been most in her element when a vortex of drama swirled around her. Whenever I reached my mind back to the school playground and pictured the gossip and the superstitious storytelling, Jeannie's face always came to mind. I think of the gossip she had spread about me in my last year of school on Mikinaak. And then my mind goes to what came after—the horrible wet thump as Rhonda pulverized her in my defense.

Jeannie was an unkind person; my first memories of her are as a preschooler, showboating her lacquered black church shoes at Sunday school to the ashamed little girl beside her who tried to conceal her clomping, two-sizes-too-large Buster Brown knockoffs under our wood paneled Sunday school table. I also recalled Jeannie's histrionics over Bird's prized moose meat sandwich. People didn't change, not their core selves, anyway. Their interests might evolve, their life experiences might deepen, but the essential archetype of a person—that remained a constant. Jeannie had always fit squarely into the box labelled *spiteful cow*.

I pull up at the address Jeannie had given me, and am greeted by a cascade of English tea roses which wrapped themselves around a white wooden arbor at the entrance to a stone path, beckoning visitors to the front porch. The front yard is like a flower market. Pink, yellow, and white roses grow in beds so large that little grass is visible, and purple phlox grows along the walkway, contrasted by bright green moss between the flagstones underfoot. Red roses twirl their stems along the length of a white pagoda that arches gracefully above a wishing well, nestled in the center of the yard. A sunny calm washes over me as I make my way to the front porch, musing that Jeannie's husband must be an avid gardener.

A woman with soft curls framing her round face comes to the door, and I instantly recognize her as a plumper version of the girl with whom I had shared the same classroom air for seven years. Kindergarten was the only year we had not been in the same class: Jeannie had been mornings, I had gone in the afternoons. It makes me feel both nostalgic and sad, thinking about how much common experience we had, yet how we are now absolute strangers.

Jeannie tugs her gardening gloves free from each finger, then wraps her arms around me in a beefy hug that leaves me a bit muddled. "Welcome, Mina. You look fantastic," she says, and pulls me into her living room.

The room has a New England beach house charm to it. The walls are sponge-painted a speckled marine blue; large photos of sea shells and starfish are displayed from picture frames adorned with white painted driftwood; a fluffy Persian cat is nestled in a ball on a nautical blue pinstripe chair, completing the room's general pleasantness. "You have an enchanting home," I say, and am surprised that I actually mean it.

"Oh, I just adore working on the house and my gardens," Jeannie beams. "My husband jokes that he feels like he's trampling through a Monet painting when he comes home from work every evening, but I know deep down he appreciates it as much as I do."

Jeannie and I chat, and I scrutinize her synopsis of the last quarter century of her life for evidence of the cruel streak that defined her as a young person. The cruelty is difficult to detect, as she describes her decision to go into nursing, and how she had eventually shifted from hospital work into home health care. But I know that if I spent more time with her, the meanness would eventually surface.

I take a deep breath. "Jeannie, I wanted to ask you about something that took place a long time ago—when we were kids," I begin. My hand instinctively goes to the leather pouch around my neck.

Jeannie winces and looks away from me. "There's a lot about that time of my life I don't like to think about. A lot of things I wish I could take back."

"Really? Like what?"

"It's...it's odd that you've come here, actually. I've made a lot of changes in my life..." She reaches up and clasps a gold cross that hangs around her neck. "One of the things that eats away at me whenever I think back to the...the person I used to be... is how I persecuted you. The way I ruthlessly picked on you... fabricating all those stories after you suffered unthinkable tragedy in your family. I'm...I'm just appalled at how cold-hearted I was back then." Jeannie reaches for a slice of lemon loaf that she had arranged on a china plate for us. She eats it steadily, then dabs at each crumb with her finger, concentrating on collecting every one, and then brushes them all to the floor, rendering the collecting process pointless. Her eyes remain on the coffee table in front of us.

"I put that behind me a long time ago," I say, in my most stoic voice.

"Did you?" Jeannie looks me squarely in the face. "I'm not sure Rhonda Doyle would be convinced of that."

My muscles tense at the mention of Rhonda Doyle's name. "Rhonda? What are you talking about?"

"All these years, Rhonda's waited patiently for you to come back. She considers you a sister, you know. And she really could have used some sisterly support, with all she's been through." Jeannie's voice took on an accusatory edge that made my face flush.

"How would you know anything about Rhonda Doyle and her emotional state?" I ask, my chin trembling. "Rhonda detested you so much she couldn't stop herself from smashing your face in."

Jeannie wipes invisible crumbs from her lap. "I have been caring for Rhonda for the past twelve years. I do home care visits with her once a week. Rhonda considers me one of her closest friends."

I wince. Rhonda still lives nearby? And is close friends with *Jeannie Baker*? And requires the regular care of a nurse? I shake my head, the questions swimming in my mind.

Finally, Jeannie takes the lead, sensing that I have lost my ability to speak. "You should take a boat over to Elsinore to see her. Rhonda can't—or at least she shouldn't—drive over here by herself to see you. She has these seizures..." Jeannie pauses. "Rhonda would never admit it outright, but she needs you, Mina. She has never gotten over how you left her family."

I am too stunned to respond. I imagine I excused myself, and somehow managed to slot the car keys in the ignition and drive home. I don't remember doing any of it, but I must have, because I find myself standing inside my living room at the bay window, staring out across the lake. Just a few kilometres across that terrifying expanse of water is the best friend I have ever known, and she needs me.

I set up a card table in front of the bay window so I can work on my laptop with the lake as my backdrop, Elsinore Island within view. For two weeks, I do nothing but write and weather angry looks from Zane and mull over Rhonda Doyle. I have so many questions. It would be easy to get ahold of Rhonda's telephone number and just pick up the phone and call her, but our friendship warrants more than a phone call after twenty years of avoidance.

I had to visit Rhonda in person.

Yet each time I think about setting my foot down on the swaying metal deck of a boat, imagine the boat setting off from the dock into nothing but open water, I grow dizzy and my heart threatens to pound through the front of my ribcage.

My entire being aches to reconnect with Rhonda Doyle.

But how can I?

CHAPTER 32

Zane goes right on disapproving of my every move, my every uttered syllable, and I carry on writing my book in a feverish haze of productivity as July creeps into August. I am more than halfway through the rough draft, and Bird and I have paired some striking prints of his oil paintings with several of the chapters.

It took several careful rewrites of the Ojibwe story chapters before I felt ready to present them to the Council Elders once more. After reading my latest draft, Flip gave me a hearty clap on the back, but some of the other Council Elders were far less enthusiastic. The book would rest in limbo until the next Council meeting. I had figured out by this point that this process was going to take far longer than I had envisioned. And I was just going to have to accept that I would never be the Mikinaak Council of Elders' literary darling.

On a dreary, rainy Saturday, I keep watch over the lake as I sit at the bay window, my computer in my lap. I am taking a break from my writing work, scrapbooking instead. My laptop screen displays a collage of beautifully coloured papers and dainty embellishments. I am putting together a page that showcases one of the rare photos

Zane had allowed me to snap since our arrival on Mikinaak. In the photo, Zane is standing on the shore, his back to the grey-blue blur of lake that stretches out on either side of him. Far off in the distance I can make out a tiny smudge of dark grey, and I take comfort in knowing that this smudge is Elsinore Island. Zane is squinting toward the camera, a small but perceivable impish grin on his face. "The constant shoving of a camera in my face, of writing a story about every half-decent day we've had together—is that a biological drive, mom?" Zane had asked, which was an unfair exaggeration. "I'll give you fifty bucks to *not* turn that picture into a scrapbook page." He had smiled as he said it.

How quickly Zane had gotten away from me. This must be what elderly ladies were getting at, when they handed over unsolicited advice in the grocery store checkout line about cherishing every minute of our young children's lives: this realization that our babies grow up far too quickly; that we will blink and they will be grown and no longer need us. But what those clucking older women had left unsaid, what they couldn't bear to bring words to, was that we must capture joy in our family life in the same way that we might slave over a hot stove of bubbling strawberries, sealing up their summer flavour for the bleakness of the coming winter. We must stow that happiness in a larder of tight-lidded jars. Because one day far too soon we will wake up and realize that every single last happy-go-lucky day has passed, and what lies ahead is a long road of surly adolescent selfishness, and a growing distance between two who were once inseparable.

Of course, not every archivist works from a need to staunch a torrent of regret. But I suspected that the majority of memory keepers were familiar with the heavy ache in the chest that asked to be relieved by chirpy images, each page of joy a tourniquet.

I arrange blue hearts and bright yellow daisies around the edges of Zane's picture, knowing he would cringe if he saw this saccharine scrapbook page. I try to block out my worries about Zane, and David, and now Rhonda Doyle. I focus on the fluffy tissue-paper digital hearts bordering Zane's photo, and concentrate solely on that one still frame where life looked easy.

The phone rings, and I am startled out of my fuzzy scrapbooking cocoon. I pick up the phone, and hear Zane's urgent voice on the other end. I know immediately that something is wrong.

"Mom, I need you to come get me. I'm at Eddy's place. Quick."

I jot down the address and am out the door before Zane even has time to explain.

I pull up to the street where Eddy's family lives, my knuckles white from their grip on the steering wheel. I squint through the rain at the house numbers until I come to the last house on the street. It is a two-storey home with an enormous wooden patio, furnished with a half-dozen round metal bistro tables overlooking a lush herb garden that occupies the entire backyard. I double-check the address I had written down. Eddy's parents run a restaurant out of the lower level of their house?

I speed my car into an empty space in the gravel parking area, and only when I hop out of the car do I notice the painted wooden sign above the entrance:

Ettie's Place.

A grey-haired woman appears in the entranceway, and I instantly recognize the friendly bulldog jowls. Ettie. The steel pin who kept Elsinore together; the cook who had elevated mealtime to an art. Ettie watches me walk toward her, her face unreadable. When I reach the bottom of the steps leading up to the entrance, her face break into a grin, jowls reaching for her ears. "It's high time, Sugarpie," she says, and holds out her arms to pull me into a fierce, cinnamon-scented embrace that feels like home.

I allow Ettie's arms to just keep on holding me. I stand there, letting her strong arms around me do all the catching up that I don't have the emotional energy to participate in. Neither of us require any details, not yet anyway, and Ettie's embrace smooths over the years and our separate struggles and carries us together right back up to present day, as though I had never left.

Ettie leads me into the restaurant, and sweeps her arm in a curved path in front of her. "It's not much, but it's mine," she says, resting her hands on her ample hips, her head held up proudly. The restaurant has a French country feel to it, with crisp white linen tablecloths and a mason jar of freshly snipped lavender on each table, and the honeyed voice of a French cabaret singer crooning "*La vie en rose*" through the sound system. In a town that boasts only one other restaurant—Bub's Family Diner, a mom-and-pop joint featuring hot hamburger platters and satisfying greasy breakfasts, this restaurant is a bold departure.

I pause before a shelf of antique books running along one wall.

"I've been huntin those down at auctions and vintage book stores over the years," Ettie says, beaming. "This year I added a second-edition Jane Austen with original full-leather bindings to the collection."

Zane, Morgan, and a third boy with tawny beige skin are playing cards at one of the round bistro tables. At the center of the table sits a platter of melted brie sprinkled with cranberries, surrounded by thin slices of baguette. The boys are laughing and jostling each other, and helping themselves to generous scoops of the gooey brie. Zane's eyes follow me as I walk up to his table. He puts down his cards and stands up. "I'm sorry I worried you, mom. I decided it was time you two were reunited. " He glances toward the exit, pink creeping across his cheeks. "I seriously do want to help you, you know." Then he gives Morgan a punch on the arm and nods toward the door. The boys fold their cards and gather their backpacks.

"Nice to meet you, Mrs. McInnis," says the boy who I don't recognize. He chases after the others as they head for the door.

"Bye, Jib!" Ettie calls after him.

"See you for dinner, Gran," Morgan calls as he jumps up and swings from the door frame before jumping down the stairs.

"See you tomorrow, Ettie. Thanks for the grub," Zane says, and flashes Ettie a warm smile for which I would have surrendered my rights to fresh water for a month. The boys tumble out the front door, and Ettie busies herself clearing away their plates and leftover food. I stand slack-jawed, staring at Ettie. She hums to herself and goes on cleaning, as though this is just another ordinary day, as though there wasn't a two-decade gap between now and the day that she and I first rubbed elbows in the kitchen at Elsinore.

"Morgan—that's my grandson— and Zane have hit it off somethin fierce," she says, as she sweeps baguette crumbs from the linen table cloth. "Thick as thieves. They act as though they've been best of friends their entire lives." Ettie shakes her head, smiling to herself. "You know, I caught Morgan and Zane down at the docks the other night, trying to catch a snapping turtle by luring it in with a hotdog, of all things. Lord only knows what they would've done with that *repugnant* creature if they'd been able to haul it up onto the dock." Ettie's smile fades and the corners of her mouth turn down. Her eyes take on a wistful look. "Those boys, the way they were huddled over that creature on the dock, they were the spittin image of two young girls I used to know."

Ettie walks over to the Open sign which hangs in the front window, and turns it around. A loud click resonates through the room as she locks the heavy front door. Then she disappears into the kitchen. "Sylvie, Chaz—how bout you two take a break. A nice long one." I overhear her say. A few minutes later, a man and a woman wearing white aprons exit the kitchen. The man has an unlit cigarette clenched between his teeth. They dip their heads at me and duck out the back door. Ettie comes out of the kitchen several minutes later with an oblong silver tray crammed with a floral china tea set and a platter of pastries. "Chocolate éclairs, beignets, and petit fours. All baked fresh this morning." Ettie motions for me to sit at the bistro table where Zane had sat earlier. She begins setting up an elaborate tea service for the two of us. "I was just thinking it's about time for a break anyways," she says, as she pours steaming tea into both of our porcelain teacups, then settles herself into the chair across from me.

Ettie takes a long, slow sip of the scalding liquid and then sets her cup down. "When I found out you were back on Mikinaak, I must have gone over in my mind a thousand times what I needed to say when you decided you were ready to come find me. Looks like Zane has done the decidin for you."

I turn my eyes away from Ettie.

"I have something to tell you, Mina McInnis. And I'm afraid it isn't pretty." She takes a deep breath. "This is harder than I envisioned. " She exhales a long, slow breath. "Okay. I'll start with something that *was* pretty: Katherine McInnis, forty years ago."

I shoot a vicious glance toward her. "I've spent the past two decades trying to forget my mother, Ettie."

Ettie nods. "I don't doubt that in the least, Sugar. But I'm sorry to say, there's more to your mother's story that needs to be told. And I find myself in the unwelcome position of the one left to do the tellin."

I press my palms against the table and close my eyes.

Ettie takes this as a sign to begin. "This story goes way back, to the time of the Elsinore regatta—the day Katherine's quick thinkin saved Mr. Doyle and our crew from humiliation. Your mother became something of a celebrity on Elsinore after that day—her silky hair and gams that went all the way up to her eyelashes didn't hurt her popularity none, either—but your mother, she didn't need to put one iota of effort into charmin our crew. For three summers in a row on Elsinore, Katherine had to fight the Elsinore men off with a stick. She was just one of those people who everyone and their dog wanted to be around."

"My heart does not contain nearly enough generosity to picture my mother young and popular," I say, glaring down into my teacup.

Ettie gives an understanding nod and nudges the plate of pastries toward me. I pick up one of the petit fours out of politeness and force one bite into my mouth.

"Elsinore staff weren't the only ones interested in your mother's comins and goins every summer, neither. Teddy was the only Doyle who ever mingled with the hired help, and I tell you, there was one staff member in particular he most enjoyed minglin with."

"I really don't want to hear about this, Ettie," I snap.

Ettie nods, but continues anyway. "One night, Teddy came down to the staff campfire, did his usual pitiful scan for Katherine, then left as soon as he seen she wasn't there. I didn't think much of it. But later that night as I was fumblin my way back to my cabin after a few too many, I happened upon them. I held my breath and stood as still as them pine trees around me. I couldn't believe it. These two young people had *no business* being together."

I lean forward, sliding my chair closer to the table. My voice softens. "Why not?"

"I'll get to that. Anyways, Teddy began dotin on Katherine in the most...ah, *innovative* ways—Katherine would wake at dawn to find a heart-shaped campfire burnin in the clearing outside her cabin door; she would return from an exhausting shift in the kitchen to find that Teddy had snuck into her cabin and carpeted the floor with red roses; one time he devised a complicated treasure hunt that had Katherine pokin around in tree hollows for love letters folded smaller than her fingernail."

I put down my pastry, the bite I had taken grating like sand in my mouth.

"It soon became plain as the nose on my face that Katherine had fallen in love with the son of one of the most...ah, *influential* men in Ontario, and she didn't seem to care one stitch that this love boat was headed on a crash course."

I sit up straighter, morbidly curious yet repelled at the same time. "She wasn't good enough for the Doyles?"

Ettie shakes her head. "Teddy was engaged to another woman. A damn near *royal* engagement. Teddy's father had strong-armed him to marry into the elite duPont family. I remember how Cissy duPont's father and Mr. Doyle smoked their Cuban cigars and nattered away together like hens the night Cissy and Teddy announced their engagement." Ettie sucks her teeth. "Poor Cissy. Teddy was so charming—she couldn't seem to see what was really goin on."

Anyone who had spent as much time as I had around ruinous men knew the type. I had briefly tousled with one of those myself, sixteen years ago.

"So, Cissy had spent the year obsessin over the finer details of her wedding decor, and Teddy spent the better part of the year obsessin over all the lovely ladies who'd be off-limits once he pledged his vows. And then he caught sight of Katherine."

My chest is beginning to tighten. I shove my chair back and stand up. "I'm sorry, Ettie. I need to leave. I'm really not up for hearing about how enthralling my mother was in her youth."

Ettie nods, then reaches over and grabs my arm. She pulls me back toward my chair, a little firmer than I would have liked. "I'm sorry too, Sugarpie, but this story needs to be told."

I cross my arms and reluctantly sit down.

Ettie continues. "Anyways—on more than one occasion I spied Katherine sneakin off into the woods after her shift in the Elsinore kitchen. Every morning, Katherine slunk into the staff kitchen with a face puffy from mosquito bites and sleep deprivation. I witnessed all of it like an...ah, *apprehensive* parent. And years later, Katherine told me the rest." Ettie lifts her teacup and takes a long sip, then carefully places it on the table between us.

I picture my mother as I last saw her: booze-bloated face, foul dishrag hair. It is impossible to reconcile Ettie's words with the mother I remembered. I feel both ashamed and disturbed that I could have such huge gaps in understanding about my own mother's life.

"As Teddy and Cissy's wedding date crept closer, Katherine seemed to just shrivel up. The only person she would have any contact with was Lenny 2-Pints, the Native guy who boated up to Elsinore every day delivering fresh goods. He's dead now, you know—this Lenny 2-Pints. Murdered over some Bear-spirit curse. I believe I told you a bit about that many years ago. There was always something suspicious about that Lenny. Anyways, he seemed to soothe Katherine, which I was grateful for. Because she looked like death warmed over.

"The night after Teddy's wedding, the Doyles hosted a massive celebration in the main Elsinore cottage—a kick-off to the three-month European honeymoon that Teddy and Cissy were leaving for in the morning. True to Doyle form, Teddy had been drinkin since twelve noon on the dot, and was feelin no pain.

"I was standin beside Teddy at the party when his sister Victoria came in from outside, a shocked look on her face. She whispered something to Teddy, but the only word I could make out was 'Katherine.' Next thing I know, Teddy's hightailin it out the door.

"I waited a while, then followed Teddy. He and Katherine were screamin and yellin at each other down at the docks. Lenny came along and had to pull Teddy off Katherine. Looked like Teddy was gonna damn near kill her.

"Anyways, the next thing I know, Teddy and Katherine take off in his boat. I had an...ah, *ominous* feeling about what was about to happen, I tell you."

A sudden coldness runs right through me. I choke on a sip of tea and Ettie hands me her cloth napkin. She rests her hand on mine and gives it a long squeeze. A sultry song I recognize as Brigitte Bardot flirting with Serge Gainsbourg, *'Je t'aime...moi non plus,'* is playing too loudly on the overhead speakers. Ettie stands up and walks over to the sound system and switches off the discordant music, then crosses the room and sits back down. This time I urge her to go on.

"I could hear the engine of Teddy's boat for a time, then it faded away to a whisper. I stood there, watchin and waitin for so long, I didn't think my guts could stand it any longer. And then I heard Teddy's distress horn. And somehow, I just knew that by the time any of us got out on the lake, it was gonna be too late.

"Years later, your mother told me everything that happened out there: She and Teddy were arguin something fierce on the boat—Teddy had a temper on him like you wouldn't believe. At one point, Teddy stood up screamin at Katherine, and the small boat lurched. Teddy went flyin, and the boat tipped to one side. Katherine scrambled to grab hold of Teddy; the boat took on too much water and slid beneath the lake like a bath toy."

My hand goes to the leather band around my neck. It feels like it is choking me. Suddenly, a loud smack comes from the restaurant's front window. I jerk, and fling scalding tea all over my lap. I turn around to see a hefty middle-aged woman with her face pressed up against the glass, eyes squinting, hands cupped above her forehead to shield the rain. She gives the window another good smack. Ettie walks over to where the woman stands on the other side of the glass, and gives the Closed sign a hard rap with her knuckle, then pivots and walks back to join me at the table. The woman keeps her forehead pressed against the glass, a betrayed look on her face, then gives the window a final half-hearted slap. She turns and trudges away. Ettie shakes her head, sucking her teeth. "Sue Gagne. One of the toughest old birds on this island, and somehow, she's managed to get herself addicted to my lavender macaroons."

I shrink down in my chair.

Ettie continues. "Teddy was three sheets to the wind, and the booze turned his limbs to lead halfway across the lake. Katherine nearly drowned trying to keep Teddy's head above water. She was a talented swimmer, but not strong enough to haul a large, wasted man back to shore. Eventually, she had to make a god-awful choice: let go of that poor son of a bitch or drown."

I stare past Ettie's shoulder. My voice comes out high and tinny. "Their argument—my mom was pregnant with Teddy's baby, wasn't she?"

Ettie fixes her eyes on mine and gives a slight nod; she doesn't seem surprised that I'd guessed.

I feel all the colour drain from my face.

"Mr. Doyle and Victoria were the ones who found Katherine. By then, the sky had turned ugly and it was starting to pour. Katherine was barely able to keep her head above water, strugglin to swim back. They never did find Teddy's body."

A wave of nausea swirls from my belly up into my skull as I struggle to make sense of Ettie's words. My voice is barely a whisper. "Teddy Doyle is my father."

Ettie slowly nods. "The following spring, Teddy fathered two babies from beyond the grave: a baby boy who would carry on the Doyle name, and a baby girl who would eventually go by the name McInnis, and whose...ah, *ambiguous paternity* the Elsinore community made a generous pact to keep to themselves."

My whole body stiffens. I hide my face in my hands. The implications of Ettie's words roll out before me, and one after another, the pillars of my identity come crashing down. I have so many questions, but I am too stunned to formulate sentences. My mouth hangs open, trying to form itself around the tornado of questions that swirl in my head. I jump from my seat and race out the door, into a storm so fierce the rain is almost horizontal.

CHAPTER 33

Ettie runs after me. I feel guilty when I look over my shoulder and see her ham hock legs lumbering to catch up, her hand on her back for support. I am soaked to the skin within a minute, the rain pelting my eyes so I am running nearly blind down the street.

"How far you gonna make an old lady run, Sugarpie?" Ettie calls out, her voice ragged.

I stop. As soon as my body is still, my last layer of composure ruptures. The tears start flowing, an outpouring of two decades of pain. Ettie catches up, and wraps her arms around me, not saying a word. I cry until my throat feels raw, and then Ettie raises my chin with one finger, to look me in the eyes.

"There is something your mother asked me to give you."

I shake my head, defeated. "I don't want anything from that woman. Whatever it is, burn it."

Ettie wipes my face with a cloth handkerchief, and laces her hand in mine. She leads me down the street, the rainwater sloshing over our shoes. We come to a red brick house with a wide verandah. Ettie sits me down in a wicker chair, and then disappears into the house. She comes back a few minutes later with an oblong yellow box. She places it on the small table in front of me.

The lump in my throat turns to acid. "I don't want to know what's in that box."

Ettie nods and places her hands on the lid of the box. "Your mother struggled with Teddy's death, and then with your brother's death, more than you will ever know. And then *you*. She never forgave herself—nor have I, to be frank—for the way she mistreated you. She fought for over twenty years to slay her demons."

I jerk my head up to look at Ettie's face, and am met with concerned eyes.

"Your mother and I reconnected years ago. A large part of me will always despise your mother for the way she neglected you, but I knew a very different Katherine *before*. And I decided I owed it to the old Katherine to help out the deeply troubled woman she became."

Ettie lifts the lid off the box before me, and I suck in my breath when I see the red leatherette cover of my mother's scrapbook.

"Your mother wanted you to have this. Personally, I don't believe your mother deserves any more of your tears, and more than once I considered not givin it to you. But I am too superstitious a woman to betray the dead. So here it is."

I remove the book from the box. My chin trembles as I look over the familiar pages, photos, and clippings I had pored over countless times as a child on my mother's lap. I turn past a picture of David and me, hanging from our grinning father's arms; newspaper clippings of a poetry contest I had won in third grade; a worn newspaper announcement of the death of Teddy Doyle. What I had always presumed to be my mother's superstitious angst around the Teddy Doyle story was something far more complex.

Time seems to come to a halt as I flip through page after page of special family moments and achievements my mother had memorialized with beautiful embellishments and thoughtful words. A burr materializes in my throat, barely permitting me to swallow. I see each edition of our juvenile *Mikinaak Howler* displayed. My mother had decorated the edges with black and white paper daisies, with a black satin ribbon running along the bottom of each page. Words come into focus from the Bearwalker interview Rhonda and I had conducted with Bird's cousin, positioned above our classified ad seeking information about the ghost of Teddy Doyle. My mind goes to the string of mornings so many years ago when I found the newsletter returned to our front porch, with angry words scrawled across it. *You were warned.* I had let that spook me for years, suspecting I had trespassed into the Ojibwe spirit world. Another piece of the puzzle clicks into place. I look up at Ettie through a lens of tears.

"My newsletter—was it my mother who was warning me to stay out of it?"

Ettie nods. "Katherine was convinced Teddy blamed the boat accident on her, and dreaded for the rest of her life that Teddy would get his revenge. Your mother feared Teddy Doyle's ghost with every ounce of her being." Ettie shrugs her shoulders, her face morose. "The last thing Katherine wanted was for you to invite that...ah, *malevolence* into your life. You shared his flesh and blood, but she feared he wouldn't be above using you to hurt her in any way he could."

I imagine David's last moments in the water and a shiver goes through me.

I stare down at the scrapbook for a long time. Slow tears trickle down my cheeks and splatter across the page. The verandah feels like it is in a slow spin. When I am finally ready to keep going, I take a deep breath and turn the page to find a cardstock frame enclosing neat rows of poker chips, each glued in the center of a sunny paper flower. I lean in to take a better look.

"Those were your mother's AA chips."

I stare at the page incredulously. With numb fingers, I flip past five similar pages lined with the coloured chips. "These are given out at sobriety milestones, right? Three months, six months, one year sober?" My voice breaks.

Ettie nods.

I slump over the poker chips and stare with wet eyes, as though on the surface of the chips I can find more details of this other life my mother had resurrected for herself.

I wipe my nose with my cloth napkin. "There must be at least fifty of these chips, Ettie. How many years was my mother sober?"

Ettie closes her eyes. "Your mother spent the majority of the last twenty years gettin sober. Unfortunately, most of those chips are twenty-four hour and one-month tokens. Each time she quit drinkin, Katherine surrendered to that program like it was her only source of oxygen. And I do believe it kept her alive. But every time she got to the fourth step—admittin to herself the grittier details of her wrongs—she just couldn't face it. Step four escorted Katherine down to the liquor store more times than I care to remember."

My fingers feel like stone as I turn the page to see one large gold medallion with the words, "Let go and let God" embossed along its arc.

"That's your mother's one-year medallion. I was so proud of the woman that day…" Ettie's voice breaks. She swallows hard.

"How was my mother before she died?" I stare down at my empty hands.

Ettie reaches out and smooths her hand over a row of my mother's AA chips. "Blue. Your mother was a dark shade of blue in here." She crosses her hands over her heart. "Katherine was never able to relinquish the guilt of losing both her children. She blamed herself for David's accident, you know. She believed that David would still be alive today if she had focused more on supervising her children, and less on the boozin. Katherine was tormented by her own relentless demons, that much is sure. She coated every mirror in the house with lipstick so she wouldn't have to look herself in the eye. Some days it was all she could do to will herself out of bed."

I fumble to turn another page, and see a line of young adults in graduation gowns, making their way through a crowded gymnasium. The scene looks oddly familiar. In neat handwriting is the caption, "Marina's college graduation, June, 1983." I shake my head and look up at Ettie. "How did she..."

"Victoria Doyle managed to keep tabs on you those first several years in Toronto, to a certain extent. She traced you through the cheques you wrote."

I think about the last day I saw Victoria Doyle, of the searing handprint her sister-in-law Cissy left across my face. I taste the sour tang of bile in my mouth as I replay the scene in my mind, overlaid with the new information about my genealogy. I bend forward, retching. But along with the disgust, I feel sadness. More family members were lost to me, without me even knowing at the time that they were family.

Ettie continues on. "When you ran away, Victoria Doyle took it harder than anyone. You were her beloved Teddy's *kin*. She saw so much of her brother in you—it was like losin him all over again when you left."

I cock my head.

"It must be difficult for you to understand all of this, but Victoria's feelings for you were incredibly conflicted. I will never know what happened between Victoria and your mother the night Teddy drowned, but Victoria has always held your mother responsible for Teddy's death. But she could also empathize with how your mother's life fell apart—things would have turned out very different for you and your mother if Teddy Doyle had lived. And then when you took off, Victoria felt partly responsible. So she saw to it that you were provided for until you had the means to provide for yourself."

I look back down at my graduation picture, imagining my mother in dark sunglasses, slouching in her metal chair as I filed by in my cap and gown. The burr in my throat seems to enlarge. How I had resented my mother and father on that day in particular, as I had peered into the sea of supportive parents, none of them mine.

"Victoria Doyle kept your mother in the loop," Ettie explains. "But Victoria made it clear the day she showed up on your family's doorstep to rescue you that if your mother did another single thing to hurt you, Victoria would personally see to it that her life was destroyed. She had collected enough of your mother's secrets by then to do so."

"There's so much I don't understand..." my voice trails off. Finally, I am able to speak again. "If my mother wanted to make amends so badly, why didn't she reach out to me once, in all those years?"

"I think that would entail admitting some awful truths, which your mother could not bring herself to do. In the end, I think she decided it would be less painful to die than to confront that mountain of shame."

I wince. "My mother killed herself?"

"Not in so many words." Ettie stares down at her wrinkled hands. "I'm the one who found your mother—in her bathtub. The coroner's report concluded that she had slipped and hit her head, probably while getting out of the bath. Her blood alcohol level was through the roof. It was a wonder she even found her way to the bathroom."

Ettie's voice sounds as though it is piped in from far away. My thoughts whirl to try to sort it all out, to grasp onto any part of the story of my family's past that I know to be true, but every memory I pull closer to re-examine looks altered. I can see where the pixels don't quite match up, where false information has been layered onto what is true.

I lift the scrapbook to my chest, and something ruptures inside of me. A new river of tears comes flooding out. Ettie hooks a finger under my chin and tilts my face square with hers.

"Listen, Mina. Your mother was a godawful parent. But you survived. And *despite* how she mistreated you, look what a wonderful job you've done raising your son. It's time to let Katherine McInnis go."

I rock the scrapbook like a child, and Ettie rests her hand on my shoulder, just allowing me to be.

After several minutes of stillness on her part, Ettie picks up the scrapbook and seems to weigh it in her hand. "I've fulfilled my promise to your mother. You've seen the scrapbook. Now I think you should give yourself permission to do whatever you want with it." Her face is solemn. "Let it go, Sugarpie."

I hug my arms, my shoulders shaking.

"This scrapbook—her *testament* to her family—is nothing more than paper and ink. And decades too late. Mina, you deserved so much more."

I pick up the book, my arm unsteady. Then I set it back down.

Ettie gives my arm a reassuring squeeze.

I shift my gaze to the overflowing puddle that spans across Ettie's driveway, then back to the scrapbook. Suddenly I am in the driveway, thrashing the scrapbook in the murky brown water. Rain cascades off my back as I hunch over and rake my fingernails from the top of the cover to the bottom, mud and leatherette gathering under my nails. Tears streaming down my face, I smear a handful of mud in wild circles until there isn't an inch of clean cover. Then I open the book and smear more mud all over my mother's carefully crafted pages. Breathless, I knead the brown mess into the paper, then hammer it with my open palm. The brown sludge squirts to the edges of the page.

"That's it. Get it all out, Sugarpie," Ettie whispers. She had joined me on the driveway, and stands over me, rubbing my back with one hand in patient circles. I turn to another page and jam the remaining globs of mud into the crease of the book.

I grit my teeth, my whole body shaking as I raise the scrapbook high above my head. As I arch up, two slender items slip from between the pages and flutter down to the driveway. One is a tattered half-sheet of paper. The other is a pink envelope. My eyes catch the word *Marina* on the half-sheet as it clings to the wet gravel. I suck in my breath.

My dirty fingers tremble as I pluck the paper from the muck. The page is crinkled, and covered in stroked-out lines of my mother's handwriting. My eyes race across the page as a fluttery feeling rises in my stomach.

At the top of the page I can make out variations on a letter opening: ~~Dear Marina~~ ~~Mina honey~~ ~~My dearest daughter~~. Many sentences have been crossed out so many times they are nothing but a thick band of black ink, and there are places on the page where the pen nib has torn through the paper. I can make out a few stroked-out lines: ~~...of all my putrid regrets, the most caustic ones are tied to you...~~

~~...forgiveness is something I wanted desperately, and which I've finally decided I don't deserve...~~

Five words at the bottom of the page remain legible.

Marina,

How I am sorry.

I sit huddled over the sodden driveway, reading the page over and over, the rain drenching my skin. The rain and teardrops turn my mother's words into illegible ink streaks. Ettie eventually leaves me to my private mourning.

Finally, I drop the note into the puddle in the driveway. With my toes, I press the scrapbook facedown beneath the murky brown water, drowned alongside my framework of beliefs about my identity. Then I stagger away, the pink envelope searing a hole through my pocket, begging me to leave it unread; to drown it too.

CHAPTER 34

The pink envelope is addressed to Victoria Doyle. I sit shivering in my wet clothes for over an hour, turning the envelope in my hands before I finally tear it open.

Victoria,
    Your suspicions all these years were right. I can't admit it to your face, but I also can't live with the idea that my secret will go to the grave unconfessed. I pushed your brother out of the boat that night.
    For years, I blamed you for the accident. I hated you for running straight to your brother that evening you caught Lenny and I in the woods. I loved Teddy, but in a way, I loved Lenny even more, and Teddy knew it. How could you not have foreseen how insanely jealous Teddy would become?
    On the boat, Teddy and I had a terrible argument. He threatened to tell the entire island that I'd fucked a big, dirty Indian, and I went into a blind fury. I didn't plan to push him, and I certainly didn't intend for Teddy's head to come that close to the prop. But I pushed him nonetheless, and the lake bled red.

I have wasted my adult life trying to blot out that night on the lake. I wonder how it will make you feel, Victoria, to learn that ever since his death, Teddy has stalked the McInnis family. He makes his presence known to me in many horrible forms, and has made it clear that he will spend the rest of my days tormenting everyone I have ever loved. My beloved son David was his favorite target.

I believe Teddy is responsible for David's drowning. Although Marina is the only one who will ever know exactly what happened in David's last moments, I know in my heart it was Teddy's doing.

So, on a morbid scoreboard, I guess our families are close to even.

Please keep an eye on Marina for me. Or if not for me, for your brother.

~Katherine

The rain pummels the ground well into the evening. Hours slip by as I sit in my living room, shivering and staring absently out the bay window at the body of water that has haunted me for over two decades. I sit and shake and process all the false beliefs I have carried for so long. *Teddy Doyle had vowed to stalk my mother's loved ones in that lake until the day she died.* But my mother was long gone.

I slip on my coat and step out into the black, wet night. As I approach the lake, my stomach begins its familiar twisting. I force each foot to take another step, closer to the shore. My legs are trembling when I reach the water's edge. Heart pounding, I lie down on my belly. I lift my hand and hold it above the black waves as they crash into the sand. My head is suddenly dizzy and the lake spins in front of me, then everything starts to go black as I look out at the horrible water. I lower my finger toward the water and close my eyes, pulling my chin down to my chest. Any second I expect the deafening telltale whine to swell in my ears, warning me of a malevolent presence nearby. My muscles tense as I bring my finger an inch above the frigid water. Bird wings flap overhead, and the waves crash relentlessly. I hold my breath, then touch the water.

I close my eyes tight, waiting for a horrible presence to attack, to pull my hand under the water. I wait, still holding my breath. Nothing. I lie on the shore, one finger immersed in the frigid lake, my entire body shaking.

I jerk my hand from the lake and walk back to the house, my legs barely able to support my weight. My chest is still tight and pounding and a migraine swells between my temples. I reach my bedroom and pull the covers up over my head, wet clothes and all. Perhaps Teddy's ghost no longer stalked me, but time had left an indelible scar. I would never set foot in Lake Huron again. Even if my life depended on it.

CHAPTER 35

The phone rings the next morning, and I drag myself out of bed, shivering. It is my realtor. "Crack open the champagne, Marina. It looks like we've got a sale. The buyers want to be in the house by the beginning of next month."

I turn my face up to the ceiling, close my eyes, and exhale a long, slow breath. Each day spent living on Mikinaak Island is like walking around with a gaping wound. After my encounter at the lake last night, I feel a renewed need to get away from the pain that surrounds this island, as unavoidable as the whitecaps that crash against our shore.

Zane comes home in the late afternoon and I ready myself at the kitchen table, wearing what I hope resembles an optimistic smile. His face and arms have grown nut brown from the time spent on his boat. When we lived in the city, there had always been a wan look about him. Zane looks more muscular now, too, as though all that time on the open water has fortified him. Looking at him like this makes me think of my time on the water with David, and how revitalized David looked during our night swims. I think about the nature of water molecules, and the attractive force that draws them to one another like magnets. Perhaps that is why both David and Zane loved the lake so much. Each of their billions of water-filled cells craved proximity to its own kind, skin cells abutting against water molecules, each molecule breathing a sigh of relief at being surrounded by its likeness. I picture David diving under the surface, and peace washing into his veins through osmosis.

Zane coughs. I blink and shake my head.

"I have big news, Zaner."

He puts his backpack down and looks up at me, not willing to part with one syllable.

"Our realtor called today. We finally have a buyer for this house. They were really keen to buy lakefront property—we're getting our asking price."

Zane shakes his head and curses quietly under his breath.

"This is an amazing gift we've been given, Zane." Desperation creeps into my voice. I needed so badly for Zane to be onboard with this decision. "With the money from the house sale, we can move back to the city. Heck, it doesn't even have to be Toronto— you can pick where we move to. You name it, we'll go there. We can put a down payment on a house of our own, and still have money left over for tuition, drum lessons, whatever you want. We'll have a fresh start with the means to get settled comfortably."

Zane's face turns the colour of a sunset. My father's old boater's adage flashes through my mind: *Red sky at morn, sailor be warned.* Zane clenches and unclenches one fist. I hold my breath and wait for the words.

"I'm happy here. I want to stay." He says, his voice breaking.

"I know you do. I'm so, so sorry, Zaner."

I wait for Zane to present more of an argument, something I can wrestle logic around to help him understand how fortunate we are to be able to start fresh in a home of our own, without the emotional baggage of living in a small town where everyone knew our family history.

An intense look burns from Zane's eyes. "We're lucky to live on this pristine fucking island populated by solid, decent people, and all you've done for four months is hole yourself up in this house and plod away, hiding from memories of people who are long gone. The memory of ghosts. Did it occur to you that awesomeness is happening all around you, and you're fucking running from it?" Spittle has formed at the corners of Zane's mouth, and a tendon bulges from the side of his neck.

"Zane, it's more complicated than that."

"My whole life, every time I turned around you were saying no—*Zane, you can't do this, Zane, you can't go there*—everything was just too risky for your precious son. And for a long time, I thought it was just your fucked up way of loving me. But it wasn't that at all. It's always been about *him*. You curbed my freedom my whole fucking life because in some twisted way, you think that's going to bring your dead brother back."

"Zane, I..." I swallow hard. "Zane, I am doing the best I can with you. You might think I'm ruining your life because right now you're trapped in the narrow, melodramatic worldview of a teenager. But the way I'm raising you is far better than any alternatives I have access to. Would you prefer that I neglect you? That I not care whether you live or die? You will never understand how I've worried over you, and all you can do is resent me for it." A painful tightness threatens to constrict my throat, and my lungs feel unable to take in air.

It's Zane's turn to rage. "You can justify your whole life away for all I care, but when it comes right down to it, you're a coward, mom. Just look at the way you've handled any difficult thing you've ever encountered. You run away. How many more times are you going to yank me out of my pathetically nomadic life because you think escaping is a solution to your problems?"

Zane isn't finished. He has a desperate look in his eyes. "And do you really think that digging around for ghost stories surrounding a tragic fucking accident that happened over twenty years ago is going to move you forward in life? What good do you think is actually going to come from circling around and around your brother's death? He's gone. It was a tragic accident, but wasting your life away isn't going to make it better. You're missing out on the present with me—*your living, breathing son*—because you're spending all your time chasing away demons from when you were a fucking kid."

Zane throws the front door open and storms onto the driveway. I follow him out.

"Zane, stop. Please. I know that you're upset right now, but—"

"Did you know there's a sacred Ojibwe place in Lake Huron where people can go to seek spiritual healing? I wonder who needs that more in this fucked up family, Madre, you or me?" He shakes his head. "Jib showed me where it is. His father took him there after Jib lost his younger brother in a snowmobile accident. Huh— isn't that something—Jib lost his younger brother." Zane is yelling now. "As in, you're not the only person on this fucking planet to have lost someone you cared about."

He glances in the direction of the lake. "I'm not sure which of us needs it more, but I think it's time I took a dive down to Broken Man's Grotto."

I turn my head toward the house, and look through two sets of windows out to the lake. A powerful wind is hurling choppy breakers the size of small vehicles against the shore. Grey clouds mushroom across the horizon. *Sailors be warned.* I stiffen.

"You get to choose, mom. You let me in on the ghosts of your past—my dad, your parents, David—everything, right here, right now—or I'm out of here."

My eyes go to the lake, and my thoughts go to the dusky blue body wedged under my parents' boat. To the metallic whine screeching through the water, to the horrible presence I knew was waiting for me. Acid fills my stomach.

Then I look at my son. Everything on the periphery falls away in an instant. Zane is at the center of my life, and nothing else matters in comparison. *Of course I choose you, Zane.*

But the words don't make it out of my mouth in time.

"You hesitated. You fucking hesitated. I hate the fucking guts of the fact that you fucking hesitated."

"Zane—"

"Too late, Marines. Too fucking late. It's over. *C'est* fucking *fini.* I'm gone. GONE!" Zane screams, and tears back in through the house and out the back patio door down to the shore. No sweater, no life jacket, just the wounded heart of an emotionally fragile teenager whose judgement I do not trust.

Zane leaps into his boat and starts the engine. I run toward him, screaming for him to stop, tripping in the sand as I rush to the shore. Hard drops of rain begin pelting down. Zane kills the engine about six feet from shore and silence falls over the lake. His hand still on the tiller, Zane looks back at me.

I stumble to the edge of the water. My son is right there, just a few steps out of reach. My baby boy who I pledged to always protect.

The dizziness begins to spin the shoreline, the blackness clouds my vision. The lake pounds a reminder into my brain that it is still the backdrop for everything I fear. I squeeze my eyes shut. *Come on, Marina. You can do this.* I stand there, foot perched above the lake, heart pounding in my ears. *Hydrogen, atomic mass 1.008; Helium, 4.003; Lithium, 6.941.*

I can't move.

I begin to sob, and Zane cranks up his engine and carves a narrow wake through the lake as though even the water should feel the brunt of his anger.

CHAPTER 36

The lake churns with hideous, white-capped waves. Clouds invade the entire sky, grey messengers of a wicked storm. I race to the house.

Bird has a boat. And he knows how to get to Broken Man's Grotto.

I call him. *Please, God, let Bird answer his phone.* The call goes to voicemail. I leave a frantic message and then slam the phone down, trying to pull my thoughts together. *You're a survivor, Marina. You can figure this out.*

I run through the house, desperate for a solution, then turn around and run through all the same rooms again. Who can I call? Who can I call? The coast guard. I grab the phone book and flip to the blue municipal pages, searching frantically for something akin to a coast guard service. There is nothing.

Just as I reach for the phone to call 911, it rings. It's Bird. I spill out the whole story in a jumbled mess.

"I'll go get Zane," Bird says without hesitating.

"Wait," I say. There is only one way to save my son. "I need to be in that boat."

"Prim."

"Please, Bird. Zane needs me to be in that boat."

"We both know that you can't..." Bird pauses. I hear him take a deep breath. "Alright. I'll leave right now. Wait for me on your shore." Bird hangs up and my breaths start coming one on top of the other. My heart begins to race and my mouth fills with a metallic taste.

I rummage through my purse, and my hand closes around the pill bottle at the bottom. Empty bottle. Hugging my chest to my knees, I focus on my breathing and curse my misplaced bravado. There is no way I can climb into a boat. And yet, I have to.

The thunder is rolling in by the time Bird pulls up to shore in a sturdy bowrider. He hops out of his boat, looks up at the murderous sky, then looks at me. He studies me silently, and assesses that I am not capable of getting on his boat.

"I'll get Zane. You stay here." He pushes his boat a few feet offshore, and jumps back into his boat, the bottom of his pant legs dark and wet. I picture Zane being tossed around by monstrous waves in his tiny boat, picture him refusing help from his friend's dad. Picture what could happen next.

"Bird, wait!"

I plunge both feet into a lake for the first time in twenty years.

I shake, and I grip the white vinyl boat seat on either side of my legs, but I do not die. A flash of lightning lights up the sky, and the rain begins to hammer down. Bird turns the key and the motor starts, and within seconds, the safe, solid ground retreats beneath a pool of unforgiving liquid. The water is choppy, but Bird reassures me that this size of wave is nothing for a boat like his. The entire time the boat plows through the rough waters, my mind focuses on two things only: getting Zane to safety, and getting myself off the water. I may have forced myself into the boat, but my mind is exploding with panic.

Bird turns his head to face me, so I can hear him over the roar of the engine. "Let's get your son back."

Bird turns back toward the lake. We sit in silence for the entire ride, tending to our private burdens as the boat lurches through the surf.

As we draw closer, Zane's boat develops from grainy abstract to clear definition, like a photo in a darkroom. I begin to make out the outline of Zane's body, standing in the boat. Doesn't he know how risky it is to stand up in a boat?

We approach, and I see that Zane is not only standing up, but actually straddling the boat. His legs are splayed, with one shoe planted on the gunwale on each side of the boat, his arms spread out to the horizon on either side of him, his head arched back, rain pummeling his face. A daring-the-gods pose. He must have heard our engine, but he gives no indication that he cares.

I call out his name.

Zane swivels his head around and stares at me as though he is staring at a ghost.

"Zane! You could be killed! Please get down from there!"

A giant swell crashes into Zane's boat, and he lurches forward but manages to regain his balance. "I'm not going to live my life in fear, mom!"

"Please, honey! Just get down and we'll talk!"

"About Che Guevara?"

"Zane, I'm begging you. Please get down!" My voice is frantic, screaming over the whining gale.

Zane jumps down onto the deck of his boat. "Too late, Madre. You can't tell me what to do anymore. And three's a crowd. I'm outta here."

He yanks on the engine cord and his boat roars to life. An enormous breaker hurls towards Zane's boat from behind.

"Zane! Look out!"

He turns to look, and the wave crashes over his boat, dipping the gunwale on one side almost underwater. Zane's body flies over the stern, his head coming within a foot of where the propeller blades churn underwater. The pull of the waves jerks the motor all the way to one side, and the boat tears off in a wide arc.

Zane doggy paddles awkwardly, the waves pummeling him. The boat cuts an aggressive curve, tearing through the lake in a circular path. Angry waves suck Zane under as he tries to escape the boat's course, but he defaults to the impotent flailing of a non-swimmer.

"Zane! Get out of the way!" Part of me can't ignore the fear that there might be something even worse waiting for Zane beneath the water.

The storm cancels the sound of my voice. Zane's clumsy strokes barely move him in the rough waves. The boat swoops past, missing him by a few meters.

The boat starts in on another circle. It swings around, herky jerky in the boiling chop of the waves, and this time the engine's trajectory leads more directly toward Zane.

"No Zane! Noooo! Look out!"

Zane flogs at the lake, gulping mouthfuls of water, his head going under the powerful waves for full seconds at a time. He makes only inches of progress out of the boat's path as it bears down on him like an insane metal beast. I can't witness this violent end to my beloved son.

I step up to the metal rim of the gunwale, raise my hands in a prayer high above my head, and dive headfirst into Lake Huron.

Frigid water stings my skin, constricting my chest. My arms pull my body up to the surface, just in time to hear a muted thump. The boat careens off on its circular course. I wrench my neck above the waves to see Zane floating in the water. His head is flopped forward, and his arms aren't moving. Behind me, I can hear Bird screaming Zane's name.

Zane's body starts to sink beneath the waves.

"No! Zane! Please, please no! Zane!"

I propel myself toward him. Fear hovers over my shoulder, threatening to overtake me, to trick me into sucking in a lungful of water. My brain screams two separate fears over and over: *Zane. Mishi-ginebig. Zane. Mishi-ginebig. Zane.*

Yet, despite the churning in my brain, my muscles remember the elemental act of slipping through water. I know that if I pause for even a second, I will be engulfed in raw panic. But I can't accept the thought of not reaching Zane. I will not leave this lake without my son.

I rope my arm around Zane's limp body. My one arm pulls us downward, my heart hammering in my throat. I pull and kick until I am certain we are deep enough to have cleared the propeller, and then I start swimming in what I hope is the direction of Bird's boat. Soon I can see the wake of Zane's propeller roiling above us, and can hear the muted gurgle of its engine.

An image of a dark creature slithering behind me flashes through my mind. *Don't look behind.* I swim faster. *Just focus on getting to Bird's boat.* I kick with all my might away from the violent drone above us.

Several feet away from us, through the darkness of the water, I can just barely make out a craggy underwater mountain sprouting from the lake bottom. I recognize the shoal as being near to where Bird had stopped his boat. I kick with all my strength, approaching the shoal. Ascending along its rugged edge, I catch a glimpse of a dark hole embedded in the rock. A cave.

A grotto.

Time stops. My mind flashes to the Ojibwe story of the underwater place of healing. I envision David waiting at the mouth of the grotto, holding his arms out to me. I could finally have the chance to explain to him how sorry I am for my horrible mistake. And David would take my hand in his and lead me inside the cave, where glimmering aquamarine *mbaanaabe-kwe* nymphs would whirl around us. He would press his forehead against mine and wrap his slender arms around me. "I accept your apology, Mina. I forgive you." His spirit would finally be able to complete its journey, and I would be free at last.

But there is no time for this. I need to get to the surface.

My lungs are burning. I probably only have another few seconds of being able to hold my breath. I hitch Zane's body tight against my side, and kick upwards.

Suddenly, I feel as though I am being sucked back down. A current of force lashes around me, pulling me under. I reel and struggle, but make little progress. A livewire feeling tingles through my scalp. *A presence is in this lake, I can feel it. Mishi-ginebig.* I scull one hand to pull us upwards, and kick with all my strength, but my force is met with a stronger counterforce. I kick my legs harder and harder, each muscle tightening like a bow string.

I strain my vision into the darkness, and lash Zane's body closer to mine. My kicks begin to grow weaker, yet still I push on. The seconds drag on in slow motion. My chest tingles. *I need air.* Darkness stretches out before me.

I kick some more, and am dragged further down.

My senses are so heightened I can hear a hundred muffled sounds in the darkness of the deep water. A muted whine comes from ahead of me. My muscles tense to snapping.

I hold my hand protectively in front of my face, my head ducked low, imagining a sharp point jutting out from the blackness, eager to pierce an unsuspecting eye. My heart feels as though it will burst with fear. *Whatever happens, I won't let go of you, Zane.*

The vibrations of an object cutting through the water hit my face first. I spring backwards. I kick my feet to propel myself backwards, and feel something brush against my cheek. I jerk back reflexively, and my hands shoot out in front of me, desperately sweeping at whatever has brushed against me. My finger snags a razor-sharp edge of rock, and hot pain immediately throbs through my hand. A red inky cloud pulses from my sliced finger, growing denser with each drum of my heart. I gasp involuntarily, and water rushes into my throat, a burning bubble that tears its way down my chest. My lungs force the water out in a fit of coughing and sucking, a horrible reflex that leads to more water burning in my lungs. My heartbeat batters in my ears and I reel around, my bearings completely lost. My chest is ready to explode, and I flail and kick and get nowhere. Pain bleeds into my chest. A whirling blackness blooms inside my head and a loud ringing reverberates in my ears. *The surface. Must get to the surface.* An agonizing need to inhale pushes every other thought from my brain. *Air, air, God how I need air.* I can see the dull light where the lake meets the sky. I hold tight to Zane and kick furiously, my entire self focused on one task: saving Zane.

My legs weaken, slower, slower, but I will not give up. *I will never let go of you, Zane.* I can see the surface of the lake, so close yet unreachable. I use my last ounce of energy to give a few last explosive kicks. I inch closer to the surface, but it is not enough.

CHAPTER 37

"Primrose! *Primrose!*"

My neck jostles from side to side, and waves slap against my face.

"Primrose! Breathe!"

My eyelids are heavy. So difficult to open. A flicker of light. *Please stop shaking me.*

I gasp and splutter, and a burning heat throbs in my chest.

I open my eyes. Bird is treading water, with me hoisted under one arm, Zane under the other. Zane bobs in the water, his eyes lidded, his arms limp.

"Primrose, are you okay?"

I look at the black waves lapping at Zane's ears. *Oh God, Zane, not you too. Please, God, I'll do anything.*

"Zane! Zaner honey! Can you hear me?"

No response.

I shake his shoulders frantically.

Zane blinks several times and then begins to cough. The water makes a sucking sound against the boat.

"Bird, help me get him into the boat. Hurry!"

"You came for me."

Zane lies dripping on the hull of the boat, staring humbly up at me. After several silent moments he hangs his head, and his whole body shakes as the tears finally find their way out. He curls himself in a ball and rocks back and forth, his head pressed into his knees. Bird's boat crashes from side to side in the waves as Zane sits there, rocking and crying.

"What happened down there, mom?"

"I don't know. I tried to swim us to safety, but then something happened..." my voice trails off.

Bird kneels down to us. "You were down there for such a long time. I dove down to look for you, but couldn't find you anywhere. And then you rocketed to the surface. But you were both *unconscious.*"

Bird's voice sounds so far away. Slap, slap. The waves continue their dance.

"Mom?"

Cold water drips from my nose. *Look at yourself, Marina.* I had been immersed in thirty-five hundred kilometres of water. *Immersed in water.* I had been surrounded by the whole of the ancient, mysterious Great Lake. So many thousands of kilometres of blameless hydrogen and oxygen atoms had permeated my pores; I could still taste their freshness in my mouth. But the fear is gone. The revelation washes over me. The fear was an element *I* had added to the equation. The scientist blind to her own biases. It had been in my power all along to split it from the hydrogen and oxygen molecules that populated the lake. The power was within *me* to overcome the fear.

I look at my son. Zane's eyes are trained on me, holding me safe in his gaze the way I have done a thousand times before with him. I knew if I asked him to, he would dive with me right then, back down to Broken Man's Grotto to find what I had thought I so desperately needed. But a mystical encounter in the depths of Lake Huron was not what I needed to be free.

I reach over and squeeze Zane's hand tightly. He stares into my eyes for a minute, then squeezes back.

I shift my gaze toward the lake. Leaning over the lip of the boat, I peer into the dark waves. "I'm so, so sorry David, but I have to let go."

I collapse in a huddle across Zane, and let the guilt flow out in long, slow breaths until I feel empty. Eventually, I raise my head and look back out at the lake. Still concentrating on my breathing, the difference strikes me. The leaden ball I had carried in my chest since my adolescence is gone. I am noticeably lighter.

Free.

Zane locks eyes with me and gives me a smile—the first whole-hearted Zane smile I have received since moving to Mikinaak. "I'm so fucking proud of you, mom."

I wrap my arms around my son again.

Zane raises his fingers to my earlobe. "Looks like you lost an earring down there."

"You know I never wear —" I gasp and bring both hands to my ears. Even before I touch it, I can sense the spray of metal that dangles from one earlobe. The silver teardrop earring. I pull the earring's curved hook from my ear and hold it in front of my face. A shaft of sunlight glances through the heavy clouds, and reflects off the earring's silver wisps. I glimpse back into the water and for a second, I think I see a flash of aquamarine beneath the surface.

It may have been nothing but the sun's reflection.

It may have been so much more.

CHAPTER 38

The view across the channel to Elsinore Island is clear and inviting. Zane selects a flat rock the size of an egg and hurls it at the lake. The rock kisses the surface of the lake four times before disappearing. Zane and I sit in the sand side by side, just close enough to one another to make my heart soar—but not too close—and watch the rings expand across the lake.

"I owe you an apology, Zaner."

Zane lies back and raises a larger, sharper rock high above the bluish-green goose egg on his forehead where the boat clipped him. I wince. He opens his hand and the rock falls, and he catches it with the same hand an inch above his eye. Then he raises the rock high above his face again. "Just one?"

My stomach tightens.

He smirks and nudges me playfully.

I take a deep breath. "All these years, I thought I was protecting you from my past, Zane."

Zane squints up at the rock and rolls it between his fingers. "And?"

I swallow hard. "It took me twenty years to figure out that the stories that go untold can affect us just as powerfully as the ones we choose to tell. I denied you an important part of your identity. I'm sorry, Zane."

Zane props himself up on his elbows and cocks his head at me. "That's not how I see it."

I turn my head. "What do you mean?"

"You gave me the gift of a blank slate, remember? All these years, I was envisioning Che Guevara as my biological father." A slow smile spreads across his face.

I let out a huge breath. "Sarcastic bastard." I pause and grin shyly at Zane. "*Literally.*"

Zane's eyes dance. He shakes his head and lets out a low whistle. "Momsario. Are you effing *kidding* me? Did you *seriously* just say that?" His face is radiant.

"I have a lot to tell you, Zane." I lean back into the sand beside my son, inch my hand over to just barely touching his, and begin.

CHAPTER 39

The dock on Elsinore Island looks exactly as I envisioned it, sitting across the bay with Zane the day before. I see her standing at the end of the dock, hands on hips, squinting as Zane shuttles me closer.

She is speechless as I climb out of the boat and Zane motors away. I walk over to where she stands, and take in her tanned skin, her short, spiky haircut, her black grease-stained hands.

"Rhonda Doyle." My chest fills with warmth at the realization that I am actually standing across from her once more.

"Mina McInnis." She points her chin at me, her face unreadable.

"You, um—you look fantastic," I say, glancing back in the direction of Zane's boat.

Rhonda looks out over the water for what feels like an eternity. "Fuckin right. The seizures are absolute magic for my beauty regimen."

We stand in silence for a moment. She turns and walks down the dock, not stopping until she reaches the end. "Well? You wanna look around this place or not?"

I hurry to catch up.

Rhonda shows me around her workshop. "I can work steady in here for up to four hours a day before things start to get a little flaky up here." She taps her head matter-of-factly. "This here's my Boatercycle fleet." She motions toward a row of five small metal vehicles lined up along the concrete floor. "The patent went through last year. A local cottage resort owner's ordered these five—the tourists eat this kind of thing up: *Made on Mikinaak* and all that horseshit."

She steers me past the various changes at Elsinore Estate, then back to the dock, where one of her inventions nuzzles against the side of the dock with each lap of the waves.

Victoria Doyle had done a run into town to pick up some supplies, and would be back on Elsinore later that afternoon. "Mom basically runs the place these days. With Fat Joe's sciatica and Ettie busy with her restaurant, mom slowly had to take the wheel. Even chops all her own firewood. You should see the pipes on her now."

I take a step toward Rhonda.

"Rhonda—" I bite my lip, "I—I'm sorry for running away from you and your mother. I was just so terrified of hurting or disappointing anyone else."

"Seems like leaving us was a recipe for exactly that. We considered you family, M."

"I know that."

I can feel the tears well up in my eyes. "Rhonda, that was a really messed up time for me. I want so badly to start over with you. Do you think we could try to pick up the pieces? I've spent twenty years longing for my best friend."

Rhonda looks me straight in the eye. She spits through the gap in her teeth and it lands in the center of the "o" on the custom *Boatercycle* decal. "Well...you're lucky I'm a welder."

"Pardon?"

"Patch jobs. *Welders know how to do patch jobs.* Come on, M—I thought *I* was supposed to be the one with brain damage here." She grins a pirate's smile.

"Tell you what. You let me take you for a spin on this work of pure fucking genius, and then we'll talk."

I glance from the Boatercycle to Rhonda. My stomach tightens. I take a deep breath, and allow a wave of calm to flow in and loosen each muscle. "If you go grab two life jackets, you've got yourself a deal."

Rhonda walks in the awkward limpy gait that has remained from her accident on the ice. I follow the jerky up-and-down of her back until she disappears into the boat shed. She reappears, carrying two bright orange life vests, and smiles as she tosses me one.

"You didn't say anything about me *wearing* my lifejacket," she says, making a loud farting noise as she tosses hers onto her seat in the Boatercycle. "No can do, M. Not even for you." She throws an arm around my shoulder, then gives it a good slug.

I can't help smiling. How I have missed Rhonda Doyle.

EPILOGUE

Each August civic holiday weekend on Mikinaak, one particular event draws families from all over the island. Fathers and sons, bosses and their employees, groups of teenage girls— a host of teams spend weeks drawing up designs, then constructing their prototypes in workshops and garages. In preparation for the cardboard boat races, only two materials are permitted for the structural integrity of the watercraft: cardboard and duct tape. Embellishments of all kinds, be they seagull feathers, beer cans, or steak bones, are highly encouraged.

Rhonda, Ettie, Bird and I stand on shore to cheer on our boys. Zane, Jib, and Morgan had toiled for weeks on their cardboard skiff. Zane even fashioned a cardboard motorbike jutting out the bow of the boat, as a nod to his Aunt Rhonda's own nautical engineering.

Rhonda, or Crazy Rhonnie, as she insists I address her in public "so the locals don't go getting any ideas about inviting me over for tea," stands in a tatty blue bathrobe, the bottom edge flapping in the wind. She jams two fingers in her mouth and lets out an impressive whistle. "Give 'em hell, Zanerman," she screams, then reaches over and squeezes my hand.

I bought a small house right here in town. In the backyard is a pleasant garden. I can gaze at the garden from my kitchen window while I plunge my hands in hot soapy dishwater. It is with great relief that my eyes meet a swathe of green growing things rather than a grey-blue expanse of lake when I look out our window. Although I can now be convinced to wade into the lake on a sweltering August day when Zane insists, water will never be my element. But braving the deep was the greatest gift I could have given myself or my son—I see it in Zane's eyes every time he looks at me.

Most weekends, Zane shuttles me over to Elsinore Island. On these visits, I often catch Victoria Doyle watching over me with glistening eyes, but I better understand that attentiveness now. Along with more complicated emotions, there is guardianship in her gaze. In some ways, Victoria has become the mother I never had. An unbreakable bond has formed between us, forged by our shared history of loss.

I have settled on a more generous view of the ugliness that lives in my family's past, have rinsed the memories clean of the blame and resentment. Forgiveness is a miraculous substance. And I now recognize something else about myself, something that must catch Victoria's eye each time she glimpses me from a distance: I am the spitting image of my mother. There is a picture of my mother's young self in the scrapbook I eventually salvaged. Each time I turn to it, I suck in my breath, startled at our likeness. I am a product of my family history, and no amount of distance can filter that from my blood.

Zane and I planted several raspberry bushes along the back fence last August, and already we have noticed new canes poking up through the soil. We were not expecting the bushes to bear fruit so soon, but this year they already sag with berries. It gives me great satisfaction to look up from my desk, out the window at those leafy bushes, and to think about their underground runners curling out in all directions. Regenerating. I picture the bountiful red berries returning each summer, and us here each year to greet them. I have found my place on this remote chunk of rock that refuses to budge from the jaws of Lake Huron. My roots, however tangled, anchor me to the gritty brown Mikinaak earth. I have found my people— every one of them flawed. I plan to remain here.

Author's Note

While Watermark is a work of fiction, the *Anishnaabek* stories that are woven throughout the novel are not my own. These are stories I encountered growing up on Manitoulin Island, where approximately one-third of my classmates were Anishnaabe. There is one exception to these Anishnaabek legends: the story of Broken Man's Grotto comes from my own imagination, as a necessary strand in the tale I set out to spin. But the rest of the stories I learned organically, growing up as a white kid on an island dotted with First Nations communities.

In high school, my best friend was a member of Aundeck Omni Kaning First Nation; I owe my knowledge of some of the more frightening Anishnaabek stories to her. Thank you Candy Corbiere, for, among other things, scaring me senseless throughout my teenage years.

Although these stories were part of the cultural landscape in which I was raised, I respectfully recognize that this is not the same thing as having ownership of them. It is my genuine hope that I have honoured these stories.

I would also like to acknowledge works I have explicitly referenced in the novel. The painting *Tree of Life* is by Manitoulin artist Blake Debassige, and can be found in the Canadian Museum of Civilization in Hull, Quebec. I also referenced *In the Domain of Lake Monsters*, by John Kirk, published by Key Porter Books Ltd, 1998.

A note about the language: I have used terms for the Indigenous people of Mikinaak and their language that reflect the language of Northern Ontario in the 1970s and 1990s. While being historically accurate, these terms are no longer acceptable in modern discourse. It is my understanding that the Indigenous people of the Robinson Huron Treaty area—the region which most closely resembles the fictional setting of Watermark—now prefer the terms Anishnaabe and Anishnaabemowin to refer to themselves and their language. I respectfully acknowledge this evolution of the language, in which Canadian Indigenous people define their identity in their own words.

Acknowledgments

I want to thank the many early readers who offered critical feedback couched in kindness as I wrestled my way through draft after draft: Aaron Farquhar, Evan Farquhar, Marilyn Farquhar, Mike Farquhar, Karma Papastergiou, Shannon Schust, Frances Wilson, Erin Schmucker, Maria Ognibene, Steve Parolini, and Phyllis Rippey. A special thank you to Neil Debassige, Darci Debassige, and Mary Ann Corbiere for reading the manuscript with an eye toward cultural sensitivity. Thank you also to Al MacNevin, who helped this manuscript along with typical Al panache.

Thank you for the amazing editing help given to me by Adrienne Kerr and Jane Warren. Working with both of you was like taking a master class in writing.

Thank you a thousand times over, Matt Heiti, for your incredibly thoughtful and generous work as the final editor. I thought *Watermark* was basically done before you came on the scene—how wrong I was.

An enormous thank you to Pieter Swinkels, the first person outside my circle of friends and family to recognize something valuable within the scribblings of an early Watermark manuscript, and to generously guide me toward unearthing more of its potential.

My unending gratitude to my wonderful agent Samantha Haywood, who pulled me from the dark abyss of unpublished authorhood, and handed me the tools to make this book fly. Thank you so much for your enthusiasm in getting this book out into the world.

To my dedicated publishers at Latitude 46 Publishing, Heather Campbell and Laura Stradiotto, thank you so much for all your hard work in helping make this dream of a published debut novel a reality.

A lifetime of thank-you's to my parents, who have always believed I was a talented writer, even when I wasn't.

And finally, my wholehearted gratitude to Thanos, who supported my stealing of many precious hours over several years to follow a dream that, statistically, was about as likely to end in success as the purchase of a Lotto 649 ticket. Thank you for unconditionally supporting my passion.